On The Devil's Knee

Craig A. Godfrey

Black Rose Writing | Texas

ISBN: 978-1-68433-571-8
PUBLISHED BY BLACK ROSE WRITING
www.blackrosewriting.com

Printed in the United States of America
Suggested Retail Price (SRP) $19.95

On the Devil's Knee is printed in Chaparral Pro

*As a planet-friendly publisher, Black Rose Writing does its best to eliminate
unnecessary waste to reduce paper usage and energy costs, while never compromising
the reading experience. As a result, the final word count vs. page count may not meet
common expectations.

For my parents Ken Godfrey 1921 – 2013 and Dorothy Godfrey 1922 – 2014. My driving force.

On The
Devil's
Knee

CHAPTER ONE
LOSS OF INNOCENCE

Boxing Day, 1914. Sandy Bay Hobart Tasmania

Frankie Mulberry was like a young songbird. Life was good. She loved life and loved her family. Were she to be honest with herself she loved her three siblings more than her strict Protestant parents, Frank and Rose Mulberry. But Frankie had flashes of guilt whenever she had these thoughts. At twenty-two Frankie still lived in the family one-storey, four-bedroom cottage on the corner of Queen Street and Lincoln Street in Sandy Bay; a sleepy village suburb to the south of Hobart. But this was soon to change.

In 1914 many would declare any unmarried daughter to be a 'spinster' at twenty-two. The less merciful suggested Frankie had already lost her youthful looks; certainly she wasn't the most fetching apple on the tree and the puppy fat of her younger years had persisted into her third decade. Slightly plump, maybe, but Frankie took care to dress fashionably. Her favourite was a high turtleneck blouse with her side swirl and low bun coiffure neat beneath her swathed mushroom and boater hat. These were popular with women in favour of female emancipation whom Frankie supported. Frank and Rose Mulberry were devoted to Frankie, as they were to all their offspring, and had not a clue to Frankie's well-kept secret …

Frankie had already married.

She had married her long time sweetheart Brady O'Connell, the mechanic son of a Coal River Valley pig farmer. It had been a registered marriage between two adults; the situation brought on by conflicting religions; that age-old chestnut – Protestant versus Roman Catholic.

Frankie looked to the mantle clock, the time passed and she knew the secret could not last forever. Frankie's marriage to Brady O'Connell – he was from a devoted Roman Catholic family, had been a fiercely guarded secret for a month now. Frankie had shared the information with her best friend, and her best friend only, her nineteen-year-old sister Bes. Bes could keep a secret, damned right she could for the two shared a bedroom and Frankie had, begrudgingly, aided and abetted her sister's own late night liaisons of late with her boyfriend Jack Carter. Sometimes Frankie thought she had been a bad influence on her younger sister, and maybe she had. Jack lived in North Hobart and worked as a boilermaker at the Hobart Gas Company. But Bes had always gone for the underdog; she seemed to be easily attracted to the wrong type. Not because Jack was a boilermaker mind. He was just a bit rough around the edges really. Frankie had met Jack twice, with Bes during the day when they were out and about together, both times on weekends, and Bes did not approve. It was soon apparent Jack was extremely possessive and immature. Sure, he was Protestant, but that meant little, now, to a young lady who had secretly married a Roman Catholic.

In other matters Frankie was proud of her sister. Bes was a strong-willed, stubborn young woman who always stood up for what was right. Presently she was a vocal sympathiser for the British women of the Suffragette movement, even though women in Tasmania had the vote since 1903.

Equality for women and *men.*

Hurrah!

This was another strength that bound the siblings.

Bes trained as a nurse at St John's Hospital in South Hobart. She had great empathy with the patients, a great bed-side-manner and loved her situation. Bes was never short of suitors either; being tall at five-foot-ten, slim with long shapely legs, fair hair crimped with an iron on occasions, that stopped at her lower back but usually, for reasons of modesty, it was styled in a chignon. It was this beauty that drove Jack insanely jealous, and they had only been meeting for five weeks now. Yes, Frankie could trust Bes to keep a secret. However twelve-year-old brother Ben and eight year old Molly were a different kettle of fish altogether. They could never be trusted. Never.

***

Boxing Day was pleasantly warm without a cloud in the sky. Out on Queen Street the neighbourhood kids played cricket. Rose Mulberry watched Ben belt the ball clean up the street. It was one hell of a hit and Frankie watched the ball hurtle towards Mount Wellington west, while Ben headed off on his first run. He loved his cricket and dreamed of playing for Australia one day. He had the arms of a strong bowler too. In fact, Uncle Johnny, Ben's godfather, used to say he was a nuggetty little bugger. And Rose loved watching her only son play. Everyone said Ben picked up his batting skills from Rose's father, Brickie Jones; so named for his brick-red hair. He had been the head brewer at Artillery Brewery in Anthill Street but sadly had passed away in 1913. Many said he took his secret recipes to the grave with him, for die-hard drinkers swore the brew was not the same these days. And Grandad Brickie loved that stocky kid Ben. Yes, he taught him a batting technique or two.

Frankie wedged the front door open and joined her mother sitting on the front porch, passing her a cup of tea. 'Did you see that? 'Rose took the cup. 'Ben just got another three runs.' A proud mother, that one. Mum and Frankie cheered along with the neighbours and together they watched the street fielders spread out for the next ball; the fielders being the eleven-year-old Thompson twins and thirteen-year-old Annie Pearson – who wanted to be a pilot when she grew up. Frankie looked across at her mother. Her stomach fluttered. She desperately wanted to tell her mother about Brady O'Connell and their secret marriage and now seemed a good time, alone with mother amongst Christmas cheer and good wishes. Frankie knew her mother Rose was no angel; Rose had been pregnant with Frankie when she and Frank wed back in '93. But Rose had not a clue Frankie was aware of this. It had been only last Easter Sunday when Frankie overheard her beery Uncle Kevin ribbing her father about it at a family gathering.

I'm twenty-two for goodness sake. I can make up my own mind. I have my own future to think of. My own destiny.

But Brady O'Connell is a Roman Catholic and father always said he would disown me if I married a Catholic.

Truth be known Frankie even suspected her father capable of violence towards such a suitor. Her father Frank had grown up in a staunch Protestant family and *bloody ratcatchers* as he called Roman Catholics, *were nought but pious infidels.* As a tram driver for the Hobart Electric Tram Company – as he had been since they first ran the trams back in the early nineties – Frank Mulberry had been known to fail to stop the tram for a Catholic priest.

Frankie's eye followed the fielders chasing the ball before her attention was drawn skywards. The day was warming up, the sky a lazy lagoon blue and not a breath of air. As the trams don't operate on public holidays Frankie knew her father was off work.

'Where's father?' Frankie asked her mother.

Rose smiled a warm smile. 'Do you have to ask?'

No. Frankie guessed she needn't have asked. The Doctor Syntax Hotel was only a stone's throw away and now Frankie remembered her father mentioning something about buying a couple of bottles of beer to have with their lunch.

Lunch!

Frankie stood smartly. She thought it best she attend to the two chooks roasting in the oven and returned to the kitchen. The kitchen was insufferable this hot summer's day, with the wood-fired oven baking two trussed chooks filled with bread and herb stuffing, along with all the accompanying vegetables,. And the plum pudding simmering in the iron pot did little to help the humidity.

***

Excited shouts from the street finally woke nineteen-year-old Bes from her nap in their shared bedroom. Brother Ben had been bowled out. Unbeknown to all except Frankie, Bes had climbed back in over the bedroom windowsill at 2am. She had been quiet as church mouse. Frank and Rose Mulberry never suspected a thing; even Tucker, the family kelpie, housed out back in a kennel, was none the wiser. Bes stepped groggily into the kitchen and studied the kitchen table a moment. Frankie had done well. Then again Frankie always did well, she was a natural housekeeper. The table was already set for lunch with the forks on the left and the knives to the right and glasses placed in front of the knives. She'd even used the special Christmas placemats Molly had made at school before the summer holidays. Yawning, Bes lifted the cloth cover from a large jug of ginger beer and poured herself a full glass. 'How long to dinner?' she asked Frankie. 'I'm famished.'

Frankie ignored Bes's question, wanting to hear the verdict on Jack whom she strongly opposed. 'So?'

'So ... What?'

'So did you talk to him?' Frankie checked down the passageway. Mother was out of sight. 'Did you finish it with Jack?' As Frankie said this she caught Bes rolling down her sleeve in a pathetic attempt to hide a bruise. 'Did he do that?'

'What?'

'That!' Frankie said angrily. Bes tugged at her sleeve. 'Mongrel. Bes you've got to stop seeing him. Why did he do that?'

'We argued.'

'About what?'

'You actually.'

'Me!'

'Yes. He knows you don't like him and he ...'

'Bloomin' right I don't like him. He's nothing but trouble Bes. You better have an excuse ready if mother and father see that bruise. How did he do it?'

'He grabbed me.'

'Grabbed you pretty hard by the look of it.'

'For goodness sake Frankie, I can look after myself.'

Bes would never do well at poker. She was a bad liar with a good heart and made unwise decisions when it came to friends, especially men.

'Mother's out the front,' Frankie said. 'Watching Ben play cricket.'

'And dad?'

'He's gone to fetch some beer. So, how does Jack know I don't like him?'

'You're hardly subtle Frankie.'

'I suppose not. But I warned you he mistreated Sally Morgan, and he ...'

'Shush Frankie. I mean it. No more talk of Jack?'

'Who's Jack?' Eight-year-old Molly appeared from nowhere carrying her favourite doll that she called Rags.

Bes. 'No one.'

'Oh. It didn't sound like just no one,' Molly said aloud to Rags. 'And why did you tell Frankie to shush?'

'Here.' Frankie handed Molly dinner plates. 'Make yourself useful.'

Instantly young Ben hurried down the passageway. "Frankie Frankie!'

'What?'

'You've got a present.'

'Really? For me?'

Ben carried a large brown parcel tied in Christmas green and red ribbon. 'Here.'

Mum was on his heels. 'A late Christmas present,' she called after Ben. 'Who's it from?'

With the lack of care only a twelve-year-old could muster Ben dropped the parcel on the table skittling cutlery. 'Be careful,' Bes said louder than she intended. 'You be careful.'

'Ben!' Mother's voice was *law*.

Ben picked up Bes's ginger beer draining the glass. 'Well Frankie,' he asked spraying spittle in his excitement. 'Who's it from?'

Attracted by the excitement, the black and white kelpie, Tucker, barked at the back door. 'It's from Brady,' Molly squealed opening the door for the family dog.

'Brady?' Rose Mulberry sounded surprised, if not annoyed. She thought, at least she hoped, Frankie's relationship with that *Catholic* mechanic had soured.

Frankie read her name on the wrapping. As far as she could guess it *was* from Brady and she was slightly annoyed he would send it to her home where her parents could see it rather than, say, give it to her yesterday when they had met briefly, secretly, to wish each other a Merry Christmas.

Mother said gravely. 'It's not from Brady, surely.'

Molly chanted. 'Brady. Brady.'

'Oh do shut up Molly,' Frankie snapped.

'Frankie!' Mother insisted on some decorum, however the parcel *was* large and the excitement palpable. Tucker pushed between legs and found a morsel of ham fat missed by the brush and shovel after Christmas lunch the day before.

'Take Tucker outside?' Mother ordered Ben.

'I want to see what's in the parcel first,' said Ben in minor rebellion. He pulled at the parcel ribbon. 'Open it then.'

'Stop it Ben,' Frankie scolded. 'Or I'll open it in my room, then you'll never know.'

Ben stepped back with a pinched face and Frankie smiled at her small victory. The ribbon untied easily and she peeled back the paper. The kitchen fell to silence while Tucker licked grease from around his mouth and barked for more.

'Ben, do as I say, put Tucker outside.'

'But mother. Can't I just ...'

Tucker placed her front paws on the table looking for any more treats.

'Now Benjamin!' Rose Mulberry raised her voice. She hated raising her voice to the children but every so often ...

'I'll do it,' Bes took Tucker by the collar and headed for the door. With Tucker's excited barking Rose wasn't fussed who took the noisy dog back to its kennel. Yet she had been disobeyed. Feeling defied she poked Ben in the back and tipped her head towards the back door.

'I'll do it Bes,' the twelve-year-old called after his sister who had already disappeared into the backyard. Ben took one last look at the parcel and decided. 'It's probably a boring old hat,' he said as he made for the door.

'It's a hat!' Molly shouted. And a hatbox was exposed.

'Told you,' Ben said disgustedly before closing the door behind him.

A hat Frankie thought. She shook the box and it rattled. *A hat and confectionery from Brady. That would be just like him. How will I explain this to mother and father?* Frankie stared at the box, her mind racing. Father would walk in any minute and she would have to account for herself. Rose Mulberry crossed her arms sternly. 'For goodness sake Frankie, open the darn thing.'

Frankie took a deep breath and lifted the lid ...

***

In that millisecond the kitchen filled with a white flash. The detonation was savage. It tore the back away from the wood framed house. The kitchen was destroyed blasting the roof into the back yard. The walls exploded outwards and all windows in the cottage shattered. Much of the house was on fire. Half a second after the blast a fireball escaped through the destroyed roof. All about was black smoke and destruction. Frankie, her mother and Molly were killed instantly. Ben was blasted down the back steps like a skittle. Bes, twenty yards away next to the kennel was thrown hard against the back fence.

In the nearby Doctor Syntax Hotel Frank Mulberry heard the explosion. Every glass behind the bar juddered. Windows rattled. Frank rushed across a paddock at the rear of the pub and along a narrow laneway between cottages and onto Queen Street ...

Into a scene of mayhem.

No man should witness what Frank Mulberry did that day. The rear of his home was demolished, but it was the bloodied and blackened remains of his wife and children that tore him apart.

Frank dropped to his knees taking his wife's torso in his arms. Neighbours were quick with buckets of water to douse flames but the fire spread quickly. Frank was paralysed with shock; all about him was a strange silence. A ringing in his ears, the muffled screams and shouts of locals and rescuers. Strangers lifted him gently, pulling him away from the remains of his little Molly, coaxing him from the horrendous sight. With his face chiselled in horror, traumatised, his mouth was wide open in a silent scream.

There were no tears. These would come later.

***

Frank paid no attention to the fire brigade. They had arrived within a short time. Supported physically by neighbours, Frank shook them free. Screaming Ben's name he found his twelve-year-old son at the bottom of the back steps. He was twisted unnaturally. But he breathed. His eyes opened staring into his father's. He tried to speak but his lungs were scorched. Frank stooped to collect his son in his arms but once again he was restrained as two other neighbours rolled the young lad onto a stretcher and rushed him away to hospital.

'Bes,' Frank's voice was hardly coherent. 'Bes. Where's Bes?'

Ted Garner, a neighbour four doors down took Frank's elbow. 'She's over here Frank. Near the kennel.' Frank looked to the fence where other rescuers knelt next to her body. 'No!' he screamed out rushing to the back fence.

'She's alive Frank,' a voice said. 'She's shook up but she's alive.'

'Oh thank the Lord,' Ted dropped to his knees next to his daughter. Bes had been knocked unconscious. She had a nasty cut on her forehead but she was alive. The kennel had taken the force of the percussion from the bomb. Tucker the kelpie however, had not been so lucky. Bes opened her eyes and reached out for her father.

'W-what happened?'

'I don't know.' Frank's throat was clogged with emotion, his words garbled.

'Mother? ... Frankie? ... Is Molly alright?'

Frank shook his head and now the tears flowed.

***

Sixteen minutes later.

Detective Inspector Charles Lloyd stood at the hall's entrance to the kitchen. He noted the time on his watch. It was 12.50. The fireman had the fire under control although smoke still poured from the iron-plate wood-fuelled oven that had withstood the blast. A fireman trudged clumsily through the back door with a leather bucket of water heaving it onto the smouldering stove.

'Jesus man!' Lloyd yelled at the young fireman. 'Haven't you blokes done enough for now?'

The fireman stood jaw open. 'Sir?'

Lloyd's assistant, Senior Constable Will Gibson, thirty-three months out of uniform now, to join the criminal investigation unit, and a similar age to the fireman, spoke for his boss. 'What Detective Lloyd is trying to say is the fire's doused now and you are interfering with a crime scene.' Gibson was more diplomatic. The fireman looked from the police to the oven, still billowing smoke and steam. Clearly the Christmas pudding had boiled dry also.

'Shove off,' Lloyd ordered. The fireman's chief officer joined them at the end of the conversation holding the nozzle of a fire hose.

'We'll take it from here,' Gibson continued the diplomacy. The chief fire officer considered his position briefly, and then nodded to the young fireman and the two made to trudge back through the kitchen wreckage.

'Not that way! Down the lane.' There was no doubting Lloyd's authority. The fireman was about to protest at the detective's attitude but out of respect for the dead – the remains of whom they had been trying to sidestep since they arrived twenty minutes earlier – he kept his mouth shut.

'If you would sir, take the side lane,' Gibson offered, again politely, defusing yet another situation. Truth was Will Gibson had served with the veteran inspector long enough to be familiar with his idiosyncrasies and defused many a situation for the hard headed, tough talking copper.

But *this* scene was particularly tough to grasp.

Detective Lloyd's watched through the shattered laundry window as the fire department retreated down the side lane. 'Idiots,' he scowled. Human remains were scattered about and in their haste the firemen had inadvertently trodden on the victims in their smoke masked madness. From where he stood Lloyd watched the firemen through a window in silence for a moment. He noted them stowing their equipment and reel in the hose coiling it about its wooden drum aboard their Merryweather chemical fire engine. The machine fascinated the inspector with its 24 horsepower engine capable of twenty-five miles an hour. And that was fully loaded; with 600 feet of canvas hose and a thirty-five gallon tank of water mixed with bi-carbonate of soda and sulphuric acid, twenty times more efficacious than just water.

They're still idiots he thought.

The inspector thread his fingers together and cracked his knuckles before running a professional eye over the remaining ruins of the rear of this once happy family home. 'It's like the destruction on the battlefields in France where this damned war's threatening the rest of the world,' he muttered to Will. Will nodded. 'Jesus Lord Will, what the bloody hell happened here?'

Neighbours had already spoken of the parcel. *It was addressed to Frankie* they wailed. *She were a lovely lass. Never in all me days did I expect somethin' like this,* another cried. *Frankie looked after me little ones when I were in hospital havin' little Jacob,* a woman five doors from the carnage fidgeted, scratching her face nervously. *She were like a mother to 'em. Oh dear god. What evil is this?*

Detective Lloyd was beyond lament. He wanted answers, not wailers. 'This parcel,' he interrupted. 'Tell me about this parcel.'

'It were a large parcel sir.'

'How large?'

'This big sir,' Tony Baker, father of five children under ten, nine cottages away, drew his hands apart like he was some fisherman describing his catch. 'And this tall.'

'About the size of a hat box,' someone suggested.

'Yes sir. A generous size hat box I'm suggestin',' another offered. 'It were addressed to Frankie but there were no address with it.'

'It was left on Alva Randall's doorstep,' someone said.

'Alva Randall?'

'Yes. Across the street.'

Lloyd. 'Oh, and when was this?'

'In the early hours of the morning she thought, 'cos she went to fetch her milk and the parcel was on her steps.'

Will Gibson looked at the inspector as if the man had not paid attention. 'It was a bomb sir, wrapped in Christmas paper ...'

'Yes yes, but why? Who for god's sake would do such a thing? This isn't France. Jesus!'

Lloyd could not avoid crushing shards of crockery under foot to inspect the epicentre of the explosion. The kitchen table was splintered, most of it blasted into the floorboards. The enamel sink hung skewwhiff, held to the wall by its pipes. All the lining of the walls were stripped of cladding and from head height two thirds of the walls were missing with most of the roof directly overhead gone. Furniture, crockery, cutlery and food was strewn about like a tornado had twisted in through the backdoor.

Instantly heavy boots disturbed the policemen's concentration. A uniformed copper stood where the hallway door once separated the kitchen from the passageway. 'Ah, Inspector Lloyd.'

'What is it?'

'The coroner's arrived sir.'

'Send him in.'

***

Doctor Walter Boyd, the Hobart Coroner, a grumpy old beggar wearing horn rimmed glasses and smoking a briar pipe, arrived with two assistants. They took a long look at the devastation. Boyd had been a medical practitioner in the army serving during the Boxer Rebellion in China back in 1899 to '01 and studied to be a coroner late in life. He'd seen death and plenty of it and knew instantly that he had a challenge on his hands. His wife Beatrice had died only two weeks earlier, but the coroner insisted on returning to work to take his mind off her death; she had lost her battle with cancer. Now he felt a flood of emotions.

His assistant, Bill Tyron and another offsider, Miss Mary Underwood stood by, also shocked by what was before them. Mary held a fingerprint lifting kit but it all seemed so pointless here this day.

Lift a fingerprint off what exactly?

With the arrival of the coroner, Lloyd and Gibson returned to the street a moment, distancing themselves from the stench of death. Out front, over a hundred sightseers had gathered along Queen Street. The inspector singled out Constable Dennis Wilson, a traffic cop in charge of order and doing a lousy job of it. 'Get rid of the ghouls,' Lloyd instructed the policeman. 'Now!'

Four constables scattered the crowd, most of whom were neighbours. Lloyd walked over to one of two police cars. It seemed only like yesterday that he would have had horse driven transport. But here they were, smart and new, reminding the detective how progressive life was these days. Tarrant automobile company in Victoria shipped the cars from the United States of America. The detective loved the T-Model Ford tourer with its four cylinder twenty horsepower engine. It even had a brass radiator and acetylene lamps with a generator on the running board. The coroner had parked alongside his transport and now Lloyd noticed some snotty nose kid was sitting behind the wheel. 'Bugger off.'

The kid buggered off. Lloyd shook his head at another constable who should have been watching the vehicles. 'What were you thinking?'

The older constable looked vague. 'Sorry sir?'

'I said ... never mind, where's Mr Mulberry, the father.'

'He's with neighbours, there sir.' And the policeman pointed to a neat weatherboard cottage with a front rose garden protected by a waist high white picket fence. 'He's with Jones and Warwick.' He spoke of two colleagues. 'And a local doctor just showed up.'

'Doctor? Good. Who are the neighbours?'

'Bowden I think their name is sir.'

Hushed voices in the hallway drew the doctor from the living room accompanied by one of the constables and Mr Bowden, Frank Mulberry's neighbour. The doctor, Scott Macrossan, a calm gentleman in his mid-forties, introduced himself.

Lloyd took the doctor's hand in greeting. 'I'm Inspector Lloyd,' he said in a whisper. 'And this is Leading Senior Constable Gibson. Is Mr Mulberry in there?' Macrossan nodded. Lloyd looked at the constable and said in a quiet voice 'I want you to watch Mr Mulberry's son. I can't have him returning to his own house. Not yet.'

'It's alright inspector,' the doctor said. 'He's sedated.'

'Oh?'

'Madame laudanum. I sedated his daughter also.'

'Ah, Bes, isn't it?'

'That's correct. She is under the pain of guilt,' the doctor said. 'She happened to be returning the family dog to its kennel, just moments before the explosion. The kennel saved her life.'

'How is she, I mean physically?'

'She has a deep cut on her forehead otherwise she is fine, physically. Mentally, it's another issue entirely.'

Lloyd nodded knowingly. 'Are either up for questioning?'

'The father is temporarily non compos mentis.' Macrossan stepped aside and Lloyd peered into the room. Frank Mulberry was stretched out on a sofa, sleeping restlessly in a sedated world of hurt and nightmares. Standing, leaning against the mantle was a uniform policeman while the owners of the house, the Bowdens, sat in silent shock. Lloyd nodded to them silently. They barely registered his presence while Mrs Bowden's face ran with tears. Lloyd looked for Bes. She sat in an armchair masked by the open door, her eyes closed, but Lloyd recognised the twitching eyelids of a woman in shock.

'Poor devils,' Lloyd muttered and crossed the room. He spoke softly. 'Stay with them constable, it's going to be a long day.'

Bes heard every word. Her eyes flashed open. 'Are you in charge?' she asked Lloyd while groggily attempting to rise from the chair.

'Yes. Detective Inspector Charles Lloyd Miss Mulberry ... Bes isn't it?'

'It was a bomb you know,' Bes seethed.

'Yes.'

'A parcel arrived for Frankie.'

'Please sit Miss Mulberry, don't trouble yourself ...'

'A bomb!' Bes screeched. 'Who'd do such a thing?'

'I don't know but we will find out.'

'You do that Detective Lloyd. Make certain you do.'

Doctor Macrossan took Bes, who was fighting the laudanum, by the elbow and steered her back into her chair. He looked to Lloyd and with a nod of his head the two returned to the hallway where the doctor closed the living room door.

'I also sedated Mrs Randall over the road,' Macrossan told Lloyd. The detective knew this to be the woman who had found the Christmas present addressed to Frankie on her front porch steps. 'But I sedated her more mildly so. The woman is devastated about what has happened.'

'And rightly so.' Lloyd turned to Will Gibson. The detectives knew Mrs Randall to be the innocent neighbour who gave the parcel to Ben to take to his sister in the house.

Will looked to the doctor. 'The corner house, right?'

'Yes. I'll come with you. There's little more I can do here for the next few hours.'

Mrs Randall busied herself scrubbing the kitchen floor. The front door was open and the two detectives and Doctor Macrossan found the woman on her hands and knees. As well as a dose of laudanum from the doctor, the woman's husband had insisted she drink a glass of brandy, cooking brandy mind, left over from the Christmas pudding, and now she was animated. Mr Randall saw the men arrive and hailed them from the back steps. The husband was a tall solid man wearing only a singlet with cuffed trousers, bare feet and greased hair parted neatly in the middle. He addressed Macrossan. 'She's been like that since you were here doctor. She won't listen to me. Scrub scrub scrub. She'll wear her arms out down to the elbows at this rate. I told her it wasn't her fault.'

'I gave that parcel to the boy,' Mrs Randall kept scrubbing, her knuckles white and her face red as beetroot. 'I gave it to him ... me ... not you Doug. Me.'

Mr Randall looked at the older copper, then to Will. 'Police huh?' he asked. Lloyd nodded. Gibson introduced them.

'Arrest me,' Mrs Randall shouted over her toil. 'Take me away. I don't care. I deserve what I get.'

'Stop it Alva,' Doug Randall was beside himself with worry. 'Leave it be girl,' he said softly but sternly.

'I can't!' Mrs Randall slopped water from her bucket onto the floor and began scrubbing hard. Doug Randall stepped inside and leaning over his wife he lifted her effortlessly to her feet. She immediately turned and beat her balled fists on his chest, but he pulled her in tightly and hugged the woman as she wept uncontrollably.

'Mrs Randall' Lloyd said with as much compassion as he could muster. 'I know you are upset but I need to ask you some questions.' Doug Randall held his wife tight and fixed the inspector with a firm eye. 'Give us a minute will you. Just a minute.' Lloyd bunched his lips, turned to Will and tilted his head to the front door.

'Wait in the front room,' the husband suggested. He held his wife at arm's length to look her in the eye. 'We'll make us all a nice cup o' tea, won't we love?'

'Tea!' Lloyd questioned impatiently.

'Yes, Alva'll make a cupper. Won't take long as the kettle's hot on the stove already. How do yer like it?'

Lloyd was about to vent his frustration when Macrossan joined them. Overhearing the tail of the conversation the doctor ushered the detectives into the front room. 'She needs a minute, inspector,' the doctor said quietly.

'It's another minute I can't spare,' Lloyd hissed under his breath.

'White with two sugars for us both, thank you,' Senior Constable Will Gibson called down the hallway.

***

The next ten minutes felt like half an hour. Finally, Doug Randall placed a tray with steaming tea pot, china cups, milk jug, sugar bowl and a plate of oat coconut and golden syrup biscuits on a serving table, in what was the family good room, with its view out onto Queen Street. 'I'll fetch Alva,' he told them in a composed voice.

Moments later the victim of circumstance sat in an armless upholstered chair between the policemen. Alva Randall had washed her face and applied makeup but the signs of anguish were etched across her once pretty face. Doug Randall fidgeted with the teapot but the doctor ordered him sit by his wife while he poured the tea.

Lloyd was impatient. 'Mrs Randall ...'

'Alva, please.'

'Alva. I am Inspector Lloyd and this is Senior Constable Gibson. Would you kindly tell us exactly what happened? The parcel was left on your porch I believe.'

The woman fought back more tears. With her husband holding her hand she finally cleared her throat. 'I went to fetch the milk out front, and the parcel was sitting on the top step.'

'So it was placed there overnight?'

'Yes, Doug and me went to bed late last night about 10.30, on account Doug was late home you see and we ate a late supper. I put two empty bottles and a shilling on the step just before bed time.'

'Did you hear anything unusual during the night?'

'No. Nothing.'

'And what time did you fetch your milk this morning?'

'It was by six, 'cos the sun comes up early in summer and the milk can be left in the sun if we aren't careful. Doug here hates warm milk.'

'How big was this parcel?' Will Gibson asked, leafing through his busy notebook looking for blank page.

'About a foot square.'

Will rolled his bottom lip and nodded at his earlier notes. 'What do you do Mr Randall?'

'Me?'

'Your work?'

'I work at Ridgley Textiles in Davey Street. I hope you aren't suggesting I ...'

'No, no sir. Not at all. You were working on Christmas night?'

'Yes I'm a nightwatchman you see. But being Christmas we were all given half shifts, that's why I came home at eight.'

'So, back to the parcel. Did you not read who it was addressed to?'

'Yes. Frankie Mulberry.'

'But you brought the parcel inside. Why did you not run it across the road and leave it on the Mulberry's doorstep?'

'We only moved here three weeks ago. We are new in the neighbourhood and I didn't know the Mulberrys.'

'We knew 'em by sight of course, to wave to like, but we never really caught their names.'

'We keep to ourselves pretty much.'

'And the parcel sat in your house all day?'

'Yes,' Doug shook his head, disbelieving. 'When I got up our boy Tommy, he's eleven, well he was shakin' the parcel when I walked in the kitchen like.'

'Shaking it?'

'Yes. He was excited. *Father Christmas came again*, he said. And he was saying what's in it do you think Pa, and he shook it a few times and it rattled.'

'Doug had to take the parcel off him,' Alva said. 'Didn't you Doug, on account he might break it.'

Doug shook a solemn face with the thought of what it contained.

'So it was addressed to Frankie Mulberry, but no street number?'

'No address,' Doug said. 'Just the name Frankie Mulberry.'

'How was it written?'

'With crayon I'm thinkin'.'

'But it was hard to read, too,' Mrs Randall said. 'Weren't it Doug?'

Doug nodded. 'It were a scrawl really.'

'Oh dear Lord, the poor sweet thing.'

Lloyd. 'So did it not occur to you to ask around?'

'Ask around?'

'Yes. To ask your neighbours if there was a Frankie Mulberry living nearby.'

'Well yes Mr Lloyd. But it was six in the morning. I thought it best to wait a while. So I put it in the cupboard and ...' Mrs Randall looked embarrassed. 'And I forgot about it.'

'Why put it in the cupboard?'

'On account of young Tommy was playing postman with it on his new billycart.'

'I made him a billycart for Christmas you see,' Doug said. 'An' Tommy was so excited he were playin' postman and riding up and down the street with the parcel. So I took it off him and Alva hid it in the cupboard.'

'It was then, this afternoon, when we saw the kiddies playin' cricket in the street that I remembered the parcel and started asking about.' Alva's eyes welled up once more.

Doug held his wife's hands in his and gave them a squeeze. 'She finally learnt Ben was the brother, he'd been bowled out you see and was sitting on the footpath ...'

'And he was so excited.'

'Who? Ben?'

'Yes, and ...' Alva managed a few words but her voice was breaking. 'He took the parcel and ran inside to give it to his sis ... oh dear god! How could I have known?' she wept.

'You said your son shook the parcel, what did it sound like?'

'Oh Lord,' Doug said. 'He dropped it once and all.'

'Dropped it?'

'Yes. Alva thought it might be full of confectionery.'

Lloyd wanted to say *that's because it was full of nuts and bolts* – shrapnel – but thought he would withhold that information, it would only add to their grief.

'One last question,' Lloyd said. 'Have you got any idea how the parcel ended up delivered to your house instead of the Mulberry's?'

'No sir,' Doug sighed. 'Not at all.'

Will Gibson spilled his thoughts to the inspector as they returned to the street. 'The perpetrator clearly had the houses mixed up. I mean both are corner houses.'

'Yes clearly. So why?'

***

Doug Randall stepped onto the street to join the detectives as they departed. He tapped a Turf from its packet, lighting the cigarette with a match before offering the packet to the policeman. 'Smoke?'

They both refused. 'Alva's been very anxious since our eldest, Harold, joined the army,' he said. 'He's training in Claremont at the moment.'

'Yes,' Will understood. 'My youngest brother's done the same, he's eighteen.' Will also felt the pressure to sign up, but policemen at home were in short supply because of the war.

Inspector Lloyd took in the scene of the porch and the step where the parcel had been placed. To one side of the house the laneway was a quagmire of red clayey mud. Someone had been digging and it continued to the front garden. Doug Randall noted the inspector studying the mess. 'We had a blocked sewer pipe recently,' Randall told the cop. 'That's the plumber's mess. They have to come back and clear it.'

'Looks like good clay,' Lloyd noted. 'My wife has a little studio in the back garden, she's a potter you see. That clay looks like it would make good terracotta.'

'Well you're welcome to it mate. Anytime you like.'

Lloyd coughed a laugh. Such an idle conversation under the circumstances. 'Thanks,' he said politely.

Immediately their attention was drawn to the coroner hurrying to meet them.

'I have some interesting information Charles.'

'A lead I hope.'

'Maybe.'

Lloyd excused himself and the two detectives left Doug Randall blowing smoke rings, to follow the coroner a short distance.

'What is it Walter?' Lloyd asked when they were out of earshot.

'Miss Frankie Mulberry was married.'

'What?'

'Yes. She was *married*.'

'Christ!' Will Gibson was the first to speak. 'But we confirmed she was a twenty-two-year-old living at home with her parents. A spinster by all reports.'

'Where did you learn this?'

'Bes just told Doctor Macrossan. He told me. Frankie was married in secret and her parents didn't know.'

'Then it is vital we find out who the husband is, or was.'

***

The three men congregated at the police cars.

'I've done all I can here for the moment,' the coroner said. They watched in silence a moment as blood-soaked parcels wrapped in cheesecloth were transported to the coroner's Ford. 'I'll have a better idea when I get the bodies, ah remains, back to the morgue.'

Inspector Charles Lloyd waited for Doctor Boyd to drive away and, taking in a deep breath, he sighed. 'Let's get on with it Will.' And the two men returned to the bombsite.

The acrid smell of burnt flesh, high explosive and the taint of spilt human blood still permeated the air. Overhead through the damaged roof, the sky was blue and all looked well with the world. Yet the devastation surrounding the two men bonded them in a quest to find the cowardly killer.

'We can safely say that the bomber has never been to the Mulberry's house,' Lloyd said. 'Otherwise he would not have left the parcel on the wrong porch.'

'Makes sense.'

'And none of the neighbours knew anything about a suitor. Yet this Frankie was very familiar with someone.'

'Clearly.'

Lloyd sighed heavily and turned back to the hallway and front door. 'I've seen enough here for today Will. Tell the men outside to secure this site. I want a tarpaulin over the open roof for starters, although I doubt it'll rain, and make certain this property is watched all night. I don't want this scene disturbed in any way.'

***

Next morning. Police Headquarters. Hobart.

Inspector Lloyd arrived at work half an hour early. He had skipped breakfast at home and now found himself staring at his office wall. His mind was blank to either rhyme or reason why anyone would commit such a crime. But peace and quiet was short lived, broken by a knock on his door. Constable Becker entered without waiting for an invitation. 'Ah, you *are* here sir.'

'What is it?'

'I took a message on the telephone earlier from the coroner, Doctor Boyd, he asked that you contact him urgently.'

Lloyd's finger was dialling before Becker closed the door behind him.

'I'm glad you called me before going to the hospital Walter,' Boyd launched into his conversation without a greeting.

Lloyd pushed the receiver tube hard to his ear and leant into the mouthpiece. 'What is it Walter?'

'Frankie Mulberry was pregnant.'

'What?'

'She was pregnant, I've been up half the night doing autopsies and when I looked carefully at Frankie ... well ... I found a foetus in the womb didn't I.'

'Are you certain?' Suddenly Lloyd corrected himself. 'I mean ... pregnant?'

'I'm staring at it right now Lloyd. I have it in a jar of formalin. It's as big as a pear so I say she was fifteen weeks thereabouts. And for what it's worth, it's a girl.'

***

Next morning. Queen Alexandra Hospital for Women.

Neighbours had raced twelve-year-old Ben Mulberry to the hospital not a mile from Queen Street within minutes of the explosion. He was found twisted like a discarded doll in the backyard where the bomb had thrown him out through the backdoor. He survived, barely. Wounds to his left arm were so severe the surgeon, Doctor Archer, amputated the limb. Sadly the left side of Ben's face was disfigured and he lost his left eye.

In the early hours of the next morning, when the laudanum had run its calming course, Frank Mulberry demanded to be escorted to the hospital to be at his son's bedside. It had been a sickening sight to see his twelve-year-old son so damaged. Ben was heavily sedated and when Lloyd and Will arrived Frank was asleep in an armchair that the orderlies had dragged into the ward for him. Ben's surgeon, Doctor Archer, who had not slept all night, ushered the policemen towards the ward. 'Will the lad survive?' Lloyd asked Archer.

'With god's help, yes.'

'And the father's here, I believe?'

'That's correct.'

'How is he?'

'Terrible. As you can imagine. And he's having mood swings from inconsolable tears to anger.'

'That's understandable.'

***

Frank Mulberry looked vacantly at the three men. They stood at the entrance to the ward all wearing mixed emotions. If there had been any expression at all from Frank, it was not identifiable. Detective Lloyd noted Mulberry's pupils had shrunk, he looked gaunt and his face and hands were clammy. Laudanum. The opiate was addictive and Boyd wondered if he had been given too much. Young Ben had also been given the painkiller and he slept soundly.

Doctor Archer had a gentle word in the father's ear and eventually helped the man out into the corridor where the four men retired to Doctor Archer's office.

'Police huh,' Mulberry underlined the word with derision. Inspector Lloyd nodded silently. 'Well? Have you come to tell me you've caught the bastard?'

'I'm afraid not,' Lloyd said. 'Not yet.'

'Who'd want to kill my daughter, sweet little Frankie? Why?'

'We will catch the perpetrator, that I promise you.'

'For now, we need to ask you some questions,' Will started a new page in his note book.

'Anything,' Mulberry fell heavily into a leather-covered chair. 'Anything to catch the bastard.'

The inspector sat on the edge of the doctor's desk, positioning himself between Will and Mulberry. He knew the first question was pertinent and sensitive and thought it best he be the one to ask.

'Did your daughter have a suitor?'

'No. Not at all.'

'Because we talked to your neighbours and one mentioned that your daughter did have a suitor some months back, a tall slim good-looking chap by all accounts.'

'That would be Brady O'Connell. He were a Roman Catholic boy chasin' my Frankie. From an Irish family. Lives near Richmond.'

Will. 'They were keen then?'

'He was. But I soon put a stop to that. Can't have my Frankie marrying some rat catcher.' Mulberry thought a moment as if to justify that statement. 'Frankie's from a good Protestant family, yes sir.'

'You were dead against the relationship?' Will asked, and immediately bit his bottom lip. *Dead* was a poor choice of words.

Mulberry looked up angrily at the young policeman as if he were stupid, and reiterated. 'He were a Roman Catholic,' he said with venom. 'Frankie were Protestant. May the two never marry.'

Lloyd rolled a discreet eye at his subordinate before taking the other chair. He sat slowly and shuffled about to face the father. 'Mr Mulberry, Frank, ah … did you know Frankie was with child?'

Mulberry sat bolt upright like he had acid thrown in his face. 'Don't be daft. No.'

'Yes sir. Mr Mulberry. Frankie was pregnant. Fifteen weeks Doctor Boyd estimates.'

'She can't be. That be impossible. My Frankie with child? No sir. Not possible I say.' The devastated father looked at Doctor Archer in denial. Searching his face for a sign it was all a mistake. 'Did you know this?' he finally asked the surgeon.

'I'm afraid so Mr Mulberry. I spoke with the coroner last night.'

'Jesus Lord. No.'

'I'm sorry this comes as such a shock,' Lloyd said. Mulberry started to hyperventilate, he struggled to breathe. Doctor Archer bailed up a passing nurse and called for smelling salts while Will poured the man water from a jug on the office sideboard.

A moment passed and Mulberry sat, mouth wide open. Incredulous. Slowly the realisation sank in. He grew angry once more and looked to Lloyd through blood shot eyes. 'Brady O'Connell. That filthy mongrel. That low life Irish pig farmer. I told her … I warned her … I ordered him stay away. Oh dear Lord, Frankie! What have you done girl?'

'You say this Brady O'Connell lives near Richmond,' Will noted. 'Pig farm you say?'

Mulberry slowly contained his emotions. 'If you drive through Richmond and cross the bridge you'll see St John's Church on the hill left. Keep driving half a mile and you'll see a road heading north. Follow that a mile or so and you'll find the pig farm alongside the river. Brady is a mechanic as well and services local farm equipment.'

'Coal River Valley?'

'Yes. The O'Connells come here in irons three fathers ago.' Mulberry's bitter words alluded to Tasmania's dark past when the majority of early settlers were felons from the prisons of Britain. 'Bloody convicts, all o' them.'

'How many live there now?'

'O'Connell's father died years back I'm told, liver disease. Brady O'Connell lives with his mother and brother, I think his name is Leroy. I seem to remember someone telling me another younger cousin helps them run the pig farm. He lives with 'em I think.'

'How old is this Brady?'

'Same as my Frankie, twenty-two. Leroy is a year older. He's also a mechanic.'

***

Afternoon, same day. Coal River Valley.

Inspector Lloyd and Senior Constable Gibson smelt the farm before they drove onto it. A gentle summer northerly saw to that. The O'Connell's ancestors had accumulated little wealth of note to pass on to their kin, for the original farmhouse hadn't changed since great great granddaddy had dug the foundations just above flood level alongside the river seventy years earlier. The pens and sties were large enough and the pigs seemed content but the aroma took some time to acclimatise to. The single storey cottage of vertical timber and shingled roof was tired, yet looked comfortable and homely with a veranda facing northwest to catch the afternoon sun.

Will steered the T-Model through the open gate and slowed well before the homestead. He pushed the clutch pedal with his foot and pressed the brake hard to the floor, finally cutting the motor by reducing the fuel supply with the mixture lever on the steering column. They had parked thirty yards from the cottage. The gentle chug of the engine gave way to the snorting and squealing of fifty or more pigs.

Will was first with boots on the ground when the sound of a woven wire fly door slammed shut on its rusted springs. Old Ma O'Connell stood on the porch and sniffed before planting her hands on her hips and staring. One moment later a wafer-thin woman with a baby perched on her bony hip joined her. The afternoon sun caused the women to squint but Ma O'Connell knew cops when she saw them, and the double barrel shotgun leaning against the wall did not go unnoticed by the lawmen.

'Mrs O'Connell?' Lloyd called out, and approached the cottage with Will at his side.

'You coppers?' the woman spat. She looked well into her sixties, although the two policemen knew her to be in her early fifties.

'Yes madam,' Lloyd said. 'I'm Inspector Charles Lloyd and this is Will Gibson, senior constable.'

'You here about the Mulberry incident?'

'You've heard then?'

'O' course. The whole country side's talkin' 'bout it.'

'Then you know we're here to talk to Brady?'

'I guess so,' she said, her eyes cold and black. 'But he didn't do it ... yer hear me. My boy's innocent. That girl's father is crazy, he called my boy a rat catcher and threatened 'im.'

'We know Mrs O'Connell,' Will said with the hint of a sigh. 'But we need to talk to Brady all the same.'

The skinny woman with child sat in a rocking chair, when behind Ma O'Connell the fly wire swung open again and Brady O'Connell stepped onto the porch planting himself in front of his mother. Brady O'Connell was a tall, slim and handsome, thin-lipped man with short back and sides parted on the left.

'It's alright Ma,' he said. 'Go inside. I'll talk to these men.' Brady looked at Will, and then stared Lloyd in the eye. 'I ain't got nuthin' to hide.'

It appeared mother and son had mutual respect for each other as Ma O'Connell sat heavily into a wicker chair alongside the rocker, where the shotgun was within reach, and said. 'If it's all the same with you Brady, I'll be sittin' right here.'

'As you wish Ma.' Brady stepped off the porch to face the policemen. 'Can we walk?'

Will nodded. 'Lead the way.'

The three walked towards the sties where the sound of pigs feeding on mulched grain ensured Ma O'Connell was out of earshot. Brady lent with his back against the wooden rails. Will assessed him a confident beggar and seemingly unperturbed that he was the prime suspect of a violent multiple murder case. 'We was married,' he said. The words as cold as his lack of emotion.

'You were what?'

'Married. Me an' Frankie married through a registrar, it would be a month now.'

'And no one knew?'

'No. Not even me Ma.'

'Where did you marry?'

'At the office of Births, Deaths and Marriages.'

'In town?'

'Yes.'

'Did you know she was pregnant?'

'Of course, that's why we married. I wanted to make an honest woman of her.'

'And no one knew, she was married that is?'

'That's what I said. But Bes knew. That's Frankie's younger sister. She's got a boyfriend and all. Sneaks out at night to meet him. It's the parents' fault, all high and mighty Protestants. We've all got the same god yer know.'

Lloyd locked his hands behind his back and watched the pigs feeding. Whatever it was they were enjoying it and the smell wasn't that bad when you became used to it. At one end a roofed enclosure gave the animals protection from the rain, but not much else. Another twenty yards past the sties Lloyd noted a mechanic's garage, open one end. From where he stood he could just make out another man inside, the older brother Leroy he imagined. He was around five-foot-eight but with broad shoulders and stocky build. Clearly this man knew the farm had visitors but he busied himself at a workbench.

Lloyd asked. 'That Leroy?'

'Yeh. Me big brother. An' that there woman with Ma is Leroy's wife Tilly with baby Joe.

'You're a mechanic are you not?'

'Yeh, me and Leroy both.'

'But you work the farm?'

'Yeh. We do both. We have to. We have our own garage here and do local repairs and I work whenever I can get the work at Cramp Brothers garage in Harrington Street. Otherwise me and Leroy make ends meet here.'

'And the pigs?'

'We rear 'em here and cart 'em to the abattoirs in Richmond.'

'Do you have help?'

'Cousin Ed mucks out the sty, helps feed and stuff like that.'

'Cousin Ed?'

'Yeh, he lives in a shepherd's hut half a mile down river.' Brady nodded to a copse of trees where an unkempt dirt track led away into the bushland.

'So Brady,' Lloyd had unbuttoned his tweed coat, opening it for some cool air. 'Who do you think made that bomb and left it on the doorstep?'

'How should I know?'

'You don't seem too upset for a man who just lost his wife and unborn to a bomb explosion.'

'Jesus Christ. What can I do? How am I supposed to act?'

'With grief. A tear might help.'

'This Ed fellow, what's his full name?'

'Ed Shelley.'

'Half a mile down that road eh?'

'Yeh.'

Detective Lloyd looked across at Gibson. Words were not necessary. As the younger cop drove away Lloyd turned back to Brady. 'So Brady, introduce me to your brother.'

'Sure,' Brady sighed. 'But I'm warnin' yer now 'e's got a short fuse and doesn't like coppers.'

'Well if he's got nothing to hide it shouldn't be a problem.'

***

Will Gibson drove the overgrown track between tall eucalypts. Like Brady had told them, he entered a clearing after half a mile where he found the shepherd's hut and the river came back into view. The one room hut was vertical hand hewn timber, with a tin roof replacing the original wooden shingles of the fifty-year-old structure. A thin finger of smoke lazily escaped the stove chimney and the one window was curtained from the inside with hessian. Will knocked on the door. It was latched from within.

A gravelly voice called out. 'Who is it?'

Will heard voices, low voices, male and female. 'Ed Shelley?'

'Who are you?' the male cried out.

'Will Gibson, Mr Shelley. 'Senior Constable Gibson. Can you open the door please?'

Low voices appeared agitated. *The voice of the law had that effect on many people.*

Will thumped on the door. 'Mr Shelley ...'

The door flew open and a young girl pushed past Will, anxious to make herself scarce. She looked fifteen, if that.

A young man appeared. 'What d'ya want?'

'Ed Shelley?'

'Yeh.'

'I've come down from the O'Connell farm. I'd like you to accompany me. My superior Detective Inspector Lloyd wants a word.'

'I'm busy. Tell 'im to come 'ere.'

'Your friend …' Will jerked his head to the young girl disappearing into the forest. 'Where's she going?'

'She lives with her parents on a farm over the hill, through them trees.'

'She's a bit young isn't she?'

'Old enough. Look, what's the problem.'

'We're here on a murder investigation so I suggest you cooperate. Now get in the car.'

***

Ten minutes later.

The five men stood facing each other in the O'Connell's workshop alongside the pigsty. The policemen scrutinised Leroy. He was shorter than his younger brother, about five-foot-eight, and stocky with broad shoulders. On the far side of the shop a mechanical thresher was in a state of repair. Will, who had an interest in machinery, caught Brady's attention as he admired the machine.

'Robey & Company,' Brady told Will. 'Ten horsepower engine. She can thresh eighty bushels of oats in an hour.'

'We're repairing it for Edgar Woolley from Campania,' Leroy added sourly. 'If yer have to know.'

'What's wrong with it?' Will asked.

Lloyd shook his head in exasperation. 'Threshers are stickin'.'

Will positioned himself to shoot his governor a discreet *bear with me a moment* look.

'You're all mechanical then eh?' Will asked.

'Me and Brad are,' Leroy said. 'But Ed 'ere couldn't fit two bits o' Meccano together.'

'That's all very well,' Lloyd's annoyance was blatant. 'But we're not here to talk about farm machinery. You all know about the Queen Street bomb attack,' Lloyd stared at Ed Shelley. 'You too I take it?'

'Yeh.'

'Yes sir!' Lloyd had taken an instant dislike to the young man. 'Show a bit of respect.'

Ed Shelley didn't appreciate being belittled in front of his older cousins. He glared at Lloyd. Lloyd returned a death stare. 'Well?'

'Yes sir,' Ed Shelley said, barely disguising a sneer.

'Can you all account for yourselves Christmas night? Let's start with you.' Lloyd looked to Ed Shelley.

'Yes.' He looked at Will. 'I was with Ellie.'

Lloyd. 'Ellie?'

'Is that Ellie whom I saw?' Will asked.

'Yes.'

'All night?'

Ed Shelley nodded and cast his eyes downwards.

'What about you Elroy O'Connell,' Lloyd enquired. 'Did you too have female company?'

'What is this?' Leroy spat back. 'Bloody inquisition?'

'Answer the question.'

'Why the fuck should I?'

'Watch your tongue boy.' Lloyd's face reddened. 'You're all suspects in a heinous crime. So I suggest ...' Lloyd stabbed his finger into Leroy's chest, 'you-answer-the- bloody-question. Do you have an alibi?'

'Yeh. Me mum, Leroy and Tilly ... sir. I was home here and they'll vouch for me.'

'I bet they will. That just leaves you O'Connell,' Lloyd faced Brady, standing so close Brady could smell his sharp breath. Lloyd scrolled an eye down the man's overalls, held by suspenders over the shoulders. 'That mud on your boots?'

'What of it?'

'Its red clay and I don't see any red clay around the farm here.'

'So what?'

'So what? I have seen that very same clay recently in the laneway adjoining the Randall's property, that's what ...'

'Randall's?'

'Yes. The Randall's live in the house where the parcel was inadvertently left. Directly across the street from the Mulberry's, on the opposite corner.' Lloyd thought he recognised a slight twitch of recognition, but he wasn't certain.

'Are you saying it was taken to the wrong house?' Brady asked.

'Inadvertently, yes. And I will bet my week's wage that if we inspect that mud on your boots closer it will be a perfect match.'

Senior Constable Gibson was impressed and he knew what was coming next. Lloyd opened his coat even further and revealed a set of iron handcuffs hooked to his trouser belt. 'Brady O'Connell, you are to accompany Senior Constable Gibson and myself to the police station in Hobart for questioning. What have you to say?'

'I'm innocent damn it.'

'If you resist I will put you in irons. Do you understand me?'

***

Late afternoon.

Brady O'Connell sat barefoot in a holding cell at police headquarters in Liverpool Street. He was far from happy and the fact he had his boots removed for examination bothered him even more.

They weren't even his for Christ's sake. His boots were waterlogged from a fishing trip and as he wore the same size boot as his brother, he wore Leroy's.

On Lloyd's orders the suspect was fetched to an interview room down the corridor from the cells where he and Senior Constable Gibson waited. The policemen sat opposite their detainee. Will was impatient to start the interview. 'The clay is a match,' he said. 'It is white clay produced by chemical weathering, forensics informed us,' Will studied his notes. 'A chemical weathering of aluminium silicate minerals, like feldspar.'

'White huh?' Brady O'Connell wore a smug face. 'Well last time I looked that muck on me boots was red. Terracotta I think you called it.'

'That's true. However the Randall's sewer pipes had rusted badly, colouring the clay over the years.'

Brady O'Connell's smirk vanished.

'We'll come back to exhibit number one, the red clay, shortly,' Lloyd leant forward placing his elbows on the table knotting his fingers together. 'How long had you known Frankie?'

'We was childhood sweethearts. I never looked sideways at any other.' Totally unexpected Brady O'Connell's face started to crumble. 'We were in love.' Tears filled his eyes. 'She was having my baby.'

Lloyd was as tough as a railway bolt. He was having none of it. Will was more empathetic.

'Well?' Lloyd pushed his chair away noisily and stood. Leaning on his knuckles like a gorilla he positioned himself close to the suddenly remorseful suspect. 'Well Brady, have you got something to tell us?'

'I didn't do it I tell you. I am innocent.'

'Where were you Christmas night, say six until dawn?'

'After Christmas dinner with Ma and Tilly, Me and Elroy went duck shootin', up river close to the village.'

'Village? You mean Richmond?'

'Yes. There's good shootin' north of the bridge.'

'What time was this?'

'After dinnertime. Mum'll vouch for us. She made turkey sandwiches with the leftovers and me an' Elroy rode up in Bevan Murray's flat tray Ford what we just fixed. He's a neighbour and we knew it would bother him none if we took his truck.'

'Where's the truck now?'

'We returned it this mornin'.'

'What time did you return home?'

'It were darkish, about nine I suppose.'

'Anyone see you?'

'What?'

'Do you know of any witnesses that will vouch for you, witnesses you saw up river, in the village?'

'Well no. Me and Elroy kind of keep to ourselves.'

'Did you shoot any ducks?'

'Ah … no actually. The buggers weren't givin' yesterday.'

'So if there weren't any ducks why did you stay so late?'

'We had some bottles of beer. The evening was warm and we sat on the riverbank and drank.'

Will thought carefully about his next question. 'You lived apart from your wife Frankie because it was a secret.'

'That's right. But we were looking for a farm to rent. A farm of our own with a garage. Then we intended to tell Frankie's parents about the marriage. We're consenting adults you know.'

'Maybe. But Mr Mulberry had a hatred for Roman Catholics. But you knew this did you not?' Truth be known Frank had made veiled threats in the past.

'Yeh, stupid bastard. But me and Frankie planned to live together with or without his blessings.'

'Did your brother Leroy know about this marriage?'

'Yes. He knew everything. But Tilly didn't.'

'Everything?'

'Yes.'

'Did *he* know where Frankie lived?'

'Yes. Actually he only asked me her address recent like,' Brady raised his brow. 'You know it's a funny thing because I thought he was going to send her a Christmas card.' Already Brady sensed he had said too much.

'Are you suggesting your brother placed that parcel on the Randall's steps? Getting the corner houses confused?"

'No, no sir I am not. I just told yer he knew where she lived. Anyway Leroy would never do such a thing, he loved Frankie like a sister.'

Lloyd looked to his subordinate and tipped his head to the door. Once they were out of earshot. 'We need to arrest Leroy.'

'I agree.'

'Go and fetch him.' Will headed for the front door. 'And Will.'

'Sir?'

'Take a uniform constable with you, he might be uncooperative. I'm sending a second car with a warrant. I want the property and in particular that garage searched for anything remotely to do with bomb making.'

***

Leroy O'Connell was not surprised to see the police car turn into his driveway the second time this day.

'Leroy O'Connell.' This time Will flashed his badge while the uniform cop at his side displayed handcuffs. 'You're to join me back at police headquarters.'

'What? Why?'

'For questioning in regards to the murder of Rose Mulberry, Molly Mulberry and Frankie Mulberry and the wilful injury of Ben Mulberry.'

'Bugger off, I told yer all I know.'

'We can do this the easy way or the hard way.' The uniform stepped forward. 'You choose.'

'Jesus.'

Leroy sat with Will in the back of the police car. As he did, Will noted the end of Leroy's little finger on his left hand was missing to the second knuckle. Leroy noted the cop staring. 'Caught in a crank shaft a year ago,' he said dryly. 'Gotta tell yer, it hurt like buggery.'

With both brothers kept apart in different cells there were minor discrepancies in their story, like timing, but they were just that, minor discrepancies. All the same Lloyd was convinced he had enough to arrest Brady on suspicion of murder. He made the arrest whilst detaining Leroy further.

At the same time he offered Leroy immunity from prosecution if he testified against his brother. When Brady heard of this arrangement he changed one vital clue that threw a spanner in the works.

'They are Leroy's boots,' he said, pearls of sweat appearing on his forehead.

'What?'

'My boots got saturated when we went shootin' at Richmond. I nearly fell in the drink. So I put Leroy's on this mornin' as he has a spare pair and we have the same shoe size.'

'Are you serious?'

'Bloody oath I'm serious.'

'So when was this again?'

'This morning?'

'Did it not occur to you they were muddy? Why didn't you clean them?'

'Dirty boots don't bother me none. Wet boots do. We live on a farm remember, besides Ma won't let us wear 'em inside no how.'

In the meantime, the police team, notably two constables and one experienced investigator, returned to HQ with the results of their warrant at the pig farm. Lloyd met the men in his office and became silently confident.

***

An hour later Ma O'Connell arrived at Liverpool Street Station with the family lawyer, another cousin of the boys, Duncan O'Connell; a round faced overweight man with the gift of speech. Ma O'Connell could be heard before she was seen … and she was mad as a disturbed bull ants' nest. The hard-faced pig farmer was not a woman to trifle with. 'I wanna see me boys.'

'You'll have to wait,' Lloyd told the woman, his tone mimicking hers. Ma O'Connell looked to her lawyer.

'Take a seat Bertha,' Duncan O'Connell told her. 'Let me handle this.'

Bertha O'Connell stared at Lloyd like she wanted to rip his throat out with her bare hands. She rubbed her chin and wiped spittle from the corners of her mouth before sitting stiffly on an uncomfortable wooden chair in a waiting room just off the front desk.

***

Due to the seriousness of the crime a special court hearing was assembled. Court was in order at 9am.

'Dynamite was found in the accused's garage,' Lloyd told the court, seriously convinced the perpetrator was standing before him in the dock. 'What use could you possibly need for dynamite?'

'We use it to blast tree roots on the property,' Brady answered swiftly. 'To clear land.'

The subject of immunity for Leroy if he testified against his brother was aired. On lawyer Patrick O'Connell's advice, he flatly refused. But already a rift had appeared in the brothers' relationship. It was also noted that Lloyd had acted above his authority and the court could not guarantee immunity. Besides, the lawyer told his cousin Leroy quietly, 'If you accept immunity from the prosecution this would act to the benefit of Brady's defence. You would appear guilty. It will serve no good purpose for either of you.'

With little to go on both men were released. In the meantime Lloyd convinced the judge another more thorough search was needed. The warrant was signed. O'Connell's property was thoroughly searched a second time, and another twenty-two sticks of dynamite were discovered in a box in a woodshed. To make matters worse Brady spoke to a reporter from *The Mercury* Newspaper, almost gloating that the police had no evidence on he or his brother.

'Why would my brother want to kill my wife?' he crowed, also explaining how the dynamite was a necessity on any farm. Unfortunately for the investigators, this was fact.

Inspector Lloyd and Senior Constable Gibson now concentrated on the Mulberry property, in particular the bomb fragments. Painstakingly the makings of the lethal explosive were gathered and even more painstaking was the dedication of the forensic laboratory who managed to piece together twenty per cent of the box; enough evidence to replicate the bomb.

'The hatbox everyone spoke of disintegrated of course.' James Braithwaite in forensics told Lloyd. 'But within the hatbox was a light wooden structure.'

'Ah, the dark brown pieces of wood,' Will stated.

'Yes, more like splinters I'd say. That's what housed the bomb. We literally had hundreds of slivers of wood to piece together.'

'I know James. You've done an amazing job.' The two detectives examined the exhibit, twelve inches by twelve, just as Mrs Randall had told them. 'It looks like tea chest packing material,' Will commented.

'Go to the top of the class senior constable.' Braithwaite agreed.

'Any finger prints?'

'We're dusting the bolts and nuts, the projectiles,' Braithwaite said. 'So far nothing.'

'Do we know how it worked?'

'I've drawn a diagram.' Braithwaite placed a clipboard on the lab bench. 'There was a tube under the lid which contained a spring under which a pin was held in place by a copper wire. The wire ran through the tubing and was fastened to the lid of the parcel.'

'So when the lid was opened the wire was pulled the pin was released enabling it to strike a shotgun cartridge, exploding the dynamite. There were at least two pounds of bolts and nuts packed in there as well.'

'Jesus Christ!' Will declared. 'I just had a thought.'

'What?'

'When we arrested Leroy I noticed an unusual gun in the garage.'

'Like what?'

'Well when questioned about it Leroy told me he purchased the gun from a neighbour, but the firing mechanism had been changed from steel to brass ...'

'By whom?'

'Leroy himself.'

'Why change the mechanism?'

'So it could be used outdoors and wouldn't rust, as a rabbit trap.'

'Rabbit trap?'

'Yes, like a booby trap. A piece of wire with a hook attached to the end runs along the side of the barrel to the muzzle. A piece of carrot is fixed to the hook and the slightest of nibbles caused the gun to fire.'

'And you didn't think this strange?' Lloyd asked shaking his head.

'Well no sir. My uncle in Campbell Town does the same thing. It all seemed so legitimate to me at the time.'

'Legitimate!' Lloyd wasn't pleased. 'Go back to the property and fetch that gun.

***

Later that afternoon.

Braithwaite at the forensic laboratory examined the firing mechanism of the rabbit gun and found it almost identical to the drawing he had made of the bomb mechanism.

'And I found these,' Will Gibson was determined to redeem himself.

'What?' Lloyd watched Will unwrap a cloth satchel and tip pieces of tubing and springs onto the bench. 'Now that I knew what to look for I recognised these. Exactly the same as the materials used in the bomb.'

Lloyd compared the evidence. He was speechless a brief moment. But there would be no felicitations. 'We've got the bastards this time. Arrest them.'

***

Two hours later Will Gibson caught up with his boss in the station canteen where he awaited news of the arrest. Lloyd tipped back his head and drained the last of his black tea in its enamel mug. 'Well?'

'Brady O'Connell is in the holding cells now sir.'

'And Leroy?' The senior constable shook his head slowly, his expression dour. 'He's shot through hasn't he?' Lloyd said.

'Not sure sir,' Will said seriously.

'Damn the man!' Lloyd heaved the tin mug across the room chipping its enamel and narrowly missing James Braithwaite of forensics entering the canteen.

'Steady on Charlie. You could do someone some mischief chucking things about.'

'Leroy O'Connell has jumped ship,' Lloyd spat. 'Apparently.'

'Oh, that is bad news.'

'Stupid bloody magistrate. Let off on a technicality. Jesus James, we had him right here!' Lloyd had a sudden thought. 'Tell me we got his fingerprints.'

'Of course,' Will said. 'And I saw that Ed Shelley was printed also when we were last at the farm.'

'Well that's a start.'

'I've left two uniforms at the farm with orders to arrest him on sight,' Will said.

'Lot of bloody good that'll do. You should have acted sooner Will. Jesus!'

'I'll send officers to the port,' Will added, leaving the room. 'And I'll put calls through to Launceston and the northwest.'

Lloyd grunted. 'Do what you must. Just catch the bastard.'

'It's not Will's fault,' Braithwaite said as the door closed behind the senior constable. 'The lads doing a great job Charlie.'

'Charlie!' Lloyd grumbled. 'Charlie? The names Charles ... James. I'm not some pantomime ventriloquist puppet called *Charlie* travelling with the bloody circus.' Charles Lloyd made it clear, his name was not negotiable.

'Inspector Lloyd,' the receptionist, Miss Dyer, with her shoulder length hair in a bow, a friendly manner and pearly white teeth, found the detective in his office. 'I searched public records like you asked and Mr Edward Shelley, Ed Shelley, does have a record sir.'

'Oh.'

'I copied the details for you inspector.'

'Thank you.' Before Miss Dyer even closed the canteen door Lloyd was reading:

Edward Aran Shelley, known as Ed Shelley had been arrested on a rape charge back in 1912. He was let off on a technicality. It was also documented that he had been found in the company of underage girls before and although this was recorded nothing untoward could be proven.

February 18th 1904 the vestry of St James of Jerusalem Anglican Church at Colebrook was damaged by fire but extinguished before it destroyed the church. Ed

Aran Shelley was in the area and arrested as a minor. No evidence could be gathered against him.

In general, anti-social behaviour against Protestants.

Where there's smoke there's fire, Lloyd thought to himself. And of an even more interesting note Lloyd read about Mrs Edith Shelley. Mr John Shelley, a known drunkard, had deserted his family when Ed was four. Mrs Shelley started a small bordello at the top of Liverpool Street and found young street girls were in demand. This, no doubt, influenced Ed and his attitude towards young women.

However, Lloyd discovered, last year in 1914 Edith Shelley was convicted of extortion and attempted murder of one of her married clients and received five years in the women's prison.

***

December 30ᵗʰ 1914

Detective Charles Lloyd looked exhausted. The Queen Street bombing had deprived him of his sorely needed Christmas break and the newspaper on his desk forecast nothing but gloom and doom ...

War!

Young Australian men were enlisting in the Australian Infantry Forces to fight alongside other Commonwealth soldiers in Europe, in droves. His own son was champing at the bit to join up. *Thank Christ he was only sixteen and looked fourteen.* Trench warfare and heavy artillery were taking their toll. Thousands upon thousands were being killed in the most horrendous fashion.

'I fear Australia is going to lose many of its younger generation,' he told Will who stood at his desk running an eye over the news headlines. 'In the last census of 1911 Australia's population was 4,455,005. The median age 24 with four per cent over sixty-five years.' Lloyd always had a knack for figures. 'Two thirds of the population are men between the ages fifteen and sixty-five ... two thirds Will!' Lloyd read aloud the heading over one article at the bottom of the front page. '*Battle at Ypres; 58,155 British dead, French 50,000, German 130,000.* It's madness Will. Unsustainable. And our lads are joining up by the thousands.'

CHAPTER TWO
WAR

Dardanelles. Turkey. Trenches near Lone Pine. 5.16pm, August 6th, 1915

Ned felt a cold chill and fought nausea. He bowed his head and prayed to a god he was having nagging doubts existed. Beside him fellow soldiers of the twelfth battalion waited anxiously, some wept silently, some shook uncontrollably. A few smoked. Many stared into the trench wall; their minds blank with faces hard and cold as tombstone. Others looked skywards as evening approached, looking to the trench lip where they had lined up waiting along the fire-step, a packed earth ledge that would launch them into oblivion.

They simply cursed.

In front of them and damned close, the Royal Navy ship's artillery exploded behind the enemy lines. The deafening roar of HMS *Queen Elizabeth, London and Prince of Wales* twelve inch guns would live with Ned the rest of his days. It was deafening.

Terrifying.

Ned watched the last of the men file into the front-line trenches. Preparing themselves. Mates grouping together so as to go over the top with familiar company. Many cursed Abdul; their enemy the Turks. They cursed his land but above all they cursed the war and the warmongers who had put them here. They cursed the British generals; stubborn, belligerent old-school warlords; poring over maps in the officer's saloon aboard the ships on the Aegean Sea, well out of range of Abdul's guns. These, Ned knew, were the very same generals with their track record of stupidity, risking the lives of the common soldier; especially Australian and New Zealand colonials like himself. Colonials considered dispensable, worth no more than, say, a wooden chess piece. It had been three and a half months since the notorious landing at Anzac Cove and as many as seventy per cent of the troops were now ill, mostly with dysentery. The men were gaunt, thin and weak. Yet camaraderie prevailed, these men were fiercely patriotic.

Ned fondled his leather dog tag like it were his talisman. Who knows? It may be. But he knew he was no more than a statistic. He read its inscription;

A.I.F.

2486,

E. B. KELLY

12th Batt.

C.E.

C.E.

Ned wanted to laugh. *Church of England. Really.* Where was god now?

For the umpteenth time twenty-year-old Ned checked his freshly honed bayonet. He ran a finger carefully down the length of its steel blade. He checked the mortise was locked onto the barrel lug of his .303 Lee-Enfield. The rifle had been stripped down, cleaned and reassembled. He tapped his slouch hat tight into place and mulled over the only advise given him by his sergeant. 'Keep yer head down lad and run like buggery.'

Now Ned was as ready as he could possibly be. All he could do was wait. Wait for the artillery to cease.

Christ I wish we could get this over with.

Ned tried to spit. But his mouth was dry as parchment. He tried to settle his nerves, concentrate, but his thoughts were continuously drowned with the din of the artillery bombardment. For three days now the bombardment had been incessant.

Three days!

Captain James McKay, a veteran of the Boer War back in '02, looked over his right shoulder along Jacob's Trench. His men were terrified. If they weren't, then there was something terribly wrong. McKay made a mental note down the line. Each man wore white bands wrapped about his arms near the elbows and had a white patch stitched to the back of their jackets. It was a smart initiative the captain thought, as Abdul's uniform was similar to the diggers and you don't want Aussies shooting Aussies. *That wouldn't do at all.*

Slowly McKay twisted his head left. The fear was palpable. Over the cacophony he heard the whispered curses and the muttered prayers. *Lambs to the slaughter,* he dared think.

Only a hand grenade's throw away was the enemy front line, and McKay too struggled with the bombardment. Over one hundred guns on board four cruisers, three warships and several destroyers anchored on the Aegean Sea were incessant. In the valley below a howitzer division added to the mayhem.

Yes, the noise was deafening. And the shells ploughed the earth raining plugs of dirt into the ANZAC's trenches. 'Thank Christ the artillery boys are accurate,' McKay's sergeant yelled in his ear. McKay barely returned a nod.

Ned unclipped the leather cover on his wristwatch. It was 5.16pm. They were attacking the enemy trenches at 5.30. The wait was gut wrenching. Ned watched a mate, Harry Grey who kept with him a small photo of his parents. Now Harry gazed at the photo and kissed it before returning it to his wallet, reminding Ned of his own family.

5.17pm

Ned's mind wandered to the day he enlisted. The bravado of that day five months ago seemed foolish now. He could die this day. Ned cast an eye to his right. The man next to him ... no ... the *boy* next to him was from Tasmania. Eric Wilcox, Ned knew, had only just turned seventeen. He told Ned he had written his own letter of consent from his father and signed it himself. He was a scrawny bugger so when they weighed him at the recruitment office he filled his pockets with rocks. But there were younger *men* amongst them. Terry Frank was a farm lad from the midlands of Tasmania and Ned knew him to be fifteen ... *fifteen for Christ's sake!* Terry told his parents he was going to Queensland to try his hand at jackarooing – he was a brilliant horseman you must understand. He lied to his parents only to front up at the enlistment office.

'How old are you?' the recruiting officer asked him.

'Nineteen sir.'

'Got a birth certificate?'

'No sir, got lost in a flood.'

'What about your parents?'

'Died in the flood sir. I got an uncle though, but we don't talk much.'

Horsemen were desperately needed to form the Light Horse Brigade. Fifteen-year-old Terry Frank was signed up. Now here he was on the Gallipoli Peninsula and, as horses were useless on this rocky mountainous terrain, he was just another foot soldier.

5.21pm

Nine minutes to go.

Ned thought of the four weeks' training at the barracks at Broadmeadows in Victoria. Four weeks. It wasn't much. Just drill, paperwork, fitted for a uniform, more drilling and straight to the Port Melbourne Docks to board the SS *Geelong*; a 450 foot 8000 ton twin-screw steamer. Crammed on board like peas in a tin they were. Luckily the five-week journey was reasonably calm, although he was seasick the first week. Then they were vaccinated and he was crook for three weeks with some fever. A week later they sailed through the Suez Canal and made land at Alexandria, Egypt's northern city on the Mediterranean. Alexandria to Cairo took six hours on a train. Ned had pleasant memories of the journey; being a country boy he appreciated the fertile land where crops of maize, cotton and wheat were plentiful. From the train station they were marched to the Australian and New Zealand camps at Mena, right at the foot of the ancient pyramids.

Each day at 6am they had roll call, drill, lectures and more drill. Occasionally they were allowed leave to visit Cairo. Otherwise they explored Giza, climbing the pyramids or riding camels through the desert.

Yes, Ned had experienced a hell of a lot the past months ...

Now he may die in a matter of minutes.

5.27pm

Three minutes to go.

Suddenly the artillery stopped. All at once. It was as if someone had flicked a switch. Immediately the silence was more unnerving than the bombardment. Every soldier remained deathly quiet. An autumn wind whistled along the trench reminding Ned how much he missed the Egyptian weather and the fresh food. Especially the watermelon, tinned fruit, fish and biscuits. His health was good then. Now four months since the landing on this godforsaken peninsula, his health had deteriorated.

Maybe if I get shot but survive, I will get sent back to Egypt for recuperation. If only.

Seconds passed. Silence prevailed. All Ned heard now was the blacksmith's grinding wheel sharpening bayonets.

Ned looked at his watch.

5.30

It was time.

They would have the setting sun at their backs.

McKay put the whistle to his parched lips and blew. Blew hard. Three sharp whistles. A shrill piercing whistle, frequent in the men's nightmares.

The signal *to go over the top.*

'Move it, move it, move!' the officers screamed. And move they did for an officer's bullet awaited any man who refused.

Ned was third up his ladder only to be kicked in the head by the man clambering before him. Ned felt no pain. Just fear. Fear and the terror of what waited. Instantly the enemy machine guns stuttered into life …

Tat-tat-tat-tat.

Machine guns spitting a hail of bullets did not take long to find their range. Men started to fall … Aussie diggers … mates.

Ned rose from the trench into a boiling cauldron of death. The front liners were falling fast. He shouted with adrenalin. A guttural unnatural roar at the top of his voice. Staring his nemesis in the face. Single shots singled out single victims, but the tat-tat-tat of the 500 round per minute Maxim guns cut men in two. Ned saw men before him slam into the earth. Some wounded. Most were dead.

All were mates.

Ned ran. *Head down and run like buggery!*

Inches to one side a mate fell; the top of his head vanishing. Ned was sprayed with a mist of warm cerebrum. Another mate took a bullet in the eye and the back of his head exploded. Ned raced towards the enemy clasping his rifle and bayonet. His peripheral vision was a blur, but he was aware men were dropping all about him while bullets whistled either side. A bullet tugged at Ned's jacket. He felt something slam his boot. Then he saw the enemy trenches. They were well fortified with log roofs. He approached at a sprint. Screaming. Firing blindly …

Crack!

Ned cranked back his rifle bolt. The spent shell spiralled free. Bolt action rammed a fresh bullet into the chamber. His aim was indiscriminate. Ned pulled the trigger ...

Crack!

A mate to his right took several bullets to the chest. His body warped and fell in front of Ned. Ned tripped and crashed into the bloodied earth of no-man's-land. Lying flat Ned wanted to close his eyes and play dead. But he was better than that. There was no going back.

All about him mates were dead or dying. With bullets peppering the earth all around, Ned rolled onto his belly and shouldered his rifle panning the barrel over the enemy trenches. A Turk's head appeared. Ned sighted him and pulled the trigger. The bullet slammed the enemy's jaw and Ned watched his target fall back into his trench.

His first kill.

Ned's confidence returned. He forced himself back to his feet. Only three yards remained ...

Three lousy yards to victory.

There was no time to think ...

Just run.

And run like buggery.

The first men reached the enemy trenches. Ned caught up as his mates realised the Turks' trenches were well protected. Log roofs had been built in place and the night reconnaissance scouts had not reported these. *This is why the bastards survived the fierce artillery bombardment.*

Unperturbed the diggers tore at the damaged sections with bare hands while others fired at the fleeing enemy below. In places the logs had been damaged and now the Aussies were firing at Abdul through gaps in the timber. The Turks were overwhelmed by the tenacity of their foe. There was to be no quarter. Ned shouldered his rifle and joined others shooting the enemy in the back as they fled. Revenge was sweet. The pain and guilt of taking another man's life could wait. For now, it was retribution.

Ned nailed his third kill.

Or was it his fourth?

It had to be *his* bullet. The Turk looked over his shoulder. Ned saw that split second of recognition. Ned pulled the trigger. A neat purplish plughole appeared in the man's forehead. It didn't seem real yet the Turk crumbled like a rag doll. Dead. Ned felt the urge to cheer. But Ned's emotions were in a whirlpool; elation was replaced by a sick-pitted nausea. The victim was someone's son, someone's father, a husband.

But it was kill or be killed.

Right?

It was as simple as that.

Wasn't it?

An enemy grenade landed at Ned's feet. He froze. But the digger at his side was a fast thinker. He rolled a dead Turk over the bomb. Instantly the grenade detonated in a muffled oomph. The body lifted a few inches and guts sprayed about them. Excited shouting followed another loud explosion. Some men had broached the northern end of Ned's trench. Ned watched as a dozen diggers followed collapsing logs into the dark maze of twisting trenches. Many Turks fled but many stood to fight. All about him was death.

So many mates dead. And dead for what?

At the edge or the trench above an Aussie appeared. He'd made it across no man's land. Ned watched him start his way into the trench when a Turk charged from behind bayonetting the digger in the back. He looked young … *So damned young.*

Ned felt anger return. A thirst for revenge he had never experienced before. Through the smoke, the dust, the mayhem Mick Maynard appeared along the trench herding a Turkish prisoner in Ned's direction. He shoved the man forward while holding his rifle to his back. Everything happened so quickly. Ned saw a knife drop from the Turk's sleeve. The Turk twisted about, raising his arm to stab Maynard. Ned was two yards away, but fast. He leapt forward plunging his bayonet into the Turk's neck.

'Fuck!' Maynard shouted.

Ned wrenched the steel free as the captive collapsed to his knees falling face first into the dirt, dead. 'Jesus Christ!' Maynard was aghast, sickened by the brutality. 'He … he surrendered for fuck sake'. But Ned was unrepentant. He stepped forward and kicked at the man's hand and it was then Maynard saw the knife. 'Jesus Christ …'

All the while the Grim Reaper glided above approvingly, taking no sides, thirsting after victims like a ravaged hound would hunt a fox.

Ned said nothing. He didn't have to; his face was chiselled with anger. He shoved by Maynard and charged after the others who ran the length of the defences bayonetting any Turk standing in their path. Officers ran ahead killing with their handguns; chasing the retreating Abdul, gunning them down before they had a chance to regroup. Others became victim to the diggers' own grenades; jam tins filled with explosives by the Royal Engineers and lit with a short fuse before throwing. Munitions were in short supply and these homemade bombs were dangerous. *Bloody dangerous.* Some exploded prematurely. Ned saw one digger lose a hand, another an eye, another his life. 5.55pm.

The enemy was on the run. This fuelled enthusiasm.

Ned found himself briefly alone. The Turk waited in the shadows but the flash of an explosion gave away his position. He ran at Ned with fixed bayonet but Ned was quicker. *Thank Christ!*

The Turk clasped Ned's bayonet with both hands. As it penetrated his belly Ned thought it just like his training … Plunging that steel into a sandbag.

Ned twisted the bayonet before sliding its long blade free. He heard the gurgle of blood in his victim's throat, the suction as the blade withdrew, the deep sigh as the Turk dropped to his knees. Ned even smelt the man's breath, a stale pungent reek of onions. Everything seemed in slow motion, silent …

And then the pandemonium of war abruptly ceased.

It was 6pm.

It had taken only half an hour but at what cost?

No Man's Land was strewn with the dead and wounded. Dead and wounded Aussie mates. It was a pathetic and sickening sight. Ned managed to score half a canteen of water, which he poured over his blood-stained face. He had mate's blood through his hair, splatters of a mate's flesh down his arms and Abdul's blood on his hands.

Briefly stone jars of rum were passed around and the lucky ones drank greedily.

The body count was horrendous. Ned found it impossible to walk the length of the trench without treading on the dead and the dying – both enemy and mates.

With the machine guns silenced, temporarily, Ned helped his mates drag the bodies aside, both diggers and Turks. On both sides the dead were piled like carcasses of meat at the abattoir. Some could be buried underfoot where they lay, others buried in the parapets. Others were dragged clear. There was no time for complacency, as they knew the enemy would launch a counterattack.

On the enemy's side the Turkish dead were laid out in a procession beside the pathway along which the enemy reinforcements had to climb. On the Australian side as many as possible, along with their rifles and kit, were laid in a depression called Brown's Dip. Many bodies would remain in no man's land, not to be buried for another five years. Ned learnt later that two thousand Australians died at Lone Pine, and six thousand of the enemy.

It was nothing less than a tragedy.

***

Ned was in shock. They were all in shock. Rum was the temporary saviour. Ned took the half-gallon stone crock offered and filled his tin mug to the brim. Shaking, he drank greedily before passing the crock to a passing digger. The man took the jar and poured himself half a mug. He said nothing. What was there to say with so much death about? The digger drank some of his rum, only a sip really, he too seemed nervous, yet he would not look Ned in the eye. Clinging to the rum jar he leant against the trench wall, his eyes darting this way and that as if he awaited another attack.

Ned didn't recognise him. 'You with the twelfth?' Ned asked. The digger ignored Ned. 'Mate,' Ned persisted. 'You with twelfth?' The man nodded, still avoiding eye contact, he sipped at his mug. Ned sighed, finished his rum and considered himself lucky he wasn't as bad off as this bloke. Ned made to walk away when an officer appeared, raising his pistol and waving it frantically towards Ned. Ned gaped down the barrel. Instinctively Ned jerked sideways. The pistol discharged ... A loud report inches from Ned's face.

The silent soldier's head exploded and Ned was splattered with more blood while the silent soldier crumbled to the trench floor, dead.

'Fuck!' Ned was aghast. 'Fuck!'

'He's one of them,' the officer said quietly, his voice calm. He holstered his Webley and Scott Mark IV. 'That man's a Hun.'

The soldiers nearest thought they had seen it all. Now this. Lying dead at their feet was a man in an Australian Army uniform. 'You men must be vigilant,' the officer said coldly. The witnesses nearest remained speechless.

'Take that wedding band off his finger,' the officer ordered Ned. Still shaking, Ned slipped the ring from the corpse's finger handing it to the officer. 'Now search his pockets.' Another man pulled a photograph free, shocked at what he saw. A woman and her soldier man, a keepsake photo so many soldiers on both sides had taken before leaving for the front lines. This one was taken in a Bavarian village. The soldier in the photo was the dead man at their feet. The photo was passed around as the officer read aloud the man's name from inside the wedding band. 'His name was Hans Fischer. He was a spy. He stole that uniform off one of ours.' The officer alluded to the Australian dead all about them.

'Bastard,' someone said. Another kicked the body.

'So be vigilant chaps. There are some enemy willing to risk their lives to get intelligence on us and with all this disorder here it's only too easy.'

The diggers were incredulous. They all knew there were German officers working with the Turks, advising them on military matters, but this was the first Fritz they had encountered.

Ned wiped at the fresh blood, smearing it down his face. He wanted so badly to dive into the sea. Now, although the Australians had pushed the Turks back, here at Lone Pine, they were still under sniper fire and pinned down within the newly claimed Turkish trenches. And the enemy were hell bent on recapturing their fortifications. There would be no returning across No Man's Land to their own trenches any time soon and Ned would have to live with the blood. No Man's Land was dangerous open space ...

And a death sentence for those who tried to cross it.

CHAPTER THREE
EGYPT BOUND

Five months earlier. Hobart early March 3rd 1915

On March 3rd nineteen-year-old Bes Mulberry started a diary. It was the size of a prayer book but not as thick with a black cotton cover and a sheath along the spine to slide a pencil. After the horrors of losing her family on Boxing Day, Doctor Scott Macrossan advised Bes it would be therapeutic. *Write down what you struggle to talk about.*

Bes wrote about her twelve-year-old brother Ben's struggle. Blind in one eye and with his left arm amputated, life ahead would be a challenge. But by March 3rd, sixty-nine days after the terrible event, Ben's humours were returning. He was young, resilient and would adapt quickly to his situation. Now convalescing, Ben was in the care of Aunt Elvira. Elvira was father Frank's sister who lived at Marieville Esplanade, Sandy Bay, not all that far from the damaged family home in Queen Street, which, for the moment, remained unoccupied.

And father, Bes wrote in her diary, *is cared for at Willow Court in New Norfolk. Being treated for mental illness and severe depression, which the doctors are confident, they will be able to cure over time, with electrical shock therapy.* Bes's only wound, a cut to her forehead, had also healed admirably.

Oh how I miss Frankie. Dear dear Frankie. And mother and Molly too of course. It is just so unfair.

Days later Bes wrote in her diary. *Ben's high spirit helps father. For a while there I thought we would lose father to depression but now he has a purpose, a duty, to look after Ben. The Willow Court doctors think father will make a full recovery* and be allowed home within a month. Although it pains me to leave them I also have a duty. Nurses are in great demand in Europe. Besides I would go mad if I stayed here at home. I need a challenge. I need a distraction.

Something else that tormented Bes was her boyfriend of five weeks, Jack. Jack showed little sympathy for her loss. Admittedly Bes had been morose and angry, but the young man, himself only nineteen, had offered little support. Less than a week after the bombing Jack was seen with Mandy Burrows, one of Bes's old school mates. It was time to move on.

May 6th 1915. I enlisted today with the A.I.F. Medical Corps at St Peters Church Hall and was told I'll be on my way to Egypt within a month.

I am especially looking forward to England (if we are ever to be sent there) and in particular London. I do believe we will sail there from Egypt, at least that is the rumour. And maybe I will meet some of the Suffragettes while I am there.

CHAPTER FOUR
A STRANGER'S LIFE TAKEN

Several weeks before Bes enlisted. February 5th 1915. Brinktop Forest. Mid-morning.

Detective Charles Lloyd hooked his tweed jacket on a branch overlooking the body and wondered why he even wore the damned thing. It was only 9.15 in the morning but the day was already shaping up to be a hot one. 'Christ, it seems hotter up here,' he complained. 'If that's possible.'

'I agree,' Senior Constable Will Gibson glanced over his shoulder from where he squatted by the victim. 'Ninety-five degrees they forecast.'

'Really? Well it feels like it's that already.' Lloyd caught the eye of the lone policeman guarding the crime scene under the shade of a myrtle-beech. He held tightly to a leafy branch stepping out into the sun occasionally to take a swipe at the fat blowflies keen on visiting the cadaver. But as the crime was at least a month old and the remains mostly skeletal or mummified, the flies had done their best work weeks ago. 'How long have you been here son?' he asked the copper.

'How long sir ... ah ... bit over an hour I'm thinkin'.'

'You haven't disturbed anything?'

'No sir.'

Lloyd loosened his tie, wiped sweat from his brow and knelt next to Will, where the leading senior constable was already taking notes.

'Jesus Will,' Lloyd said in a quiet voice. 'She's hardly dressed like a country-girl. So what's a lady doing all the way up here?' Lloyd spoke of Brinktop Forest atop a slight hill overlooking Coal River Valley. The body was hidden in a copse of black wattle and small gum trees.

'Who found her?' Will asked.

'A local lad, a shooter – up here rabbiting.'

Will stood, stretched and took another close look at the perimeter of the site. 'Well she wasn't dragged here, at least there's no sign of her being dragged.'

'So she walked.'

'Exactly. And of her own accord. I'd say she was either on a stroll or she came up here to meet someone.'

'I'm inclined to think the second scenario is more likely.'

'But I can only find *her* footprints, there in the dried clayey earth,' Will pointed to a clear patch of land a yard square where nothing wanted to grow. 'No other prints, except, possibly, the rabbit shooter's.'

'Then have him checked.'

'Could it be self-murder inspector? She hung herself maybe.' She was after all lying under a horizontal branch perfect for such an eternal endeavour. Will then pointed to a weathered belt off a fawn-coloured Mackintosh still adhering to the decayed flesh, lying near the body.

'Impossible.'

'Sir?'

Lloyd took up a broken stick and began poking about in the woman's skeletal throat. Within seconds Will caught sight of what his governor had been after. Slowly a tightly rolled red handkerchief appeared. 'I doubt she put that there herself Will,' Lloyd said. 'And I suggest she was strangled with that belt.' The detective then used the stick to draw attention between her legs where the remains of a sanitary towel showed. 'She was also menstruating.'

Eight feet away was the victim's mauve Dolly Varden hat with a veil and a matching umbrella. These appeared to have been placed together. 'She does not however, appear to have been sexually interfered with. Although it's a bit hard to tell now. Not in her condition.'

'Sir?'

'Well she could have had consensual sex with her killer and redressed.'

'Consensual?'

'Yes Will.' The wily old sleuth had noticed something Will hadn't and drew the young policeman's attention to the remains of a brown and green rug tangled in bracken. 'I admit it's hard to see,' Lloyd said, 'but that appears to be a picnic rug. Now you don't bring picnic rugs to a crime scene. There are no signs of food scraps; a chicken bone for instance, although the devils would most likely have chewed them up.' Lloyd was speaking of Tasmania's *hyena*, as he noted fresh devil scats in the vicinity.

'Devils? Up here sir?'

Lloyd rolled the fresh scats with the stick. 'Look carefully. There's traces of undigested hair, bone and the feathers of small birds.' Will was impressed. 'Believe it or not I read up on animal scats for another case once. It's remarkable what one remembers.'

'So you think she came here for romance only to end up like … like this?'

'I'd wager on it Will. The weather would have been warm enough, around mid-December.'

Will turned back the badly weather-beaten lapel of her coat to reveal a gold-framed cameo. 'There's also remains of a pearl necklace about her throat,' he told Lloyd.

'Any sign of a handbag or purse?'

Will. 'No.'

'So,' Lloyd stood, stepping into the shade. 'She was a woman of certain means who wasn't raped and she wasn't robbed. By all accounts this death has taken place sometime during this summer.' Lloyd ran his handkerchief between his collar and neck, it felt suddenly hotter.

'This's interesting.' Will pointed with the toe of his shoe to an empty beer bottle overgrown with grass.'

'Ah, good.' Lloyd poked the twig he was holding into the neck prising the bottle free. 'This may have prints.'

***

The straining motor of a Model T Ford truck rolled towards them cross-country up the gentle hillside, from the Orielton to Richmond main road, where their own Ford was parked. *Any steeper and they won't make it.* Charles Lloyd shook his head. Will noticed the governor's anguish. 'I guess it's a long walk to the road with that body on a stretcher.'

'I guess so Will.'

The two detectives watched Doctor Walter Boyd, a passenger in the Model T, with one foot out on the running board ready to jump free, while Mary Underwood, his trainee in forensics, struggled at the wheel over the rocky terrain. Mary cut the motor just outside the copse of trees and the Ford backfired sounding like a firecracker.

'Walter,' Lloyd said walking over to meet them.

'Charles. You've met Mary before I believe.'

Lloyd touched his tweed Brixton flat cap. 'Good day to you Mary. And I do believe you have met Senior Constable Gibson.'

Mary nodded politely and immediately slid a canvas stretcher from the tray on the back of the Ford with the agility of a dock worker. 'Any prints of note?' Mary asked, dumping the stretcher and reaching in for her Gladstone bag of finger print equipment.

'This may be useful,' Lloyd said holding out the beer bottle. Mary took a shoebox from the truck and carefully stored it.

The coroner studied the cadaver a long minute while Lloyd aired his views. 'So how long do you reckon Walt'?'

'Hard to say. The weather and the state of her health would make a difference to the decomposition.'

Lloyd looked at his old friend sagely. 'How did I know you'd say that? Just a ball park?'

'Ballpark. I'd say four to six weeks.'

'That's what we thought.' Lloyd unhitched his coat from the tree and threw it over his shoulder. 'We've seen all we need to see here Walter so we'll leave you to it.'

CHAPTER FIVE
THE CAIRO CHAMELEON

Cairo. Mena Army Camp. March 30th. 1915

Archie Bryant had never thought too hard about past civilisations. That is until he gazed at the land of the Pharaohs out the train window. The troop train carrying Archie and the rest of the 13th Battalion from Alexandria rattled through the Nile Delta and over desert sands towards Cairo, and every soldier bar none was in awe of the magnificent spectacle to their west. The pyramids. The three most prominent and spectacular monuments were silhouetted against a magnificent sunset – an artist's palette of red, yellow, orange and blue. They appeared in the distance through one oasis after another. Oases of tall slender date palms, some as high as eighty feet. There was not one man amongst them who, only two months earlier, had ever dreamed they would stand before these wonders of the ancient world in their own lifetime.

'And we thought we was headed for France,' Archie told a mate. 'Who would 'ave thought, eh?'

They could almost taste the excitement.

From the Cairo train station the soldiers were marched to Mena Camp, Giza, some six miles west, at the foot of the pyramids, and on the edge of the Sahara Desert.

'You're gunna love it here lads,' a sergeant, who arrived months earlier, barked at the men. 'It's all sand and more sand. You'll drill in sand, march up to yer ankles in sand, you'll eat sand and just to top it off you'll shit in sand.'

The midday sun was hot, damned hot. This didn't bother the blokes from Queensland but Archie and his Melbourne mob sweated like buggery.

Like all the men around him, Archie had been impulsive, enlisting without hesitation to help the Mother Country fight the Hun. After passing medical checks – including a dental tent called the *chamber of horrors*, where many men with bad teeth had them extracted on the spot – he spent eight weeks in a Melbourne training camp. Archie was even inoculated against cholera, and didn't that bloody well hurt.

At the camp he was fitted with a uniform, learnt drill and was fixed with identity papers and dog tags. Archie found the training relentless; yet occasionally interesting, including semaphore signalling.

Archie preferred to keep to himself, a loner if truth be known. But that's difficult for a man thrown amongst so many other single men where avoiding company, ironically, only drew attention. Reluctantly he acquired mates, Rex Johnson being one. Rex was nineteen, a likeable farm boy from Campbell Town in Tasmania. Tall and thin as a rake he had blonde hair, blue eyes and was damned handsome. Mind you the lads didn't have to be handsome to be accepted. The army requirements for recruiting were: a bloke had to be over five-foot-six-inches with a thirty-four inch chest expansion and between nineteen and thirty eight years old. But as the war progressed and men died, the rules changed. The age limit grew older for starters. On the voyage they each received one shilling per day for 50 days. This doubled as they entered the war. Of course corporals were paid more at nine shillings, a lieutenant one pound, a colonel seventeen shillings and sixpence and a Brigadier two pounds five shillings. Not that Archie or Rex could ever aspire to those wages.

***

After two months' training the recruits endured a six-week sea journey across the Indian Ocean – the first week was spent struggling with seasickness. They sailed through the Suez Canal and finally set a welcome boot on dry land at the ancient home of Cleopatra – Alexandria.

Mena Camp was well established by the time Archie and his brigade arrived. Roads serviced the tent city – home to thousands of Australian soldiers – with names such as Artillery Road or Canberra Road. The officers, engineers, artillerymen and light horse had their own individual areas. There was even a post office. On the outskirts of *town*, local Arabs had set up their own shanty cafes and bars. For the moment, on the surface, life looked all right.

***

The new arrivals were drilled relentlessly. After weeks at sea they needed to be whipped into shape and with the news Britain had declared war on Turkey the rumours were that they would be deployed sooner than later. Sundays, after compulsory divine service, the men had free time to explore the environs of Giza. An area where Arabs with camels or donkeys would pester them for a photographic portrait with the pyramids or sphinx as a backdrop, or a short camel ride over the desert. Many soldiers climbed the pyramids.

Archie and Rex stood atop the second largest pyramid; the largest being impassable at the top, with its capstone still in place. The view was magnificent looking to Cairo or west across the vast desert. From the peak Mena Camp was like an ants' nest four hundred and eighty feet below. It was also not for the fainthearted for the flat top, where the gold-covered capstone had been removed in antiquity, was only a few feet square in area and the pyramid dropped away at forty-five degrees in every direction. Overhead was nothing but the blue sly.

'Forty centuries look down on you,' Rex said sagely standing with his hands on his hips in awe of his experience.

Archie. 'What?'

'I read that in a book at school,' Rex said. 'It was Napoleon Bonaparte who said it. *Forty centuries look down on you.* He stood right here where we are over a hundred years ago. He was talking to his generals and his words were meant for the thousands of French troops camped right down there where we are.'

'Crikies. Napoleon,' Archie looked impressed. 'You mean that Frog bugger at Waterloo?'

'That's him.'

'Well bugger me.'

'Julius Caesar stood right here too, two thousand years before Napoleon.'

'Did you read that in a book too?'

'Yeh.'

'Clever bastard aren't yer?'

Back on the desert, Rex carved his name into one of the pyramid's limestone blocks with his bayonet, brought along especially. *Rex Johnson 1915*. He passed Archie the blade. 'Your turn.'

'Nar.'

'Why not? You might cop a bullet in France. At least you can immortalise yourself here.'

Archie jumped from the two-ton block onto the sand, ignoring Rex. On a sand hill several hundred yards away a bunch of soldiers were taking it in turns mounting camels and having their portrait photographs taken with the Arab handlers. 'Let's get our own portrait made,' Rex said. 'You an' me on a camel each, to send home like.' Archie remained silent. 'Archie? What do you say?'

'No thanks.'

'Why?'

'I just don't want to, alright?'

'It's only a shillin'. It'd be a marvellous memento to send home to your mum and dad Archie. Come on ...'

'Jesus Rex, I don't want my photograph taken.'

'But why?'

Archie was flushed. The day was hot and his temper flared easily. 'Just leave it. All right?'

'Christ. Forget it.'

CHAPTER SIX
THE BATTLE OF WAZZIR

Cairo. April 2nd. 1915

Cairo was a modern and cosmopolitan city. Many buildings of Cairo's established business district were, strangely enough, of European architecture. Although the French only occupied Egypt for a three-year period, 1798 – 1801, they left behind the powerful influence of Napoleon Bonaparte's French middle class. On the other hand, it was the British who had left their traditional footprint, as they had occupied Egypt and the strategically priceless Suez Canal for twenty-seven years now, since 1882. The National Bank of Egypt on Tahrir Square, for one, was a good example of British influence and would not look out of place in London, or Melbourne for that matter. Yet it was the myriad of mosques and the legacy of the Ottomans that gave the city its exotic identity. These austere, almost fortress-like buildings from the Ottoman occupation, with their overhanging bay windows of elaborately carved wood, were the most prolific.

The boys of the 13th Battalion were in awe. Several large squares – public meeting places – serviced the city central, with narrow streets and alleyways snaking away from these plazas, leading into the heart and soul of the authentic sector of the Arab city. Here the sights, sounds and smells of the ancient metropolis truly shone.

The lads marvelled at the variety of food available on the streets; pigeons stuffed with rice, roasted on spits next to shawarma. Or red and green stuffed peppers with paprika and cayenne or falafel served up with Egyptian bread, the boys heard was called pita.

The smells were extreme, exotic and exciting.

Street peddlers sold tea from huge brass urns strapped to their bodies. Women, balancing water pitchers on their heads, led donkeys through the alleys hauling carts loaded with sacks of grain. Many women wore black, their faces covered with a black veil, with black ankle length trousers. Egyptian businessmen wore western style suits with sandals on their feet and the traditional fez hat on their heads, while many wore the full-length coat sleeved kaftan and traditional Arab headwear.

For country boys from Australia it was exotic, another world entirely.

The soldiers wandered down tight lanes filled with Arab cafes, bakeries, spice stalls and confectioners. Metal workshops were many, all spilling into busy bazaars; bazaars offering everything from brass spittoons to fly-switches – or maybe an antiquity from the days of the pharaohs, fresh from the forger's kiln.

Watching over the metropolis were slender hundred-foot minarets springing up from the mosques towards Allah's Heaven. From these minarets the Aussie soldiers heard the Salah – a haunting prayer sung by the Moslem muezzin – calling to prayer those devoted to Islam.

Allahu Akbar the prayer cried out. God is great.

Archie Bryant had rarely experienced love. At least that's what he told Rex. Not true love anyhow. For Archie it had always seemed forbidden fruit. Certainly he had had the occasional liaison but his ill temper had the girls guarded. Only once did he truly fall for the affections of another. Mandy was sixteen at the time, and Archie nineteen. But that occasion was doomed from the start. To begin with Mandy's father had words with Archie. There was bad chemistry between them. Mandy was also a virgin, and to be quite honest, Archie was looking for more. Now in his early twenties, Archie felt life owed him. And here he was, standing outside a brothel in Cairo bold on beer and cocky as a rooster.

Archie had wandered the alleyways into Haret el Wasser, an area of Cairo occupied by many drinking establishments and bordellos. He was in the company of Rex and a dozen other mates, for an unaccompanied soldier would soon be robbed. The soldiers had a pass from Mena Camp until 11pm. It was dusk on Good Friday and darkness approached to shroud the devil.

Archie and his mob were already intoxicated when they joined the hundreds of other soldiers in the streets of Haret el Wasser. The streets were in party mood. It was a fiesta, a carnival of rakishness and depravity. The girls were obliging and the young men rowdy and crude. The myriad of bars set up, seemingly overnight, sold cheap adulterated grog and the humid Egyptian evening reeked of ammonia where men had pissed in the alleyways. They sang crude ditties while others savoured cheap sex in darkened doorways. Archie was spellbound for he had never been subjected to such debauchery.

A dark-skinned beauty caught Archie's eye. And he hers, but for different reasons. Archie's beer-fuelled bravado translated to gullibility in the eyes of this Nubian siren. Archie thought her skin the colour of dark Cadbury's chocolate with shamelessly exposed breasts, large, firm and shaped like papayas. The woman touted on the steps of an arched doorway, entrance to a six-story house of pleasure. Like an inn sign may advertise its name with an illustration, the fille de joie's exposing attire advertised her promiscuity and the delights within.

Archie was smitten, while the whore was as attracted to the soldiers' piastres as were the men to her flesh.

'Many many pretty girls inside,' the Nubian siren said in strong accented but well trained English. 'You men come, many many girls ... you choose.'

'Garn Archie,' Rex laughed.

'I ... ah ... dunno.'

Nineteen-year-old Jack shoved Archie hard in the back and Archie stumbled forward. Archie's temporarily lost pluck was soon restored amongst cheers as the siren took Archie by the wrist, hauling him inside. His mates tripped after him.

Nothing prepared Archie for the opulent splendour of the Ottoman interior. The men lumbered drunkenly into the foyer of what appeared a large hotel. Cane furniture was scattered about on Persian rugs accompanied by ebony sideboards and secateurs inlayed with mother of pearl. Egyptian men mingled with soldiers; some – who clearly were already sated after their masculine urges – sat on low sofas smoking shish. Others drank watered-down whisky while leaning against walls, walls adorned with built in display cabinets exhibiting Ottoman Iznik pottery; pleasing to the eye blue and white vases and plates. Huge alabaster urns displayed indoor plants. To Archie it seemed no expense was spared.

Archie noted various ornate entrances leading off to dimly lit corridors behind drapes of hanging glass beads. Directly ahead a main arch, in the shape of a lotus plant with columns of black and white chequered alabaster, tempted those with more coin than sense towards a grand carved wooden staircase. This lead to the upper levels of debauchery. The electric and gas lighting was subtle, setting the mood while traditional Egyptian music – harps, lutes, drums, flutes and cymbals – percolated through the merriment from the upper floors. Here the officers were pampered.

Aussie digger Ted spat a glob of chewing tobacco into a brass spittoon. 'Shit!' was all he could think to say. 'This'll cost a pretty penny.'

The chocolate-skinned beauty ushered the soldiers in from the doorway. 'Come,' she purred, barely audible over the ratbag chatter of dozens of other soldiers with the same intent. 'Come, you follow.'

They stood in a tight knot, their heads pivoting, taking in the sights, the exotic smells of rose water or apple tobacco and the eastern music. Slow to react, wary, they finally fell in after Archie who was still in the clutches of this beautiful hostess.

The hostess took the men into a drawing room. She clapped her hands and at least twenty young women traipsed into the room in well-rehearsed order.

'You choose,' the hostess said.

Eric, the clown amongst the group asked. 'What about you love? How much?'

'Too much for you soldier boy.'

Drunken laughs.

'Ah, come on.'

The Nubian beauty stood two inches taller than five-nine Eric. She leant in stroking his right cheek. 'I am hostess, yes. I not for sale.'

'Bugger.'

The groans of disappointment were hushed. 'These girls,' the Nubian beauty said, sweeping her arm towards the tantalizing exhibits. 'You pay two shillings. They pretty, yes? Two shillings half the hour.'

'Two bob, Christ,' someone coughed. With soldiers pay at one shilling a day, two bob wasn't a bargain.

Tiger Smith was tempted. 'Half hour huh?' He rubbed the stubble on his chin.

'Half the hour, girl make you very very happy.'

'How much for five minutes?' another lark laughed. 'Cos that's all Tiger needs.'

Tiger blushed. 'Bugger off.'

'Half the hour is set time,' the hostess answered. 'Half hour good, yes?'

'I'll go 'alf hour with that one.' Clearly impatient, Kevin pointed at a petit black girl with long straight coal black hair and the whitest teeth he had ever seen. He stood eagerly flashing a florin.

'Go Kev,' a few shouted.

The Nubian beauty clapped her hands and the commitment was made. The young Egyptian took Kevin by the hand and the two passed through a beaded curtain and melted into a passageway softly lit with red lanterns.

'Jesus,' Tiger said, his face one of amazement. 'That was bloody quick.'

'You're next Tiger.'

'Nar.'

'Go on. You know yer want to.' For all his mouthing off of late, it seemed Tiger had lost his nerve. 'Lost yer balls Tiger?' one lag called out.

'Bugger off.'

'I'll take … *her*,' Archie cut the jeering short. 'Archie. You mongrel,' Rex smacked his lips and fidgeted anxiously.

Archie's choice was surprisingly ordinary. But the young lady, possibly Arabian Chinese had an extraordinary aura about her. Enchanting would probably describe her best. She did not smile, preferring to remain stern-faced but something about her attracted Archie. Exotic? Definitely. But was it simply a challenge? Her silky black hair was cut short and tightly knotted. Her exposed breasts, whilst not overly sized, were firm with large and pointed caramel-coloured nipples. She wore ankle length silk trousers the natives called shintijan and a silk scarf trailed over her shoulders. Archie stood silently still moment, almost in a trance.

'Archie.' Rex prodded.

Archie snapped from his silent reverie back into the surrounding din of drunkenness and degeneracy … back into the realisation he was about to lay with a total stranger. He sensed heart palpitations while a stirring in his trousers drew him into the real world about him. 'Two shillin's yer say?' he said in a croaky voice staring directly at the half-caste femme fatale.

'Ah … you like Silk Road,' the Nubian said.

'Silk Road?'

'Yes. You have good taste soldier boy. Silk Road, she exotic, yes?'

Archie swallowed hard.

'Good man Arch',' Rex was impressed.

'Christ Archie,' another laughed. 'She'll eat yer alive.'

'He hopes so,' Eric grinned, casting a lascivious eye over the remainder of the girls.

'I'll 'ave this one,' Bill said digging into his pocket for a florin. The ball was rolling. The choices made.

'What about you Baz,' Eric called down the line to Barrie, one of the more conservative of the group. 'There's a nice little plump one there. That's your cup of tea ain't it mate?'

'You know I have a sweetheart at home.'

'You know I 'ave a sweet 'eart at 'ome,' Eric mimed.

'Bastard! Haven't you blokes heard of venereal disease?'

'What?'

'Venereal disease … the pox.'

And their officers *had* warned them. Any soldier who caught the pox would be sent home in disgrace with his pay book marked accordingly. He would be shamed before his family and god help them if they had a sweetheart or wife to answer to.

'Girls clean,' the hostess protested. 'Girls inspected weekly. They show certificates.'

'Certificates!' Eric cried out triumphantly. 'Well there yer go lads. Hear that Baz, the girls all got certificates. Are yer sure mate yer don't wanna …'

'Piss off Eric.'

Six punters took up the challenge; the remainder followed Barrie to the bar and the Nubian beauty returned to the street.

***

Archie stood in the doorway of a first-floor room off a corridor. He tackled mixed emotions. Tadita, for that was the name she told him, led him by the hand into a small room smelling of stale perfume and sex. Archie could feel his heart pounding in his chest as the anxiety persisted but so did the lustful anticipation. The furniture was sparse, the décor exotic but these small bedrooms, designed for coupling and nothing else, were the old hotel guest rooms divided in two by makeshift partitions; a necessity when a city is inundated with thousands upon thousands of single men and space is premium. And the groans, cries and screams of copulating were barely discreet.

Tadita closed the door and locked it. She reached out her hand. Her English was non-existent but body language prevailed. Archie dug into his pocket and gave the woman a hand full of piastres, more than two shillings worth clearly, from the twinkle in her eye, but like many other soldiers he still struggled with the exchange rate. Now, without the encouragement of his mates and without a beer in his hand, Archie's nerve was tested. But Tadita was an experienced whore, she had seen it all before and besides, the clock was ticking.

Tadita sat on the bed and reached out for Archie's hand. He swallowed hard and mumbled some useless words the woman could not understand anyway. Tadita patted the bed next to her. Archie sat. Tadita closed the gap between them, took Archie's hand and placed it on her breast. Tadita was used to the calloused skin of the working class Australian. If it had been a discomfort it didn't show. For Archie, holding the supple flesh was surreal. He felt his face flush. Tadita encouraged him to fondle both breasts and he marvelled at the texture, like firm jelly and the weight seemed similar. Tadita said something in Arabic. The words seemed poetic, calming and above all friendly. Reclining on the single bed under a window facing the street Tadita lifted her shintijan. She was naked underneath. Archie was scarcely subtle, staring at her mons of wiry black hair. Archie swallowed hard. At Tadita's beckoning he lay beside her and she caressed the outside of his trousers. Already semi-aroused he felt himself harden, vanquishing all modesty and anxiety. Lust conquered. Archie lifted his shirt over his head, threw it to the floor and unbuttoned his trousers. Tadita wiggled out of her costume and lay on her back massaging her breasts and moaning suitably, pouting her lips, professional to the end. There was no turning back. Not now …

Archie knelt on the bed before the whore, his knees sinking into the feathered mattress and was about to position himself when … suddenly the window to the street was ablaze with fire.

Archie snapped about in time to catch a massive fireball roaring past the window outside. It exploded onto the street below. Tadita threw Archie aside and they both clambered to the window. Apparently a burning mattress had been launched from the floors above. Excited drunks cheered in the street, gathering about the flames and fuelling it with furniture now cascading from the bordello's upper windows. A riot had started. Tadita shouted something at Archie and stabbed a finger towards the door.

'Jesus Christ! What the hell?' Archie was as shocked as the woman. The flames spread fast and the early evening darkness was aglow. The bedroom filled with red and yellow light while the street filled with shouting, yelling and anarchy.

Archie stood at the window frozen in shock a moment. Suddenly what sounded like gunshots snapped him to attention and he realised his naked body was on display to the rioters in the street only one floor below. Archie cupped his shrinking manhood and leapt off the bed dressing faster than he had disrobed. Tadita shouted once more, screaming at him to leave as she too dressed.

Another flaming pile dropped from above and into the street. Archie took one last look out the window. Now a hundred soldiers had gathered, drawn by the uproar of a revolution. Arab property owners, servants and some brave civilians tried to control the mounting skirmish, but they were outnumbered by hundreds of angry soldiers. Several fights broke out. More mattresses and bedding plunged to the street. It soon became clear furniture was being set alight and thrown from the floors above. Tadita flew into a rage and started pummelling Archie who pushed her aside and fled to the foyer where Rex and a couple of others were gathered. 'What's goin' on?'

'It's a riot Archie,' Rex shouted back. 'The bastards are getting their just desserts.'

'What bastards?'

'The bloody Jippos have been ripping us off for months, they water down the booze which is already shit and the whores have doubled in price, apparently.'

An entire inlaid ebony cabinet was pushed down the stairs beside them, shoved by drunken Australian and New Zealand soldiers. Archie heard the whistles of the local police but they were pathetically outnumbered and beaten back immediately. Outside, the numbers swelled into the thousands. It was pandemonium. Now, out on the streets, Archie could see several buildings, brothels five and six storeys high, were in flames.

Haret el Wasser was a war zone.

And they were more than two thousand miles from the front line in France.

The soldiers ran riot. Their animal instincts and pent up anger unleashed. The local fire brigade arrived, only to have their hoses hacked with knives, axes and bayonets. It was mayhem. The British Military Police, the 'red caps' as they were known, stood no chance against the rioting diggers. Soldiers ransacked many of the brothels, shoving the girls out onto the street along with their pimps, furniture and clothing; which was all set alight. Maoris of the New Zealand forces, which were estimated to be one in ten of the New Zealand soldiers, were particularly savage.

Archie followed a burning piano pushed out the hotel door and down the front steps into the rabble. He was keen to distance himself before law and order took precedence. But more than once he was shoved into the fray. Angry, he lashed out. Suddenly he was taken from behind, a strong arm around his throat. Archie could not see his attacker but managed to free himself before elbowing the man in the jaw. He twisted about to finish the job with a right hook when he recognised the man was military police. The MP, overwhelmed, snatched Archie's dog tag and ripped it from his neck, but Archie vanished into the chaos.

On Haret el Wasser the larrikins vented their anger. For many it was a game, a punch up to let off steam. For others, it was personal. Archie, like many, was simply at the wrong place at the wrong time. Finally, Lieutenant Malcolm of the 9th Light Horse created a piquet line with ninety-five of his men and the battle weary diggers retreated at the point of bayonets.

This act of violence was inexcusable. But the men had had enough, enough of the watered-down high-priced grog and enough of the expensive whores. Besides, many had caught venereal disease.

Certificate my arse!

Archie heard later that more than two thousand cases of the pox – *wounded in horizontal combat* – were currently being treated, putting much pressure on the medical corps, with an average stay in quarantine being thirty five days. 1344 men were to be sent home, disgraced. The brass was not happy.

Archie found Rex and Eric some blocks away as he made his way through the deserted bazaar towards the trams, which would take them to Mena Camp. They were sharing a bottle of looted brandy. Archie took a decent mouthful and shuddered as the spirit burnt his throat. 'Jesus Christ that was somethin'.' He took a second guzzle and passed the bottle back to Eric, already befuddled with drink.

'How'd you go with Silky Road then, eh?' Eric ribbed Archie.

'Don't ask.'

'What?' Rex danced in front of Archie. 'Wha' do yer mean, don't ask? Did yer do the act or not?'

'Did yer see the piquet soldiers?' Archie dodged Rex and his impertinent question.

'Yes mate. Bastards spoilt the fun.'

'They was rippin' dog tags from the necks of anyone caught lootin',' Eric said, his red eyes wide and darting about with excitement.

'I know,' Archie said. 'They got mine.'

'Oh Jesus Arch. How?'

Archie told of his punch up. 'It was self-defence for Christ's sake.'

'Then drink up lads. We best be getting' back to camp, there's goin' to be a shit fight when the brass hear of this.'

***

The last tram for the ten-mile trip back to Mena Camp for the night was pulling away as the lads entered the square. And it was crammed with soldiers. Even the roof, the exterior and the running boards were dangling soldiers like bats in a cave.

'Shit!' Archie cried out. 'We've missed the bloody tram.'

Up ahead the lads saw hundreds of drunken men already struggling to hike back to camp.

'Bugger that,' Eric, ever the jester, had a plan. 'Watch this.' Fuelled with grog he threw a handful of piastres to a boy with a donkey who had been selling tea from an urn. As Archie and Rex watched on, he donned the boy's smock over his shoulders and pulled the Arab headwear low to hide his face. Eric mounted the donkey and rode alongside the tram shouting at the top of his voice. 'The Sultan's coming, the Sultan's coming.'

It worked.

There was an immediate uproar of drunken men peeling away from the tram, dead keen to glimpse the revered Sultan.

Archie, 'What the bloody hell?'

The drunken soldiers ran about in several directions looking for the esteemed Muslim Sovereign. Eric disrobed, deserting the donkey and the Arab attire and clambered on board the tram. 'Now!' Eric urged the other two, turning to wave them aboard. Archie and Rex didn't need much encouragement and were next on board. Seconds later, when the rabble realised the deception the tram filled once more.

'Clever bugger aren't yer?' Archie laughed, thumping Eric on the back.

CHAPTER SEVEN
POOR SAPS

Next morning.

The official Proceeding of the Court of Inquiry at Mena Camp proved a farce. Certainly, witnesses came forward and described the unfortunate event in detail, but true to Aussie mateship, each witness spoke of the culprits being the New Zealanders. *Apparently no Australians were involved.*

'No Australians involved you say?' the inquiry panel asked, incredulous.

'As far as I could see,' one officer told the board. 'The men were all New Zealand privates.'

'No Australians?'

'No sir.'

Of course not, the guilty larrikins laughed.

Apparently, Archie and the lads heard, the New Zealand inquiry blamed the Australians.

However fourteen dog tags had been collected indiscriminately. That was fourteen Australians who were definitely there and fourteen men from whom the army wanted retribution. Fourteen out of thousands. And Archie was one of them. They would be made an example of.

'Archie Bryant, A.I.F. 13th battalion,' Colonel Rupert Bygraves ran an eye over Archie, standing to attention before him. The colonel saw a strapping young man with a fine physique. For this reason ...

'You are to be consigned to the Royal Engineers as a sap.'

'A sap sir?'

'You *do* know what a sap is, do you not.'

'A sapper, a tunneller sir.'

'That is correct. You want to act like a rat you can live underground like one. Your first employment however will be digging latrines for 5th Battery Field Artillery.'

Had the colonel known, this disposition suited Archie just fine. For one, he would feel safer underground and would come into contact with fewer soldiers. Loner Archie Bryant was led away immediately for latrine duty.

***

Usually chosen from the ranks of enlisted miners, bricklayers, blacksmiths and carpenters, the sappers were a fearless mob. In a nutshell, Archie knew his employment would be in the dangerous pursuit of tunnelling beneath the enemy trenches, planting huge amounts of explosives, retreating to a safe distance and then blowing the enemy to Kingdom Come.

That's it in a nutshell.

Captain Graham Walters of the AIF Royal Engineers, a stout man in his early forties with a handlebar moustache and an air of imperialism about him that bordered on annoying, addressed the new recruits. Archie stood at attention with thirty others in the midday sun. Walters walked the single line of soldiers inspecting them carefully.

'At ease,' he eventually ordered. 'I know that some of you are suffering from the nasty beverages offered by the Jippos at Wazzir last evening. Then so be it. An afternoon's exercise will soon sweat it out of you.'

No one smiled.

'Many of you are here because you are experienced coal miners, you will be the *face men,* by that I mean the men who will do the clay kicking and timbering ...'

'Clay-kicking sir?'

The captain stood face to face with the man who dared interrupt. 'Name, soldier?'

'Fry sir.'

'Yes Fry, clay-kicking. They're the men who dig the face of the tunnel. Do you have a problem with that?'

'No sir, it's just that it's all sand 'round 'ere sir.'

'I'm talking about France man,' Walter shouted into the soldier's face for the benefit of all. 'You others,' the officer continued, 'the less experienced,' and Walter's eyes narrowed towards Archie, 'the less experienced drunkard rabble-rousing troublemakers will be a secondary group called *mates*. Mates will be timbermen, baggers and runners-out. That is shoring up the tunnel and removing the clay for the diggers. In other words making the tunnels safe and keeping them clear. The good news is, face men will be paid six shillings a day and mates will get two shillings and tuppence.' Walters singled out Fry. 'That's two shillings and tuppence more than many of you are worth.'

Archie couldn't believe his luck. He had been accused of something he was innocent of, and his punishment was to join the sappers, an elite group of men whilst his pay doubled.

'That's the good news,' Walters said. 'The bad news is the work is dangerous, bloody dangerous, savvy?' There were no signs of disapproval. 'Now, which one of you men is Archie Bryant?'

Archie snapped to attention. 'Me sir.'

'Step forward.' Archie stepped forward. 'Fry, Williams, Bennett and Macintosh, step forward.' The five men stood to attention, eyes forward. 'You men will report immediately to the Duty Sergeant in charge of digging the new latrines for the Engineers at the end of Artillery Road. Quick march.'

***

The new latrines were well under way by the time the new recruited sappers arrived at the Engineers camp at the base of the Great Pyramid. Stripped to the waist they joined other engineers digging the pits; each thirty feet long, one yard wide and ten feet deep. Carpenters fitted bench seating – seats of ease – the full length of the excavation, while canvas sunshades were erected overhead. Modesty was a stranger in such situations.

It was late afternoon when Archie's life took another fateful direction. 'What's that?' Archie pushed his slouch hat back on his head and wiped sweat pouring from his forehead. The man next to him, Wayne Melville, had struck an object with his shovel and, what at first appeared to be shells and broken glass, crumbled from the latrine wall at their feet. Wayne picked up the neck of a black glass bottle. It was thick glass with a bulbous neck and lip. Archie stooped to collect what he thought were shells only to realise they were broken clay tobacco pipes. He recognised the old pipes, for his granddaddy smoked something similar when he was a kid.

'Jesus!' Wayne said. 'Did the pharaohs smoke pipes?'

'I don't reckon mate. These aren't *that* old.'

'What ya got there?' One of the other diggers, Frank, took the opportunity to lean on his shovel and take a break.

The Duty Sergeant appeared. 'Come on you blokes, sooner you dig the bloody holes the sooner you can get out o' there.'

'Christ Sarge, can't we have a smoko?' Wayne jammed a broken pipe into his mouth and puffed away.

'Leave that shit and get on with it,' the sergeant shook his head. 'I want to get outa here too you know.'

'What is all this anyway?' Archie asked.

'That,' another digger joined them, 'is rubbish left by Napoleon. Bill Tanner found a pipe with French writing on it the other day.'

'Well I'll be buggered.'

No one suspected the profound effect this discovery had on Archie. He had never been all that interested in history but after standing on top of the pyramid, in the very footsteps of Julius Caesar, Mark Antony, Napoleon and even Lord Nelson, and now this ... this tangible evidence of Napoleon's occupation of Egypt a hundred years earlier ... well, it was a turning point. Fate had left its calling card.

Against his better judgement, Archie found a new level of camaraderie in the Engineers' mess tent. After washing at trestles in buckets of water the new recruits dressed and joined their colleagues at tea. Even the food was better here. Sure, the vegetables were *queer* compared to what they were used to back home and the butter, made from buffalo and goat milk, was unsalted. But the meat soup was generous and tasty with plenty of grains.

Over tin mugs of hot sweet milk tea, Archie showed off a half pipe he had salvaged from the latrine find. 'Probably smoked by Napoleon himself,' Archie told onlookers.

'Yeh, right.'

'You like that old shit mate?' Tom Barnard sat on the bench seat opposite Archie. He had been watching his colleague with interest.

'Yeh, sure.'

'A mate found a Frog coin in that hole too today.'

'Oh.' Tom had Archie's attention. The other lads picked up their tin plates and cutlery and moved to the wash buckets. Archie and Tom watched them a leave. 'Tom Barnard,' Tom said, offering Archie his hand.

'Archie ... Archie Bryant.'

'You one o' them troublemakers at Wazzir last night eh?' Tom asked, but not in a disagreeable manner. Archie nodded, unoffended. 'What I should o' said,' Tom went on, 'was you one o' the unlucky bastards what got caught?'

'Yeh.'

'Bastard eh. It was a bit o' fun though,' Tom grinned. 'Jesus Christ I've never had so much fun. Gave them bloody Jippos what for huh?'

'Yeh.' Archie wanted to tell the soldier of his own experience. Tadita for one. But thought better of it.

Tom Barnard picked up the pipe lying on the bench. 'Do you like the really old stuff?'

'How do yer mean?'

'The ancient stuff, stuff o' the pharaohs?'

'Like the pyramids?'

'Yes, but antiquities from them days.'

'Antiquities?'

'Yeh mate. That's what they call the really old stuff. The lads are digging up bits and pieces from time to time.'

'Like what?'

'Wait here. I'll be back in a mo.' The soldier hurried off to his tent, returning moments later. He looked about to be certain they weren't being watched. "ere, check this out.'

Tom slipped a small figure into Archie's hand. It was a small Egyptian mummy-like figurine in a turquoise glaze, about four inches long and appeared to be made of clay. Archie had never handled such an artefact, but recognised the appearance from books he had seen at school as a boy. He turned the figure over in his hand to reveal symbols running down the full length of its back.

'Hieroglyphs them symbols are called,' Tom said with a distant smile.

Archie was smitten. 'How old is it?'

'Christ mate, thousands o' years.'

'Where did it come from?'

Tom looked about once more. Hardly subtle. He leant closer. 'It's out of a tomb. Some lads, sappers like you and me, dug the side out of tomb when we was diggin' latrines for the medical officers at Heliopolis.' Archie knew of Heliopolis but hadn't been there. It was a new district settled only ten years previously outside Cairo where a huge palace had been turned into a troop hospital. 'Do yer like it?'

'It's … it's … fascinating, yes.'

'You can have it for two bob.'

'What?'

'I'll sell it to yer. Two bob.'

'Are you sure … I mean … it's a great find.'

'Sure I'm sure. Me and the lads 'ave found all kinds o' stuff. Do yer want it or not?'

Archie's frugal upbringing caused him to be wary. 'Two shillings, it's a bit rich mate.'

'Two bob, that's only a day's wages, now yer a sap.'

'I'll give you a shillin'.'

'Jesus. You run a hard bargain. Tell yer what, one and six an' it's yours.'

'Done.' Archie pocketed the figure and took one shilling and sixpence from a coin purse in his pocket.

Tom closed a calloused fist around the two silver coins and stood. 'That's a good price cobber, the dealers at the bazaars are selling stuff like that for ten bob to the officers, especially the Tommys,' he said using the colloquial name for the British troops.

Neither soldier took much notice of a lone figure fiddling at the next trestle, surreptitiously wiping the table top. The figure watched Tom depart, and sat beside Archie before he had a chance to stand. 'Garfield Gardener, corporal,' he introduced himself with a sloppy handshake.

Archie. 'Hi.'

'Field Ambulance with the twelfth,' Gardener said.

So what?

Gardener. 'Mind if I join you?'

'Well I was about to …'

'Won't take a moment.'

Archie was wary. He had noticed this bloke before, a corporal in his late twenties, and thought he had been watching him. 'What won't take a moment?'

Garfield looked about, rubbing his chin. 'Well ... I couldn't help notice you purchase a clay figure from Tom, an ancient figure.'

'So?'

'Well would you mind if I take a look at it?'

Archie sighed heavily, signalling impatience. But the bloke was a corporal. Archie presented the statue.

'Nice,' Garfield rolled it over in his palm. 'Very nice. Did Tom tell you where he found it?'

'Somewhere near Heliopolis.'

'Of course. Have you got any idea what this is?'

'Figure from the time o' the pharaohs,' Archie said lamely.

Garfield took a small magnifying glass from his pocket to study the hieroglyphs on the back. Finally reading out loud, 'I am Metjen. Son of chief scribe Minnakht.'

'You can read that?'

'Of course. I graduated in ancient civilisations at Sydney University.' The corporal studied the artefact closer, his eye magnifying comically through the lens. 'This is called a shabti. An archaeologist told me they were left in the tombs to serve the dead in the afterlife.'

'Serve?'

'Yes, like servants. Some tombs had hundreds of them. This one would be around the time of Pharaoh Seti 11.'

'You know your ancient history then. How old do you reckon?'

'Three thousand years approximately. Do you want to sell it?'

'No,' Archie answered smartly. He had other plans.

***

Archie slept well that night, ensconced beneath a woollen blanket against the chill of the desert night upon his new camp stretcher. Around him, within a tent of twenty other snoring men, Archie sank into a heavy sleep, eventually dreaming of the ancients who came before him and the treasures they left behind in the sands of time.

Over a breakfast of salted porridge other thoughts plagued Archie. The entrepreneur in him surfaced and Tom Barnard's parting words mulled over and over: *'That's a good price cobber, the Jippo dealers at the bazaars are selling stuff like that for ten bob to the officers, especially the Tommys.'*

Archie fidgeted through Sunday prayers. But by noon he was on a tram heading to the bazaars of Cairo and in his pocket was the Egyptian tomb figure wrapped in a handkerchief.

***

Afnan Mubarak was a resilient Egyptian. Like a Nubian spitting cobra she could survive in a dry savannah. She had the cunning of a desert rat, a shrewd miser in every respect. It was said about the alleyways of Cairo that she still had the first piastre she ever made. Too mean even to celebrate her own seventieth birthday this year, Afnan Mubarak sat in the shadows of her ill-lit antique shop, situated at Khan el-Khalili, one of Cairo's oldest souks and built in the early 16th century, so Archie had been told.

Once entering the narrow alleyways of the bazaar Archie experienced anxiety. A sense of danger even, accompanied him into the claustrophobic labyrinth of merchant stalls where anything and everything changed hands daily. Archie prided himself on possessing a good sense of direction, however, the twists and turns disorientated him and although he had an address written on a card, each request for directions left him more anxious.

Shopkeepers hassled him in passing, but the temptation to stop and look was soon marred by unwelcome attention from vying shopkeepers. Most were demanding, some bordered on aggressive and Archie felt like a fish out of water, admonishing himself for venturing here alone.

Shop 1116 was clearly marked in western and Arabic numerals beneath a hand painted sign that read *Mubarak Antiquities*. Her shop was four times the average frontage and, unlike the small-time dealers, she had a glass window. Archie stood a moment, grateful to have finally found the shop, and studied the dusty dirty window. Items on display were piled from the sill to ceiling with every antique imaginable to a country lad from Australia. Both Western and Arabic items were represented; be it musical instruments, a framed portrait, a brass lantern, hand beaten silver or ancient antiquities. Archie saw a figure similar to his amongst dozens in the window; some blue glazed some the earthy colour of clay. He tried the door. It opened. A bell over the door heralded his presence into the dimness ...

Behold, a stranger enters.

The obese antique dealer sat amongst elevated cushions where she reclined behind a glass top counter. Archie's immediate thought was one of a bull seal he had seen sunning itself on a beach back home ...

She looks like she could bite too.

Archie shook the image clear from his thoughts. 'Mornin',' he said in his most confident voice.

The woman gestured curtly with a nod and a sour face. Without any hint of subtlety she looked the soldier up and down before sniffing loudly. 'What you wan'?'

As Archie's eyes adjusted to the light he noticed the fat-faced merchant had a silky white beard to one side of her chin. Her pupils were like black eye peas, the whites jaundice yellow and now that he noticed the missing teeth – with the few remaining a burnt umber – he caught her breath, and shifted back a step.

'Well?' she insisted.

Bugger it. In for a penny in for a pound.

Archie unravelled the ancient figure and placed it on the counter. The woman didn't flinch. She showed no emotion but allowed her eyes to focus before picking the piece up for examination. She felt the weight in her hand and knew it was genuine. She took up a magnifying glass on the counter, and closed one eye, casting it over the artefact. She read the hieroglyphs on the back. The artefact could have been cast in solid gold but she showed no reaction. Slowly the old Egyptian looked back to Archie. She noted his dirty fingernails. 'Where this from?' she asked, her face as expressionless as the figurine she held in her chubby little hand.

'Heliopolis.'

'Hmm.' The woman grunted. 'Where in Heliopolis?'

'I don't know. I bought it from another soldier who found it digging latrines.'

'Huh. Soldiers dig, dig, find many things yes?'

'I guess so. How much ... I mean how much will you give me for it?'

'Huh! This shabti very common. No worth much. You know name shabti?'

'Yes.'

'Many many shabti put in tomb with mummy. Many many.'

'So what's it worth?'

'Piastres or pennies.'

'Shillings.'

At the word 'shillings' Afnan Mubarak pushed the shabti back across the counter. 'I give you sixpence, not a penny more.'

'Sixpence. Come on its gotta be worth five shillin's at least.'

'Huh!' For the first time the woman laughed. 'You keep shabti, maybe it give you good luck where you go soldier boy.'

'Four shillings then.'

'No, no four shillings. One shilling. Last offer.'

Archie groaned a sigh and cast an eye around the shop. 'Do you mind if I look around?' he asked. Another grunt was taken as permission granted, even if he didn't have much money to spend and she knew it.

'Look. No touch.' The dealer watched Archie carefully. She read his naivety. Archie was undeniably fascinated with the shop. He had never been in an antique shop before, only recently reading in an English magazine, The Spectator, that they even existed, like the curiosity shops in South Kensington. This was extraordinary. Then, amongst the Ottoman curiosities, the Arabic beaten brass and the French porcelain, Archie saw something he knew about. An Eastman Kodak Company. Rochester camera with black painted body and leather bellows. He knew it to be Format 8 with 1.5/8 by 2.1/2 inch exposures on 127 roll-film. It had fixed focussing with a clear viewfinder and a film advance indicated by a red window. It was the bees knees and almost new. Archie's cousin had one and Archie had even taken two photographs with it himself. That must have been three years ago, and this camera looked about the same age. But the greatest advantage was that the Vest Pocket Kodak, as it was marketed, would easily slip into the pocket of his army tunic. Archie picked the camera up without thinking. The merchant sat upright. 'How much is this?' he asked.

'Too much on your pay soldier boy.'

'I've used one like this before,' Archie said, almost defensive. 'How much?' he asked again, not put off by the woman's impertinence.

'Five shillings.'

'F-five. It's not new.'

'I know this. How much you give me?'

Archie was taken aback. He knew the Egyptians liked to haggle over prices but was not prepared for her offer.

'I ... ah ... I'll give you two shillings.'

'Bah! Five shillings I say.'

Archie looked in his purse. Bad move. This act was akin to accepting the woman's price. Archie counted two shillings and eight pence, some in piastres, and was relying on the sale of the shabti.

'Well?' Mubarak said impatiently. Archie pinched his lips and with a sigh returned his purse to his trouser pocket. The dealer's eyes narrowed and she rubbed her hooked nose a moment in thought. 'I tell you something.'

'What's that?'

'You give me shabti, I give you camera.'

The ancient figure cost Archie one shilling and sixpence. The camera was a bargain. Archie asked. 'You want to trade huh?'

'Yes. You deaf? I trade. Deal?'

Archie returned to the counter with a satisfied grin and thrust his right hand in the woman's face. She was aware of this western custom, shaking hands to make a deal. For the first time Afnan Mubarak allowed a wry smile curl the corner of her mouth, and she raised her grossly large arm. Anyone would have thought Archie had singlehandedly purchased the Eiffel Tower in Paris the way he shook the fat sweaty hand. When he remembered. 'Ah, do you have film?'

'Film sixpence.'

'Sixpence!'

'Yes. You wan or what?'

Archie was defeated. He passed her the sixpence and was given one roll of Kodak film in a brown paper wrapper. Afnan Mubarak slipped the shabti under the counter and dropped the coin into a small cash box before locking it with a brass key on a leather strap about her neck. Clearly she had unfinished business and watched Archie reading the instructions on how to load the film. 'You wan' make money?' she asked quietly, should there be stray ears hiding amongst her legion of *objects of virtu*.

'Money?'

'You wan' to make money? Sell things to soldiers?'

'Like what?'

Afnan Mubarak held Archie's eye long enough to convince herself she was not making a mistake. Finally she picked up a small brass bell on the counter and with a flick of her fat wrist she gave the bell a brisk shake. An Arab boy appeared from behind a heavy Persian rug draped over a doorway behind the woman. A doorway that had gone unnoticed until now. The boy was eleven or twelve, a rather unkempt looking lad in traditional Arab clothing with a weathered red velvet fez on his head. Words were exchanged in Arabic.

'Go with Youssef. He no speaks English but he show you something in back. You look. Come back. We talk.' Archie stood speechless a moment, aghast. 'Go!' Afnan Mubarak said impatiently, her voice raised. Archie looked to the boy. He looked harmless enough. He circled the counter and followed Youssef into the darkness of a short passageway before entering a large windowless storeroom lit by an oil lamp and filled with shelf after shelf of antiquities. The fat merchant's words returned to Archie; *Soldiers dig, dig, find many things yes? This shabti very common. No worth much.*

Not worth much, Archie whispered to himself while casting a sharp eye over the shelves. *Bullshit!*

Woodcarvings of half jackal half human gods, pottery statues, alabaster jars with baboon heads and hundreds upon hundreds of shabtis in various conditions, various materials and a range of sizes, all stared back from the floor to ceiling shelves. Archie was astonished and made a mental note to visit the Cairo museum when the opportunity arose. He looked to Youssef who grinned back proudly.

'Can I touch?' Archie asked, certain he was standing before a priceless collection of antiquities. Youssef shrugged. *No English.* Archie made to pick up a shabti. Youssef suddenly smiled and nodded approvingly. Archie picked up a large figure, eight inches and turquoise blue like the one he had. It was mummy-like with the headgear of a pharaoh and with crossed arms at the chest. The body was covered in the ancient written language, the hieroglyphs. It was also decidedly heavy and looked less refined in detail than the one he sold the merchant. Youssef said something in Arabic motioning Archie to return to the shop. Archie was about to replace the shabti when Youssef placed a hand on Archie's hand, pushing the figure to his bosom and signalled, *keep it. Follow me.*

'Ah you like faience I see,' Afnan Mubarak looked pleased with Archie's choice.

'Faience?'

'Blue glaze. Same as one you sell me. The Egyptians, they like thees colour. Is called faience.'

'Oh. It's very nice, yes.'

'Nice!' The old lady laughed at Archie's description. 'That is 19th Dynasty, 1280 B.C. You know what BC mean?'

'Ah yeh, of course,' Archie lied.

'What?'

Archie felt a fool for lying and being caught blind. 'I've forgotten.'

'Hmm,' Afnan Mubarak was starting to like this naïve Australian. He seemed perfect for her cause. 'BC mean Before Christ. That what English speaking peoples say. Before your Jesus Christ born see.'

'Yes, that's right. I remember now.'

'How much moneys do you think faience worth?' she nodded her fat head to the shabti, still in Archie's clutches.

'Oh! I don't wanna buy it.'

'I no ask you to buy it. I ask how much it worth?'

'I couldn't even guess Mrs ...'

'Madam. You call me Madam. No Mrs.' The sharpness of these words was instantly softened by a light smile. She dug fat fingers into a small box of confectionery and placed a caramel in her mouth. Rolling it with her tongue to one side to avoid bad teeth, she said, 'Twenty pounds that shabti worth.'

'Oh.' Archie used both hands to place the statue carefully on the glass counter top.

'Huh.' The dealer wiped icing sugar from her mouth and chuckled. 'But I sell to you, one pound.'

'Oh I'm not interested in buying Madam. I came to ...'

'Listen me.' Afnan Mubarak fancied herself as a good judge of character, and she knew a fraud when she saw one. 'What your name?'

'Name?'

'Yes. Name?'

'Archie ... Archie Bryant.'

'You listen me Archie. You buy shabti, one pound and you sell to soldiers for two, three pound maybe more, yes.'

'But I can't afford to pay you Madam Mubarak.'

'No. Maybe you no afford this shabti.' And she flicked an irreverent finger at the figure on the counter. 'But maybe you chose from other shabti. Something not so much moneys. You buy from Madam Mubarak and sell to soldiers. You some back tomorrow and buy more. Madam Mubarak make you rich soldier.'

Archie looked long and hard at the statue. 'This no true,' the merchant said picking up the shabti Archie had chosen.

'True?'

'Shabti is no true... how you say in English ... faux ... fake.'

'What?'

'Yes, fake. All you see is make in bazaar.'

Archie was aghast. He swallowed hard looking into the other cabinets full of antiquities. 'This true,' Afnan Mubarak said of her stock on display in the shop. 'Well most is true. Very very old from pharaohs, yes. But what you see out back room is fake. We make much moneys together, you and Madam Mubarak, yes?'

At that moment Archie felt a bond with this seventy-year-old crook; the naïve young Aussie soldier and an old hand at an ancient game ...

Deceit.

CHAPTER EIGHT
RACKETEERS ABROAD

Lance Corporal Peter Barton knew a bargain when he saw one. He was immersed in the history of this exotic land of the pharaohs and had already acquired two other small ancient items purchased from Arab boys in the streets of Cairo. One piece, a pottery scarab beetle seal with hieroglyphics, and the other a shard of pottery from a large jar painted with ducks, lotus leaves and hieroglyphics. The shard was the size of a cigarette packet, which he wrapped in an embroidered souvenir silk scarf for his mother. These he had posted back to Melbourne along with letters and a photo of him mounted on a camel with the Sphinx and the pyramids in the background.

Now, this sapper Archie Bryant, on latrine duty at Mena Camp, had *dug* a small green glazed mummy-like figure, also with hieroglyphics. It was in perfect condition and Corporal Barton paid Archie eight shillings for it. Yes sir, Lance Corporal Peter Barton knew a bargain when he saw one.

Archie wasted no time. With the freedom of an evening pass from Mena Camp Archie regularly trammed to Cairo with other men from his brigade. But he had no problem losing them once they dispersed in small groups; some dining in cafes, some in the drinking establishments and some revisiting bordellos unaffected by the Wazzir incident. For all they cared Archie Bryant was wasting his pay on whores. Meanwhile Archie hurried to Madam Mubarak at the bazaar.

In the short period of one week, eight shillings became four pounds. Four pounds became nineteen. Nineteen became thirty-three. Archie was over the moon and Madam Mubarak was happy to add Archie Bryant to her stable of fraudsters.

The fact Archie was one of eight working for the Madam had not occurred to Archie. Three were Australian, one a New Zealander and four were British Army. But with forty thousand men in the Egyptian Expeditionary Forces gathering in Egypt for a major attack in Europe, Archie's dealings attracted little attention.

Archie's favourite ruse of discovery was to have an *artefact* hidden in his pocket, and then, when he had a witness or two, he would crumble away the side of a trench with his shovel and the *ancient artefact* would tumble to his feet.

'Oh my god!' was Archie's favourite line. 'Would yer look at that?'

With witnesses to back his claim in the mess tents that night, Archie had the perfect provenance. No one ever doubted his claim; especially as he moved about the mess tents and bars and cafes of the Arab shantytown on the outskirts of Mena Camp, rarely rubbing shoulders twice with previous customers. And to this end Archie went to great lengths to remain aloof and discreet; that is until Corporal Garfield Gardener appeared once more from nowhere one night, as Archie took a smoko before lights out.

'Lovely evening Archie,' the corporal said in an annoying monotone, approaching from behind. 'How's it going?'

'Fine.' Archie was alert. He had a bad feeling about this bloke the first time he met him in the mess tent, a week or two ago. He had tried to avoid him like the pox. Now here he was. Archie looked over his shoulder and took a last draw on a half-smoked Turf. He made to flick the cigarette into the sand and leave but Garfield placed a hand on Archie's shoulder pressuring him to remain seated.

'Stay. Finish your cigarette.' The bloke was only a corporal but a good half dozen years older Archie guessed, yet his tone was more an order given by a major general. Garfield sat on the bench seat next to Archie, staring ahead towards the darkened shape of the pyramids, now lost in the moonless Arabian night. 'Have you heard the news?'

'News?'

'Yes, about the big push?' he asked Archie, his irritating voice reminding Archie of Peter Houghton, a school kid everyone picked on half a dozen years ago.

Archie was curious. 'Big push?'

'Yes. The 9th, 10th and 11th Battalions are to be deployed in a matter of days.'

'Oh?'

'That's the word. Off to Alexandria and then Marseilles apparently. Then we train to the Somme.'

'Blimey, no, I hadn't heard.' Archie studied the soldier a moment. 'You're with the twelfth aren't yer?'

'That's right.'

'So what about the 12th and 13th?' Archie asked of their Battalions.

'Haven't heard. But clearly we'll be next to move out ... the twelfth that is. Actually the destination is very hush hush. No one really knows where we're off too. There have also been rumours we're headed for Lemnos.'

'Lemnos?'

'Near Greece. Close to Turkey.'

Archie finished his cigarette flicking it in a spiral of sparks across the sand. He stood.

'I'm knackered. See yer tomorra.'

'How's business?' Garfield asked sharply before he lost Archie's company.

'Business? What business?'

'You know what I'm talking about.'

'Sorry?'

'Come come Archie. You've quite the reputation of late. The man to see ...'

'Man to see?'

The corporal held Archie's eye briefly but Archie felt his face would give away his secret and so he stared back into the desert night. 'The man to see, if one fancies purchasing a little something of the land of the pharaohs, is you Archie Bryant.'

So that's what the bastard was up to, Archie thought to himself. He could be trouble and Archie wondered how much he knew. If it was the sale of antiquities, well it was hardly illegal. Lots of soldiers were doing it. But dabbling in the black market with forgeries ending up in the hands of officers, well, that could see him court-martialled.

'I have been fortunate.'

'Fortunate. So you have.' Garfield tried to look Archie in the eye but Archie was as evasive as his dialogue. 'You've been exceedingly fortunate old boy. That's what.'

Archie had had enough of this game, he stepped to face the man planting his boots apart with his hands on his hips 'What are you trying to say mate? Spit it out.'

'Alright. Keep your shirt on.'

'Keep me shirt on! Say what yer wanna say or shut it.'

'Easy. You're talking to a corporal.'

'I don't take fools easily Gardener. Say what you came here to say or bugger off.'

'Very well.' Garfield took a bronze oil lamp from his pocket. Archie recognised it immediately. He had sold it to a sergeant in artillery and made one and a half quid profit. 'Recognise this?'

Archie scratched his chin grinding his teeth, stalling for an answer. 'Yeh,' he finally said. 'I sold that to a sarge in 11th's artillery.'

'That's right. And it ended up in the quarters of Major Denis Kinnock.'

Archie's face reddened. 'How?'

'How? Your sarge sold it on to the major, didn't he? You see Major Kinnock's become quite the collector and has got together a small collection of antiquities. Most of it quality too, except for this.' Garfield weighted the lamp in the palm of his hand.

Archie, 'How did you end up with it?'

'I am on friendly terms with Major Kinnock's valet, private Max Quin, who invited me to evaluate the Major's artefacts. I asked to borrow it ...'

'Evaluate?'

'Yes. He knows of my interest and expertise. I picked the lamp as a fake immediately.'

'A fake! Now listen sport ...'

'Don't play games with me Bryant. It's a fake. The detail poor. It was made yesterday. And you've been selling dozens of fakes the past week or so. Made a pretty penny too I should imagine. What I want to know is, where are you getting the stuff from?'

'Don't be daft. I haven't got a clue what you're on about.'

'If you don't cooperate I'll see you exposed and you will be sent home in disgrace.'

Garfield Gardener stood to face Archie. He sensed success. Looking about them, to be certain they were alone, Garfield lowered his voice. 'Look Archie, all I want is a piece of the pie. I know you're making good money out of it and there is plenty to go around. Besides, with my contacts we can sell more upmarket pieces and make more money in the short time we have left. I've seen a set of four alabaster canopic jars sell for two hundred pounds to a Britain at the embassy; I know a fake twelve-inch tall bronze of the god Osiris sold for three hundred pounds to a British general. I know the items are out there, I just need to know where and how. We can do this together.'

Archie wanted to throttle the bloke there and then.

'Besides,' Garfield said quietly, 'I am already heavily invested in this.' Archie's concerned expression quietly questioned this comment. 'I've already assured Major Kinnock that this,' and Garfield toyed with the lamp in his hand, 'is the real thing. So, what do you say?'

Archie took a deep breath and turned to face the pyramids, his hands back on his hips. His mind raced. Suddenly his mouth felt dry and he smacked his lips in contemplation. He could see he had little choice. Finally, after what seemed ages, he spun about to Corporal Gardner. 'All right. But we do this on my terms.' Garfield's face brightened. It had proven easier than he thought. 'On my terms,' Archie reiterated. 'Understand?'

'Yes, yes, we'll make a great team, you'll see.'

'Meet here after tea termorra,' Archie grumbled and walked away disgusted with himself.

***

Madam Mubarak thought little of Garfield Gardener the moment she met him. And the first moment she had alone with Archie she warned him to watch his back. She was however, impressed with the corporal's knowledge of Egyptian antiquities and saw the opportunity to increase her own wealth with minimum risk. Archie too, was impressed when the initial storeroom at the back of Mubarak's shop was bypassed for another locked vault where *the good stuff* was stored.

Corporal Gardener stood aghast gaping at a carved and painted lid from off the sarcophagus of a 25th dynasty noble's wife, Tjenety, 750-656 BC It had been looted a year earlier and now Madam Mubarak thought it a good time to move it on, while there were so many buyers in Cairo. Garfield Gardener swallowed hard as he ran a respectful hand along the polychrome decoration and hieroglyphs, which had lain in a dark tomb for over 2600 years. All about him were genuine museum pieces sharing the musty storeroom with hundreds of quality fakes. He was speechless.

***

At sixty-three General Delbert Sedgwick Kinsley was the archetypical stick in the mud, high-ranking British army officer. He had served in the Boer War as a colonel and was then promoted to Brigadier and now, in 1915, he was one of those heading the Expeditionary Forces in Egypt, as a Lieutenant General. A position of responsibility and trust. A stick in the mud he may be, and set in his ways, yet dull and unadventurous he was not. And all for the wrong reasons. In the last six months stationed in Egypt he had accumulated considerable wealth, being an instigator of the plans to keep the existing Egyptian government in check. This body made autonomous decisions, like the requisitioning of fodder for the occupying equestrian forces and insisting Egypt sell Britain its cotton for well below market price. This caused resentment from the local authority but the old general just kept accumulating baksheesh through another of Corporal Garfield's network of contacts, General Kinsley's orderly, Edmund Cornish. Cornish played the middleman – between the black marketeers and the general. Outside daily business, on behalf of the Expeditionary Forces, General Kinsley had also developed a passion for antiquities; collecting an extraordinary number of artefacts and smuggling them back to Kingsley Manor in Sussex, an inherited residence of a mere eighty rooms. For Kinsley, in Egypt he was like a child in a confectioner's, he had the pounds and piastres and Cairo was well stocked with sweetmeats and toffee. The moment Garfield saw the sarcophagus lid he knew he had a buyer in the general who resided at Shepheard's Hotel in Cairo, where he lodged during the armies sojourn in Egypt.

Two evenings later Garfield and Archie met Edmund Cornish, the general's orderly, as arranged at the rear of the Shepheard's Hotel. Cornish was one of those pathetic snobs, a man with a common background who had ascended *that* ladder. A social climber, one in Archie's circles would say. *Good luck to him for his success*, Archie thought, *but yer don't have to be a bloody snob about it.*

Cornish observed the two Australian volunteers with a level of contempt. Certainly, on all accounts they were neat enough for soldiers but there was no denying it, they *were* colonials. Uncouth was the word that came to mind. He stepped from the servants' entrance at the rear of the hotel and, recognising Garfield signalling in the shadows, he crossed the courtyard to meet Archie and Garfield waiting under fig trees.

'Evening,' Garfield smiled cautiously. His previous meetings with the general's valet had always been formal.

'Who's this?' Cornish asked of Archie without pleasantries, conscious to remain in the dark shadows himself.

'Archie Bryant, it was he who first found the lid.'

Archie tried the friendly approach. 'G'day.'

'Where is it?' Cornish ignored Archie.

Garfield alluded to a handcart behind date palms at the edge of the grounds where Madam Mubarak's boy Youssef waited. Keeping to the shadows the three men moved to the cart. Cornish took a surreptitious look about him, ever aware. He nodded to Youssef who lifted the canvas veil to reveal the lid belonging to the sarcophagus of the ancient noble's wife, Tjenety. Cornish inspected the artefact with great care. If he was impressed he did not let on. Cornish nodded briskly and Youssef replaced the cover. Immediately a disturbance caught their attention back at the servants' entrance to the hotel. Archie looked over his shoulder to catch the figure of a large man silhouetted against the passage lights behind him. Archie guessed it to be the general, General Kinsley. The red glow of a cigar temporarily lit his corpulent face as he focussed into the darkness, while a small pug dog brushed by his trousers, skipped down the steps and ran to a courtyard lamp where it pissed profusely.

'Wait here,' Cornish ordered and walked briskly to meet the general.

'He's a right toff,' Archie said of Cornish when the orderly was out of earshot.

'Yes well, just keep it nice eh?'

Archie tapped a Turf from its packet and offered one to Garfield who he knew didn't smoke. Garfield paid no heed, busy observing the body language of the general and his valet. Meanwhile the pug pissed. Archie crouched down, 'Here boy,' he whistled and the dog came over to investigate. Archie gave the small animal a neck scratch and it rolled onto its back for a belly rub.

'Pugnacious,' the general called over. 'Pugnacious. Here boy,' General Kinsley's voice was husky, probably from the cigars. As Pugnacious obeyed his master Cornish returned. 'Here,' he passed Garfield a fold of bank notes Archie recognised as Sterling. 'Fifteen hundred. It's all there.' It was clear that it would be unacceptable to check the amount. Archie was impressed; the general was not a haggler and Cornish was his eyes and ears.

Cornish ran a final check, lifting the canvas then replacing it. 'Get your boy to follow me,' he said loudly for Youssef to hear without acknowledging the Egyptian. Archie and Garfield watched as Youssef pulled the small cart over to the hotel stables where the general's military staff car was garaged. Once the artefact was secure in the vehicle, Cornish returned to the two soldiers.

He directed his words at Archie. 'I trust you men will be discreet.'

'Of course.' Garfield said in all seriousness.

'Quite. The general has also instructed me to inform you he is pleased with his purchase and is in the market, so to speak, for future finds.'

'Certainly. You can tell the general he will have first refusal on anything we come up with.'

'Actually,' Archie said. 'There is this.' Garfield froze. *What's Archie up to?* Archie took a large pottery faience scarab seal from his trouser pocket. 'It's from the same tomb,' he lied. 'Tjenety's tomb.' Cornish took the paperweight-sized artefact and looked at it closely. He rolled it over in his palm. Looking back towards the hotel where the general was still enjoying his cigar in the evening air with Pugnacious tucked under one arm.

Cornish. 'How much?'

Archie didn't hesitate. 'Two hundred.'

'T-two hundred?' Cornish eyeballed Archie and Archie held the man's gaze. Two hundred *was* excessive but it *did* come from the same tomb as the sarcophagus lid. There followed silence as the orderly weighted the item in his hand as if he was some museum expert. Which he was not. 'Wait.' Cornish returned to the general.

'What the bloody hell are you doing?' Garfield hissed at Archie.

'Relax mate.'

'Relax?' Garfield was ropable. He snatched Archie by the shirtfront without thinking and pushed him against the trunk of a thick palm where they were masked by the tree and lost in the darkness. 'The bloody things a fake!' Garfield's hissed.

Archie kept his calm. 'I wouldn't be doin' that mate.' Archie's left eye twitched. He looked down at his crumpled shirt. Garfield relinquished, sucking in a deep breath before releasing his grip.

'It's a fake,' Garfield repeated more calmly.

'Don't you ever ... ever, do that again,' Archie said with a vacancy in his eye that unnerved Garfield. Garfield also sensed coldness in his accomplice's steely eye he had not noticed before.

'But it's fake Archie,' he said, his voice faltering.

'Did you hear me sport?' Archie reiterated, straightening his shirt.

'Yes ... yes.' Garfield felt defeated. 'Sorry.'

'Yes,' Archie said in a soft voice. 'It's a fake. And those two drongos are no more expert than you and me. So as I said, relax. I just got us another hundred quid each.'

'You there!' Cornish reappeared. 'Archie is it not?'

Archie turned to face the general's valet, *cool as a cucumber*. 'Archie, yes mate, that's me.'

'Where did this come from?' Cornish held the scarab in one hand. Garfield fumbled nervously.

'Like I told yer, it's from the same tomb, the very same tomb as Tjenety's coffin lid.'

'Yes, but where did you acquire this?'

'It were brought to me by an Arab lad who knows I ... I ah ... shall we say dabble in such items.'

'As was the lid, what?'

'That's correct.'

'Hmm.'

Garfield stepped forward, his face now lit by light from a nearby street lamp. 'Do not feel obligated Mr Cornish. It was after all an afterthought, wasn't it Archie?'

'That it was corporal. That it was.' Archie reached out. 'Don't feel obliged old cobber,' he told Cornish. 'We have many other clients.'

Cornish stepped back closing his fist around the artefact. 'No!'

'No!'

'I mean, the general will take it. Two hundred you said.'

'Spot on.'

'Here.' And Cornish pushed more banknotes into Archie's open hand.

'Jesus Christ Archie,' Garfield managed when they were alone. 'I thought we were in for it then,'

'Oh yea of little faith,' Archie replied passing Garfield ninety pounds.

'Ninety?' Garfield said. 'He paid you two hundred.'

'Yes but it cost me twenty. That's ten each leaving us ninety each profit.'

Garfield had no choice but to accept Archie's word as Archie pocketed the one hundred and ten pounds difference in the knowledge the fake scarab only cost him five.

'What if they find out it's fake?' Garfield said. 'I've only sold the general the real stuff in the past.'

'Don't worry about it corporal Gardener, we'll be fightin' the Hun in France if he ever does find out. Besides, he's buyin' illegitimate antiquities and beyond his means I would say, what can he do, tell the police?'

'What do you mean beyond his means? The man's wealthy.'

'Yes he's wealthy. But by what means? I've heard stories.'

Garfield had heard the same gossip. He knew Archie had a point and at this stage he did not need reminding they would be in the front line in the very near future.

***

If it wasn't an alabaster jar selling for four times its purchased price it would be a mummified animal … a baboon or cat maybe, for a quick profit. These animals, considered sacred in ancient times, were popular souvenirs amongst the officers. Archie very smartly accumulated over fifteen hundred pounds, all exchanged into Bank of England notes overprinted with Arabic by the treasury, for use by the Expeditionary Forces anywhere in the Mediterranean. A one-pound note was equivalent to 240 piastres and the tight roll of banknotes felt great stitched into Archie's kitbag.

Whenever possible Archie took himself to the Egyptian Museum in Cairo. He was in awe. Fascinated. Nothing prepared him for such splendour. The massive elongated stone building had a central arched entrance, the likes of the Arc de Triomphe in Paris, with arched cloisters either side. A massive glass dome on top allowed natural light to stream into the grand exhibition hall, where the largest exhibits – like the statues of Ramses the Great – as tall as a four-storey building were displayed.

Archie walked silently between glass case after case of artefacts. He gazed with reverence at the mummified bodies of pharaohs in their sarcophagi, astounded at the quality and quantity of everyday items used in these ancient times. It was surreal for the country boy from Australia. And Archie read up on these ancient peoples. He read about Upper and Lower Egypt, learning about dynastic periods; Early Dynastic, Old Kingdom, Middle Kingdom and New Kingdom, amazed how this ancient civilisation spanned several thousands of years.

But most importantly Archie was amassing a small fortune along with this knowledge. Knowledge he used to authenticate his nefarious dealings. Everyone liked a story. Provenance they called it, whether truth of fiction.

But the end to Archie and Garfield's racketeering enterprise was in sight. Training intensified on the rifle range, mock attacks were practised daily as were trench digging, pack drill and route marching.

Along with the engineers, Archie's sapper unit training broadened into surveying underground with miners' instruments to maintain correct direction, engineering and even lectures from geologists trained in the understanding of the earth's surface and subsurface conditions. He was trained to identify if the ground between the attacker and the objective was mineable; both for northern France and surprisingly, the west coast of Turkey. Meaning that the surface soils and the strata beneath, that is the local geology, could be easily excavated with normal tools, for the saps would have to carry shovels with them.

'Turkey huh?'

'Yeh mate, I hear the third brigade, that's the 9th, 10th and 11th Battalions including the 1st field company engineers are already on Lemnos Island,' one of the engineers confided in Archie.

'Lemnos? Where the bloody hell's that?'

'Not far from Turkey mate.'

They were even taught a few Turkish phrases considered useful. Like Halt – *Doo-er*. Hands up – *Eller yukari*, and even throw down your rifle – *Selagh brack*.

'Bloody useful, yeh right,' Archie grinned. 'I'm sure I'm gonna stand there with me rifle pointed at the bastard while I try and remember *Selagh brack*.

'We'll be underground mate, you might want to learn *help I'm stuck!*'

Until this comment Archie had not considered the possibility of a cave-in and being trapped in a tunnel ... And the thought terrified him.

***

Days turned to weeks. The streets of Cairo were less crowded, now the lads had sailed from Egypt and made their assault on the west coast of Turkey at a place called the Dardanelles. This was now common knowledge. Archie knew his time in the antiquities business was over. He had amassed a tidy sum – three thousand two hundred and forty quid; take or leave a few bob. He purchased a leather money belt, converted his money into thirty-two one hundred pound notes sterling and fed them, carefully folded, into his belt.

Corporal Garfield Gardener had left Egypt with the Twelfth Battalion Field Ambulance before Archie's Battalion, and Archie learnt later he had been a part of the original landing in Turkey.

For now, Archie and his battalion drilled and trained in tunnel warfare, fourteen hours a day. All Archie could do now in his spare time was wait. He made several more visits to the Egyptian Museum and in his rare spare time Archie took photos of the pyramids, the sphinx and the streets of Cairo.

***

The Sunday before they were to leave Egypt, Archie stood alone before the Sphinx – with its mythical human head on the body and haunches of a lion – all half buried in the sand. The light was perfect for photography. Archie framed the famous landmark with stone ruins in the foreground. He snapped the photograph, when two fellow Royal Engineers approached. 'Here, Archie,' one called out. 'Give me the camera and I'll take a photograph with you in it ... and the pyramids behind you.'

'Thanks mate. But I'm right.'

'Come on,' the sapper walked up to Archie and grabbed at the camera.

'I said I'm right!' Archie flared. He could smell beer on the bloke's breath.

'Jesus mate. Keep your shirt on.'

'Why?' the other sap asked. He knew Archie to be a bit of a loner and didn't take to him that well. 'Everyone wants a photograph with the pyramids mate.

Here, I'll get you a camel to sit on.' The man whistled and three Arab camel handlers jogged in their direction. The first man, a toothless Bedouin in tattered ankle length kaftan, thobe and sandals, vied for business.

'Up, up,' the Arab told the sapper and the camel dutifully fell onto its knees and squat.

'It's not for me mate it's for him,' the soldier pointed to Archie.

Archie grew irritable. 'I told you I'm right. Right?'

'Come on Archie. 'Your mum and dad would love a photo. Get on.' He squeezed Archie's shoulder.

'Fuck off will yer.'

'Jesus. It's only a photograph.'

'I don't want a photograph with the bloody camel.'

'Yeh but your family would,' he persisted.

'I don't have any family ... all right?'

'No family?' the first one said.

'Shit, sorry mate. Well what about one for your album?'

Archie turned on the sapper, his eyes fixed and angry.

'Sor-ry,' the man said and walked away leaving Archie to deal with three pushy camel wranglers.

CHAPTER NINE
NURSES OF WAR

Indian Ocean. April 1915

Bes finally sailed on HMAT *Benalla* as a part of a convoy of 28 transports, including NZ ships. Sailing from Hobart to Melbourne the ships rendezvoused at King George Sound – a wide deep harbour off Albany on the south coast of Western Australia. Eventually the convoy sailed across the Indian Ocean to Colombo on the west coast of Ceylon. Then, five and a half weeks after leaving Australia, HMAT *Benalla* sailed through the Suez Canal in another convoy at night.

Bes wrote in her diary;

Well I signed up for ... quote; 'Free passage: from, and return to, Australia either by 2nd class mail steamer or by military transport.' I was given one free uniform and am to be paid seven shillings a day as a staff nurse.

Bes made few friends on the voyage over.

During the day I usually find a secluded corner on deck and read novels or teach myself French.

At night she would often cry herself to sleep.

Most ladies are really not my company or I simply find it too difficult, what with the horrors of Boxing Day fresh in my mind. However, one nurse, Melbourne lass Janet Stubbs, made an effort to befriend me.

Curly red-headed Janet was three years older than Bes, yet naïve for her extra years. Bes picked her for a virgin immediately; there was something of the church-going, girl next door about her, and it was Bes's worldly outlook that attracted Janet to her. Eventually Bes opened up to Janet, finding that talking about her shocking ordeal *was* therapeutic. Also Janet had lost a younger brother to scarlet fever; so in a sense they had common ground.

'I had a boyfriend once,' Janet confided in Bes one morning, gazing over the port gunwale towards the Indian Ocean's eternal horizon. 'Max Randwick his name was. He was a plumber ... made plenty of money too,' Janet's gorgeous green eyes looked into Bes's with a hint of pride. 'At least he seemed to always have money. Took me to Luna Park he hid.' Janet's voice faded and she stared back at the passing ocean.

Bes guessed this liaison did not have a happy ending. 'Well don't keep me in suspense, what happened?'

'Have you ever been to Luna Park,' Janet avoided Bes's question. 'It's in St Kilda.'

'No ... no I haven't. The only time I have been to Melbourne was on board this ship a few weeks ago.'

'Oh ... Luna Park's fun ...'

'Max Randwick,' Bes persisted. 'What happened to him then?'

Janet looked coy a moment and Bes thought her face blushed but it could have been the setting sun. 'We were together a month. He was great fun. A bit of a lad now I look back ...'

'And?'

'Well he ... he wanted to ... you know.'

'And you didn't?'

'No! I certainly did not.'

'I've got news for you Janet. They all do.'

'I know, but ... why? Why spoil everything? I want to marry and have children.'

'So how do you think you make babies, Janet?' Bes did not mean to sound patronising, but she did.

'Yes ... but ... well I guess I'm old fashioned.' Janet suddenly realised her friend's candidness about the forbidden implied she was hardly innocent herself. 'Have you ever ... you know.' Bes looked surprised at the question, not that it troubled her, more so that she was not expecting it. 'Oh please forgive me Bes,' Janet took Bes's arm. 'I did not mean to pry, it's just that ....' and her voice trialled away.

Bes shrugged. Was she revealing too much of herself to her new friend?

Janet's face broke into a grin. She looked Bes in the eye once more. 'You have haven't you?'

'Been with a man?' Now Janet's face reddened and Bes knew it not to be the sun. Bes felt energised talking to Janet and her devil-may-care attitude exposed itself once more. 'Yes Janet. I have had two lovers in my short time on this planet.'

'T-two! Golly.'

Bes had a moment of guilt. She'd had a tryst with Herbert Foster last year. Herbert was a printer's apprentice. They were both eighteen and he was her first. Jack was her second and Bes's guilt stemmed from the night before the bomb blast, when she met Jack in the middle of the night. 'So,' Bes shook thoughts of her culpability free and demanded from Janet. 'What happened to Max Randwick pray tell.'

'I didn't see him for a week and then someone told me they saw him in Bourke Street holding hands with Patsy Sellers.'

'Oh.'

'I went to school with Patsy Sellers, she was always a ... what's the word?'

'A scarlet woman,' Bes said.

Janet giggled. 'I was going to say a flirt.'

CHAPTER TEN
ARCHIE'S LANDING

Gallipoli. Late afternoon May 9th 1915.

Archie Bryant felt his stomach churn. He had had an irritable bowel lately and put it down to his diet on board the troop ship the past week. But then again it was just as likely nerves. The first lads had landed at Gallipoli at dawn on the 25th, two Sundays ago now, and news of their progress reaching Lemnos Harbour, from where the attack was launched seven hundred and fifty miles from Turkey's coast. The news had not been great. Sure, they had pushed the Turks back up into the hills and the Aussie diggers had dug in.

But at what cost?

More than two thousand Australians killed on the first day Archie heard. Two thousand out of twelve thousand who made the landing on the first day! Much of this had been hearsay and rumours. *But where there's smoke there's fire.*

Two thousand dead. Thousands more wounded.

Archie climbed clumsily over the side of the destroyer where they were anchored well out on the Aegean Sea. Out of enemy artillery range. It wasn't easy clambering down the rope netting into waiting landing craft, especially weighted down with a seventy-pound haversack on your back and an Lee-Enfield .303 rifle slung over the shoulder. Each man carried his own rations; tins of bully beef and a canteen of water to last two days. They each carried two hundred rounds of ammunition, dressing kits and a portable spade for digging, along with six empty sandbags. The bayonet was strapped to their belt. The sappers had to carry a pick as well. Archie was pumped, his veins rushing with mixed emotions.

As Archie and the Royal Engineers of the 13th battalion were rowed ashore, enemy snipers took shots at them. But these shooters were inaccurate, firing from well back in the hills where the Turks had been scattered by the men who had landed on the 25th April.

'Yet the bastards are still close enough, so beware,' the barge skipper told Archie. 'They are still trying to force us back into the sea.'

***

The late afternoon sun was low on the horizon casting a bright orange hue across the Gallipoli Peninsula. From the water Archie noticed the hills and cliffs directly behind the beach, now known as Anzac Beach, were honeycombed with dwellings; dugouts shovelled into the hillsides, reminding Archie of cave dwellings. The dwellings were covered against the elements with whatever was at hand. The lucky ones had canvas tarpaulins. Some managed to construct walls with their sandbags and others salvaged timber from wrecked barges or supply crates to make wooden frames to shore up the earth. Furniture consisted of shelves and cupboards built from biscuit boxes, while tables were constructed from tinned bully-beef crates. Some even managed a tarp for a floor covering.

'Looks like a mining camp,' Archie told the bloke next to him.

The rowers stowed their oars and the tenders scraped over the round smooth rocks of the beach. Archie and his mates were ordered out. Some soldiers at the stern leapt over the gunwale only to plunge chest deep in the water with all their kit. Archie was more fortunate. He stepped ashore from the bow ...

And into a world of organised pandemonium.

It was no picnic.

Archie saw his first blood. Stretcher-bearers shoved past the new arrivals, rinsing their blood-soaked stretchers in the sea before hurrying back into the hills to the front line. Archie's attention was drawn to the hundreds of wounded men lined along the beach waiting to be evacuated to the hospital ships. But more sobering still were the rows of dead soldiers wrapped in shrouds and lined at the high tide mark awaiting burial.

'That's nuthin',' Archie heard one veteran of the original landing tell the stunned new arrivals. 'Yer should 'ave been ere the day of the landin'. There were thousands and thousands of the poor buggers.'

Beyond the hospital tents, barely above high water mark, Archie saw his first Turks. Twenty or more prisoners sat in an enclosed corral on the beach, their fates unknown. And every square foot of the small beach, about six hundred feet north to south, was alive with activity. Ammunition deposits were stacked fifteen feet high. Supplies for field kitchens, medical supplies and all the paraphernalia of warfare was stored along the rocky beachfront. All awaiting dispersal into the field.

'Move it, move yer mongrels,' a sergeant on the beach, a hardened forty-year-old boilermaker from Bendigo with a hearth-brush moustache, screeched over the din at the new arrivals. 'Get your arses up the bank. Now! Move it.' Archie followed the men before him, towards an area he learnt was named Shrapnel Valley. And he would find out it was called Shrapnel Valley for good reason as a bomb exploded overhead blasting a thousand lead bullets earthwards. Pellets showered down like hailstones. The man in front of Archie fell, the top of his head bloodied and another took a ball passing through his bicep, continuing through his right arm and splintering his rifle butt. He too fell to the ground, crying out in agony.

He had been ashore six minutes!

'Stretcher bearers!' the sergeant screamed.

Head down, Archie ran, stumbling over the uneven landscape. He kept on running until they reached the cover of the steep embankment where the earlier soldiers had dug in like rabbits. Suddenly the severity of warfare hit home. This was real. Very, very real.

For Archie the war had arrived.

***

Archie's boatload was herded up the steep hill, more a cliff face if truth be known. 'Right you bastards,' the sergeant yelled. 'Dig in and keep yer fuckin' heads down.' The new arrivals looked lost, including Archie. 'Well come on ladies, don't just stand there. Get yer shovels out and dig ... yer saps ain't yer?'

Archie and the others looked along the hill face. Dugouts were situated in tiers the full length of the hillside where small groups of men huddled in their shelters smoking, heating bully beef over small fires, playing cards or simply waiting the next bombardment.

'Home sweet home eh?' Duncan Peters said with a wry smile, tossing his haversack to the ground and stepping on it before it rolled down hill. Archie had grown fond of Duncan. They had met on the troopship. Duncan was a jackaroo from New South Wales; short, but a tough little bugger in his nineteenth year with blue eyes and blonde hair. He called a spade a spade and that's what Archie liked about the bloke. Duncan took up his entrenching tool, a folding shovel, and stabbed the embankment, staking his claim like a Ballarat goldminer. 'What say me an' you share this plot Arch',' he said, studying the other two-man dugouts only feet away.

'Sure.' Archie did likewise, taking a moment to look out across the Aegean Sea from whence they came.

'Look on the bright side Arch', at least we have a view.'

'Yer, ya got that bit ri ...'

Instantly another overhead shell burst. A deadly shower of lead balls peppered the cliff face. Old hands along the hillside had heard the whistling shell approach and ducked for cover. The less experienced paid for their ignorance.

'Stretcher bearer!' someone screamed out not too far distant.

Archie and Duncan had been lucky, but along their ledge one man lay with a bloodied head. He wasn't moving. Another screamed in pain while his arm hung loose by skin from the elbow.

The sergeant picked himself up from where he had dived to the ground. His face was ashen. 'Dig in you fellas, and make it snappy,' he said with more empathy. 'And be aware, you may dig up a body.' He watched the looks on the men's faces. 'Aye, that's right. Some o' yer mates were buried here in a hurry, the day o' the landin'.'

***

The days soon ran into weeks and Archie and Duncan settled in nicely. They had no choice. They dug further back into the hill than most, shoring up their dwelling with timber from broken crates scrounged from the cove. With the excavated dirt they managed to level an area outside the entrance, widening the tier. 'Sort o' like a porch, eh Arch'?' Duncan laughed, a lumpy hand rolled cigarette jiggling from the corner of his mouth. On this *porch* they managed to cook their meals and brew tea. Each man had to cook his own rations and to do this they had to risk snipers to gather firewood. Breakfast was tea with sugar, no milk, six biscuits – a hard tack that had to last all day – a small piece of cheese, a quarter pound of jam and one rasher of bacon. Lunch was a billy of tea only and the evening meal, teatime – was a stew of bully beef with billy tea, no milk. Day in day out.

Monotonous.

Archie looked at his bully beef; fatty and bubbling in the skillet over a smoky flame, and had a thought. 'What would you order for yer last meal Dunc'?'

'Wha'?'

'Yer last meal. They're gonna hang yer for somethin'. What would yer order to eat?'

'Oh, that's easy. Bacon and eggs, oxtail soup and trifle with clotted cream.'

With this image in mind the two novice soldiers were lost a moment in a culinary reverie.

***

May 19th 1915

For the most part Archie and Duncan were busy digging trenches or assisting the Royal Engineers with the infrastructure.

Then, army intelligence received a Morse code warning that a major enemy counterattack was imminent. Also observation aircraft had warned that vast numbers of enemy reinforcements were marching across the peninsula. And Archie and his mates were ready.

It came at 3.30am.

The Turkish army made a massive attack, determined to push the enemy infidels back into the sea. However the allies were prepared.

For the Turkish forces it was a terrible failure. Of forty-two thousand soldiers, three thousand lay dead along the front line ridges and ten thousand were wounded. Archie heard the Anzac losses were one hundred and sixty killed and four-hundred-and-sixty-eight wounded. Charles Bean, the official war correspondent wrote:

The dead and the wounded lay everywhere in the hundreds. Many of those near the Anzac line had been shattered by terrible wounds inflicted by modern bullets at close ranges. No sound came from that terrible space ...

***

May 24th

Archie and his mates struggled with the stench of death. Thousands lay where they had died, now rotting in the sun, bloated with flies. But, on the 24th, Archie was to witness a rare act of humanity during warfare. An armistice was planned. A truce declared with both sides delegating burial parties to inter the victims beneath the battlefield in hastily dug pits. Like so many others, Archie walked no man's land in a daze. Death was all about them yet Archie struggled to understand how blasé they had all become. Aussie diggers shared cigarettes with Turkish soldiers. They exchanged souvenirs, a button or a coin. Duncan drew Archie's attention to the high table-topped hills behind the enemy lines where hundreds of people gathered.

'Who are they?'

'They're locals,' an officer said, also amazed at what he was witnessing.

'No!'

Hundreds of Turkish civilians had taken advantage of the ceasefire to come and see the battlefields for themselves.

It was all so surreal.

And for a few brief hours the shooting ceased.

***

The weeks passed. The weather grew warmer. Archie and his mates soon hardened to the hardships and sights of warfare. They completed a road to cart weapons and equipment to the men dug in at the battlefield ridges. Another road allowed field guns to be moved into position. When they weren't building piers at the cove to land supplies they dug wells, with only moderate success. Where possible they dug latrines near the trenches, for the soldiers had no choice but to relieve themselves in open pits. Archie and his mates dug trenches and in particular, tunnels. The tunnels were the most dangerous work, tunnelling beneath the enemy trenches where hundreds of pounds of high explosives were stowed in silence. A difficult and dangerous endeavour. They were then detonated. Of course, the enemy did the same and it was not unheard of for two tunnels to meet ending in hand-to-hand combat underground. Although Archie had been spared this terrifying ordeal.

Collapses were common also, and at least once in the first week Archie had to be dug free from a cave-in after an artillery shell exploded too close for comfort.

The days were hot but worse than the heat were the flies. Big fat flies bloated from feeding on the cadavers, where more dead bodies, both Aussie and Abdul, were mostly left where they fell. If approached, the flies would lift from the corpses by the thousands in a black cloud. But any attempt to retrieve the dead was fraught with danger, as Turkish snipers were everywhere and any man foolish enough to lift his head above the parapet of a trench was almost guaranteed to die from a sniper's bullet.

There were to be no more truces.

No armistice.

Then there were the rats, also bloated on death; there were snakes too, but more feared than snakes were lice. These tiny wingless insects lived entirely on human blood. Many men shaved their heads and rubbed kerosene into the skin. Lice were everywhere, in underclothing, in shirts and trousers. There was no avoiding them. The lucky soldiers were able to swim in the sea and naked men on the beach amongst the ordinance was a common sight. They were also a favourite of the Turkish sniper and swimming could be hazardous.

***

Wednesday. May 29*th*

Archie and the Royal Engineers were ordered to return to Quinn's Post, a fiercely defended trench system and desperately sought by the enemy. It was known that Turkish trenches had advanced once more, and they were only a grenade's throw away. It was time to blow them apart.

Major FR Edgeworth had been a geologist before the war and a natural choice to lead the sappers. By his own admission he had been a trifle overweight when he enlisted but the Egyptian heat and now the army diet had forced half a stone from his fifty-year-old frame. He was tall, sporting a long neck with little tuft of whiskers growing on his throat. But he had a pleasant demeanour and constantly spoke of how he missed his beloved wife, Audrey. His first assignment after the landing had been to search for water, to dig wells; however this was unreliable and fresh water had to be barged in from Lemnos Island and severely rationed.

For Archie, Duncan and the tunnellers, spoil removal was a big issue. Aerial reconnaissance from observation balloons or enemy aircraft could easily spot spoil heaps and give away the tunnels' locations. Unskilled soldiers were used to bag the dirt and remove it well away from the location, dumping them in old trenches or shell holes. This had to be done in the dark of night. During the day the bags of dirt were stored in laybys dug into the tunnel walls. Also before dawn, the trail the carriers took had to be raked over and covered with bracken; otherwise, once again, from the air a trail could be seen leading from the tunnel to the dump site, inviting the enemy to bombard the tunnel with artillery.

Archie scraped the earth from the tunnel wall with a bayonet rather than hack at it with a pick, for the enemy had listening devices and listened for the enemy diggers. It was laborious work. Laborious and very dangerous. One method of listening for the enemy tunnelling towards you was to drive a wooden stake into the earth wall and bite into it feeling for any vibrations. Silence was paramount and dry sand was trolleyed into the mines to deaden footsteps.

Saps working with Archie bagged the earth for carting away. Other men made the tunnel secure. A sill was first cut and made level before the floor was put in place, the two uprights or legs were slotted into the sill and then the roof slotted in the same way. A sandbag would then be shoved in behind to keep it tight. Importantly all timbers had to be accurately measured and cut before being carried underground.

Securing timber was a major problem. The saps had to scrounge what they could, for timber was in huge demand for shoring up trenches, making duckboards, dugouts and building huts.

Archie also learnt surveying skills in the use of box sextants, compasses, miner's dials and levels, for once underground the men had to maintain the tunnel in the direction of the enemy trenches. Military surveyors provided accurate trench maps based on aerial photos taken by observation balloons. But these changed daily and if tunnellers were suspected beneath them the enemy deserted that trench and all the sappers' efforts would be wasted.

But what really fascinated Archie was learning explosives. Archie learnt the British alone employed thirty-six different types of explosives for mining purposes. They all produced slightly different effects when put into action. Major Edgeworth explained explosives generally fell into two classes, low and high.

'Low explosives are a form of combustion which burns gradually through the charge, producing large amounts of hot gases under pressure, creating a slow explosion. With high explosives, the detonation is much more rapid with the complete charge combusting at the same moment.'

'Like black powder?' Archie suggested.

'Exactly. High explosive gases are sudden and enormous pressure is released creating a shock wave, a sharp blow if you like, rather than a slow push.'

The enemy trenches near Quinn's Post lifted from mother earth in a massive mushroom of dirt, rock, timber and soldiers. Archie was afforded a front row seat, observing the sappers' handiwork through a periscope made from shaving mirrors. He saw bodies and body parts, cartwheeling in slow motion, blasted from the comfort of their trenches along with machine guns, ordinance, lumber and even shit; apparently the nearby enemy latrines were in the firing line as well. Debris, detritus and human waste showered down. The diggers – for that was the nickname now given to the Australian soldiers – cheered manically.

Abdul was mad. Mad as hell. The hornet's nest had been broached. Surviving enemy machine gun posts on the periphery of the bombsite opened fire immediately. Stuttering indiscriminately. Sweeping swarms of lead towards Archie's trenches in pointless retribution.

Score board: Abdul – two dozen dead.

Diggers – nil.

But imbalance would not last.

***

June 4th
Whilst the war of attrition dragged on at Anzac Cove and up into the hills, the British had their own battles at Cape Helles, south of the Anzacs. On June 4th they launched the Third Battle of Krithia, breaking through the Turkish lines with the loss of six-thousand-five-hundred allies to the enemy's nine thousand. But the advantage was lost when they did not reinforce the new position and the Turkish counterattacked.

What a terrible waste of life, Archie thought.

***

June 18th
Fifty-five days after the landing the Royal Engineers completed the piled jetty at the cove, Watson's Pier. It also happened to be the centenary anniversary of the Battle of Waterloo, good enough excuse for a celebration. Archie and his engineer mates were invited to a 'gala' dinner to feast on the special menu of *Hors de Combat,* or *Boeuf Galee d'Australie* and *Charlotte Russe avec Anzac bisquite especiale.* These delicacies were actually tinned turkey and salmon washed down with rescued wine, medicinal whisky and a secret stash of beer. The highlight, though, for those too drunk to walk *home* to their dugouts was a *carriage service,* being pushed up the hill in wheelbarrows.

Archie heard later that the officers ate crayfish.

***

August 3rd
Archie and his saps heard whispers. A massive offensive was being planned. They heard twenty thousand extra British troops had landed further south. At Anzac Cove it was learnt the Australians were to attack at Lone Pine while the New Zealanders, Australians, British Indian Sikhs along with the Ghurkha Rifles were to climb into the Sari Bair Range and take Chunuk Bair, strategic high lands.

This was exciting news. The clock was ticking.

CHAPTER ELEVEN
ARCHIE'S BAPTISM

Trenches. Lone Pine. Gallipoli Peninsula. Turkey. First light, August 7th[th], 1915
The months had passed by Archie Bryant, and the war of attrition bogged down. Neither side had an advantage. For the most part Archie dug tunnels, trenches and latrines. He aided the Royal Engineers to manufacture home-made bombs with high explosives packed into bully beef tins, with short wicks. He helped construct wooden structures and built roads, pathways and dug steps into the cliff faces to the front line.

In his spare time, he and his fellow lodger and sap Duncan Peters expanded their own dugout, pushing back into the steep embankment a good six feet, well out of Abdul's shrapnel range. They managed a sandbag wall to knee height at the front and shored up the roof and sides with extra scrounged crates. At the front they built their *kitchen*; a small hearth of rocks to boil the billy and heat their bully beef. The bully beef of course was a staple, there was no avoiding it lest one was to starve, and the billy tea was bloody awful. Water for the tea was carted to the dugouts in old kerosene or petrol drums and no matter how well they were scrubbed, there was no ridding the water of the essence of fuel. At least the tea was hot and wet.

Occasionally they managed to trade an onion or two from trophy hunter Whisper Morris five *doors* along. Whisper – who acquired the nickname back home where he never shouted a drink – had contacts with one of the officers' cooks and he would swap an onion for, say, a Turkish cap or some other souvenir gathered from the battlefield. Hence the tag trophy-hunter. The most sought after souvenirs were the German Lugers or other side-arms used by their Turkish allies. Whisper was a hoarder and his dugout was crammed with souvenirs. He called it his 'museum'.

Rarely was Archie involved in combat, but he was reminded daily of the dangers on the front line as they watched the parade of *body-snatchers* – that's the nickname the lags gave the stretcher bearers – carting the wounded down from the trenches to the beach. Certainly, Archie had taken the odd pop shot at Abdul, but mostly he was armed with a shovel.

Until August the 7th – the day after the massacre at Lone Pine – when Archie and other sappers were ordered to the battlefield. Tunnels were required.

And urgently.

***

Back at Lone Pine.
Bodies lay everywhere. Many enemy, many Aussie diggers. Far too many. Some lay in groups where hostile machine guns cut them down like weeds. Some were alive with horrific limb wounds incapacitating their crawling to safety, for enemy machine guns were still trained across no man's land, even though the diggers had captured the Turkish trenches at Lone Pine. Some cried out for mother, it was pitiful and there was nothing their mates could do to save them. And it was now abhorrently clear to survivor Ned, of the 12th battalion, that the distance they had covered was no longer than a tennis court, line to line. It had been madness. Thousands of young men ordered to run into a furnace of sizzling lead.

Ned had survived. Sure he had cuts and bruises *but hey, he was alive*. A measure of bravado and relief descended on those that made it to the enemy line. And they had a right to be proud. They had captured the enemy trenches and, with fixed bayonets, they pushed the bastards back.

But the dead lay knee deep and one officer would write in his diary, *the dead carpeted the ground and the only respect we could possibly pay them was not to step on their heads.*

During the night after the massacre the Turkish counterattacks were vicious. Many diggers suffered from dysentery but they put up one hell of a fight, keeping Abdul at bay. Some managed to shift the enemy corpses. Many bodies filled the fortifications – and in some places, they blocked the enemy trenches completely. Other bodies were pushed out onto no man's land. Some were dragged into communication trenches and left in piles.

It was a scene from hell. A scene from Armageddon.

And all during this, enemy counterattacks were expected. During the night 'A' Company and finally 'D' Company filed through the trenches to swell the diggers' numbers. To replace the dead.

By sunrise the sweltering summer heat brought the flies. And the flies attracted the rats. *The bastards were everywhere.*

Amongst the new arrivals, Archie and the 13th sappers were speechless. They stood in reverent silence staring at the carnage. Never had they seen so many dead. But their reverie was short lived. They had a job to do.

In charge of the 13th battalion sappers, Major FR Edgeworth, assembled his crew in a tight niche off to one side of the occupied enemy trenches. He was clearly disturbed by the bodies, particularly the Australians. They all were.

'We have been ordered to tunnel under enemy trenches some fifty yards north-east. Lieutenant King, the man leading this latest push, is of the opinion Abdul has built a new HQ there and is preparing a major assault to recapture these trenches. I needn't remind you blokes we must act fast.'

'What else's bloody new?' one lag groaned.

'Yes. Well ... Archie,' King singled out Archie.

'Yes Sar.'

'Johnson here,' and the Major nodded to the soldier next to Archie. 'Johnson has the co-ordinates. Take Bronson and Dalton with you and start digging the face immediately.'

The digging went on into the night and all the next day with digging teams. By the second night they had positioned the tunnel at a depth of twenty feet, ten feet below the enemy trenches. Reconnaissance had informed them that the Turks had re-established their HQ and by using a doctor's stethoscope to listen in at the tunnel ceiling they learnt the enemy trenches were being lengthened, the fortifications strengthened and, most importantly of all, the nearby enemy trenches were being re-occupied. It was decided another massive attack by the enemy was imminent. All the while Archie and his crew dug, shored up and dug further; removing the soil during the dark of night so as not to be seen. And when the air became stale they used blacksmith bellows to pump fresh air down the tunnels

Archie's biggest fear was that the Turks were also tunnelling. This meant there was always the possibility that the enemy would detonate first. The thought terrified all the saps who, for this reason, worked silently so as not to be detected. Finally after seventy-two hours the explosives were positioned. Soldiers trolleyed in thirty-pound petrol tins of high explosives with one man in front of the trolley, his back pushed hard against the drums while the trolley was eased down the steep incline.

Different explosives were used. Black powder being the most common, then wet gun cotton, Blastine, and finally Ammonal. Archie was informed today's charges were Ammonal; an ammonium nitrate-based grey powder that was three times more powerful than gunpowder. One advantage was that a naked flame or even a stray bullet could not detonate it. A standard detonator and primer were required for firing, or a slab of guncotton incorporated into the charge. Archie learnt the Ammonal had been stored in petrol drums as the product was susceptible to absorbing moisture. The drums being to waterproof the explosive.

During this tense period the Turks made several counterattacks. The bodies piled up. With the trenches so close a grenade war ensued with both sides lobbing hand bombs at each other. The Turkish bombs had long fuses and the Aussies found they could catch them and throw them back. But Abdul soon learnt to shorten the fuses and many Australians lost hands, eyes or worse, their lives.

CHAPTER TWELVE
THE GOBLET

Ned's life had become surreal. He had become blasé about death. Numb to the horrors about him. In the years to come, doctors would use terms like shell-shocked for some men, crazy from the constant artillery. But Ned was different. The truth was Ned had become a renegade. A maverick. His uniform was in disarray, he hadn't washed in weeks; nay, months. He'd disowned his Christian god and like many others he now took his mind off this pestilence by souvenir hunting the enemy cadavers.

A macabre past time. But everyone, it seemed, was in on the act. First a button or an enemy belt buckle with the ubiquitous Turkish crescent and star. A stray wallet produced a fold of Turkish kurus and a Turkish officer's dress sword with an engraved blade was a prize indeed.

'Nice sword,' one bloke commented. He sucked on the remains of a Turf while using his rifle muzzle to push the leg of a corpse back over the parapet. 'Officer's sword huh?'

Ned looked to the pathetic pile of enemy bodies at the end of his trench and nodded warily. There was no guilt. Death suddenly felt ... well ... so normal.

'Tell yer what,' the bloke went on. 'I'll swap yer for this.' He pulled a German luger from inside his jacket. 'Fully loaded and I got twenty extra rounds.'

'No mate,' Ned said. He liked the sword and besides if he was caught with a hand gun it would most likely be confiscated. Handguns were for officers only. 'I'll hang onto me sword thanks.'

Archie was the last out of the loaded tunnel. Using sign language the sappers set their charges, tamped down the drums and wired the ton weight of explosives before retreating. His mates sealed the entrance while the charge lead was unspooled to a safe trench some hundred yards distant. Major Edgewood was notified and a report sent to Lieutenant General Sir William Birdwood. Birdie, as the men called him behind his back, was telegraphed through a wire service to his HQ at the beach. Birdie gave the order to proceed immediately.

For safety reasons Ned and his mates were ordered back from the front line to the safer rear trenches, along with the saps. Those who could, watched the enemy trenches through periscopes and those close to the major heard the countdown …

'Three, two, one … fire!"

The ground shook to a muffled rumble not unlike an earthquake. Archie and Ned watched a huge mound of earth rise from the underground while a mass of flame leapt skywards.

Everyone cheered. The enemy were caught totally unawares.

As dirt and rocks showered down the few Turk gunners who had survived, opened fire, shooting blindly through a mist of smoke and dust. But the damage was done. Once again Ned and his mates were ordered over the top. They charged the enemy line and with minimum sacrifice were able to occupy the new trenches with the Turks, dazed and panicked, pulling back a hundred yards.

Leading the charge, Ned was one of the first at the crater, a hole twenty feet wide and sixty feet long. The explosion had gone upwards and then followed the trench lines in both directions. Enemy dead were everywhere, there must have been fifty or sixty Ned guessed. The few survivors who could, had scattered for their lives to trenches further back. Ned heard a crack and a bullet tugged at his torn jacket, reminding him that snipers were still about. Ned dropped to a crouch clambering down into the crater. Other diggers gathered at the crater rim but soon scattered when one was shot in the arm by another sniper.

Ned's addiction to souvenir hunting had him scouring the crater when he noticed what appeared to be a stone wall. It was not unlike sandstone blocks the colonial builders used back home. On closer inspection it appeared to be a cellar but there had not been any buildings on Gallipoli Peninsula, not that Ned knew of anyhow.

A cellar?

Ned slid down the incline standing before the wall. An avalanche of rubble followed, gathering at his feet and his disturbance threatened to cause another landslide and bury the *cellar* once again. Ned noticed a small opening and dropped to his knees to peer inside. Visibility was poor, however there was enough light to peer inside. Ned froze. A human skeleton stared back at him, its twisted bones disturbed by the explosion. Ned was used to death, by god he'd seen enough. He was numb from the saturation of this bloody war. But a skeleton?

Ned crawled in the narrow opening, but his body masked the light. Fiddling about in his pocket he found his matches, sparked one and realised he was staring into a tomb. Terracotta pottery, offering bowls to the gods, were scattered about, as were double-handled amphora and pottery oil lamps. Ned now realised the sarcophagus had been broached by the bomb, tipping the human remains onto the floor. The match burnt Ned's fingers. He cursed and lit another, this time illuminating what appeared to be a small bronze goblet with ornate embossing about its rim. Ned squeezed in further reaching for the vessel when something caught on his knee amongst the rubble. Ned was about to discard the object when he noticed it was a terracotta lamp. Or part thereof. In the poor light he thought he could make out the figures of two people. *Were they copulating?* Suddenly Ned heard distant voices. Excited voices. Other soldiers were on their way. Ned snatched up the vessel, withdrawing from the tomb and with one carefully displaced stone he caused a cave-in. And the tomb was instantly re-buried.

'Well well.' Ned spun to face a tall well-built soldier; a sergeant, three stripes. He appeared over the lip of the crater, his eyes fixedly on the bronze goblet. 'Where on earth did you find that?' Sergeant Garfield Gardener slid on the loose rubble down into the crater to join Ned.

'May I?' He took the small six-inch goblet from Ned before Ned had a chance to protest. 'How interesting,' Garfield fought the excitement the artefact gave him. 'And a lamp, an erotica lamp no less.' Ned closed his fist about the broken lamp but the sergeant held onto the goblet, turning it reverently in his hand. The patina was a greyish green and Gardener thought one could be forgiven for thinking it was bronze, but he suspected otherwise.

He noted embossed olives and olive branches in the metalwork and recognised it to be Roman, 3rd or 4th century AD. Dirt crumbled from around the lip and a Latin inscription became apparent circling the outer rim. But the vessel was in need of conservation and the writing difficult to read. Garfield rubbed dirt from the rim with his thumb when one word caught his attention, *and* his imagination. A name. He was certain it read Pinarius. Immediately the goblet became very desirable.

No, more than that ... very, very valuable.

'Well?' Gardener said matter-of-factly, trying hard to conceal his excitement.

'Well what?' Ned said curtly, noticing the Red Cross armband of *Field Ambulance* wrapped about the sergeant's arm for the first time.

'Where did you find this?'

'Right there.' Ned stabbed a finger towards rubble at their feet.

Garfield's brow furrowed. 'Really?'

'Really.' Ned reached out but the corporal pulled back. 'Hang on moment. I'd like to inspect it properly but this isn't the time or place. But I needn't tell you that, need I.'

As if the two men needed reminding, an enemy machine gun chatted close by and other Australians gathering at the crater's rim, scattered as bullets peppered the ground where they stood. Garfield stiffened. Aware. Ned seized his chance and, snatching back the goblet, he made for cover.

'You can have a closer look back at the trenches,' Ned called over his shoulder.

'Hey!' Garfield shouted after Ned who had scurried back up the crater as fast as one of the cadaver rats. Ned ignored the corporal. 'Hey!' Garfield yelled again. 'I'll take you up on that offer Edward Kelly.'

Ned turned as his name was called out. *How the bloody hell did he know my name? I haven't even seen the bastard before.* Garfield caught the look of surprise on Ned's face and pinched the dog tag, hanging about his own neck, between his fingers. 'Dog tag!' he called out with a smart-arse smirk.

Ned shook his head and disappeared back into the fray where within minutes the Turks regrouped, forming a massive counterattack and Ned carrying his precious goblet was forced to retire to the original Australian front line.

Archie Bryant and Duncan Peters managed to get drunk that night. Rum was considered an essential for the saps. Given that the tunnels were damp, dim, dangerous, poorly ventilated and permanently perilous, the rum ration was doubled and many saps simply held out their mugs and looked away, so the orderly just kept pouring. Some sappers, like Archie and Duncan, stored their ration in their water bottles and traded it for luxuries like a piece of fruitcake, bread or cheese.

They weren't maudlin drunk but they managed to render themselves *happily pissed*. They fried onions, exchanged for rum, over their campfire and even managed to score half a loaf of bread. They sang songs around the fire and laughed at Abdul's weak attempts to spoil their fun with intermittent shrapnel bombs exploding overhead.

It proved to be the frying onions that attracted Ned to Archie and Duncan's party. Ned had performed well at the front line trenches and was rewarded with furlough back to the beach. The first thing Ned did was take that long dreamt-of swim in the Aegean. He washed his clothes in the seawater and even managed to score a tin mug of fresh water to clean his teeth and finally shave two week's growth of bristle from his chin.

Life wasn't that bad Ned thought, as he sought his way to Whisper-Morris's dugout. Whisper-Morris being the soldier with the souvenir museum in his dugout, Ned wanted the man's thoughts on his recently acquired goblet. Shuffling carefully dugout to dugout, Ned followed the light of dozens of lanterns; some kerosene and others slush-lamps – these were fat-filled tobacco tins with a wick.

That's when Ned smelt the onions and the toasting bread.

'Evening fellas, havin' a shindig eh?' The fumes of Navy rum in Archie's dugout had not gone unnoticed either. Archie nodded, folding the remaining toast around his fried onions and shoving them in his mouth.

'Mind if I join yer?' the stranger asked.

Archie looked at the wiry soldier. He was shorter than Archie with a square jaw and chiselled features and red hair. He looked a strong bastard too.

'Sure,' Duncan spoke first. 'Care for a rum?'

'Is the pope a catholic?'

'Here.' Duncan passed Ned his tin mug and Ned drank a decent draught, sighed with satisfaction, took another pull and wiped his mouth with the back of his hand before handing back the mug.

Ned shot a hand towards Duncan in introduction. 'Ned Kelly.'

'Ned Kelly ... yeh right. And I'm Captain Thunderbolt!'

Of course Ned had been down this road a thousand times. His Ma named him Edward without a thought of the consequences. Christened and Baptised as Edward Kelly it was too late to change it and as Ned grew up the jokes went in one ear and out the other. Ned's straight face confirmed the name. 'You're serious aren't yer?' Duncan scratched his head.

'Bloody oath.'

'Fark! Yer mum and dad must 'ave a sense o' humour.'

'Yeh, well ... and you?'

'Duncan Peters and this ugly mug is me fellow lodger Archie Bryant.'

'G'day.' Ned was hardly subtle, looking at the fried onions remaining, warm in the pan at the edge of the fire. 'Onions! Jesus you blokes done all right.'

Duncan. 'Want the rest?'

'Or ... really?'

'Yeh mate.'

'Jesus, thanks. I'm so hungry I could eat the crotch out of a low flying duck.'

Duncan tipped the caramelised onions onto a piece of bread and the two saps watched Ned sit awkwardly with what looked like a Turkish officer's sword at his hip and other items tucked into his belt.

'Yous are saps aren't yer?' Ned asked. He wasn't about to receive a medal for that observation, not with the lads' picks and heavy duty shovels on display.

'That's right,' Archie acknowledged. 'You were in the big push on the 6th eh?'

'Yes mate,' Ned's voice trailed away and Archie thought he'd leave it at that.

So many casualties.

'Thought so. Saw you there today.'

'You blokes made a bloody mess up there,' Ned said of the explosion.

'Oh?'

'I mean in a good way mate. Bloody big hole eh?' Ned studied the two saps a moment. 'Say, check this out.' He lifted a small satchel tucked into his belt and passed Duncan the goblet. Archie recognised the handled vessel, maybe six inches high on a short wide stem with a bronzy green-grey patina, as an antiquity. Duncan gave it a cursory inspection and passed it to Archie.

'Where'd you get this?'

'Found it didn't I?' Ned exposed the broken lamp. 'And this too.'

'Will yer look at that?' Duncan said. 'It's people shaggin'.'

'Yeh,' Archie said. 'Erotica it's called.'

'Where did yer find this stuff?'

'In that friggin' big hole you blokes blew today.'

'You're kiddin' me.'

'No mate. I was first in that crater. The explosion exposed a tomb or somethin', I saw a skeleton and bits o' pottery and I grabbed them.'

'Jesus!'

'Yeh Jesus.'

'What are you going to do with 'em?'

'Sell 'em I reckon.'

'How much?' Archie asked, far too enthusiastically.

'I dunno.' Ned was suddenly cautious. After all it wasn't every day a treasure like this showed up. 'Maybe I'll just hang onto 'em. I was on me way to show it to Whisper, to see what he made of it like. I've got other stuff here too I know Whisper collects. But then I bumped into you blokes.'

'Other stuff like that sword eh?' Duncan acknowledged the fancy officer's dress sword hanging in its scabbard from Ned's hip.

'Yeh.'

Duncan looked back to the goblet in Archie's hand. 'That looks old.'

'Bloody oath.'

'I mean really really old. I heard the city of Troy ain't that far from here. You know the Trojan horse and all that bullshit.'

'Yeh well,' Ned looked vague a moment. 'Nice talkin' to yer.' Ned finished his bread and onions and stood, arching his back in a stretch, before making his way over to Whisper-Morris a few dugouts further along the cliff face.

Archie and Duncan watched silently a moment, each lost in their own thoughts and the embrace of mother rum. 'That thing looked bloody old Archie,' Duncan finally broke their reverie. 'Wonder what it's worth?'

'Be worth a few bob I reckon mate.' Archie was saying no more. He had never spoken of his black market antiquity dealings in Cairo, and thought it best he didn't. For one thing everyone would want to know how much money he made and where it was now. He fingered his money belt discreetly and took another swig of rum.

'Archie!' Archie heard his name called through the stillness of night and looked about warily. Somewhere down the valley he could hear the colonel's gramophone playing the *Marseillaise*. Otherwise the night had grown dark with only the faint slither of a crescent moon watching over the land of the Ottoman. But the fire illuminated Archie like a limelight. 'Archie Bryant! Is that you?'

Archie wasn't exactly ecstatic to see his old partner in crime, Garfield Gardener. The tall soldier pushed his way in front of other dugouts to reach Archie; finally squatting by the campfire. Archie forced a smile.

'Garfield,' he acknowledged rather curtly.

If Garfield was offended it didn't show. 'I was going to say fancy seeing you here, but hey, we were all headed here one time or another. When did you arrive?'

'May. May 9th.'

'You missed the fun then.'

'Fun?'

'Abdul's welcoming party. The landing. Bloody bullets everywhere.'

Archie shrugged. 'I see you're a sergeant now.'

'Yes. With all the men around here ...' his voice trailed away. He meant to say being killed but couldn't manage the dark words. 'Well ... promotion comes quick like.'

Garfield looked at Duncan. 'You with the 13th too?'

'Yes Sarge,' Duncan acknowledged the three stripes on the man's arm. 'Duncan Peters.'

'I'm Field Ambulance with the twelfth, we're camped down the valley.'

'Yeh, right. Rum Sarge?' Duncan passed his mug.

'Don't mind if I do.' Gardener drank, before asking. 'Say, don't suppose you blokes know of an Edward Kelly, around here?'

'Edward Kelly? Archie couldn't help himself. 'You mean Ned Kelly?'

'Well yes.'

'They hung 'im in Melbourne back in the '80s,'

'Funny bugger aren't you? Good to see you haven't lost your sense of humour Arch.'

'Yeh ... well.'

'Ned Kelly?' Duncan said. 'Wasn't that …' Archie stood abruptly kicking Duncan in the process. 'Nar,' Archie said, realising something was afoot between this Ned Kelly bloke and his old nemesis the sergeant. 'No Ned Kelly's round 'ere. Not that I know off.'

'You sure?'

'Come on Garfield, there's thousands o' men here but with a name like that everyone would know.'

'Fair enough.'

'What's this bloke done anyhow?'

'Done! Nothing. He's just a friend of a friend who asked me to get a message to him … from home.'

'What was that all about?' Duncan, naturally curious, asked when Garfield was out of earshot.

'Nuthin'.'

'Bullshit Archie. That's Ned Kelly talkin' to Whisper over there right now,' Duncan tipped his head to Whisper's dugout less than thirty feet away, where they both knew this Ned Kelly bloke was chatting to Whisper inside his shelter.

'I just don't like the bastard.'

'Who, that sarge?'

'Yes mate. I knew him in Cairo and I … well I just don't trust him, all right?'

Duncan took his pocket watch from his haversack. 'Jesus, nine thirty already.'

The clouds over the bay had cleared and what moonlight there was sparkled blue sapphires in a neat trail from the beach out to the warships. Tonight the Turks had been thoughtful. There had been no more bombardments and all was peaceful with the world. For the moment. Archie fancied he could hear the snores emanating from the thousands of hand-dug caverns honeycombing the hillside.

'I'm hittin' the dirt,' Duncan was barely coherent through a yawn. Immediately a dark figure appeared. Making his way back along the embankment face was Ned, who found Archie in the dark, dousing the flames to save the firewood for another night.

'You've got a suitor,' Archie said.

'What?'

'Do you know a Sergeant Gardener, Garfield Gardener?'

'No, why?'

'Well he knows you. He was here looking for you.'

'When?'

'Twenty minutes ago.'

'Oh. What did you tell him?'

'Told him I've never heard of yer. Told him Kelly was a common name. So was Ned.'

'Sergeant you say?'

'Yer.'

'Tall skinny bastard, strong lookin' bugger?'

'That's him.'

'He hassled me for this.' Ned tapped the little sack hanging from his belt. That sounded like Garfield all over, Archie thought. 'He turned up at the crater just after it blew.'

'He did?'

'Yes mate.'

'Strange. The bloke's with Field Ambulance. I wonder what he was doing on site so quickly?'

'Your guess is as good as mine mate,' Archie said, but he knew better. Garfield Gardener was up to his old tricks in this ancient land. Why, Archie had heard archaeological discoveries were being made all down the peninsula. Just twenty miles or more south, at Cape Helles, French troops uncovered ancient artefacts when they dug trenches, and the French army immediately authorised an archaeological excavation. They believed they had located the important city of Elaeus, Archie heard, located at the tip of the peninsula.

And there was a war on for Christ's sake!

Then again all the old generals throughout history took ancient treasures as trophies, Archie reminded himself. 'So what did Whisper have to say about the goblet?' Archie asked.

'He said it's real old like. Ancient he said.'

'No shit?' Archie said and hoped his words didn't sound sarcastic.

'Roman, he guessed. Whisper said he read about Troy and stuff back home. He's seen pictures.'

'Yes, but Troy wasn't Roman you know.'

'Even I knew that,' Duncan muttered from the dark of his bunker.

'Oh? Yer both know a bit about history then?'

'A little.' Archie noticed the sword missing. 'Sell the sword to Whisper huh?'

'Swapped it for this.' Ned held up a pocket watch on a fob chain dangling it a moment. Archie watched its silhouette swing hypnotically with the sparkling Aegean behind it. 'Its German hallmarked silver. The spring's stuffed but I'll get it working. Easier to transport home than that sword.'

'Yer goin' home then?' Duncan shifted on his dirt mattress searching comfort.

'You're a cheerful bastard,' Ned said.

'Where is it ... the goblet? Did you sell it?' Archie asked.

'No mate.' Ned tapped the satchel hanging from his belt.

'And what did Whisper have to say about it?'

'Said it was really old.'

'We know that.'

'Yeh ... well. He didn't seem to think it was worth much.'

'Well there you go.' Archie was about to pressure Ned into selling when Ned slipped the sack free and said. 'Listen ... ah,' Ned looked about. The three men were alone. 'I think this, goblet or whatever it is, is pretty special ...'

'Special?'

'You know, valuable. And with that sergeant lookin' for me, it could be trouble.' Ned paused. Archie waited. 'Look, you blokes are saps. Yer don't have to stick yer neck out for Abdul all the time. Christ yer underground for most o' the fightin'.'

'What are yer tryin' to say sport?' Archie took offence, pushing out his chest. 'That we aren't soldiers?'

'Jesus no! I didn't mean that. No, it's just that ... well here,' he pushed the wrapped goblet into Archie's hands. 'Look after it for me will yer. An' this too.' He passed over the broken lamp. 'I wanna keep 'em away from that Gardener bloke, and I'm livin' in the bloody trenches most o' the time. I've got nowhere to hide the damned things. Tell yer what, we'll go halves when I finally sell it. I'm sure it's worth a pretty penny.'

Duncan poked his head out from the dugout. 'Thirds,' he said.

'What?'

'Me an' Arch'll look after it for yer and we'll go thirds.'

Ned thought a moment. 'All right, give me the rest o' that rum an' it a deal.'

'Done.'

'And write yer names and numbers on 'ere,' Ned passed Archie his half empty cigarette packet and a small lead pencil. Archie jotted down his name followed by his service number, 2486. Duncan did the same.

'Security eh?' Duncan said slipping a smoke from the pack for himself before handing the packet back.

'Let's call it a receipt.'

'Fair enough. Here.' Duncan passed the half-gallon stone jar to Ned when Ned realised his mistake.

'Shit! It's near empty.'

'Now now sport,' Duncan laughed. 'There's enough left in there to get yer legless.'

CHAPTER THIRTEEN
BES IN EGYPT

Egypt. June 7th 1915

HMAT *Benalla* arrived at Alexandra, Egypt. Bes and Janet were two of fifty nurses, twenty doctors and six hundred soldiers on board. Although they had enlisted with the Australian Army Nursing Service the government had offered them to the Queen Alexandra Imperial Military Nursing Service Reserve or the QAIMNSR for short. They were, in other words, under orders from the British Army.

Bes's diary entry for June 7th

The docks at the northern most Egyptian city of Alexandria were in disorder, to put it mildly. Our luggage, and all the medical staff's luggage, was dumped on the wharf higgledy-piggledy amongst the kit for six hundred soldiers. We nurses had no choice but to wait while the mess was sorted.

Four hours later they were on board the train to Cairo, rattling south ...

... on wooden seats with slats missing and no cushions. The six-hour journey was most uncomfortable; however the scenery was beautiful, exotic even, and helped take our minds off our disposition.

But what awaited them in Cairo was totally unexpected.

Heliopolis, Cairo. June 1915

Like many grand hotels in Egypt, the Heliopolis Palace Hotel had been commandeered by the British Army, who in turn had offered it to the Australian Medical Corps for the Australian wounded at the futile Gallipoli campaign at the Dardanelles on the west coast of Turkey.

At a cost of two and a half million pounds, Heliopolis Palace Hotel was built by the Belgian king and an English syndicate. Fortunately for the war effort the hotel had proven a white elephant, the main reason being they were not granted a casino licence and now war had killed any prospect of that relatively new phenomenon, tourism. The Palace Hotel was renamed, *The First Army General Hospital*, or the *F.A.G.H.* as all departments were pigeon-holed.

Now, over one thousand wounded soldiers were cared for within its opulent interior. Even the King's Room – a lavish suite with its opulent furnishings – was now the primary operating theatre. The Grand Banquet Hall was turned into a convalescent ward with over one hundred beds.

Stained glass windows illuminated marble staircases by day, with clusters of electric lights by night.

I have been assured there are ten thousand electric globes in place here. But what Janet and I are really excited about is, there are hot and cold baths and showers in our lodgings where the nurses and doctors occupy the first, second and top floors.

Orderlies and lesser ranks were housed in the hotel servants' quarters in the basement

And as if this establishment was not large enough a second General Hospital was located at Mena camp, Bes was informed, but she and Janet had the good fortune to be stationed at Heliopolis.

The two friends were lost in wonder, in awe amongst the alabaster, the marble and the granite grandeur of the Hotel foyer. It was the most extraordinary and luxurious hotel either had ever seen, let alone to be working and living in.

'Grand isn't it?' Bes turned to face the voice. 'You're one of the new arrivals are you not?' the voice asked Bes and Janet. Bes was always wary of strangers but these were unusual times and this man could very well be their principal.

'Ah … yes. We just arrived.'

'On the train,' Janet added as if there had been options.

'Yes of course,' the voice answered Janet, but clearly he only had eyes for Bes. 'Robert Galloway,' he said, and offered his hand, first to Bes. 'Doctor Robert Galloway actually,' he corrected. 'Best be formal I guess. But ...' he looked about, the coast was clear. 'Call me Rob outside the hospital.'

'Nice to meet you Doctor Galloway,' Janet said cheerily. 'I'm Miss Stubbs.'

'Yes, quite.' He gave Janet's hand a gentle squeeze before looking directly back into Bes's blue eyes. 'And that's my friend Miss Mulberry,' Janet said before adding awkwardly. 'Nurse Mulberry.'

'So,' Galloway looked a little uncomfortable. Most nurses swooned when they met the tall, dark and extremely handsome surgeon. But this long-legged beauty seemed oblivious. 'So do you know where to go first?' he asked.

'No we don't, 'Janet answered for both of them. 'Do we Nurse Mulberry?'

'No we don't *Nurse* Stubbs,' Bes said. 'But my guess is that the good doctor here is about to show us,' she added affably. 'Isn't that right Robert?'

***

The converted hotel-hospital was immense; it seemed it would never end. Finally at the end of the west wing Doctor Galloway left the two at the entrance to administration.

'Here ladies, sign your life away in there. Matron Gwyneth Garrett is on duty today I do believe; she'll steer you in the right direction.' There was a moment's awkward silence before Galloway added, 'I guess I'll be seeing you on the wards.' The doctor delivered Bes the most disarming smile. 'Nurse Mulberry ... I ... ah didn't catch your first name.'

'No,' Bes allowed the faintest smile escape. 'No you didn't.' Bes turned on her heels and walked into the administration ward.

Janet went to follow. 'Her name's Bes,' she whispered to the doctor, her face a picture of conspiracy. 'And I'm Janet.'

'Oh you *are* a flirt Bes Mulberry,' Janet was an excited schoolgirl. 'A real lush.'

'A lush!' Bes grinned, feeling good about herself. 'That's not a nice thing to say. You were hardly subtle yourself Nurse Stubbs.'

'Well he was rather gorgeous,' Janet gushed. 'Don't you think?'

'He was alright, I suppose,' Bes smiled inwardly, for she had a feeling they would meet again, and soon.

For all its grandeur the massive hospital soon revealed its true colours. The colours of blood and infection, the stink of septicaemia, vomit and open belly wounds. Shrapnel wounds seemed to be the worst where artillery shells exploded overhead; shredding on impact, spiralling bread knife sized chunks of razor-sharp iron spinning through the trenches. Limbs were severed, eyes gouged, heads decapitated, intestines exposed. And there were wards and wards of the wounded and dying. But as conditioned to the damaged bodies as Bes had become, Bes had nightmares about her family; themselves ripped apart by a coward's bomb.

***

Three weeks later.

Bes walked the corridors of the dying, the crying, the moans and groans of hundreds of badly wounded souls. All were men. Most were young. Many would die. It was gut wrenching. Boxes of straw caught the falling limbs of amputees under the operating table. Where possible modern nickel-plated operating theatre trolleys were in use but more often than not old wooden benches and dining tables had to suffice. White tablecloths commandeered for surgical clothes were saturated with the blood of the brave and unfortunate. Where possible electric lights were used; however many an amputation or abdominal operation was conducted near windows taking advantage of the Egyptian sun.

As a nurse in Hobart Bes had witnessed trauma; children run over by automobiles, a stockman trampled by his horse or the cruelly burned. But here in Cairo the battlefield wounds ...

War was a bitch.

An announcement resonated in the corridor drawing Bes's attention back to the land of here and now. 'Nurse Mulberry.' The man's voice was that of a familiar stranger. 'Bes Mulberry, I do believe.' Bes turned back to face Doctor Robert Galloway. He looked even more handsome than the first time they met. Bes, who had been lost in a reverie temporarily, barely smiled, yet she nodded politely. Galloway played his hand cautiously. 'Doctor Galloway ... remember me ... Robert?'

'Yes of course,' and Bes added before she thought, 'How could I forget?'

'I'll take that as a compliment,' he said.

'Oh ... I meant ... ah ....'

'Never mind.'

'I haven't seen you around since we first met,' Bes said without thinking. *Blow! Will he think I've missed him?* Bes reprimanded herself.

'They've had me in surgery at No.2 Stationary Hospital,' he said. Bes knew of the other hospital at Mena Camp. 'Those boys on the Dardanelles are copping a what for.'

'Yes, will it never end?'

'Terrible business.' Doctor Galloway struck while the iron was hot, so to speak. 'I say, are you on a break perchance?' Bes was about to lie; tell the man she was busy. But truth was, she *was* on a short break. A short shrug of her shoulders answered the doctor's question.

'Then would you care to join me in a cup of tea?' he asked.

Bes sighed, yet capitulated, fearing she would appear ungrateful or worse, prudish. Besides, she was famished. Bes accepted.

***

Mess tents had been set up in the grounds behind the hotel, lost between rows and rows of field ambulances delivering the latest victims from the horrors of Gallipoli, fresh from off the Alexandria train.

'It *is* Bes, is it not?' Galloway asked as he pulled a chair from under a table for Bes.

'That's me. Just staff nurse, Bes Mulberry,' Bes did not mean to sound subservient.

'Then I am *just* Doctor Robert. But please call me Robert.' He looked about as he pulled his own chair free. 'That is unless we are working together. *Neville* would never approve, eh?' Bes knew the Neville, Robert spoke of, to be Neville Shaddock the sixty-one-year-old Director of Medical Services who ran the hospital with the iron rule of antiquated Victorian values.

'Then we must not upset the good Doctor Neville Shaddock, must we?' Bes was coming across somewhat short with the man, but she didn't know why. Truth be known she liked what she saw of him. And he was a gentleman, seemingly genuinely interested in her.

The pot of tea arrived and a three-tier stand of sandwiches, cakes, pastries and confectionery – which Robert insisted on ordering – was placed on the table. It appeared some of the European-trained Egyptian cooks were kept employed in the Army run hotel-hospital, for service to the officers. Bes did not hold back, devouring egg sandwiches with watercress and some strange spicy pastries. 'Delicious.'

'I'm glad,' Robert smiled taking small bites from a pastry. 'This is goat I'm thinking,' he said of his pastry. 'And the egg in the sandwiches would be pigeon.' Bes thought if he was trying to shock her he needn't bother, she loved it all. In particular, Bes adored a sweet jelly like confectionery flavoured with rose water. She ate three pieces while Robert sat back, one leg hooked over the other and watched her with interest, sipping tea as if he were with the queen.

'You like that confectionery?'

'Hmm,' Bes found it difficult to talk.

'Turkish Delight they call it. At least that's one thing Abdul got right, eh?'

'You a Kiwi?' Bes finally managed to ask.

'Lord no. What made you ask that?'

'Well you often finish a sentence with eh … like the Kiwis do, and you have got a slight accent.'

'Well the accent is probably because I'm from Queensland and the 'eh' is probably because I have worked with a few New Zealand doctors since arriving in Egypt. And you.'

'I'm from Tasmania.' Bes studied the man a moment. 'And in case you are wondering, no, my grandfather was not a transported convict.'

'Huh!' Robert laughed, showing off his perfect white teeth and for the first time Bes noticed a small mole on his upper forehead. 'Convicts eh?' he leant forward to lower his voice. 'Now there's a word we don't hear too often. I think I may have a skeleton in my closet there somewhere, but my mother would never talk about it.'

Bes finished her second cup of tea and they held eyes briefly while Bes wondered what his intentions were. He seemed genuine enough. Or was he just being friendly? Did he simply want someone to chat with, or was he attracted to her? Robert showed little interest in the food so Bes had no qualms about finishing the sandwiches. As her appetite was satisfied her thoughts wandered again. What was she doing here anyhow?

High tea with a doctor no less, what would mother have thought? Mother.

Bes had an involuntary moment of morose flashbacks.

'Are you all right?' Robert asked.

'Sorry, I … I was …. just thinking about home. My mother actually.'

'Oh. Is everything alright?'

'Look I'm awfully sorry. I must leave.' Bes stood clumsily taking her purse from her apron.

'Is it something I said?'

'No. No not at all. It's just …' Bes fished about for a few coins.

'Please. This was my pleasure.' Robert made an allowance for the women's independent movement sweeping the civilized world the past decade and added. 'Maybe another time.'

Bes nodded an awkward thank you and hurried away.

CHAPTER FOURTEEN
NED'S DEAD

Five days later. September 1915

It was not as if the bullet that hit Ned had his name on it. Everyone joked it would. Same for *every* Tom, Dick or Harry, wasn't it? But could the Turks even spell these Australian names? One thing was for certain; Ned didn't feel the half-ounce German manufactured projectile as it slammed his shoulder skipping over bone before spinning unfettered through his neck. On a positive note it missed major arteries.

Ned was unconscious as two *body snatchers* rushed him down Bolton's Ridge and along the shoreline to Anzac Cove. There was a lot of blood. At the casualty clearing station Ned was declared dead. The stretcher-bearers were confounded.

'We thought he'd make it.'

The doctor shook his head. It was something he had done a lot of lately. As was the situation on Gallipoli, Ned's body was taken by the bearers to be discarded at a burial site in Shrapnel Valley. Here his dog tag was removed, personal belongings taken from his pockets and his body placed in a long row of fellow cadavers awaiting burial – a service that was conducted each evening. So it can only be imagined the reaction from the twelfth battalion chaplain when Ned's painful groaning drew the man's attention to the wriggling shape beneath the shroud.

Ned had lost a lot of blood. But his wounds weren't necessarily death threatening. He was rushed back to the hospital tent, his wound dressed and when they thought him stable enough he was transferred to a hospital ship.

Three days later Ned was able to keep down some hot barley soup in a hospital bed at Mudros on the island of Lemnos.

Back from the dead, they all joked and Ned laughed along with the rest.

***

Within a fortnight Ned had been transferred once more, this time to Heliopolis in Cairo. *Back where he bloody well started.*

It was not as if twenty-year-old Ned was a handsome lad. He was a wiry strong, stocky bloke with tight curly red hair – well he did have curly red hair that is, until the hospital shaved it off to rid him of lice. But it was his sense of humour Bes went for, and god only knows they needed a good laugh.

'Crikey nurse, I'm bald,' Ned feigned a distressed face as he rubbed his functioning hand over his spiky dome. 'Yer could light a match on this.'

'Well as long as you don't burn the hospital down,' Bes answered. 'How's that shoulder today?'

'Not bad.'

Truth be known it ached like buggery.

***

Days turned to weeks, weeks to a month. Ned's wounds proved superficial. Superficial as in the bullet had skipped across bone but damaged muscle and left a nasty scar. Mentally, Ned had new values also. For one thing the near death experience had made material wealth less important. Ned lived for today, grateful to be alive, yet feeling guilt for his mates still in the firing line. By the end of October Ned was back at Mena Camp on light duties. Although he protested that he wanted to return to his mates on the Gallipoli Peninsula and finish what they started, there were persistent rumours that an evacuation of the Dardanelles was imminent. Ned was refused his demands and ordered to wait until his battalion returned from Turkey, for a bigger battle awaited them all, on the increasingly futile Western Front. With this in mind Ned volunteered to join the Twelfth Battalion Sappers, and the days passed quickly in training with the Royal Engineers.

Bes missed the prankster sapper Ned when he left hospital. Many a down time she had shared a pot of tea and listened to Ned's stories, as wild and unbelievable as many of them were. But she was a good listener and Ned was quite the raconteur.

At Mena Camp the talk was now all about France. The Hun and the allies were in a stalemate and it was clear they would all soon be re-assigned to the Western Front. But Ned could not stop thinking about the nurse, that affable angel with the friendly bedside manner, Bes Mulberry. *Sure she was a good looker.* But Bes was more than that to Ned. She was caring, intelligent and worldly.

***

Janet was an incurable romantic, an inveterate admirer of her friend Bes's ability to attract men without realising it. Janet didn't think Bes naïve, just unobservant maybe.

'It's from that Ned, isn't it?' Janet was gushing giggles as Bes opened a personal letter sent to her in Heliopolis with a postmark from Mena Camp army post office.

'Settle petal,' Bes told her friend, unable to hide her own suspicions that Janet was right. Bes unfolded the paper and turned her back on Janet to read the letter's contents.

'Well?' Janet skipped in front of Bes.

'Well what?'

'It's from that soldier you spent so much time with. The one with the shoulder wound ... what's his name ... Ned. Isn't it?'

'Golly Janet,' Bes said playfully waving the letter about so her friend couldn't see. 'You're such a stickybeak.' Janet dodged and ducked and finally, bursting with curiosity she snatched the letter. 'Janet!'

Janet avoided Bes's protests and read aloud. *'Please don't think me forward, but would you be interested in meeting me for tea at The Sovereign Hotel this Thursday at, say, 2pm ...* oh Bes, he's smitten.'

'Stop it,' Bes grinned.

'That's tomorrow Bes. Thursday.' Janet read on. *'I realise you may not be able to get a message to me at such short notice, however I will wait at the front entrance for you anyway, in anticipation. Please don't feel obligated, I will understand should for any reason you are not there to meet me ... yours faithfully, your true friend, Ned ...*

Oh Bes. How sweet. He has nice handwriting also. You must go.'

Bes managed to snatch the letter back. 'Where's the Sovereign Hotel anyhow?

***

Bes found the hotel near Tahrir Square in central Cairo. An old-school British Hotel, yet accepting of the common soldier. Ned was overjoyed. 'Bes!' he called out across the busy street, whipping off his slouch hat in a gentlemanly salute, only to reveal a tight red haired mat where his shaved hair was finally growing back. 'Jesus ... I mean gee ... I really didn't think you'd make it,' he said rather clumsily.

'Why?'

'I mean, well I wasn't certain you'd be able to make it.'

'Well here I am.' Bes was having second thoughts why she allowed Janet to talk her into this rendezvous. But she soon relaxed, seeing a happy and positive face for a change.

'And here you are indeed. Gee, it's real terrific to see yer.'

Bes wanted to say *and it's good to see you too*, but restrained herself. What she saw in this rather earthy soldier she wasn't certain. But now she was here, *in for a penny in for a pound,* as her Aunt Jessie would say.

Inside British etiquette struggled with Egyptian traditions. But unlike the more affluent Shepheard's Hotel overlooking the River Nile, the service was a little more relaxed at The Sovereign.

Ned launched into conversation. 'I'm so pleased you came,' he reassured her.

'Me too.'

Bes already knew Ned was one of three boys to Jim and Flo Kelly from Flemington in Melbourne. Samuel Kelly was the youngest brother at twelve but Ted Kelly, Ned's eighteen-year-old sibling, had just been sent to Gallipoli and Ned wasn't too happy about it. 'He's impulsive Bes. I'm worried about him and mum expects me to keep an eye on him but I'm stuck here, ain't I?'

'He'll be fine Ned, you'll see.' But Bes's voice lacked conviction. Ned insisted Bes order for them. A pot of tea for two with a plate of sandwiches took nearly half an hour to arrive. Neither, however, were bothered, enjoying each other's company more than Bes wanted to admit.

Ned spoke with pride of his dad who fought the Boers back in '01 as a light horseman. 'And you?' Bes asked. 'You didn't join as a light horseman?'

'Never learnt to ride Bes.'

'Oh.'

'I know, living at Flemington an' all. Crazy ain't it?' Ned picked up a wedge of sandwich and pushed the bloater paste and relish, crusts and all, into his mouth. Bes couldn't help smile. Ned was down to earth, nothing like Robert the doctor, and she liked down to earth. 'You've never told me about your parents Bes,' Ned said through a mouth full of sandwich. Bes took a small bite of her own sandwich and thought a moment. She must have appeared serious for Ned said, 'I don't mean to pry, tell me if'n yer don't want to talk about 'em.'

Doctor Macrossan's advice resonated in Bes's mind ... *It would be therapeutic to talk about it.*

And Bes talked.

***

Anzac Beach. Six weeks earlier.

Sergeant Garfield Gardener of the Twelfth Battalion Field Ambulance looked at the pile of dog tags sitting on his converted crate desktop and sighed. A true heartfelt sigh. It was one of his responsibilities to write to the mothers and fathers or wives of the dog tag owners, informing relatives of their great sacrifice, and the chore was nothing less than repetitive. A task to be certain. A bloody chore. Sitting at another *desk* in the chaplain's tent, Reverend Herbert Peach wrote with empathy, momentarily taking a time to meditate on his task.

Maybe he was asking god for assistance.

At a nearby trestle any personal items belonging to the deceased – like diaries, letters, watches, mementos – were sorted for postage back home accompanied by the letters of condolence. Garfield poised with pen to paper, selecting dog tags like a lottery. The whole bloody war was a lottery. Some won, many lost. He read the first tag:

AIF

3193

Donald E. Stott

9th Batt.

RC

Garfield rubbed his forehead in thought, as if that would help, and plucked a regular condolence opener from his meagre repertoire;

It is with great regret ... I regret to inform you ... I am writing to you to express my sincerest sympathies ... Please accept my greatest sympathy ... it is with the deepest sympathy I write ... your husband/ son was admitted to hospital on the June 19th but died of his head injuries, chest injuries, shrapnel injuries ...

'Jesus!' Garfield blasphemed. The reverend chose to ignore him. He had heard a lot worse of late. Garfield picked up a handful of leather discs and read them indiscriminately; Mitchel, McPherson, Hill, Taylor, Reid, Bedward, Kelly ...

Kelly! He studied the tag closer:

AIF
2486,
EB KELLY
12th Batt.
CE

E. Kelly!

'No,' Garfield heard himself say aloud. 'Couldn't be.'

'What couldn't be?' Reverent Peach asked.

'Oh ... ah ... this Kelly fellow, I knew him.'

'I am sorry sergeant. Were you close?'

'No ... it's come as a shock that's all.' Garfield looked across at the two men sorting personal items at the trestle. 'Kelly,' he said aloud. 'Are there any of Ned Kelly's belongings there?'

'Ned Kelly?' the reverend questioned.

'Yes I know. Apparently his parents were ignorant to the fact Ned was short for Edward.

'Kelly,' one sorter said. 'Yes Sarge, I seen a Kelly here a moment ago ... here.' He held up a packet of Turf. 'And a pocket watch. Looks like a Hun watch Sarge. Souvenir I reckon.'

'There's something written on the fags,' the other man said.

Garfield Gardener picked up the cigarettes and smiled.

Well well, he thought to himself, and he mulled the name written on the packet over and over in his head ...

Archie Bryant ... Archie Bryant.

***

The next morning found Archie at *the* beach, Anzac Cove, looking for drinking water. He woke thirsty, parched, and slipped away while Duncan snored beneath his blanket. It was 6AM and British sailors were flogging tins of condensed milk and beef extract. Without Duncan's knowledge, Archie buried the goblet and his money belt in the dirt beneath his bedding but had kept a few coins for such an occasion.

Milk two shillings a tin, beef one shilling. Trust the Tommys to make money out o' the Aussie diggers, Archie thought. And bought two of each.

Archie walked to the water's edge and took a look back inland. With the difficult terrain rising steeply from the beach, the diggers still managed to put every inch of land to use. The elaborate system of dugouts was truly a rabbit warren and Anzac Cove had turned into a self-sufficient community with shopkeepers, chaplains, doctors, dentists and barbershops. Church services were conducted in the open with the chaplain conducting communion using biscuit boxes and a cloth for an altar.

Archie stripped naked and waded into the water amongst twenty or so other like-minded soldiers. It was cold but reinvigorating, but short-lived as Turk snipers started taking pot shots at them from their hidden perches way back up the in the hills. Luckily no one was hit until *Beachy Bill*, the nickname given to one well-hidden Turk artillery gun, lobbed a shrapnel bomb, which exploded over the bay wounding three swimmers. It was time to evacuate the water. Refreshed, Archie managed to score an empty drum and a ration of fresh water. The water stank of kerosene but at least he could make a billy of tea and hopefully the condensed milk would help disguise it.

Wishful thinkin' matey.

Back at the dugout Duncan was animated, angry, and Archie's salutation was not appreciated. 'Christ Duncan, yer look like somethin' the cat dragged into the house.'

'Ned's dead!'

'Who? What?'

'Ned, that bloke we met last week, the bloke what give us that old mug thing he found to look after.'

'Jesus! Dead? How do you know?'

'Your friggin' mate was 'ere wasn't 'e?'

'Who?'

'Sergeant Garfield bloody Gardener, that's who.'

'Jesus!' Archie's eyes darted to his bedding. It was in disarray but the dirt beneath it was undisturbed. 'What did he want?'

'You Archie. You.'

'And?'

'And he kicked about in the dugout like he was lookin' for somethin'.'

'Bastard! What did he say?'

'Well he wanted to know where you was. Where was yer anyway?'

'Getting your breakfast yer miserable bastard.' Archie sat the water drum next to the campfire ashes and threw Duncan a can of milk. 'Well come on then, get the fire started.'

'Is that it? Yer friends been killed and you wanna make tea?'

'He wasn't me friend Duncan.' Archie realised his choice of words were inappropriate. 'Look mate. That's bad news but this is war mate. Blokes are getting' killed every minute.'

'What does the sergeant want with yer anyways Arch?' Duncan's tone mellowed with the thought of hot sweet milky tea.

'How would I know?'

'It's that mug thing ain't it? The one Ned told us look after.'

'So the prodigal son returns eh?'

Archie recognised the voice instantly and the hairs on his neck bristled. He turned to watch Sergeant Gardener approach along the cliff face, careful not to lose balance and slide down the embankment into the next row of dugouts. 'Sergeant,' Archie said curtly, his unsmiling face hardly disguising his disparagement.

'Back from the beach I should imagine. You look pleasantly refreshed.'

'What do you want Garfield?' Archie spat with the precision of a cobra.

'Sergeant Gardener, soldier. I'm a sergeant now remember,' and as if to accentuate the comment he raised an elbow to display his stripes.

'What do you want ... *sergeant*?'

'That's better,' Sergeant Gardener stood on the narrow shelf of the dugouts modest *porch*. He faced Archie who refused to budge. Archie faced off a moment. He could smell cherry on Garfield's breath and guessed he had recently cleaned his teeth with Mawson's Cherry Tooth Powder, a luxury item here on the battlefield. At that moment thick smoke spiralled from a campfire nearby below and the two were in the thick of it. 'Let's walk,' Garfield said with a cough, doing his best to fan the smoke away from his watering eyes. Easing away from the cliff face the two walked silently a few minutes along a goat path on the safe side of Shrapnel Valley.

'You know Ned Kelly is dead?' Garfield finally said.

'Yer, Duncan told me.'

'I'll not beat about the bush Archie, where have you hidden the goblet?'

'What goblet?'

'What goblet?' Garfield mimicked. 'Now how did I know you'd say that ... what goblet?'

'I don't know what yer talkin' about.'

'Pull the other one Archie.' Garfield stroked his chin thoughtfully before saying. 'What say I tell you what I know, eh?'

'Fine.'

'You and your sapper friends blew the Lone Pine HQ. Well done, well done indeed. In doing so you have opened a huge elongated crater that just so happens to have exposed an ancient tomb. Ned Kelly, front line soldier is first into the crater, admittedly under great risk to his personal health. But the man's an intrepid souvenir hunter and is used to taking such risks. He discovers said tomb, souvenirs a bronze goblet and somehow managed to rebury the tomb before yours truly, that's me, stumbles on Ned holding the goblet.'

'You souvenir hunting too?' Archie said with a stab of sarcasm. 'Rifling through dead men's pockets no doubt.'

'I'll choose to ignore that comment. Now yours truly,' Garfield continued, stabbing a finger into his own chest, 'yours truly has a brief moment to hold this goblet and quickly inspect it before one, other diggers approached, and two, the enemy was close by and keen to recapture what they had lost.' Garfield eyeballed Archie. 'With me so far?' Archie nodded indifferently. 'Now this is the interesting bit. I rubbed some dirt free from the rim of the goblet and read the name *Pinarius*.' Garfield waited for a response but was not surprised at Archie's ignorance. '*Pinarius*, heard of him? No of course you haven't.'

This is when Archie felt like punching the man.

Garfield strutted, head high in the knowledge he knew more than Archie ... a great deal more. 'Quintus Pinarius was a famous general at the time

Emperor Constantine the Great moved the capital of the Roman Empire from Rome to Constantinople, hence the name of the city Constantinople ... Constantine, get it.'

'I'm not stupid.'

'No,' Garfield bit his bottom lip nodding sagely.' No, that you're not Arch.'

'So what's this got to do with the price of eggs?'

'Quintus Pinarius controlled a Roman settlement somewhere up in those hills,' Garfield nodded in the direction of the front line. 'It was a barracks of two battalions, a thousand foot soldiers a piece, with a settlement of several hundred civilians surrounding the fort, you know, blacksmiths, bakers, candle stick makers, all that is required to make the world go round.'

'So?'

'Well this General Pinarius amassed a fortune in taxing the merchants who needed to sail through the Dardanelles to trade in Constantinople.' Garfield now saw a slight twitch of interest in Archie's expression. 'Back to the goblet. Now us scholars know the tomb has never been found. The Roman settlement has never been located. Schliemann ... have you heard of Heinrich Schliemann?'

'No.'

'Well Schliemann discovered the lost city of Troy, just north of here, back in the 1870s. He was a most successful archaeologist and actually found treasure at Troy.'

'Treasure?'

'Priam's treasure in fact.' Archie was interested but daren't ask who Priam was. 'Priam was the legendary king of Troy during the Trojan War ... the Trojan Horse. Remember that in your history lessons at school.'

'Yes,' Archie said, pleased with himself.

'Yes, well. Schliemann looked for the Roman settlement. Legend told of it being here on this peninsula but no one knew where. One would think if anyone was going to find it, it would be Heinrich Schliemann. But no. Then presto! Your explosion uncovered Pinarius' tomb, only to have it disappear again immediately lost once more. Now Ned is dead. So where is this goblet Archie? It is my belief it will lead us to the old general's loot.'

'I wouldn't have a clue Garfield.'

Now it was Garfield's turn to twitch. 'Rubbish Archie. Your name was found on a cigarette packet in Ned's pocket when he died. I spoke to Whisper-

Morris and he recalls seeing the goblet. He also told me Ned spent some time in your company the night he too met Ned Kelly. Not only that but Duncan Peters' name was on the packet also and Duncan told me that Ned left the goblet with you both. So, Archie, where the hell is it?'

'Duncan's full o' shit.'

'I think you're the one full of shit Archie.'

'Duncan was pissed that night, we both were. Got on the rum. So bugger off Garfield, I can't help yer.'

'Just remember who taught you everything Archie, everything about antiquities.'

'So, I don't know what happened to the bloody goblet. All right.' Archie shoved by Garfield and made his way back up the path.

'I'm not finished yet Bryant,' Garfield yelled after him. 'You hear me?'

'You stupid bastard,' Archie was furious. He threw Duncan against the dugout where a chunk of roof collapsed. 'I should kill yer, yer traitorous bastard.' Archie lifted Duncan by his shirt and tossed him aside once more.

'No Arch. Jesus! What's the problem?' Duncan was a big lad, strong, but he was in no position to fight back when his opponent was so angry.

'You told that arse Gardener about the goblet.'

'No Arch, I never, honest.'

'Bullshit! He told me, you told him, Ned left the thing with us.'

'I never Arch. The bastards played yer for a fool.'

'I oughta crown yer one here and now.' Archie balled his fist and bent his elbow.

'You're not listenin' Arch. I … shit … I told Whisper.'

'Told Whisper what?'

'I told him Ned left the what's it, goblet yer say, with us for safekeepin'.'

'Yer didn't tell Gardener?'

'No mate. Honest. Just Whisper.'

'Shit!' Archie mellowed. 'Well you're still a fuckin' idiot. Jesus.'

'Sorry Arch. What's the problem anyways?'

Archie studied his mate. They'd shared this rat hole over four months now. When was it ever going to end? The diggers weren't advancing and the Turks weren't retreating. He offered Duncan a hand and hoisted him to his feet. Both men were covered in dirt from the collapsed roof. They shared a laugh and poured the tea, but not before tipping one whole can of sweetened condensed milk into the billy. Archie sat, leaning against the embankment. What did he have to lose? *Nuthin' really …*

And he told Duncan Peters his whole story, including how he had left the goblet buried in the bottom of his kit when some bastard stole it.

Now that bit wasn't true.

The area now notoriously named Lone Pine remained a front line hotspot for weeks to come. Archie and the sappers blew up several more tunnel systems and all were successful. However the war of attrition continued. Archie heard the useless British general, General Hamilton, had been replaced by General Munro, and there were rumours that an evacuation was being planned …

Now that *was* good news. Good news indeed.

***

November 13th

Word quickly reached the men. The Minister for War, none other than Lord Kitchener himself, was visiting Anzac Cove. It had been a hush hush visit with minimal fuss; after all it would not do for Abdul to be made aware. He was ushered by ANZAC'S top brass, namely Lieutenant General Sir William Birdwood, the man in charge of the Australian troops. Birdwood was a brilliant strategist and his men loved him; unlike Britain's military leaders on the peninsula, who all too often were appointed for their social status with little military experience. And to make matters worse they were incompetent and unapproachable.

'The King asked me to tell you how splendidly he thinks you have done,' Kitchener told the hundreds of men gathered about him near the beach, before inspecting the front line. 'You have done splendidly, better even than I thought you would,'

Archie thought this a momentous occasion and hurried through the soldier's shantytown and down the hillside to the gathering, in a valley safe from enemy artillery. On his person Archie carried his Vest Pocket Kodak with four photos remaining.

A tall slender man in his sixty-fifth year, Kitchener struck a handsome pose in his British uniform of blue combat jacket, woollen jobcar britches secured with puttees to knee high leather boots and sporting a long walking cane. He turned towards Archie during his speech and Archie managed a clear photograph capturing him with his handlebar moustache and clean shaved chin. Archie took three photos, discreetly of course, and was winding on for a fourth when he recognised general Delbert Sedgwick Kinsley amongst the top brass entourage. Kinsley had been the British General in Cairo to whom he sold the fake pottery scarab faience with its hieroglyphs. And for the enormous sum of two hundred pounds. Archie felt it unlikely the man would recognise him from that dark night in the hotel courtyard but he was taking no risks and dissolved away.

'Nice little camera that.' The deep voice belonged to tall willowy man with wire rim glasses, pointed features, a small thin mouth and an enthusiastic studious face beneath his wide rimmed rabbit felt hat. Archie had seen the thirty-six-year-old Sydney Herald correspondent Charles Bean, now employed by the War Office, on many occasions around Anzac Cove, but never had they spoke.

'What was that?' was Archie's response, nervous that he was about to be reprimanded for taking photos, frowned upon by the higher ranks. Although Charles Bean wore an honorary captain's uniform he remained a civilian.

'The Vest Pocket Kodak,' Bean answered. 'Nice little camera.'

'Oh … yes.'

'Excellent for this kind of work.' And Bean tapped the side of his nose with a surreptitious smile.

'Oh I … I just snapped a photograph of his Lordship … I …'

'Don't worry man, I'm not bothered. I saw you take a snap or too, jolly discreet camera, I was thinking of buying one myself but I'll have to wait until London I should imagine. May I …' Bean reached out.

'Yeh sir, sure. Go for it.' He passed the war correspondent his camera, astounded that he was even having this conversation with the controversial historian.

'120 roll-film is it not?'

'127 I believe. I've one shot left on that, my first roll.'

'Really. Tell you what, I'll snap the last film of you and get it developed here for you.'

'Really?'

'Certainly. I'll even make you prints.' Bean limped slightly and Archie remembered hearing that he was shot in the leg that fateful day at Lone Pine; wounded as an observer of the battle.

'That's jolly decent of you sir.'

'It would be a pleasure. Stand over there.' And Bean directed Archie to pose where Lord Kitchener could still be seen in the background.

'Oh ... ah ... I rather not if you don't mind ... take my photo that is.'

'Very well, it's your last shot. You take one of me then.'

Archie couldn't believe his good fortune. He snapped the correspondent and passed him the camera.

'Do you know where my office is?' Bean asked Archie of his bungalow come dugout, photographic dark room and quarters. Archie nodded. 'Call by in a day or two then.'

***

On the strength of this visit to Turkey Lord Kitchener made his decision. An evacuation was ordered.

Days later Sergeant Garfield Gardener found Archie with the Royal Engineers, setting wire netting in front of the Australian trenches. The idea of the wire fence was to fend off the hand thrown bombs lobbed by Abdul. This way they exploded harmlessly in no man's land. Sergeant Gardener had become more and more threatening towards Archie as the evacuation of all allied troops on the Gallipoli Peninsula was now imminent. In that case, in Garfield Gardener's eyes, General Quintus Pinarius' tomb would be lost forever. Or worse still the Turks would discover it.

'You don't know the importance of what you have Bryant,' he argued, using Archie's surname when he was angry.

'Look Gardener,' Archie returned the formality. 'You know where the tomb is. In no man's land. And I told you the goblet was nicked from the dugout. It could be anywhere by now.'

'Why don't I believe you? Because I know you too well Bryant.'

***

Ned Kelly had told Archie what he saw that day in the crater; a sarcophagus, a skeleton, a few wine amphorae, broken pottery once holding food for the general in his afterlife, and the bronze goblet. A bronze goblet Archie knew now was silver. That alone should fetch a decent price on the black market when he returned to Cairo.

Archie paid two visits to Charles Bean's office and was told both times the captain was visiting other areas of the peninsula. There was more pressing business afoot. The evacuation for one. A massive operation that would have to be organised in great secrecy, should Abdul discover the plans and massacre the remaining evacuees. For this reason Archie went about his business – the photos would have to wait.

***

November 25th
Duncan sat by their campfire desperately trying to thaw his mitten-covered hands over the flames. The cove awoke this day to a light snowfall and all in all the weather was miserable. Close by Duncan observed two military police approach their dugout and warned Archie.

'They're headed over 'ere by the looks of 'em.'

Archie craned his neck around the sand bags to focus through a cloud of frosted breath. The two MPs spoke to occupants further along the cliff face, where they were directed towards Archie. A third MP promptly joined them, a Tommy soldier, a rare sight at Anzac Cove.

'Private Archie Bryant?' the first officer asked Duncan as the three reached the dugout. Duncan shook his head vigorously in silence. Archie crawled out into the open and stood to face the men. 'Who wants to know?' He sounded cocky and to be quite honest, he felt like it. War does that.

'You're under arrest.'

'What?'

The Tommy spoke next. 'You're under arrest for defrauding a British general.'

'Piss off!' Archie was angry. He knew what this was about but the fat old bastard was dabbling illegally in the black market.

The Tommy clamped Archie's arm with a tight fist. Archie stared at the man's hand before fixing him with a death stare. 'I wouldn't be doin' that if I was you.'

'Oh,' the Tommy tried to pin Archie's arm behind his back but Archie pulled free and struck out, punching him in the jaw. The MP slipped in the frost, sliding off the ledge before landing heavily on the dugout terrace ten feet below.

'Christ Bryant,' one of the Australian MPs yelled. 'What the hell.'

'I don't take threats lightly.'

'You're to be arrested man. Now you strike an officer. Jesus.'

'Arms out soldier,' the other officer shouted. He presented handcuffs. 'You're under arrest.'

While the British military police officer clambered up the crumbling icy gravel of the steep hill side, his pride shattered, Major FR Edgeworth, in charge of the 13th Royal Engineers made his entrance passing the dugouts. 'Leave that man be, that's an order.'

Edgeworth had been tipped off at the beach about Archie Bryant's impeding arrest, and for what? Fooling an old fool, especially a British fool. And he was incensed. 'Leave that man be lieutenant. Leave him be now.'

'Sorry major but this soldier is to be arrested.'

'Not on my watch, lieutenant.'

'The arrest is under orders of General Kinsley of the British Armed Forces.'

'British Armed Forces,' Edgeworth spat. 'Exactly. And you Tommys have no jurisdiction to come here and arrest an Australian soldier. Especially on some trumped up charge of what ... selling the general some trinket souvenir.'

'Major, in all respect I ...'

'Bugger off.'

The two Australian officers looked lost. But if that *was* the charge it seemed awfully unreasonable, especially as there was a war on. The British glared at Major Edgeworth a moment before admitting defeat. He turned to Archie who couldn't hide his smile. 'You've not heard the end of this Private Bryant.'

'Thank you sir,' Archie stood to attention after the MPs retreated.

'Yes, well. Let this be a lesson. Don't get into the sandpit with a Tommy general. And he's right you know, you haven't heard the end of this. They'll be back.'

'Yes Major.'

'Now finish whatever you were doing and report to Quinn's Post ASAP. You too Peters. The Turks have settled in up there and we've work to do.'

CHAPTER FIFTEEN
QUINN'S POST

November 25th

Quinn's Post overlooked Monash Valley, Shrapnel Valley and down to the cove itself and with the evacuation in the planning stage it was imperative to push the enemy back from any sightseeing advantage. With the plans for evacuation came winter storms, unbearable weather, snow. Well below, the ground was hard and dry but near the surface was difficult toil with the freezing weather and frozen soil.

It had taken three days to dig the charge tunnel and lay the explosives silently beneath the Turks trenches only a grenade's throw from their own. With the explosives tamped down, the charge set and the entrance being sealed, all that had to be done was to pull back the diggers in the advanced front line trenches and detonate. But Abdul had other plans and hand thrown bombs were lobbed by strong arms into the Australian trenches. At first diggers managed to throw some back. But the wily enemy soon shortened the fuses. Men were killed and many wounded before they could retreat.

Archie made his exit from the sappers' tunnel into mayhem. Several hand bombs exploded nearby. With help he sealed the tunnel and turned to make his escape when a Turkish grenade landed at his feet. Archie didn't hesitate. Scooping up the bomb he heaved it out of the trench. But it slammed into sandbags, dropped back onto the firing step and exploded.

Archie was less than ten feet away.

He never felt the shards of metal shatter his nose or slice through his cheek. The pain would come later. But he knew he was hit. He knew it was bad …

And Archie Bryant slipped into darkness.

CHAPTER SIXTEEN
BES & ROBERT

Heliopolis. Cairo. Late in the year 1915.

War brings out the best in some and the worst in others. With the shroud of death hovering overhead some nurses threw caution to the wind. At an institution like the Military Hospital at Heliopolis, love was a free commodity only at the expense of one's reputation. And that could be very expensive. For the common soldier, the bordellos of Wazzir continued to be a rich source of gratification.

For Bes there was no shortage of suitors. Five months had passed by. The wounded came in their thousands, many were repatriated back to the battlefield and many were sent home bandaged and broken. However, just as many died and were buried in the ancient sands of Egypt, in the very same desert as Egyptian peasants, Roman centurions, Bonaparte's soldiers and the almighty Pharaohs.

Bes had recently farewelled Ned who had sailed for France with an advance party of the Twelfth Battalion sappers. It was only after he left that absence made the heart grow fonder. At times they had seemed an unlikely couple but there was a rare quality in her stoic soldier friend, and Bes found her thoughts often centred around him. Certainly he was shorter than her, not particularly handsome and rough around the edges some might say. But he was thoughtful; generous with what little he had and had a wonderful sense of humour.

'Yes, I will miss him,' Bes told her friend Janet. 'But there's a war on you know.' Truth was, Bes was terrified of falling for a man who might desert her for an enemy bullet any time soon.

As if these thoughts weren't bad enough, Bes received a letter from her Auntie Jessie in Hobart. Her father Frank Mulberry had died in Willow Court Mental Institution. He never did fully recover his mental health before he died, the doctors agreed, of a broken heart. Bes was devastated. Her mother and sisters gone and now her father. On a positive note Aunt Jessie had moved into the family home in Queen Street, as brother Ben's guardian. Ben was doing fine, the letter read, and was back at school. And the neighbours had all chipped in to restore the house. Initially Bes wanted to return home but her conscience prevailed; there was a war on and her services were desperately needed.

With Ned gone and the sad news of her father, Bes desired distraction. Robert, that is Doctor Robert Galloway, had also become a good friend over the months. But for different reasons, on Bes's side that is. She saw him more as a colleague. Bes told Robert everything she had to tell him and he to her, well most of it, that is.

A target of their amusement was often the sixty-one-year old director of medical services, Doctor Neville Shaddock, who struggled with twentieth century medicine.

'Old Neville's a bit like the geriatric warlord generals in England,' Galloway huffed into his cup of Ceylon black tea. 'Wrestling with the fact that men on horses wielding sabres cannot attack machine guns, and win.' Bes had to agree. As angry as it made her, she felt her hands tied against the bureaucracy of this pointless war. Bes reached for another crust-less potted salmon sandwich and felt a pang of guilt knowing what Ned had told her of the diet the diggers were enduring in Turkey. But she was starving and these rare high teas were a highlight of her free time in Cairo.

'Why do the English call this high tea anyhow,' Bes said of the four-tiered silver salver groaning with delicacies. Delicacies from cold meats, brown bread and pigeon pie to walnut cake, chocolate roll and current teacake. Here at the Shepheard's Hotel in Cairo it was difficult to believe there was a war on at all.

'High tea?' Robert Galloway asked. 'As opposed to low tea?'

'Yes.'

'Well this is high tea served at a dinner table; a low tea is served on an independent low table.'

'How silly of me. Why didn't I think of that?'

At nearby tables some heads turned towards the main entrance. Bes followed their eye line. 'Well goodness me, speak of the devil.'

Robert looked discreetly over his shoulder and there was old Doctor Neville Shaddock himself being shown through the busy restaurant to a table for two by the window. 'And he's with Matron Maisie Stanford,' Robert said. 'The sly old goat.'

'He has a wife back in Oxford does he not?' Bes asked.

'I do believe so.'

'You've never told me why *you* haven't married,' Bes said to her colleague only to blush slightly. Did this sound like she was flirting? *Maybe she was.*

'I simply haven't found the right person.' Robert held Bes's eye. He was an intelligent good-looking man, terribly handsome in fact with a fine figure to complete the package. 'You know,' Robert placed his empty teacup back on its saucer and tipped his head towards Neville Shaddock. 'I heard that old fool remonstrating with one of the black ward assistants for *shirking* her duties, as *he* put it, because she had menstrual pain.' Being medical staff it was not the subject matter that disturbed Bes rather than the fact that, *here we go again*, whenever she spoke of his past he changed the subject. 'He accused the poor girl of hysteria brought on by her menstrual cycle. *It is a notable fact that hysteria*, he said aloud to other staff, *hysteria rarely occurs among women of civilised nations.* Where on earth did he get that reasoning from?'

'Yes. Where indeed?'

They finished their evening with a walk along the Nile. The late setting sun struck gold upon the lateen sails of a felucca, gliding lazily on a calm river. The setting was as romantic as one could wish for in wartime. Leaning side by side against a rail they stood in silence a moment, staring west towards a sun the size of an ostrich egg, magnified on the horizon. The air was still, the evening balmy, delivering the exotic aroma of street food. For a brief moment Bes thought Robert was about to put his arm about her waist. Suddenly Robert stiffened, 'Goodness!' he looked at his watch. 'I didn't realise what the time was.'

'Time?' Bes was confused. They were not rostered back on until six in the morning.

'I told the chaps I'd meet them at the club.' Bes knew Robert spoke of the Gentlemen's club at Gideon Hotel along the river. 'I'll see you to the tram,' he said.

'No.' If Bes was disappointed she hid it well. 'I'll be fine.'

'A young lady should not walk down the street unescorted,' Robert offered Bes the crook of his arm to usher her towards the tramlines.

The offer to take his arm was too little too late. 'Seriously. I will be fine. I can look after myself.'

'Are you certain?'

'Go.'

'Goodnight then.' Robert made to give Bes a peck on the cheek. It would have been just that. A peck. But she moved away smartly and headed for the Heliopolis tram.

CHAPTER SEVENTEEN
RESURRECTION

Heliopolis Hospital Cairo December 3rd.

Somewhere close by a man cried. It was a pathetic sob. A continuous weep. At first Archie thought he was dreaming. His hearing returned, sharp and clear. He heard voices, women's voices, the soft pleasant tone of females he had not heard in months. Were they angels? Archie opened his eyes only to be assaulted by a fierce and bright light. He slammed them shut and found he was staring at a faint translucent pinkness that was sunlight shining through a window onto his face. Carefully he opened them again, blinked and allowed a moment for his vision to adjust to the brightness. Now he stared at a high ceiling tastefully moulded in floral patterns with electric lights hanging from fancy carved ceiling roses. The sense of smell returned and he caught a mixture of ethanol fumes with chlorine and the metallic smell of blood. Archie realised he was in hospital. The weeping continued and Archie new it to be the patient in the next bed.

'There Bill, there there,' the angel said softly, calmly. 'Has the pain returned?' Bill answered weakly in the positive. 'I'll fetch more laudanum.'

Archie tried to turn his head but a terrible pain shot down his neck. He realised he had a tube running down his throat into his stomach. He gagged. Immediately panicked with claustrophobia Archie instinctively pulled at the tube, gagging noisily. He felt his face. It was bandaged. With the tube removed and terrified that his entire head was bandaged Archie cried out. But thankfully his eyes were uncovered. He ran fingers down his face, his mouth was exposed but he could not feel his nose.

'Matron!' the angel called out. 'Someone fetch matron.' As footsteps hurried away Archie felt soft hands take his, carefully but firmly, pushing them back to his side. 'Keep calm now Archie.' The angel's smooth fingers stroked Archie's bare chest in a soothing action to accompany her tranquil words. 'Relax Archie. You are in hospital in Cairo. You are safe now.'

Archie tried to speak but his voice wouldn't cooperate. His throat was parched but the angel knew. She seemed to know everything. Gently she raised his head slightly, propping another pillow beneath him and he felt something cold and hard pressed to his lips. A glass straw. Archie sucked at the water, gulping the delicious liquid through his cracked lips, like a thirsty dog.

'Now now Archie, not too much.' The angel kept her voice calming and Archie relaxed a little. 'You can have some more in a little while.'

'I had a tube down my throat.'

'That's how we have been feeding you.'

'Feeding me ... what ... what happened?' Archie finally managed in a croaky voice he hardly recognised.

'You were wounded at Quinn's Post. You have been sleeping.'

'Sleeping. What day is it?'

'Friday.'

'Friday!'

'Friday, December the 3rd. Yes Archie. It's been eight days.'

'Eight days asleep?'

'Matron will explain.'

Bes stepped aside as the matron took charge. 'How long has he been awake?'

'Just now,' Bes said. 'I'm pretty certain.'

'Notify Doctor Galloway.' Matron Dorothy Gilchrist studied Archie a moment. His eyes were wide and frightened but she had seen it all before and far too often, now this damned war was heading into another year. Archie tried to slow his breathing, aware that he was anxious, and focussed on the matron. She looked in her late forties, a robust woman with greying hair and a slight Scottish accent; or was it Irish?

'You have been in a coma Mr Bryant.'

'A coma? The nurse said I was asleep.'

'Well I suppose you could say that. You've had a cerebral trauma. Shrapnel I believe, all too common I'm afraid. Anyhow you have had a sudden loss of consciousness in a cerebral haemorrhage.' Archie looked vague. 'The brain gets a surprise by the accident and shuts down.'

Archie remembered only too well now.

Quinn's Post. The hand grenade. The white flash.

Gilchrist held her hand before Archie's face. 'How many fingers am I holding up?'

'Three'

She fanned them slowly one side to another watching the patient's reaction. 'At least your sight seems unimpaired.'

'Why is my face bandaged?' Archie asked, terrified of the truth.

Matron was not about to hold back. There were hundreds of similar cases and she had other wards to visit. Archie noticed the woman's chest rise and fall heavily as she took a deep breath. 'You have severe cheek trauma and you have lost your nose completely. Should we remove that bandage one would see clearly your tongue and down your throat, with your mouth closed.'

Matron explained how, with the aid of anaesthesia based on chloroform and ether, Archie's face was stitched where possible.

Archie felt tears well up. Matron noticed. 'I'm sorry Mr Bryant. Doctor Galloway will visit you shortly, should you have further questions.'

Further questions! Is she serious?

Minutes later, aware that the patient would need counselling and a hand to hold, Bes Mulberry returned to Archie. 'More water?'

'Please.'

'Now drink this.' Bes exchanged glasses and gave Archie laudanum. The effect was instant. She took Archie's hand in hers and waited. And Archie fell back into a deep sleep.

***

Two days later.

Conscious that someone was close by, watching, Archie opened his eyes to be greeted by the angel. Bes stood between the patient and the Egyptian late afternoon sun beaming through the hospital window, unaware a ring of light haloed her head.

'My angel,' Archie said, relaxed in the knowledge this friendly face was before him.

Bes. 'How are you holding up?'

'Better now you're here.'

'That's the laudanum.' Bes held eye contact a moment wondering if the patient was once a handsome man. She had sponged him the past eight days and he certainly had the fine figure of a man. She helped Archie drink water. 'You'll be able to drink some chicken broth today. Hungry?'

'I'll say.'

'Did Matron explain … tell you of your wounds?'

'Apparently half my face is missing,' Archie tried to make light of the situation but it hurt to smile beneath the bandages.

'Well …' the truth was, half the man's face was missing or knotted. 'At least you still have your sense of humour,' Bes said instead.

Archie reached out and Bes took his hand as a counsellor. 'It's going to be a long road Archie, but I can see you are a strong fellow. We'll see you through.'

'I know you will and I thank you for it.' Archie squeezed Bes' hand. 'Bessie, my angel.'

'Bessie? The name's Bes. Anyhow how did you know my name?'

'I heard Matron call you Bes the other day. Tell me Bes, how did I get here?'

'You were pretty badly knocked up. You were patched at the field hospital and finally taken to a hospital ship where you sailed to Alexandria and were transported here by train.'

'What a pity I missed the trip.'

'Yes well. We thought we had lost you a couple of times, as maintenance of respiration and blood circulation is first priority. But as I said you are a resilient man Archie Bryant.'

***

The days passed. The pain was handled with the laudanum. The boredom had to be managed by sleep. Archie felt his strength returning while he drank three meals a day, all chicken broth, through a straw. By the end of the first month he was sitting up playing cards or chess with other patients in similar circumstances. Others played draughts while some learnt languages, like French or Arabic.

It had been five days before his doctor made it to his bedside. Doctor Robert Galloway seemed pleased with the sapper's progress. His dressing was changed every second day and his humour improved; although bouts of depression clouded over him from time to time. But it was always Bes who managed to encourage a broken smile on that wounded face.

***

December 25th 1915 Heliopolis. Egypt.
It was Christmas Day. Yet the mood in the ward for those managing the pain, and their demons, it was a jolly occasion. Only the day before Archie had his stitches removed using nitrous oxide to dull the trauma and later a carbolic acid solution wash, to prevent infection.

The wards filled with the aroma of roasted turkey, thick gravy, cranberry jelly and roasted root vegetables; all garnered by the officers and hospital orderlies from sources best left undisclosed.

As long as there was a war the black market thrived was the answer Archie received when he saw the feast.

Archie's Christmas dinner, of course, was cut into tiny pieces which he swallowed with some difficulty, but the French wines served with the meal – and drunk through a straw – aided its passage. After plum pudding Captain Jackson of the 9th Artillery entertained the men by tinkering at the keyboard of a borrowed piano while the nurses sang Christmas carols.

It wasn't home with the family, but close enough.

'Archie!' Archie heard his name called from the end of the ward. 'Archie!' he turned awkwardly to see his old dugout mate approach, a kit back over his shoulder.

'Duncan?'

Duncan stopped at the end of the bed and swallowed hard. He had been warned by the nurses what to expect but it still came as an awful shock. And now, for Archie, it was the first time he realised he had such a speech impediment, with damaged lips and mouth he salivated uncontrollably, especially when he spoke. Hospital staff had ignored this problem and so Archie had assumed he was perfectly coherent.

'Mate,' Duncan floundered for words while Archie smiled awkwardly. Duncan took the best approach possible. 'You look like something the cat dragged in.'

'Get stuffed!' Archie croaked a laugh and Duncan could see the pain it caused.

'Seriously mate,' Duncan stood next to the bed where Archie was propped up on pillows. 'How is it?'

'The truth?'

'Yes mate. The truth.'

'It's not too good.'

Duncan took his friend's hand in his and gave it a manly pat with the other. He could see now there was no nose behind the bandages. 'The nurse told me yer lost yer nose.'

'Yeh. Ask me how I smell.'

'How do yer smell then?'

'Terrible.'

Duncan laughed at the old vaudeville joke. 'Same old Archie underneath I see.'

Archie noted the kit bag. 'So what's with the kit, yer stayin' the night?'

'No mate,' Duncan laughed again. He spun it about so Archie could read his name stencilled on the canvas. 'That's yours.'

'What? Really?'

'Yes mate. I brought it back from the peninsula. We were evacuated on the 16th. Spent a few days on Lemnos then we sailed for Alexandria. Got to Cairo this morning so here,' Duncan plonked the kit bag on the bed, 'Merry Christmas.'

'You're a real mate Duncan. Thanks cobber.' Archie looked at the kit bag knowing there wasn't much in it but clothes and toiletries. But something hard pushed through the thick material. 'What's this?'

Duncan was clearly excited balancing on one foot then the other. 'Have a look.'

'It's not ... is it?'

'Don't ask me mate, have a gander.'

Duncan helped Archie rummage through to the bottom of the kit bag realising immediately it *was* the ancient goblet. 'H-how the bloody hell?'

'I knew yer was bullshittin' about someone nickin' it 'cos yer wasn't that worried. So I had a scratch around, then I thought 'e's a friggin' sap ain't he? He's buried the bastard, and voila, as the frogs say.'

Archie brushed dirt of the goblet and held it to the light. It truly was a beautiful piece of ancient tableware.

'And I suppose yer wonderin' what happened to this too, eh?' Duncan lifted his tunic to reveal Archie's money belt holding up his britches. 'But I'll be needin' another belt to keep me strides up Arch, I've lost a stone since the landing.'

'Ah mate … I don't know what to say.'

Duncan passed Archie the belt. 'Say thank you.'

'I'll do better than that.' Archie unzipped the fastener and peeled away a one hundred pound note. 'Here. Buy twenty belts.'

'No Arch, I can't accept that.'

'You can an' yer will. I don't wanna hear any more about it. You've earnt it, right?'

'Jesus Archie,' Duncan face reddened. 'Truth is me mum could use this back home. Thanks mate.'

'When are you off to France?'

'Couple months they reckon. We're back at Mena now. More drill. Same friggin' sand. I'll come an' visit again soon, bring yer some chocolate eh, it'll melt easy in yer gob. Say, while I'm here give me yer address back home an' I'll look yer up sometime.' Duncan slipped his pay book from of his pocket along with a pencil, and turned to the back pages used for contacts. 'Where exactly are yer from anyway?'

'No fixed address Dunc, leave me your address and I'll write yer when I settle down.'

'Sure mate.' Duncan scribbled on a page and tore it out of his pay book. 'Well I best be off. The lads are playin' the officers at cricket after our Christmas lunch … can't miss that.' Duncan touched Archie's shoulder in a farewell gesture, when he remembered. 'Oh yeh, Captain Bean, remember him.'

'Charles Bean?'

'Yeh. Well he sends his condolences and he gave me yer photos all nice and developed.'

'Really Duncan! You're too much old mate.'

'They're in yer kit, in a brown paper envelope. The camera's in there too.'

'Have you looked at them?' Archie asked.

'Of course. You got some nice mementos there. There's one o' you and me in the dugout.'

Archie felt about blindly in his kit bag slipping the envelope free finally shuffling himself completely upright, better to view the photographs. One by one he inspected his handy work. The photographs taken in Egypt were particularly clear. The desert light was perfect. 'There's the one of you and me Arch.' Duncan picked the dugout shot free. 'You know mate I'd love to have that photograph, of me and you like.'

Archie remembered letting his guard down when he allowed Spider Jones, another sapper, take their photo. 'Maybe I can post you a copy when we get back home, eh,' Archie suggested.

Duncan looked disappointed. He loved that photo. 'Why not now Arch?'

'Now what?'

'Give me that one and you can get another one printed from the negatives.' Duncan picked up the photograph.

'No!' Archie snatched it away, immediately annoyed with himself for acting so abruptly. 'Sorry mate, I'll get yer a copy, I promise.'

'Sure … sure thing. 'Duncan was clearly surprised until he realised it was probably the only photo that Archie had of himself before the horrific wound. 'Well,' he sighed. 'I better be off.'

Duncan stepped through the huge doors of the palatial converted hospital and back into the Egyptian sun. Christmas Dinner and cricket beckoned, but as he walked to the tramline he had a nagging feeling that Archie's promise would be broken.

Archie finished inspecting the photographs. He was pleased, the camera had taken better quality photographs than he expected. He studied the snap of Lord Kitchener, proud that he had been a witness that ever-important day. But then something caught his attention. Sergeant Garfield Gardener was in the background. Archie felt his anger grow. *Bastard*. But then he also recognised the man standing next to Garfield, and busy conversing in a serious manner, was General Delbert Sedgwick Kinsley's orderly, Edmund Cornish. The realisation hit Archie like a bolt of lightning.

Bastard! Now it all made sense. Gardener had set him up. That's why the Military Police were after blood. *Bastard!*

Time heals all wounds, or most wounds at least. The months passed and although grossly disfigured, Archie's skin healed and the mental scars became manageable. One constant that Archie read with interest was news from the Western Front. The war, now touted by imaginative journalism as The Great War or even World War, seemed it would never end. Whole villages were wiped off the face of the earth whilst the death toll was devastating.

Then the news Archie never wanted to read appeared before him;

Sapper Duncan I. Peters Australian Infantry Forces Number 2914 of the 13th Battalion Royal Engineers. Roman Catholic, was killed by an artillery shell on the 19th of July at the Battle of Fromelles in French Flanders.

Archie didn't make friends easily, but he could count Duncan as one of them.

CHAPTER EIGHTEEN
A CALL TO BLIGHTY

June. 1916 Heliopolis. Egypt.

Archie sat in a cane wheelchair on the lawn in a convalescing garden at the Heliopolis hospital where he relaxed in the Egyptian sunshine, alone with his thoughts. Although the air was still the cicadas made a racket in the sycamore trees. The sky, Archie thought, was the sharp blue of an ancient faience statue. Archie soaked up the sun, his face unmasked and the warmth felt great on his skin. He felt at peace with the world. Although he suffered mood swings. Archie's face was unrecognisable. It looked like a wild animal had gnawed him. On the bright side this deformity attracted little attention as he shared his ward with dozens of similar victims.

'Here you are. I thought I'd find you out here.' Bes looked stunning, even in her uniform. Archie had grown extremely fond of the cheerful nurse; they had grown close over the months. Bes was not one to judge or be distracted by the horrific visage before her. 'I've some good news,' she smiled that warm smile Archie treasured in his dreams.

'Good news? For you, or me?'

'You.'

'Oh?'

'You're about to be sent to England.'

'England. What on earth for?' Anxiety crept up on Archie. He was happy here. In Cairo. With Bes.

'It's called plastic surgery. There is a ground-breaking procedure by a New Zealand surgeon called Doctor Harold Gillies. He reconstructs damaged faces.'

'Oh? How?'

'I can't say exactly. Doctor Galloway will explain. But you will have a new and handsome face reconstructed.'

'A New Zealander you say.'

'Yes, but he is in England. He has set up a surgery in Cambridge in a Military Hospital at a place called Aldershot.' Archie's mood changed. 'What's the matter, aren't you excited?'

'I'll miss you.'

Bes's naivety surfaced. 'And I'll miss you too Archie.' Bes stood in front of the wheelchair taking both of Archie's hands in hers. Truth was she had made close friends with many of the men in her care. 'We can write to each other,' she said in a tone of regret. Regretting that she was failing him in some way.

'Bes ...' Archie hesitated. His eyes welled up with uselessness. The fact was he had fallen for this angel. He was besotted. For the first time in his life he was really in love. 'Bes,' he said, squeezing her hands to the point of discomfort. 'Bes ... I ... I love you.'

'And I love you Archie,' Bes said with the innocence of a young schoolgirl. 'And I'll miss you too. Cheer up, you're about to get your life back, pretty much anyway.'

'You don't understand Bes. I love you. If I could I would marry you.'

'M ... marry!' Bes stepped back, shaking her hands free. 'Archie, what are you saying?'

'I'm in love with you Bes. I ... Oh Christ what am I saying?'

'No Archie ... I ... we are friends. I am your nurse and you are my patient.'

Suddenly Archie's mood turned dark. 'Jesus I should have kept my mouth shut!' He groped at sympathy. 'Why would a beautiful woman like you ever want such an ugly specimen like me?'

'Now Archie. That's not fair.'

'It's that Galloway isn't it. That Doctor bloody Galloway. It's him you want isn't it?'

'I'm not staying here to be berated Archie Bryant. Not by you or anyone.' Bes turned to leave, fighting back tears of her own.

Archie's eyes were now cold and dark. 'He's married you know.' Bes stopped in her tracks, her mouth wide. 'Yes. Didn't know that did you? He's got a wife and child in Geelong.'

'No. No Archie. You have the wrong doctor.'

'Oh do I?'

'How do you know this? How could you possibly have learnt this?'

'I heard him talking. I heard him talking about you to that Jewish doctor he is friends with, the small bloke with the grey hair.'

'Doctor Myers.'

'That's him. You and Galloway had afternoon tea and cake at Gibson's Tea Rooms recently and the waiter spilt milk on your dress.'

Bes was stunned. There was no denying it. That had happened. Archie must be telling the truth.

'He told Myers you and he were close and Myers asked him, *does she know about Theresa and your son back in Geelong?* '

'When … how …'

'I had taken myself to the lavatory. It was late. They were doing their rounds and they didn't know I was in the cubicle.'

'Theresa could be his sister.'

'No Bes. His answer was, *you're joking old chap, why would I tell Bes about my wife?*'

'Goodbye Archie.' Bes's voice broke. She could take no more. 'Good luck in England.'

***

Cambridge Military Hospital. Cambridge. England. July 1916.
The red brick and stone military hospital had opened in 1879. But the consequence of ruling an unwieldy empire was a huge strain on British infirmaries. Afghanistan, the Zulus, Pakistanis, Iranians, the Boers, the Burmese, the Boxers, all took their toll. They all wanted a fight. It was soon deemed necessary to extend the military hospital and in 1893 two angled pavilion wards, their designs loosely borrowed from ancient Greece were added, one each end of the main rectangular building.

Although Archie had no difficulty walking he was wheeled through the front door beneath an elaborate clock tower, reminiscent of the decoration atop a six-tier royal wedding cake, Archie thought. Out front oak and wattle trees flourished and the lavender was in full bloom, permeating the surrounds with its delightful scent.

Archie met the pioneer surgeon, Doctor Harold Gillies personally, not long after arriving at the hospital. He was immediately assessed as a candidate for the latest facial reconstruction surgery that came to be known as plastic surgery. Doctor Gillies – the thirty-three-year-old nose and ear surgeon and pioneer of this procedure for deformed soldiers – was a New Zealander born in Dunedin. With receding thin hair and a rather thick brush style moustache to compensate, Gillies was softly spoken with a commendable bedside manner and a certain confidence. The confidence of a man who was prepared to take risks for the advancement of modern medicine. He realised the need for his ground-breaking procedure, when confronted by the horrendous injuries from the Western Front. Sixteen per cent were facial injuries, flying shrapnel being common. Particularly badly burnt were the airmen who had survived fiery crash landings.

In the past patients were left with facial deformities that would make it difficult to breath easily, eat or drink. Gillies saw the need to repair these faces. The authorities agreed and Gillies was given the go ahead to set up Britain's first plastic surgery unit at Cambridge Military Hospital at Aldershot.

He was truly a hero.

***

'How are you holding up?' Gillies asked Archie.

Archie wanted to say, *how do you think*? But forced a smile that pulled his face taut. The discomfort was obvious but Gillies needed to examine Archie. 'Do you know how this procedure works?'

'I believe you make a cast and reconstruct somehow.'

'That is correct. Men who have lost … men with parts of their face disfigured are being fashioned prosthetic custom-made masks. It's in its infancy you must understand and we are learning daily but overall the results are most positive.'

Archie listened intently. Anything was better than his current state. He had looked in a mirror once, and only once, and fighting depression was a struggle. But there was an aura of positivity in this doctor's voice and Archie, hanging on to every word, found his New Zealand accent comforting.

Historically survivors with major facial injuries were left disfigured with difficulties seeing, breathing, eating and drinking; as well as looking horrific.

'Step one will be to make a paper mache mould over your face,' Gillies said. 'This will be to capture the right shape. The exact shape you understand. Once we have this mould we sculpture attachments to replace the damaged sections of face. These are made from paper-thin copper. When finished we have professional artists paint on the facial features and skin. This is done while the mask is on the patient so as the skin artists can match tones. For patients missing eyes we employ master glass smiths to create cut glass eyes baked with enamel.' Gillies spoke passionately, clearly a proud man. 'A bulb of glass is blown and colour applied. The eyes are baked and the colour set. The eyeball is then cut to fit the patient and carefully polished. But this does not affect you Archie.

'How does this ... mask, or part of, stay on my face?' Archie asked.

'We'll furnish you with a pair of glasses which are clear glass you understand, not optical lenses, and the mask is held in place by these fake glasses.'

Doctor Gillies presented a portfolio of previous patients. Before and after photographs. For the first time Archie attempted a genuine smile. 'And these men are pleased with the result?' Archie asked.

'Very pleased, Archie. For the most part these men can lead normal lives, some back in the work force, many continuing a happy married life.'

'That's fascinating.'

'Archie,' Doctor Gillies closed the folder and sat in a chair opposite. He leant forward to face his patient. 'I have also pioneered a surgical technique called tube pedicle surgery skin-grafting.'

'Right,' Archie said warily.

'Tube pedicle skin-grafting is where I separate a flap of skin, but not detached, from a healthy part of the body and stitch it into a tube which is then sutured to the injured area. Like your cheek. A period of time is then allowed for the new blood supply to form at the implantation site. Later it is detached, the tube opened and the flat skin stitched over the area that needs covering.

'My god. You can really do that. And it grows ... like a new cheek?'

'In a fashion, yes. But it is time consuming, convalescence requires months. It takes time for a new blood supply to flow to the treated area.'

'One thing I have plenty of, doctor, is time.'

'It means you won't get home for another year of more.'

'There's nothing at home for me anyway.'

'Oh? No family.'

'No.'

'I'm sorry to hear that. Let's look on the bright side Archie. New face, new man and maybe you'll meet a lovely lady, fall in love and live happily ever after.'

'Maybe.'

CHAPTER NINETEEN
A TACTICAL ABORTION

Fromelles, French Flanders. July 1916.

The Germans had captured the small but significant village of Fromelles almost two years earlier during the Race to the Sea, when the Hun marched across northwest Europe. Fortunately they were thwarted by French and British troops before they reached the English Channel. But Fromelles had remained German occupied by the enemy ever since, where the 6th Bavarian Reserve Division had dug in and held the village, supported by strategically positioned army units along Aubers Ridge, high ground to the northwest of the village.

Two months earlier in May, the British 8th Division tried to take the ridge but suffered devastating losses; eleven thousand killed Ned heard. Spies noted it took German soldiers an entire week to bury the dead.

Now, four days earlier on the 15th, preparations were well underway for a massive offensive in which the Australian 5th Division were to be involved – of which Ned, fresh from Egypt, was one of thousands – under the command of Gallipoli veteran Lieutenant General Sir James McCay. But Brigadier General Harold 'Pompey' Elliott, commander of the Australian 15th Brigade, part of the 5th Division, was not convinced the attack was well planned, and made his views known to Field Marshal Haig.

A Major Howard was sent to hear Elliott's views and the two men observed the field of attack from no man's land. 'What are your grievances?' Howard asked Elliott.

'For a start you are relying on Australian artillerymen who are inexperienced. And our guns are unreliable. The distance to be covered across no man's land is also variable. 'Look.' Elliot pointed out the variations with some distances between allied and German lines of up to four hundred feet. 'That's a long distance when one is being shot at by machine guns. You will also notice much of the ground is waterlogged due to all the rain we have had. And the Germans have a clear view from their fortified machine gun posts in those damned concrete pillboxes.'

'I see.'

'Be frank, Major, what is your opinion of the outcome?'

'A bloody holocaust.'

'Then I trust you will report this unsatisfactory situation back to Haig.'

Grievances were aired, apparently on deaf ears. The attack on Fromelles and Aubers Ridge was to go ahead.

***

Fromelles, French Flanders. Wednesday July 19th 1916. 11am.

The heavy artillery barrage had begun two days earlier, intensifying by the hour. The ear-shattering boom was continuous. The ground shook as the sixty-pound Howitzers destroyed infrastructure, while eighteen-pounder guns damaged the enemy trenches and some of the dreaded barbed wire barricades.

Underground Ned's shoulder was killing him. The bullet wound at Lone Pine from August 12th last year pained him immensely but he never complained. His only regret was that he would never be able to play cricket again. Yet he accepted light duties and was trained in setting the detonating charges, joining the Aussie sappers in Flanders. For Ned this new employment was exciting. He was to be a part of the first Australian offensive on the Western Front, and would not have to fire a shot.

Ned had been re-assigned to the Australian 5th Division and along with the 1st and 2nd he sailed from Egypt to Marseilles in late March 1916. From Marseille they travelled north by train to Paris, marvelling at the beautiful French countryside, rich in forests and green meadows with delightful chateaux and ancient farmhouses. On a sombre note he saw many women – widows in black.

But the people were friendly, cheering as they passed and Ned would always remember the young French girls blowing them kisses as the trains passed by.

Fromelles was a typical village in French Flanders. Red geraniums in full bloom burst from the window boxes of the quaint seventeenth and eighteenth century cottages. The churches all appeared medieval, surrounded by fields of potatoes, corn, wheat, cabbages and pumpkin. Unfortunately, it was behind the German lines ...

And soon to become rubble.

Ned sat in the tunnel twenty feet below the Sugarloaf and almost directly under a section of the German front line. He was anxious. He had lost his nerve of late and had an eerie feeling all was not well. For days now the men had dug in silence. The tunnel floor being covered in a carpet of sandbags to dull sound of the men scratching and gouging at the Flanders clay, rather than hacking at it noisily with picks. For it was suspected the enemy were doing exactly the same. Only the day before one of their *listeners* thought he heard creaky truck wheels nearby. Ned came up with a listening device, an eighteen-pound shell case with a bayonet running through the base. The lid was the lid of a tin cigarette case and was connected to a wire to the top of the shell case. The device was placed flat against the wall. With one man holding the tin to one ear, any enemy digging nearby would be heard. But now the bombardment above made listening difficult.

***

Meanwhile above, both the Australian and British infantry prepared for a major attack, the plan being to break through the German front line and take the villages of Fromelles and Auber; to make it impossible for the German's to move further into France.

They would go 'over the top', bayonets fixed, at 6pm.

Lieutenant-General Hacking had the men, the artillery and ammunition for a four-thousand yard front. But plans changed constantly and Brigadier-General Harold 'Pompey' Elliot, the Australian commander, and also a veteran of the Gallipoli landing, had been given only two and a half days to prepare his men for this major attack; even after airing his grievances to Field Marshal Haig.

On the 17th and 18th of July the Royal Engineers laid duck-boards and tramways to the front line to bring up equipment; rifle and machine-gun ammunition, sandbags, explosives, scaling ladders, digging tools, portable foot bridges and all the heavy hardware required to win a battle. Telephone cables had to be buried and regimental HQs set up. The artillery also had to be brought forward and new emplacements dug. It was exhausting work.

All very well. But the Germans had occupied this part of the line for nearly two years now. They were well entrenched and knew the terrain intimately. The allies did not.

The Germans had built a tram network to bring in huge amounts of hardware. They had built a parallel line alongside the front line trenches with tramlines branching off towards the rear. These supply lines joined up with supply depots where horse-drawn or petrol-driven vehicles could collect supplies from the commandeered French rail system. They had buried a telephone network for communication and also electric cables for lighting, powering water pumps, concrete-mixing stations and other amenities. Put simply, they were too well prepared. And old cavalry generals wanted to pit foot soldiers against a vicious, well-armed adversary.

***

While the Australians laboured into the previous nights, Ned and his mates dug two serious tunnels towards the German lines.

Now, on the morning of the 19th, Brigadier-General Elliot watched the German front line through his binoculars. He had never seen anything like this at Gallipoli; hundreds of heavy artillery pieces firing all at once. He watched the sixty-pounders explode causing huge upheavals in the ground while allied shells shrieked overhead and, hopefully, weakened the German front line.

After the massive bombardment many enemy lay dead behind the lines. But thousands and thousands more waited in their concrete bunkers, deep dugouts and bungalows safe underground. Now with the shelling ceased, these men climbed from their hiding places and manned their machine guns in secret.

Waiting ... while their own artillery retaliated causing havoc with their attacker's preparations.

CHAPTER TWENTY
MEET THE ANTI-CHRIST

4.55pm

Although it was suspected it could happen, no one was prepared. The explosion was a dull thud, not a large charge by any means, but the tunnel ahead of Ned collapsed trapping and killing the five sappers in the front line. Ned was the only one at 'D' stage on the Royal Engineer's plan – where he prepared detonators by the light of a small kerosene lantern. The collapse was followed by muffled shouting and instantly the wall of the trench next to him caved in. Ned was defenceless, confronted by three enemy sappers, all training pistols directly at him.

'Hande, wo wir sie sehen konnen,' the leader, a sergeant, shouted. *Hands where we can see them.* 'Schnell, schnell!'

Ned knew no German but he understood. *Bloody oath he understood!* Slowly, deliberately, Ned put his hands in the air. The second man pushed through the opening grabbing Ned's arm roughly, pressing his pistol into Ned's cheek. He touched him down looking for weapons. He unsheathed Ned's bayonet strapped to his hip as a dagger, threw it aside and shoved Ned into their own tunnel. Already Ned heard voices, fellow diggers, rushing in to investigate. He was about to scream a warning when the first man slammed his luger grip into Ned's face chipping a tooth, drawing blood. The third German pushed Ned aside and heaved two grenades down the Australian's tunnel.

'Lauf,' the leader shouted. 'Lauf, schnell!'

Ned was forced onto his hands and knees and, in single file, one enemy in front and two behind, they crawled some distance in total darkness. Ned guessed they traversed forty, fifty feet through this claustrophobic passageway, much of it an un-shored *raw* tunnel relying on the strength of the clay. Minutes later Ned felt a welcome breeze. A fresh draught in off the battlefield. The tunnellers entered an ill-lit chamber above their narrow passage; a chamber some twelve feet by twelve to which they gained access by climbing a wooden ladder.

Ned wiped his bleeding lip on his sleeve and looked blankly at a tall thin-lipped middle-aged officer with purple blotches over his cheeks.

'Ah … was haben wir den hier?' *Ah … what have we here?*

A rapid conversation followed before Ned was led to the enemy trenches above where he recognised that ever familiar trench smell; a combination of damp earth, high explosives, blood and guts.

'Du sprichst Deutsch?' the officer asked Ned. *Do you speak German?*

Ned remained tight-lipped. 'Nein, naturlich nicht.' The officer prodded Ned forward. If Ned was not so terrified with the thought of his own execution he may have shown some interest in the enemy trenches. He did note the German trenches were better situated and organised than the allies. The land above these trenches however, were also littered with the dead. Ned knew this to be due to the British artillery bombardment that had been constant the past three days. These men were angry. He was trapped in a spider's web.

And Ned was nothing to them. Revenge could be sweet.

Now the big guns had fallen silent. Any strategist knew this to be the prelude to an attack.

'Bewege es!' the sergeant spat. *Move it!*

Ned was led through a maze of trenches some half a mile back from no man's land. They stopped at the entrance to an underground bunker. Finally Ned was shoved roughly in the back, almost tripping over a white terrier dog on the threshold to a stair landing, a wooden stair leading down to an underground bunker carved from the clayey earth off the main trench system. Inside was oppressively humid and a fug of cigarette smoke hung in a haze barely penetrated by the electric lighting. Waterproofed against the lowlands water table it was poorly ventilated. Ned could also smell schnapps and sweat. Maps were pinned to the vertical timber walls, with four-tier bunks on two walls and a dining table in the centre. A small makeshift kitchen seemed to provide all the comforts of home, with a stove for cooking and warmth. A chimney disappeared through the ceiling. Ned estimated they were a safe twelve feet below the surface. He saw one officer sitting at the table with four sergeants and two corporals. Although the officer had his coat thrown over the back of his chair, with his holstered luger beneath it, Ned recognised the yellow and geometric grey insignia of a first lieutenant.

Ned was prodded to one corner where he was forced to sit on the floor and exhibited like a zoo animal. The white terrier ran to one particular corporal, a man sitting alone, jumping onto the soldier's lap and licking his face. This corporal, a lanky pale man with hooded eyes looking older than his 27 years, rubbed the dog's belly and studied Ned with contempt. Had Ned known; he was an orthodox, unhappy disagreeable soldier, prone to argue and whom even his comrades thought odd.

'*Life's a struggle,*' they would hear him complain. '*So why change it?*'

'Name?' the officer asked Ned in English.

'Edward.'

'Edward who?'

'Edward Kelly.'

'How long have you been tunnelling?'

'Long enough.'

Ned didn't see the assault coming. He was instantly cracked on the head by the sergeant who captured him. Clearly the man was fond of pistol whipping.

'I said how long?'

'Ten days.'

The officer threw a clipboard with paper and a pencil at Ned's feet. 'You draw me a plan. I want full plan of your tunnels yah, their connection to the trenches. I want depths. Where are the batteries, the magazines, the officers' headquarters … you understand? Now draw.'

Ned pushed the board away with his boot. The sergeant lifted his Luger to crack Ned on the head once more but the officer blocked the blow.

'You do these thing for me and I'll see you treated goot. You understand?'

Ned ignored the officer and looked stoically at the floor. But the officer was a patient man and decided on a psychological approach.

'You English cannot possibly win thees war.'

'I'm Australian.'

'Yah, you Australian … you cannot win thees war. Australia. England. France. Imposs-eeble.' The officer bunched his lips a moment. 'Yes. I treat you goot. You tell me what I need to know. You owe these English dogs noth-ing.'

He looked at the white terrier. 'Like Foxl here.' The dog pricked its ears and looked at the officer, its head on a tilt. 'Foxl here strayed across from English trenches. Corporal here look after Foxl now. He's mascot for us. But who knows, maybe Foxl he is spy. Spy for English, yah?' The officer tittered coldly at his attempted humour. 'No matter spies. We Germans are far superior. Your generals are fools. We can see everything you do from Aubers Ridge, Ja.'

The corporal wearing the white blue colours for the state of Bavaria continued to stare at Ned, the hatred in his cold black eyes unchanging. Ned held his stare. *Bugger the bastard.*

The officer noted Ned's defiance. 'The corporal here was a trench runner in 1914,' the officer said. 'I am certain you know thees things, the trench runner running dispatches between trenches is the most dangerous labour of all, and he won an iron cross, second class, for his bravery. Show him corporal.'

The corporal continued stroking the terrier but looked coldly to his black iron cross pinned over his cold heart.

Ned wanted to answer, *why the hell are you telling me that?* But he remained silent. The other soldiers smiled amongst themselves and Ned had the impression this corporal was not liked by his colleagues.

'You see,' the officer continued, enjoying the attention. 'This corporal is clean-shaven god-fearing man, he is a non-smoker, he shuns drinking and he does not make use of the French belles. Yet he wears an iron cross. He is a brave man Edward Kelly. A brave man indeed, yah?'

Ned's mind raced. Death was at his doorstop. Would it be quick? Would he be tortured? A bullet between the eyes? Or maybe they wouldn't even waste a bullet on him. Maybe they would stick him with a bayonet like he did to the Turks at Gallipoli.

'So my friend,' the officer said now squatting in front of Ned. Squatting on his haunches he picked up the clipboard and pencil. 'So what is it to be?' he leant in close and Ned caught the not unpleasant smell of garlic and paprika sausage on the man's breath.

'Well?'

'Fuck you and fuck your mother!'

The blow that followed from the sergeant's pistol laid Ned out on the floor while the officer rose to his feet and started with his boot. First kick to the chest and the next to the head. Ned felt his eye close. He drew his hands up to protect his face.

Suddenly whistles went crazy. Shouting followed and the distant sound of battle grew into a crescendo.

The allied attack had begun.

The Australians had finally made their move at Fromelles.

The lads were out of the trenches at last. Charging the Hun. Bayonets fixed.

'Up, up!' the officer screamed. 'Der Angriff hat begonnen!'

The German soldiers filed from the bunker. 'Corporal Hitler,' the officer ordered the corporal.

'Yah, Herr Lieutenant.'

'Guard this man with your life.' The officer's eyes narrowed. He had *unfinished business with this bastard Australian soldier*. 'Guard this man well Adolf. I will be back shortly.'

Corporal Adolf Hitler stood as the officer hurried from the bunker. He bolted a bullet down the barrel of his Mauser and aimed at Ned's chest. 'Ja Herr Lieutenant. Es wird mir ein Vergnug sein.' *It will be my pleasure.*

If Ned had a watch he would have known it was 6pm; the very time they were to detonate the charges he and his mates had dug under the nearest German trenches, several hundred yards back towards his mates.

Corporal Hitler wanted to put a bullet in this bastard Australian's head. He'd killed before in battle and if he were to be honest with himself he enjoyed it. English, Australian, French; they should all die by Germany's hand.

Yes, he enjoyed killing, and would do it again.

But for now he had to *mollycoddle* this prisoner for the officer's pleasure.

The humidity in the bunker was taking its toll. Outside was pleasantly warm, sunny even. A lovely evening for a stroll.

Except there's a bloody war taking place.

The corporal sat once more and picked at a piece of jerky, chewing it as he trained an eye on Ned. Ned lowered his eye, not wanting to antagonise this soldier further. Not right now at least. The corporal shifted in his seat, pleased at the signs of subservience from his prisoner. Ned let his eyes wander his surrounding ...

When he saw the officer's luger.

It was slung over the chair in its holster where the officer had left so abruptly.

Outside the chatter of the Maschinengewehr 08 machine guns was incessant. Ned felt sickened. He had survived Lone Pine, now he knew his cobbers were being slaughtered overhead in no man's land. The smoke of battle was drawn into the bunker, along with the shouts, the chatter of murderous machine guns and the screams of the dying.

Hitler fidgeted. He was clearly uncomfortable on prisoner duty. A loud shout was followed by a thud. A body hit the landing. Hitler spun about. Ned dived for the luger. He slipped it from the holster. Safety catch off ...

When Hitler fired.

The .303 splintered the bunks behind Ned. Hitler wrenched back the bolt. Another bullet chambered. Aiming blind he fired as Ned clouted the rifle aside with the Luger. The bullet burrowed into the wall. Ned charged his adversary, pinning the man's throat to the wall, he jammed the muzzle into Hitler's heart ... And pulled the trigger.

Nothing. Click! Nothing.

The 9mm Luger was faulty, *that's* why the officer left it behind. For the briefest of moments, a split second, Ned looked his adversary in the eye. Eye to eye, Inches apart. And Ned sensed an evil he had never experienced before ... Ever.

In that split-second Ned fancied he saw Satan himself, so powerful was the hatred within. Ned raised the Luger and crushed it against the corporal's head. The dark eyes rolled back in his head and the soldier crumbled to the floor, unconscious.

***

Less than two minutes later Ned hurried from the bunker into mayhem. Dressed as a German corporal he weaved amongst the panicked Germans. Only a furiously barking terrier knew the truth. All about the two and quarter mile battlefront was wreathed in smoke from the heavy artillery. It afforded some cover. But Ned had to make his way across four hundred yards of no man's land to the allied lines.

Thousands lay dead or dying.

Not in his wildest dreams could Ned have thought he would have to witness such horror, not all over again. Unbeknown to Ned the Germans had counterattacked most of the afternoon, causing chaos in the Australian and British trenches. Also unbeknown to Ned the Australian infantry attack was failing ... And badly.

Survivors from the 59th and 60th battalions were bogged down in shell holes and shallow dug ditches in no man's land. Ned passed one man bleeding to death, both legs blown off. Another man close by, so damned close by, was victim to a mortar which exploded spiralling him into the air a dozen feet before crashing limply back to earth, stone dead. Ned passed an officer kneeling in death, gripping his pistol pointed towards the enemy, his head drooped foreword, where he was shot through the neck, dying instantly.

Ned just ran.

He ran for his life, running along the German front line. If any German gunners noticed Ned they would have been confused. For this reason he avoided being shot by the enemy.

As the smoke lifted most of the German machine guns had a clear shot from Sugarloaf, with other machine gun posts on both flanks mowing down advancing soldiers in a cross fire. It was futile. Another waste of Australian youth. And the toll on the officers also was frightful.

The 54th Division did worse than most. They lost all company commanders and many junior officers in the first half hour, many dying before leaving their own lines.

The 54th's commander however, Lieutenant-Colonel Walter Cass, made it to the German front line without a wound and few casualties. He immediately set up a temporary HQ in a German dugout with a large dining table, armchairs, stove, electric lights and wallpapered walls. Clearly all looted from the French chateaus. A well-stocked wine cellar was also surrendered.

It was all so surreal amongst the death and destruction.

Cass bunkered down, but unfortunately, to the commander's east and west, the enemy held on to their positions. Now they moved forward, effectively cutting off the Australians in these captured trenches.

Ned dropped into a trench captured by the 54th. He was unarmed and it was inevitable that an Australian should capture him. 'Stand to yer bastard.' Ned froze. He stared into the barrel of a loaded Lee-Enfield.

'I'm Australian!' Ned said as calmly as possible. The digger twitched the muzzle. 'Hands in the air.' Ned threw his hands skywards but the movement panicked the soldier. He fired and the bullet grazed Ned's right arm.

'Jesus Christ,' Ned screamed out. 'I'm Australian.'

The soldier was having none of it. He attacked, driving the rifle butt into Ned's belly. Ned doubled over. 'I'm Australian!' he moaned. Another digger appeared and together they tumbled Ned into the captured officer's dugout. Lieutenant-Colonel Cass looked up from a table covered in German maps.

'Prisoner sir, caught him just outside.'

Forty-year-old Cass, sickened by the German advantage, glared at the German corporal. 'Shoot him!'

'Sir?'

'I said shoot him.'

'I'm Australian,' Ned pleaded. 'From Flemington. Edward Kelly.'

If this didn't sound like subterfuge nothing did. 'Edward Kelly.' If it wasn't so serious the commander felt he could laugh. 'Edward Kelly … Ned Kelly. Right. Shoot him.'

Cass's dark eyes were intense. His thoughts racing. He had an entire division waiting orders. Both soldiers manhandled Ned back towards the entrance and certain death.

'I fought at Gallipoli,' Ned shouted. 'Under Field Marshal Birdwood … Birdie!'

If Cass had difficulty with the accent of his own diggers the Field Marshal's nickname *Birdie* caught his attention.

'Jesus Christ man, what are you doing in that uniform?'

'I'm a sap sir, I was captured in the tunnels. I managed to escape from behind the German lines by wearing this.'

'Well get it off before you *are* shot.'

'Yes sir.'

Cass ordered the soldiers. 'Find Ned here a uniform before he goes back up top.' All present knew where that uniform would have to come from …

No man's land.

***

The unknown soldier lay in a shell hole weeping. Crying out for his mother. With so many thousands of dead Australians surrounding him, with so many bullets zinging back and forth it was not unknown for two bullets to collide head on. With the deafening roar of artillery, fire, smoke, screaming and the stench of slaughtered men, the war had taken its toll on this unknown soldier. The soldier had tipped over the edge into madness. Shell shock was a beast many men were burdened with. The not knowing; not knowing when the bombardments would stop, not knowing if you were to come out of this hell alive and if so, in one piece. Lying next to the unknown soldier in the shell hole was his dead companion. And slumped across the mud was the body of his commanding officer. Now here he was. Alone. Lost in a world of madness. A nervous wreck crying for his mother. Through the tears, the mud and the splattered blood of his mates running down his face, the unknown soldier did not register the behaviour of two other soldiers in the shell hole. They were fellow diggers stripping the uniform from an Australian cadaver.

'Who are you with Kelly?' Lieutenant-Colonel Cass asked Ned who was pulling on the dead man's uniform.

'The 5th sir.'

'You're a sap you say?'

'Yes sir.'

'Then get back to the fifth's HQ while you can. They're going to need all the saps they can get. Get back before Fritz counterattacks, and dig in soldier. Blow those bastards to kingdom come.'

'Yes sir. Thank you sir.'

Ned hurried to ground level. The scene in the trenches was worse than Lone Pine. Bodies from both sides lay two and three deep in places. Ned wanted to retch, but held back. Picking up a rifle and ammunition belt he climbed over the sandbags of the German front line and started across no man's land. Smoke from a bunker fire drifted before him but thankfully this stretch of battlefield was void of conflict. Instantly a sniper bullet whistled close by Ned forcing him to dive into a shell hole. He stumbled over a corpse, a fellow digger, wearing only underclothes.

No!

Surely he wasn't wearing this man's clothes.

Australian stretcher-bearers from Cass's captured trenches hurried towards Ned. They slid in the mud down into the shell hole also, and as the smoke lifted Ned saw the unknown soldier. He cried like a child, blabbering sentences no one could understand and calling out for his mother. It was truly pathetic. The stretcher-bearers rolled the soldier onto the stretcher and climbed awkwardly from the hole. Without a word spoken, the men took advantage of more smoke, and were soon lost to sight.

Ned leapt from his cover and ran for the Australian front line. It seemed both east and west the battle still raged and Ned estimated he was somewhere near the middle of the entire defensive front; an area the Australians had taken. But somewhere, well hidden, snipers watched his movements and bullets tugged at the dirt at his feet. Ned hit the ground, hiding behind bodies. The occasional shell burst or bullet sung by, but Ned crawled on his belly, worming between bodies of the dead and the wounded.

'Help me,' one man cried out in excruciating pain. But Ned saw his intestines exposed. There was nothing he could do. 'Help me. Please.' Ned crawled over to the man. He was a young infantryman. Ned's age. He took the muzzle of Ned's .303 and put it in his own mouth. He looked up at Ned, pleading. Ned stared the lad in the eye. *Please*, he begged.

Ned looked away and pulled the trigger.

When he looked back the action had removed most of the soldier's head.

Now Ned threw up.

***

The unknown soldier was finally delivered to a field hospital safe behind allied lines by the two stretcher-bearers. He had not a clue what was happening to him. He was assessed temporarily insane. This *war neurosis*, as some called it, was caused by continuous exposure to exploding shells. The man had succumbed to shellshock like so many before him. Not being wounded, he was placed in a chair, shaking uncontrollably, white with fear some noted. 'And a man suffering shock,' an orderly told Ned at a later date, 'loses his nerve and can't be relied in battle ever again.'

'It'll be Blighty for him.'

Ned knew Blighty was the colloquial name for a ticket back to England for recuperation.

'Many soldiers sent back to England with shell shock are treated like cowards,' the orderly said. 'No one understands it.'

No previous war had used so much heavy artillery and it was the constant exploding of shells nearby that caused this reaction. Lunatic asylums, disused spa and mental institutions were all commandeered to house these men. Solitary confinement, disciplinary treatment, electric shock treatment, shaming and physical re-education and emotional deprivation were all used as treatment.

None of them worked.

CHAPTER TWENTY-ONE
BAPTISM OF FIRE

Bes in France early July 1916

Marseille was a far cry from Cairo. Located on the south of France near the mouth of the Rhone, Marseille, or Marseilles as the French spelt it, is France's third largest city after Paris and Lyon and one of the most important trading ports in the Mediterranean. But there was little time for sightseeing as Bes, friend Janet and the Heliopolis crew were herded onto trains destined for Paris and then the Western Front.

Alarmingly the constant, distant boom of artillery could be heard a hundred miles from the front lines. It was as sobering as it was terrifying. The women had all heard the stories, they had read the statistics of the dead, the wounded and the dying. Now it was becoming a reality.

***

Guyver Air Field. South of the Somme between Soissons and Vauxbuin.

Setting up a Field Ambulance Casualty Clearing Station so close to an airfield was not the smartest of moves. But casualties amongst airmen were high and the top brass deemed it necessary. July 10th was a Monday. The medics and nurses from Cairo weren't even unpacked when they had their first taste of war in France.

In the distance Bes and Janet watched the huge airship. It seemingly hung in space like a monstrous hot-air filled sausage. They had seen pictures but never in real life and now, between the airship and the flying machines buzzing about like angry hornets, Bes was fascinated. All the nurses were.

They listened to the far-off pop, pop, pop of the Lewis machine guns as the French pilots tried to fly close and shoot down the reconnaissance Zeppelin. But the German gunner in his foreword turret atop the rigid airship was returning fire at a steadier pace; keeping the *hornets* at bay while the massive craft made its escape by climbing to heights the airmen could not.

Standing close to Bes and enthusiastically watching the action was French mechanic Jean Pare. 'Tres bon, oui?' He planted his hands firmly on his hips. 'Ees magnify-icent to watch thees airmans. Very brave, non?'

'Oui,' Bes replied. 'I mean yes,' Bes answered, without taking her eyes off the conflict high above, some three miles distant.

Twenty nurses in Bes's team from Heliopolis had been assigned to a medical camp on the perimeter of the French airfield. On arrival they had felt safe within a canvas marquee emblazoned with huge red crosses. Now they were not so certain.

With the airship out of reach the French aircraft returned. Minutes later the *hornets* grew in size until Bes could hear the whining Nieuport 17 motors approaching. They appeared insect like with their twin wings protruding from a wooden frame with a canvas skin, silhouetted against gathering grey clouds. With a range of 155 miles they had spent their maximum time in the air. Besides, Jean Pare assured Bes, he had identified seven enemy kills in half an hour from where he stood. Bes was mesmerised. One by one, five lightweight bi-planes bounced back along the runway to safety.

'Merde! Ou se trouve Marcel?' the mechanic yelled over the din of the dying propellers. *Where is Marcel?*

Everyone looked skywards.

One pilot climbed awkwardly from his open-air cockpit with blood running down his arm. He would need medical attention. Bes noted bullet holes in a jagged line through the fuselage where they stopped at the pilot seat.

'Where is Marcel?' Jean Pare asked again in his native tongue.

The wounded pilot and one other said they last saw Marcel climbing after the Zeppelin as it ascended. They signalled for him to return but he ignored them.

'Idi-ot.'

'Regardez!' Another French mechanic levelled a finger to a black dot high above. A bi-plane dropped through low cloud diving towards them at full throttle.

Enemy or foe?

The black dot grew closer and closer, the engine wound tight as a coiled spring, wailing its descent.

'Jesus Christ!' someone shouted. 'It's Fritz.'

People scattered. The nearest cover was the hanger two hundred metres away. Janet and the other medical staff made for the tents, trusting in the armour of the international Red Cross painted on its canvas. Captivated, Bes had left her escape too late and found refuge behind a horse drawn supply wagon.

The flying machine was out of control.

The screaming motor barely disguising the screams of the pilot.

Suddenly Bes's wagon shifted. The horses were spooked. Whinnying in fright they broke into a gallop while barrels and crates tumbled from the cart.

Immediately Bes was in the open. The warplane plunged towards the airfield. Bes froze.

Now she saw the pilot. Bes caught a glimpse of French markings. Instantly the pilot's screams were hysterical laughter. The plane levelled at a hundred feet. Dropped belly first to ten feet …

And roared directly over Bes. Bes felt a gush of wind. She heard maniacal laughter. And then the screaming engine climbing once more.

Suddenly the airfield filled with admirers. Men of the French flying corps rushed back onto the tarmac shouting with excitement, waving furiously.

Chanting. *Marcel, Marcel, Marcel.*

The French flying machine did one lap of honour before the pilot cut the engine and dropped gracefully onto the runway where he taxied up to the gathering. Marcel Arquette threw a leg from the cockpit and slid onto the lower wing with the grace of a knight dismounting his stallion. He peeled one leather glove away at a time before removing his flying helmet and goggles. His admirers gathered around him but he pushed through his enthusiasts, clearly attracted to Bes. Bes stood firm. She was stunned. Furious. Furious at his insolence. Angry he should be so reckless. The ace pilot stood an arm's length before Bes, and looked her up and down, wearing the smirk of a serial chauvinist. Bes was incredulous. Speechless.

'Bonjour mademoiselle,' Marcel Arquette bowed slightly. 'I 'ope I deed not fright-en you too much,' he almost crooned in strong accented English.

Slap!

Bes didn't hesitate. She stepped forward and gave the airman a slap around the face that even surprised her. The mechanics and other pilots cheered. The nurses gasped.

'Mon dieu! Mademoiselle. You have such strong arms, no?'

Bes could see she had knocked the young buck down a peg or two. And he *was* a young buck, her age at a push she thought.

Mind you he was devilishly handsome.

'You sir, are a reckless imbecile.'

'Imbecile! Ees French word, yes? You speak French?'

Bes had been studying French in Cairo. But now was not the time. 'So is idiot,' she said, and stormed away.

'He is rather gorgeous,' Janet said hurrying to catch up with Bes as she stomped back to the nurse's camp.

'Dangerous! That's what he is Janet. Dangerous.'

'Dangerously handsome I should think,' Janet said with a giggle. 'And my, can he fly an aeroplane. Wow!'

'I say, you knocked him back a peg or two.' Doctor Richard Pringle was impressed. Bes had only met the head physician that morning and she was already making an impression. Very tall, maybe six three, and skinny. Doctor Pringle was from Toorak in Melbourne. He had volunteered early in the war and was given the rank of colonel with a crown and two pips to sew on his tunic. At forty-three he was still a single man, of not particularly handsome features made less attractive with his shaved head, unbecoming for an officer. The fact was, like so many other soldiers of the trenches, Richard Pringle had suffered head lice back at the Dardanelles. And as the barber told him *the best way to get rid of the bastards is a shaved head and kerosene.*

Now, for reasons of convenience, or was it fear of the *bastard* lice returning, he chose to maintain his bald pate. 'He's jolly well deserved a good slap for some time,' Pringle went on about Marcel Arquette. 'Good for you Nurse Mulberry.'

Bes was a little embarrassed. She thought she might have gone too far. But the fact was, she thought she was going to die there for the briefest of moments.

'Thank you Doctor Pringle. He did scare me somewhat.'

'Well tally-ho I say. Now.' Richard Pringle looked to all the nurses who had gathered in the mess tent. 'Things get a bit hectic around here. But I am an informal chap and I insist you all call me Richard. There's a war on and I'll leave the formalities to the stuffy English down the road, eh what?'

***

Bes and her colleagues soon learnt that the Australian Infantry Forces were to take their first action on the Somme in a week or so. Loose whispers spoke of a series of attacks to be made with the aim of wearing down the enemy, for breaking through the German front lines was near impossible. Pozieres Village was strategically important and further north, Thiepval was mentioned. Key to these attacks would be aerial reconnaissance and aerial attacks to keep the German's Fokkers from dropping bombs on the advancing ANZACs.

'And casualties amongst the airmen is extremely high,' Richard told the gathered nurses. 'Shamefully higher than the Hun I am told.'

'Why is that Doctor?'

'Richard ... remember?'

'Richard! Why do we have higher casualties?'

'I'm told the Germans spend a lot more time training their pilots. The allies, sadly, take more risks.'

Bes thought of the French pilot Marcel Arquette and his recent foolhardy stunt and thought she understood.

'I have been told on good authority that the major push is to be soon, as early as the twentieth maybe,' Richard said. 'All the airmen based here will be involved and it is our duty to tend to the wounded, of which we anticipate there will be many.'

A tour of the Field Ambulance Medical Unit followed. There were casualty clearing stations, advanced dressing stations, tents for stretcher bearers, nursing orderlies, tented wards, operating theatre, cookhouse, washrooms, horse stables and garages for motorised ambulances. The average tented ward was eighteen feet wide by thirty feet long. Fifteen-foot tent poles supported the canvas where the cover fell away at forty-five degrees to six-foot walls. Thirty sturdy ropes hammered into the soft earth anchored the entire marquee. Apple crates served as bedside tables and Bes noted the camp stretcher beds were all blanketed with different bed linen; all donated or commandeered from local villages she was told. However each bed had an army issue blanket. Each tent ward accommodated a dozen beds with legroom only between each leaving the nurses a corridor from the entrance to the exit at the foot of the beds.

On the perimeter of the camp were open-walled tent shelters, six in all with red crosses on the canvas. These were the emergency preliminary examination tents, large enough for one operating table. From here the badly wounded were assessed before theatre, amputation or whatever lifesaving action the doctors deemed necessary.

The nurses' quarters were much smaller tents, with four women to each. The lucky ones had a few chairs or maybe a dressing table, mostly salvaged from ruined properties nearby. All the tents were stitched with huge red crosses. But the proximity to an airfield made them fair game.

Directly behind the hospital camp was a mobile kitchen. Huge soup kitchens were built to prepare hot food and where possible, transfer hot rations to the trenches. The kitchens were open air and under the cover of tents where possible. A corral maintained some animals for slaughtering and huge cauldrons simmered over fires in the open. Unfortunately these catering camps were occasionally hit by artillery and in that situation the only hot food a trench soldier could hope for would be bully beef in a tin heated by matches.

***

Before dark each evening the celebrations would start. The laughter and shouted coarseness of drunken pilots carrying across from the French airmen's quarters. Occasionally they ceased before midnight. Often they partied into the small hours of the morning. No one chastised the young airmen. Many of their lives were destined to be cut short. Pilots enjoyed a respect few of the boots on the ground could ever dream of. They drank wine, Chartreuse and brandy. They crowed about their kills. They slapped each other on the back and boasted about how many women they had bedded.

Occasionally Bes and Janet enjoyed a glass of wine themselves, for the local wine was excellent and cheap. And occasionally they would creep silently over to the pilots' wardroom at the rear of a timber hangar and steal a peek through the windows. More than occasionally they would catch the local prostitutes vacating the mess and returning to their villages with extra coin in their pockets.

'You must admit,' Janet told Bes one night as they lay awake on their stretcher beds, 'He is awfully handsome.'

'Who?'

'Who? Who do you think I mean ... who?'

'If you are thinking who I think you mean then you are talking to the wrong girl.'

'Oh really. I've seen how you look at him.'

And Bes was guilty as charged. She had seen Marcel Arquette on three occasions since the altercation, each time he was about to embark on a flying patrol, but he always threw her a wave and a smile. Bes ignored each and every one of them. Also, unbeknown to Bes, Marcel had caught Bes spying through the wardroom window more than once. At twenty he had bedded many French girls, a German, an Austrian and two English women.

'But I would like to lie with a kangaroo,' he joked to his mates.

'Here's one hundred francs you cannot,' Gabriel Bossier, a fiery red-headed Norman, emptied his pocket of coins and placed the bet on the table.

'One hundred? You miser Gabriel,' Marcel said. 'I will take your bet for two hundred, not a franc less.'

'Two hundred then,' the other airmen said. 'But it must be the nurse who slapped your ugly face.'

'Of course. Who else?'

'Then I'm in too,' Henri Vigneau fetched the money from his purse. By the time the bets were all laid Marcel had gambled one thousand francs on his own sexual prowess.

***

The next day. July 10th.

'Bes Mulberry isn't it?'

Bes turned sharply as her name was called. Marcel Arquette stood back from Bes's tent, dressed smartly in a clean uniform with his hands behind his back. 'Bonjour mademoiselle.'

'What do you want?' she asked sharply.

'I just want to apologise ... apologise for my be-havior the other day.' Bes was impressed with the man's grasp of English and dearly wanted to test her French but was not confident. Not yet. 'Yes well,' Bes maintained a stern face. 'It was a silly thing to do.'

'Silly?'

'Stupid, then.'

'Ah yes ... you call me idi-ot, oui?'

Bes stood proud, offering the meanest of smiles.

'Yes, yes. I deserve that word. Idi'ot. But I come to you now with peace ... how you say. Peace ...'

'Peace offering.'

'Yes, yes. Peace offering. Et voila!' Marcel produced a posy of flowers from behind his back. 'Here.' He stepped forward and reached out with his offering.

'Where did you steal those?' Bes said, refusing the gift. 'From someone's window box?'

Marcel feigned shock and horror, then grinned. 'I did actually, but thees, thees,' he said taking a chocolate bar from his pocket, 'I bought in the village with my own money.'

Chocolate. Bes hadn't eaten chocolate since Cairo. She reached over and took both the posy and the chocolate. 'Thank you,' she said bluntly.

'Well?' Marcel smiled.

'Well what?'

'Well will you for-give me mademoiselle? I am so sor-ree I frighten you, but you must realise I was full of excite-e-ment for shooting down the enemy.'

'Yes, well don't do it again.'

'Non non, never. Can I call you Bes mademoiselle?'

'If you must.'

'Yes, I must. And you call me Marcel.'

Bes was warming to the young pilot. He was genuinely remorseful for his behaviour and it was all done and dusted and ... *he was frightfully handsome.*

'Au revoir Marcel.'

'No au revoir mademoiselle, you say bonne nuit.'

'Yes of course. Bonne nuit.' Bes turned to return to her tent ...

'Pard-on ... Bes.'

'Yes?'

'Tomorrow I have ... *trois patrouilles* ... ah three patrols over Amiens yes. Amiens and Pozierres and St Quintin but I will be on the ground après midi ... late afternoon. Please, it would please me muchly if you would join me in the vill-age for evening ... ah ... *mange* ... ah, eat ... dinner I think you say?'

'Oh I don't think ...'

'Of course she will!' Janet appeared, throwing back the flaps to their tent. 'You'd love to wouldn't you Bes?' Bes gave Janet a death stare. 'Bes?' Janet said with less confidence.

Bes sighed, turning back to the young airman. She looked to the posy and rolled the chocolate bar in her hand. 'Early you say?'

'Oui, yes. I can borrow my friend's motorbike and we can be in vill-age by six.'

Bes had seen enough artillery-bombarded villages to experience its sobering effect, and memories of her own home, after that terrible explosion on Boxing Day flooded back as if it were yesterday. Bouclé was a tiny village of two hundred people, thereabouts, but as at July 1916 it was not strategically significant and was well behind the allied front lines. It boasted a bakery, a blacksmith, an inn, two chapels, a butcher and various tradesmen who worked from their homes; namely a cobbler and a seamstress. Cheese and fresh milk could be obtained at a small dairy farm on the eastern extremities of the village.

Marcel parked the 1904 Peugeot motorcycle behind the inn and entered the premises through the backdoor where he ushered Bes directly to the small parlour. They were the only patrons in the room. Three older men drank quietly in the bar next door.

Bes was chuffed. A small table for two was pushed hard against the parlour window with the view across the paddocks. A half-burnt candle poked into a bottle smoked and crackled while melted wax dribbled down the neck where it set like tears. A red tablecloth showcased two white dinner plates and bone handled cutlery.

'You like?' Marcel asked as he pulled Bes's chair out from under the table and waved a theatrical hand for her to sit.

Bes maintained a measure of haughtiness. 'Yes ... very impressive.' Bes sat. Marcel fetched a bottle of red wine already opened and placed on the small parlour bar by a jolly and friendly innkeeper who was determined to keep a low profile. Bes wondered if he had been paid to do so. Marcel poured two glasses. 'Theese wine ees from Bordeaux,' Marcel noted, pouring two glasses.

'That's south is it not?'

'Oui, yes. Ees south west, on the ... *cote du golfe de Gascogne.*'

Bes had only drunk white wine in the past but found the red wine surprisingly agreeable. The innkeeper placed a basket of freshly baked baguette on the table with butter. Bes didn't hold back. She hadn't had butter since Cairo, and that was made from goat's milk. The fat salty delicacy brought back memories of home and Bes considered how so many things are taken for granted. But it was the rich red wine sauce the rabbit was cooked in that softened her attitude towards this handsome Frenchman. He said he shot the rabbit himself, but Bes did not believe that for one moment.

Marcel spoke of his adventures in the sky telling Bes he had been flying for three months now. He had shot down nine German aircraft, he said, and told of how he and two others brought down a reconnaissance Zeppelin last month.

'I could feel the heat from ... from 'alf a mile ... as the hydrogen gas she explode into flames.' Bes thought if he doesn't stop talking she would eat the entire rabbit herself. 'And I see the pilot and crew, they jump from the flames ... one thousand feet they fall to ground.' And Marcel slapped his hands together to simulate impact.

'Oh, how awful.'

'Awful? What this word awful?'

'Terrible. Sad.'

'No terrible. No sad. Thees bast-ard Hun they come to my country and kill women and children. Bast-ard. I kill all of them. More wine. Drink.' Marcel drained his glass like it was beer and slopped two more. Flying aircraft and facing the enemy high above the battlefield made men of boys, but occasionally the boy showed through when their boots were on the ground. The boasting bravado, Bes put down to his youth, reminding herself he was about her age, twenty.

'The Hun, he outnumbers our aircraft three to our two,' Marcel went on. 'And they have better command posts, yes. But we allies are superior fighters in the air.' Marcel drank deeply and wiped red wine staining his lips. 'Especially *nous Français* ... ah ... we French, *Oui*? Best fighters up there,' and

Marcel stabbed a finger towards the ceiling. He leant forward as if he was to part with a secret. 'I tell you true, some-theen else about Anglais pilots.'

'Yes?'

'I am told eighty per cent of Anglais pilot casualties are pilots what fly less than twenty patrols.'

'Really?'

'Really. They are overworked, flying several patrols a day, for weeks and months on end. Unless they were killed first. Many many Anglais airmens are unskilled.'

Marcel forked a large piece of purple rabbit meat from the pot, slopping gravy on the tablecloth before cutting it in two and shovelling a chunk into his mouth. 'I tell you some-theen else mademoiselle Bes,' he said mulching meat. His table manners were hardly gentlemanly. '*Nous Français*, we manufacture more flying machines and faster than the Germans also.'

'Who? The French?'

'Oui. Even the Eng-leesh are dependent on *Français* ... ah ... how you said ... engine, yes. Engine and aircraft frames. They had only sixty planes in August 1914. But Bretagne has a grand industrial base, yes, and will soon be leading aviation, that's for certain.'

'Crème Brulee they call thees thing.' One shallow stone crock was placed on the table between them by the innkeeper. Two spoons. Marcel took up one spoon and tapped the layer of toffee crust still smoking around the edges, atop the egg custard.

'Here ... open mouth.'

Before Bes could protest Marcel reached across the table and spooned the custard into her mouth. It was either that or wear the delicious sweet down her bodice. The warm egg and cream vanilla bean custard was the best Bes had ever tasted, and the toffee was a perfect accompaniment.

'*Tres bon, oui?*'

'*Tres bon,*' Bes smiled. She was mellowing to the Frenchman. And Marcel warmed to her smile. Evening gave way to a moonless night while the conversation continued well into a second bottle of wine. Marcel proved to be a listener after all. Life was not *all* about him. Bes told of her growing up in Sandy Bay, she told Marcel about Tasmania, even explaining the island's dubious origins. Bes spoke of her family and finally talked of the horrific Boxing Day that destroyed her family back in '14. Marcel was aghast. With all the horrors of war that he had personally witnessed the past year, nothing he could imagine would equal what Bes had endured. Marcel reached across the table and took Bes's hands in his. Feeling Bes's pain, his gesture was genuine and not the usual action of a serial libertine. If Bes was surprised she didn't show it, accepting the deed as genuine sympathy, *and god only knows she sorely missed it.*

'I ... ah ... I do not know what to say Bes,' Marcel's words were fractured. He took a long draft at his wine. 'And the po-leece, they never catch thees man?'

'They arrested a suspect but his lawyer got him let out on a reprieve. Not enough evidence they said, while they investigated further. Then he disappeared.'

'Disappeared?'

'Vanished. Took off. Ran away.'

'Mon dieu. Eet was him, you think?'

'It certainly looked that way.'

'But why?'

'I don't think we will ever know.'

With the second bottle drained Marcel blew out a huff and squeezed Bes's hands once more. 'Eet ees time for nice conversations, *oui?*'

'*Oui.*'

Energised, Marcel jumped to his feet and stepped to the bar. Bernard,' he slapped the bar calling to the innkeeper. The jolly landlord returned to the parlour. '*Chartreuse s'il vous plait.*'

Marcel returned to the table with a bottle half full of green liqueur. 'Chartreuse ... wait until you taste thees. Made by the Chartreuse monks who live in the Chartreuse Mount-ains.' Marcel poured two small heavy bottomed glasses no bigger than eggcups. 'Sante a toi,' he said, lifting the glass to his lips, he threw his head back and drank the lot in one mouthful. 'Ah,' he sighed. Undeniable approval. Bes sniffed at her glass.

'Smells herbie.'

'"erbie?'

'Like herbs.'

'*Oui, oui,* ees 'erbs, flow-ers and plants.'

'Plants?'

'Big secret. No one they know thees things.'

Bes felt the best she had for some time. Her initial chilled attitude had melted away. Marcel Arquette had proven quite the gentleman, even if his table manners were wanting. Outside the inn the July evening was balmy and Bes found she did not need the jacket and shawl she had brought along. Besides, the wine and Chartreuse had warmed her blood.

Marcel stood by the motorbike leaning his back against a corral fence built to keep dairy cattle in order. Bes joined him, feeling completely relaxed, and thinking this crazy pilot looked even more handsome, if that was possible, in the faint light spilling over them from the inn.

'I enjoy this night very much,' Marcel said.

Bes stood next to him, facing the paddock. 'So did I Marcel. And thank you.' Bes felt alchemy afoot. A chemistry between them that was catching her totally unawares. 'Marcel … I …'

'*Oui.*'

'I'm sorry I slapped you.'

'Oh that!' Marcel laughed.

God! Bes even loved the man's laugh; his mouth wide-open showing off his perfect white teeth. 'I deserve thees slap I am thinking.'

'Yes you did,' Bes answered with a cheeky smile. 'But maybe I shouldn't have slapped you so hard.'

'Hard? You call that hard?' he said, and laughed once more.

'Oh!' Bes said playfully. 'You want a really hard slap do you?' She moved across to confront him, restraining his wrists while she feigned another slap but Marcel pulled her towards him until they were face-to-face. Marcel straightened, drawing Bes towards him even more. Bes drifted closer still. Their bodies connected and the Frenchman stole a kiss. For Bes it felt right. She threw caution to the wind and returned the affection. Their lips parted and Bes felt Marcel's tongue exploring hers. This was something she had never experienced before and it sent electrical sparks through her body. They kissed long and hard. Marcel felt Bes's firm breasts push against his chest and Bes felt Marcel's manhood stiffen against her groin as he embraced her in his powerful arms.

Finally Bes pushed away. Against all temptation, against all desires and following her moral upbringing she must remain chaste this night. *Why?* She wasn't sure. Bes wanted him so badly, but thoughts of her mother and father looking down on her was sobering enough. 'Let's go,' she whispered.

Back at the camp all was quiet. The battlefields were eerily still. Even the pilot's mess was in darkness. Marcel parked the bike in the hangar, so as not to wake the camp and walked Bes to her tent.

'Thank you for a lovely evening Marcel,' Bes said quietly. 'I enjoyed myself. *Bonne nuit.*'

Marcel held Bes's hand long enough to know his position. He would be fighting the enemy in the sky the next day and continue his challenge on the ground tomorrow. But was Bes a challenge? He was loath to admit he had fallen for this *kangaroo nurse*. A pang of guilt cast a shadow over the Frenchman's conscience. He had let his guard down. The charade was over. All bets we off, were they not? Marcel Arquette the libertine had fallen in love.

'*Bonne nuit, mademoiselle Bes.*'

CHAPTER TWENTY-TWO
DUELLING SALIENTS

Mid July 1916
It appears I have a suitor, Bes wrote in her diary. *A Frenchman and a pilot no less. What would father think? His name is Marcel (and I'm certain he is Roman Catholic) but we have enjoyed each other's company for almost a week now.*

***

Two days later.
Marcel and I have become quite close and I would be devastated if anything happened to him.

    An old French lady came to the camp last evening selling silk scarves and I bought one for Marcel in the colours of the tricolour. He looked so handsome with it tight around his neck and said he would wear it always.

Writing a diary was invariably a release from the stresses of war. But the war continued in all its ugliness.

***

All generals agreed. The battle of the Somme – as the infamous war of attrition had become known – was wearing everyone down. It was wearing both sides down; bogged in the lowlands mud, buried under plateau dirt and sunk within a million shell holes filled with blood-stained water since August 1914. Hundreds of thousands of lives had been wiped from existence, nearly all of them young men.

Field Marshal Douglas Haig, commander of the British Expeditionary Force on the Western Front since 1915, had not expected the war to go the way it had. Desperate to rid France of the German invaders, Haig needed his army north in Belgium, but the Germans were too well embedded along the River Somme with their elaborate defences and fortified trenches and machine gun posts protected by reinforced concrete pillboxes. Consistently, any ground taken by the allies was challenged in counterattacks by the Hun, to regain their losses; for the Germans were under strict orders from their Kaiser Wilhelm 11, also the King of Prussia, who stubbornly resisted failure.

'A fish rots from the head,' Marcel told Bes.' And the Kaiser ... he is a big fish.'

The villages of Thiepval and Pozieres were of strategic importance. They were integral to the allied success and must be taken at any cost, for German-occupied Thiepval was situated in a salient in the British lines, and the British were trying to spearhead their own salient into the German's existing salient, along the Somme.

It was an impossible situation.

'Win over Pozieres and we will have the Hun on the run,' Bes heard an Australian officer, Colonel Murray, crowing. 'We will have the bastards on the defensive and the war will be won.'

'But at what cost?' Doctor Richard Pringle shook his head solemnly. 'Men are being torn apart by artillery and eviscerated by machine gun fire ... on both sides.'

Already the offensive had continued through the summer months, and now a wet autumn had arrived and a brutal winter approached.

'The loss of life is tragic, shocking,' the colonel persisted. 'That is why we must take Pozieres.'

'Murray is right of course,' another officer weighed in. 'Take the high ground at Pozieres and force a breakthrough in the German's line.'

All very well, in theory.

***

July 12th

Bes knew Gabriel Bossier to be one of Marcel's best friends and she didn't like or trust the redheaded pilot. For one thing, he knew Marcel and she had become good friends, yet he flirted with her whenever he had the chance. He even allowed himself brush seductively against her once, when they were forced to pass through a narrow doorway together, but Bes gave him the benefit of doubt. Now here he was with a minor leg wound and in her care.

Gabriel took Bes's arm. 'Vais-je vivre?' he said with a flutter in his green eyes. Clearly he was not in any pain. Bes now had a reasonable grasp of the French language but feigned ignorance. 'Will I live?' Gabriel asked again, this time in English.

'Yes,' Bes answered. 'You'll live.' Bes pulled her arm away with undisguised distaste.

Two more French pilots were brought in this day. One with bad burns and another, Joshua Dagenais, with a bullet wound to the shoulder. Dagenais' wound was stitched and dressed and he was left to convalesce side by side with Marcel.

Hours later Bes sensed she was the main subject of their obviously lascivious conversation and managed to position herself for a brief moment, and listen.

'Que pensez-vous de la pute de Marcel?'

Mongrel, she thought. If I'm not mistaken he said, what do you think of Marcel's whore? Whore! How dare he?

'Je pense que vous avez perdu votre pari, mon ami'

'Votre pari? Your bet?' Bes said aloud to the pilots. 'What bet?'

'Ah so you do understand French,' Gabriel said in his native tongue.

'Yes. More than you know. What bet are we talking about?'

If there was ever a chance for Gabriel to discover the truth and maybe, just maybe, win the bet, he said, 'Marcel made a wager that he could bed you.'

Bes felt bile rise in her throat. Devastated yet defiant, she rushed outside.

***

Marcel was busy in the hangar with Andre Auclair, aviation mechanic, a five-foot eight-inch Lyonnais with dark greasy hair and a dark complexion. The cowling was removed from Marcel's Nieuport and the two men were deep in discussion peering into its engine compartment. Marcel heard footsteps approach and turned to front an angry nurse.

'Bes?' Marcel's voice had suddenly lost its usual confidence.

'We must talk,' Bes seethed.

'Oh ... ah ... I was ...'

'Now Marcel!'

'Tu vas,' the mechanic shrugged. 'Aller ... Go.'

Bes, clearly angry, stormed away to where they had privacy. All the same her voice rose. 'I trusted you. I thought you were a friend!' she reproved. 'A friend!' Bes threatened a raised hand. 'I should slap you like I did the first time. You deserved it then and you deserve it now.'

'What are you talking about?'

'You had a bet with Gabriel that you could ... could bed me.'

'Oh that.'

'Oh, so you admit it then.'

'Bes ... I ... Jesus. That was then ... how you say ... fun with the mens. That was just stupid talk.'

'How could you?' Bes fought back tears. She wasn't going to cry. Not now. Not ever.

'Bes ...' Marcel stepped forward reaching for Bes's hands but Bes crossed her arms and stepped back.

'I really liked you Marcel. I thought you were different, but you're no better than the animals you fly with.'

Marcel stood silently, frozen in speechless stupidity. He watched as Bes stormed out of the hangar without looking back. What *had* he done? He felt himself falling for this Australian. For the first time in all his juvenile philandering life he suspected he was in love. Now this.

Bes immersed herself with her colleagues. Since meeting Marcel she had neglected them. Now she enjoyed their company and spent much of her free time with them. Anything to keep Marcel at bay. And Marcel did try but Bes was a tough nut to crack. Marcel had pierced her armour just slightly, but now the armoured plates were bolted together once again. She dined in the doctors' mess. Played cards with the orderlies. They even borrowed a horse and buggy and Bes took her colleagues to the inn Marcel had taken her to. But whatever the situation the war was commander in chief, and Bes kept a daily record in her diary.

I'm told three Australian Divisions of Anzac Corps One are now attached to the British advance led by Lieutenant General Hubert Gough, she wrote. *Gough is a reckless old man they say. He wants the Australians to attack immediately. But I've been informed the Australian commander, Major General Harold Walker will have none of it. He demanded he would not risk his Anzacs until adequate preparations were made. Hooray to him I say. For this reason the attack is re-scheduled for 12.30am on the 23rd. The Australians are to attack the village of Pozieres, not far from here, from the south, advancing in three stages half an hour apart.*

Bes learnt from airfield officers that, unlike their mates at Fromelles four days earlier, the Australians would be given a better chance of survival at Pozieres. They were to crawl across no man's land undetected in the dark of night, and then, when the whistles sounded they would only have a short run to the German line.

'At Fromelles the diggers were sacrificed, having been sent against enemy machine guns in the early morning sun,' Bes's source said in disgust. 'Fromelles was nothing less than a massacre. But this attack on the village of Pozieres will be different. By day break on the 23rd the Australians will have the village of Pozieres almost surrounded and the Germans on the run.'

July 15th 1916. Bes added in her diary. It has been two and a half weeks since we arrived here. The French airmen have turned out exactly like I suspected. And they certainly don't know how to treat a lady. They have giant egos but I will concede they are so brave. Not a day passes by without more wounded pilots being brought to us. Although we are primarily here for the airmen we receive many others, for all the other hospital camps are overworked. This war is a crime against humanity. So many wounded with ghastly injuries. So many dead. Each day at least one airman is killed or does not return from the patrols. Some days several don't return and we only hope they have been taken prisoner and been shown some respect by the Germans.

***

Evening of the 22nd

Bes was awestruck. It was as terrifying as it was amazing. British and German heavy artillery duelling with fierce shelling, a frightening display that lit the night sky for miles around. At 12.30am the allied guns were elevated to bombard well behind the enemy front line trenches. This gave the Australian

1st and 3rd Brigades a chance to attack, where they rapidly captured the trenches south of Pozieres. By 1AM the Australians had captured their second objective; south of Albert-Bapaume Road. However fierce resistance from the Germans to the east, slowed the advance. By 4AM the Australian's had extended their front line diagonally across the village south.

Bes couldn't sleep.

***

First light. Next morning. Over Pozieres July 23rd 1916
Bes watched the Nieuport 17s and the Spad V11s scramble, lifting into the wind like toy kites and rising steadily for the clouds. Their mission? To shoot down enemy aircraft bent on bombing the advancing troops on the ground at Pozieres.

As squadron leader Marcel Arquette was the first in the air. With his eyes wide with adventure he stared back at Bes through his flying goggles, with his woven scarf trailing from the cockpit like some heroic champion. Bes watched on, her arms stubbornly crossed. But despite her misgivings, Bes knew the German pilots were already in the air, and she made a silent prayer for Marcel. Bes made a silent prayer for all the airmen. They were certainly a courageous lot despite their testosterone-driven chauvinism.

Bes knew the German Albatross D.11, with their Daimler engines and twin machine guns, and the Mercedes driven Fokker DR1, were superior flying machines for climbing and conducting sharp turns and rolls. But the Frenchmen were superior pilots.

British airmen would also be in the sky flying their Sopwith Camels armed with synchronised twin Vickers machine guns firing between the spinning propeller blades.

'How does that work?' Bes had asked Marcel. 'Why don't they shoot off their own propellers?'

Marcel explained how the machine guns were fitted with cams with two lobes set at 180 degrees, directly timed off the drive shaft to match the propeller passing. 'Prior to this,' Marcel explained to Bes, 'the machine gun was mounted on top of the wing and the pilot had to stand in his open cockpit and let go of the controls to shoot the damned thing.'

'*Dangerous!*'

'Terrifying.'

'But the Engl-eesh Sopwith Camel,' Marcel went on. 'Thees two-winged flying machines have increased lift and are cap-able of make-een high G manoeuvres ... and with their shortened wing span they make sharper rolls and turns, yes.'

From a thousand feet Marcel could clearly see the German trenches with their tell-tale white chalk deposits shovelled aside. It was nearly 6am and Marcel and his squadron of French flying machines could make out the Australian advance. The Australians had been given lengths of pink cloth to sew on the backs of their tunics so the pilots would recognise them.

Then, as expected from the north, ten German Albatross D.11s dropped beneath high cloud, the port side of their fuselages golden with the new day's sun. They were maybe two miles distant and there was no knowing if they had seen the French airmen. Marcel signalled to the pilots closest who broke formation and climbed up into the blanket of cloud overhead. The other French pilots were quick to follow. Within minutes the two squadrons closed in on each other. Each flying at over one hundred miles per hour. Now they were upon each other.

But Marcel and four other Nieuport 17s were above the Germans. They dived. Each singling out one Albatross. The chatter of machine gun fire was instant, swamped by the deafening buzz of rotary engines.

Immediately three German aircraft were in difficulty. Bi-plane wings, wooden frames, spars and ribs with canvas skins and external bracing wire were no match for British Vickers machine guns manned by angry Frenchmen. Marcel dropped sharply by the starboard side of his target. He opened fire. His bullets smashed into the radiator and boiling water scalded his adversary. Marcel heard screams. He caught a glimpse of a tortured face ... blistering with the heat. And the Albatross spun out of control nose-diving towards the battlefield.

But there was no time to gloat.

Marcel saw the black cross out the corner of his eye. A black cross framed with white emblazoned on the enemy wing. The Hun was manoeuvring into position. Trying to line Marcel in his sights. But Marcel was a veteran. He made a viciously sharp right turn. This caused a dangerous spin but it threw him out of harm's way. Marcel corrected the spin into a steep dive. Suddenly he pulled up, climbing, gaining precious height. A fireball one thousand feet below confirmed Marcel's first kill. Now the Hun he had shaken off desperately tried to reposition himself … but had not a chance.

Marcel found himself in the perfect position on the climb. He was closing in on the underbelly on the next victim. He did not hesitate. He pulled the trigger squeezing off fifty or so rounds. They shredded the lower fuselage and as the fabric tore away it exposed the cockpit and a wounded pilot. Marcel had the briefest of moments to fire another burst before he whipped by his target … with only feet to spare.

There were no screams. The Hun had taken several bullets to the neck and face. The Albatross flipped, its canvas skin trailing away as it ripped from the frame. Marcel looked over his shoulder. His fellow pilot Rene was now prey. Two German planes were closing in fast.

And the Hun's Albatross D.11s had twin guns and they were faster. Marcel pulled up into yet another steep climb. Almost vertically, close to a stall. But using his height advantage he rolled and dived once more with a Hun in his sights. But Rene was directly in line. If Marcel fired now there was a chance he would hit his fellow Frenchman. Marcel's brief pause cost Rene dearly. The Hun on his tail opened up. The first swarm of lead passed by his right wing but the shooter now had his range. He tweaked the machine gun once more and pulled the trigger … a long burst.

The first two dozen bullets peppered Rene's wing. The next dozen riveted the fuselage behind the pilot's seat. But one unlucky shot caught Rene in the back. The bullet punched through his flying jacket …Skin. Bone …And heart, making its chaotic exit spraying blood over the control panel.

Marcel saw Rene slump forward, dead.

The plane went into an uncontrolled spin peeling away from the action in a death dive. Marcel screamed in anger. He managed a tight turn placing himself at right angles to the Hun, who, for all his success, had not seen Marcel. Marcel opened up in a furious barrage of lead. His aim was true. Marcel's stuttering Vickers burying several bullets in the starboard side of the Hun before at least two slammed into the German's chest. Marcel pulled up at the last minute.

It was close. Damned close.

Marcel flew over the adjacent German. His wheels skipping across the Huns upper wing. Marcel turned in his seat, desperate to locate another Hun. But his attack had been so aggressive the remaining Germans had turned back. Five hundred feet below Marcel saw Rene's flying machine pound into the earth, a crumbled skeleton of wood and canvas and he knew somewhere amongst the wreckage was his friend's body. Marcel checked his fuel gauge. Quarter tank, he would have to return to base. Searching the sky around him Marcel located nine French pilots. They had lost three to the Huns six. He signalled the closest to return to base. They would have to refuel and come back out again, for it was common for each pilot to conduct at least three such patrols in one day.

***

Twenty minutes away as the crow flies, Bes and her medical team had their hands full. Sixty-seven badly wounded were delivered by ambulance motor vehicles and horse-pulled wagons from a nearby skirmish that had taken more victims than survivors. All surgeons, all doctors were frantically trying to save lives. The exterior operating tables were saturated in blood while straw-filled baskets beneath the tables – rapidly filling with severed limbs – oozed gore at the doctors' feet. The Red Cross tents were frantic and Bes and her colleagues could barely keep up with the stitching, dressing and quiet reassuring words into the ears of the dying.

So it was little wonder Bes and the others did not hear the droning motors of two approaching enemy Albatrosses, each with six bombs pegged to their outer fuselage, ready to be unclipped and dropped by hand onto the medical station. The leading aircraft flew low. The pilot knew there were no guns manned at the hospital tents. He slowed slightly and dropped two bombs; each twenty pounds weight of high explosive. The other pilot flew over the airfield releasing his first two bombs over the main hangar.

Now Bes heard the engines roar overhead.

She looked up expecting to see Marcel waving back like a madman. Instead she saw the dreaded black cross of the Hun. Bes saw the bombs falling. She heard the Albatross climb again and would not forget the sardonic wave of the enemy pilot. The first bomb landed amongst the nurses' tents. But Bes knew all hands were in the hospital marquees. The second bomb crashed through the red cross of an operating shelter.

Bes was horrified.

Amongst the fireball that mushroomed from the target she saw cartwheeling medics and mannequin-like bodies flop heavily back to earth. Their valuable lives taken by a cowardly act. Instantly the north end of the hangar, three hundred yards away, exploded. Incendiary bombs had hit a fuel supply. Medical staff rushed out into the open. Outraged, horrified, they watched the two pilots climb and bank the craft for another attack.

But through the black smoke Bes noticed other aircraft approach. Her heart sank. *Surely*, Bes thought, 'they can't be bombing helpless patients.' But then Bes recognised the Nieuport 17s. Marcel was leading.

The two German planes were engrossed in a second attack. Marcel signalled his comrade closest, Gaspard. The other pilot knew exactly what he had to do. They had worked as a team so often they could read each other's minds. While Marcel peeled away climbing sharply, Gaspard approached the nearest enemy from the side firing early to distract him. Caught unawares, the Hun aborted his bombing to retaliate against Gaspard ... but it was too late.

Watching, cheering from the ground, the medics observed Marcel diving from above. He fired a brief burst into the upper wing and fuselage before diving past the enemy and managing a tight turn only feet from the ground. Marcel instantly pulled up into a near-vertical climb. He banked sharply and dived a second time.

And Bes could hear Marcel's boast yelling in her ear.

This is why they call me knight of the air ...

The Hun powered ahead for quarter of a mile before turning to starboard in a tight turn to try to attack Marcel. But Marcel was already on his tail. The vertical dive had increased his speed to 150 miles per hour. Marcel had the Hun in his sights. He fingered his trigger and pulled hard.

Nothing. The ammunition belt was jammed.

Marcel stood, yanking at the belt. Trying to rail the Vickers back into the cockpit. But it was futile. He was a target not to be missed. The second Hun flew in from the west, the sun behind him, pouring dozens of rounds into Marcel's aircraft.

Several hit the fuselage. The lower wing began shedding loose fabric.

But Marcel wasn't hit. Cursing, Marcel sat heavily, still on the tail of the Hun in front while the attacker on his port side flew close overhead.

Too bloody close!

Immediately Gaspard appeared from the southeast. He had the second pilot sighted. He fired a burst and Marcel felt the whistle of Gaspard's bullets pass by him. Gaspard's target banked to the left and like an angry wasp he counterattacked. Gaspard also banked ... But left his underbelly exposed.

The second German flew directly at him firing relentlessly. Twenty ... forty bullets hit Gerard. Marcels friend would have taken half a dozen bullets at least, through the cockpit floor, through the pilot's seat and through Gaspard. Marcel caught a glimpse of Gaspard spiralling out of control and then, seconds later, falling in a trail of smoke.

Marcel was sickened. He punched his dash. Revenge would be sweet. Marcel maintained full throttle. He was still gaining on his target. But he was unarmed ...

Unarmed yes. But dangerous.

Marcel decided to land on the Hun's upper wing. Force the bastard into a crashlanding. Speed wise he still had the edge. Marcel opened the throttle further. He could smell the petrol. His motor was screaming. Marcel climbed, sped forward and came down heavily on his adversary.

The Hun was totally bemused.

He tried evasive action but Marcel let his Nieuport 17 settle on the Hun's upper wing. The weight was too much. The Hun sank twenty, thirty feet. Marcel wanted to force the German to land amongst trees.

A certain death.

But again the second German plane appeared. He had to keep his burst short for fear of hitting his partner. The Hun squeezed the trigger. His shots were wide as he sped towards Marcel. But instantly two or three rounds hit Marcel's engine ...

His wooden propeller splintered. Sparks arced off the propellor shaft. The fire spread rapidly.

Fuelled by the rushing air the flames licked about Marcel's feet, hungry for the fuel tank beneath him. The second aircraft shot past and Marcel saw his chance to abort, save himself from his folly and land quickly as possible.

But the fire had other plans.

Searing heat rushed up Marcel's legs. He felt his trousers catch alight. Fire licked about his jacket and it was then he realised the fuel lines were severed and it would only be moments before the fuel tank was broached and he exploded mid-air. But luck shared Marcel's cockpit ...For the moment.

The tank remained intact. However the engine cowling caught on fire. With the wind feeding the flames Marcel was doomed. He managed to bank back towards the airfield. Marcel guessed he was only at three hundred feet. Pushing the stick forward he felt the craft drop sharply. At the same moment the flames blew directly into Marcel's face.

He felt his skin blister. The pain was unbelievable. Marcel closed his eyes but the flames burnt his eyelids. He jerked the lever and the Nieuport dived sharply.

Bes had seen everything. As Marcel flew towards the runway on a steep angle she could see him clearly. He was on fire. There were no screams in pain or fear. Just the whining motor, the thrashing of a splintered propeller and the shredding fuselage of a plunging aircraft in flames.

Marcel's flying machine hit hard. The engine mount burying itself in the dirt. Marcel was slammed against the dashboard. A fire team raced forward with buckets of water and sand. Bes was quickly on the scene. The fire was intense. Bes screamed his name. Defying death Bes pushed into the flames but two men pulled her back. There was nothing anyone could do. Marcel's face turned briefly to face Bes. It was a surreal moment. One fire-fighter managed to throw a bucket of water over Marcel. His face sizzled. His skin bubbled. And ever so briefly his head jerked in an unnatural dance.

'Marcel!' she cried out, and again she had to be restrained. Bes was certain he looked at her briefly. 'I love you,' she mouthed between uncontrollable sobs. Bes thought Marcel managed a faint smile. A smile through the torturous pain.

'Back, back!' someone shouted and the petrol tank, although near empty, exploded, collapsing the aircraft completely into a pyre for a French hero.

CHAPTER TWENTY-THREE
SAFE FROM THE GUNS

Five months after the Pozieres.

Days turned to weeks and weeks to months. There was no respite. Five months had passed since Marcel Arquette's dreadful demise and each day the pain in Bes's heart gnawed at her wellbeing. Each day the horrifically wounded were brought before Bes in what seemed an eternal parade of death and destruction; all the results of mankind's inhumanity. Nevertheless Bes persevered amongst the blood and gore that was a constant reminder of Boxing Day 1914.

Camp hospital supervisor Doctor Richard Pringle was no fool. He had heard of Bes's past, only recently ...

Everyone was just so damned busy. Busy for gossip too, apparently.

He was amazed at her resilience. Amazed how Bes managed to conduct her duties the way she did. But now he understood. Boxing Day 1914 in Sandy Bay must have been extraordinarily tragic. And then to have witnessed Marcel Arquette's horrific death; a heroic pilot of whom he knew Bes had once been fond and had misunderstood; it was time to act.

***

It was November and the mud and slush now synonymous with the Western Front was everywhere. There was no avoiding it. Bes brushed fresh snowflakes from her greatcoat and scraped her boots before entering the colonel's winter lodgings; a timber shed, which had been erected for him before the snows arrived, complete with a potbelly stove. Doctor Pringle sat at a card table writing under the light of a kerosene lamp. Bes thought he looked an old man, although she knew the veteran of Gallipoli to have recently turned forty-four.

'Ah Nurse Mulberry,' he looked up and over his reading glasses. 'Bes.' Pringle delivered a warm fatherly smile. 'Take a pew.' Having said that, it was not as easy as it looked. Every available surface seemed to be covered with paperwork. He stood his full six foot three and cleared the upholstered chair in front of his *desk*, which Bes recognised as a discarded chair from a ruined chateau; loose horsehair stuffing and all.

The doctor's smile had been exchanged for a solemn frown. 'Just doing my letters.' Bes knew he spoke of letters to the mothers and fathers of dead soldiers. 'Ghastly chore. Simply ghastly. But I'm getting a dab hand at it ...' And his voice trailed away. 'Since I have written so many.'

'I don't envy you doctor.'

'No ... but I must say I manage to make them all a little different and quite original.'

'Oh.'

'Yes. You see they write back to me asking questions, questions like who was he with when he died. Did he have any last words, and things like that? And I can hardly write back that the poor chap was screaming curses or was yelling obscenities while being held down by four stretcher-bearers.' Richard Pringle picked up a fluted-cut glass and was about to take a drink. 'Oh, please forgive me. Would you like a sherry? Major Griggs brought me back a bottle from Blighty when he was on a week's leave.'

'Thank you.'

The doctor fossicked amongst boxes of the deceased knickknacks and found another glass – also souvenired from a ruined chateau – and poured. 'It's an Amontillado from Spain. Very scrumptious.' Bes drank half the sweet syrupy wine in one mouthful and there was a moment's silence.

Pringle looked over the top of his reading glasses once more 'Scrumptious, what?'

Bes nodded.

'Well I suppose you are wondering why I asked you to see me so I'll get on with it. I'm assigning you and Janet to Queen Alexandra's Military Hospital.'

'In London?'

'Yes. At Millbank on the River Thames near Westminster.'

'But, Doctor Pringle ...'

'Call me Richard.'

'Ah ... Richard, I'm ah, needed here. We're all needed here. This ...' and Bes waved a hand at the correspondence piled on the man's worktable.

'You've been through enough Bes. Janet told me about your family. Terrible business. Simply terrible.'

'But I ...'

'I've made my mind up Bes. Please don't argue with me. And I'm sending Janet along as well. God only knows you need friends in this world. We all do.'

***

London. Early December 1916

Bes wrote up her diary when opportunity arose ...

However, the journey to London on the ambulance trains is not all beer and skittles. Us nurses have been put to work, and rightly so. We joined the evacuation with the wounded and sick from the casualty clearing stations near the front line. From here to Boulogne takes twenty hours. For the badly wounded this is a nightmare. One such patient was a badly wounded Royal Welsh Fusilier, Robert Penthouse. I was told he suffered his horrific head wound in a village cemetery when a piece of marble headstone shrapnel embedded in his eyebrow. I can only pray he will survive the trip. The orderlies could not transfer him from his stretcher to a bunk for fear of starting a haemorrhage in the lung and he had already been on the stretcher five days.

One officer told me he saw a cattle train used as an ambulance train from Rouen, with all the wounded as they were, picked up off the battlefield, with septic open wounds full of straw and dirt.

Thankfully our ambulance train is sixteen cars, including ward cars with thirty-six tiered beds each, a pharmacy car, two kitchens, a personnel car and a brake and stores van.

Bes wrote little about her voyage across the channel to Dover where the wounded, the sick and the medical staff were transferred onto another ambulance train destined for Victoria Station in London. Bes and Janet however, were shown to a regular passenger train at Dover Harbour Station, where they shared an overcrowded carriage with soldiers given a week's leave.

These men travelled *back to Blighty* with the mud of Flanders still caked on their uniforms and boots. Some even joked to Bes how they had shot a bullet through their hats so they could boast a near miss to their families.

One man spoke of his brother who had four day's leave, Bes wrote. *He had slept on the ground in trenches for so long that he couldn't sleep back in his own bed. His mother found him in the morning sleeping on the bedroom floor.*

Others were keen to return and kill the enemy. These men were lost in Blighty. They would have a hot bath, a good sleep and maybe go to the pub where they had only old men for company.

Twenty-two and a half months after leaving Hobart Bes Mulberry and her friend Janet Stubbs arrived in London, and fell in love with the big city.

I love London, Bes wrote in her diary. *I have always wanted to visit and golly-gosh, here I am. At Victoria Station thousands of new recruits were being loaded onto the returning trains. I couldn't help it notice many are older men.*

As the government had passed conscription, any childless male between the age of eighteen and forty-five was eligible to be called up for duty.

Almost as many women were there, to see the men off to war. Mothers, wives, sisters are all are shedding a tear or two. And the flower lady selling posies was doing a roaring trade.

Bes was also quick to note how many women were doing the work of the absent men;

From road tarring to traffic wardens and even railway guards.

***

Queen Alexandra's Military Hospital at Millbank on the River Thames in Westminster was a long walk when tired and carrying a kit bag. Bes and Janet would discover the underground train carriageway later.

The hospital was opened in July 1905 but by 1914 it was the British Army's general hospital. The elaborate Edwardian brick frontage showcased stone features including a bow window supporting a decorative gable to the front entrance below. Timber sash windows featured throughout and the nurses were advised – for those who required prayer – that there was a chapel at the rear.

After registering Bes and Janet were issued smart new uniforms. The British standard. Ankle length skirt and apron with a huge red cross sewn onto the bodice and tight fitting scarf-like caps. All white and nicely starched. They were then shown their lodgings and called for ward duty within the hour.

Only days later Bes wrote in her diary:

We witnessed a Zeppelin raid over London last night. They are terrifying machines hundreds of feet long and filled with hydrogen. But this makes them vulnerable. This one was shot down by a British pilot. The huge aircraft exploded high over London and we all watched and cheered as it came crashing down to earth. And Bes felt compelled to add a matter-of-fact footnote: *Marcel told me that Germany ceased all sausage production because the intestines of cows used for sausages were required to make the skins for the Zeppelins leak-proof hydrogen chambers. A quarter of a million cows are needed for one Zeppelin I have been told. It is hard to imagine.*

It was also hard to imagine, the war had followed them to London.

CHAPTER TWENTY-FOUR
ARCHIE ARRIVES IN LONDON

London. May 1917.

Archie's pioneering skin graft by Doctor Gillies was a success. Much of the cheek was now enclosed and the eyebrow was rebuilt although his chin and nose had to be reconstructed by the copper foil method. The painted result was nothing less than miraculous. Archie stepped onto the streets of Cambridge on February 11th 1917, fifteen months after he was wounded at Gallipoli. This action alone took great courage, for all the hospital staff were accustomed to his appearance, yet the members of the public were not. While his face reconstruction was a marvel of modern medicine, his face still resembled that of a mannequin.

Most adults, aware of the procedures through newspaper articles, were subtle voyeurs. Children however were a different entity completely. Archie held back the anger. He fought the tears.

With the silver Roman goblet and the erotica lamp firmly concealed within their cloth bag, Archie caught the train to Victoria Station and trammed to South Kensington, West London. Here Archie had read, in the Country Life magazine discovered in the hospital library, there were many antique and fine art dealers situated. Some still traded, in spite of England being at war.

Noel Langston of Langston Fine Arts, High Street, put the terracotta lamp aside, but turned the goblet carefully, reading the Latin inscription around the rim through his wire rim glasses. Archie took the opportunity to wander an eye over the shop. The furniture looked old. *Bloody old!* Had he known, he was looking at 17th century English oak, 18th century French tapestries, cabinets of fine silverware and pewter. One thing Archie did understand was that nothing was priced and there was plenty of dust. Archie guessed business was down; there was after all a war on.

If the dealer was taken aback by Archie's appearance he did not let on, besides the exquisite antiquity he held before him held his attention. 'Where did you acquire this?' he finally asked. Archie explained how it was found in a shell hole on the Gallipoli Peninsula, omitting that it was not he who found it and the fact it came from a tomb.

'How terribly interesting.' The tall lean man in his late seventies, Archie surmised, and smelling strongly of camphor, handled the goblet with respect, whilst dismissing it as nothing out of the ordinary. He was shrewd enough to realise this soldier knew enough about it for it to be ancient, and as excited as he was – knowing its rarity – he conveyed a lack of interest. 'You are not the first soldier to bring Roman pieces in here you know. I've other pieces dug in France also, including Neolithic tools.' Langston nodded to a glass cabinet with several flint tools on display.' Archie showed little interest. 'This too is a Roman piece you know,' he said. 'Possibly 3rd to 4th century AD. ... do you know what AD means?'

First mistake! Archie smouldered under his mask. *Do not talk down to me yer snobby bastard.*

'Of course.'

'Quite. Well that makes it around sixteen hundred years old thereabouts. The lamp is the same period.'

'Well they *were* found in the same hole.'

'Yes. Well. But that does not necessarily make them valuable. The Romans occupied England for four hundred and fifty years you know and Londoners have been digging up these kinds of things for some time.'

'So you're sayin' yer not interested. Fine. I'll take 'em elsewhere.'

'Oh I didn't say that young man,' Langston was cunning as a fox. 'They still have an intrinsic value. I mean this goblet would look fine in a museum and ...'

'How much?'

'H – how much. Oh, let me see now.' The wily old dealer studied Archie over his wire rim glasses before making a casual re-inspection of the goblet. 'Well ... I ...'

'I know it's silver not bronze.' Archie quickly added, hoping this would up the price a few quid. 'Well then?'

'I'll give you two pounds for the lamp, mainly because of unusual design and ten pounds for the goblet.'

'Ten pounds. Yer jokin' aren't yer?'

'No sir. I was not ... joking, as you say.'

'Ten quid. It's worth ten times that.'

'Twelve pounds. That is my final offer.'

'Fine. I'll take the two quid for the lamp.' Archie snatched the goblet, rewrapping it. 'But as for this. I'll go elsewhere.'

'Oh ... wait. I might have been a little hasty. On consideration I could go to fifteen.'

Archie kept wrapping.

'Fifteen guineas that is.'

'Guineas, pounds ... fifteen ain't enough.'

'Twenty!'

'Yer getting' close mate but ... nar ... I'm takin' this to the British Museum. I have a feeling it's as rare as hen's teeth.'

***

Days later. May 1917

Sergeant Garfield Gardener stood outside Langston Fine Arts, High Street, South Kensington. Blowing warm breath into his mitten covered fingers, he hopped boot for boot; the frost coming up from the cobbles being conducted through his hob nailed army boots like refrigeration coils. Despite the cold he was transfixed. On display in the shop window was the damaged terracotta erotica oil lamp he had seen with the goblet that afternoon in the shell hole at Lone Pine. He leant in close, his breath fogging the glass. Yes. Definitely. There was no mistaking it. The naked figure of a laurelled Roman, an orator maybe, coupling with a naked woman with pert breasts and large hips. Beneath the erotic pose were the initials QP. There was no doubt in Garfield's mind, QP for Quintus Pinarius the Roman general. He looked about for the goblet but of that, there was no sign.

Garfield tried the door. Locked. Being the middle of winter London grew dark early, shops closed early, especially antique businesses in a time of war.

He cupped a hand over the door pane, peering inside. A single gas lamp burnt at the rear of the shop. He saw movement and tapped on the glass.

Noel Langton saw the Australian soldier before the soldier saw him and guessed immediately the man was selling not buying. He watched the figure out on the street desperately trying to look into the shop and was in half a mood to ignore him, but the memory of the silver goblet nagged him. He opened the door a few inches. 'Can I help you?'

'I've some antiquities from Egypt you may be interested in.'

'Egypt. Like what exactly?'

'Shabti, nice large ones in faience, a carving of Anubis, a set of beads off a mummy and Ptolemy period coins. All small items I collected myself while in Egypt, small items I know will sell.'

'You know the Egyptian antiquity market by the sound of you. You had better come in.'

And not too soon, Garfield thought. *Freeze the balls off a brass monkey out here.*

Slipping his haversack from his back Garfield entered the shop that wasn't much warmer than out on the street. At least there was not the icy breeze.

With the artefacts spread on the glass top of a low cabinet Garfield negotiated the twenty pounds offered, up to twenty-eight. But something plagued Garfield. The goblet for one, he was becoming obsessed with it. 'Tell me Mr Langston. I couldn't help it notice a Roman terracotta lamp in your window, the one with the couple ... ah ... shall I say enjoying themselves.'

'Oh yes, it's a recent acquisition.'

I'm sure it is.

'I couldn't see a price on it.'

'It's twenty pounds sergeant.'

Garfield puffed out his cheeks and made a suitable whistle, but he had already made his mind up. 'Then sir, you give me eight pounds instead of twenty-eight and I'll take the lamp.'

'Really.'

'Really.'

'Very well.' Langdon crouched beneath the cabinet where he kept a small cash tin. 'And here's me just thinking how you Australians drive a hard bargain.'

Garfield helped himself to the lamp out of the window while the antique dealer fetched the eight pounds. 'You bought *this* from an Australian did you not?'

Suddenly Langdon became wary. 'Ah, yes. As a matter-of-fact I did.'

'I know because I have seen that lamp before. It was a stocky built man, five foot eight thereabouts about twenty-five was he not.'

'That would be him. But he had a face disfigurement.'

'Disfigurement?'

'You know. He has suffered a trauma and has had his face reconstructed. It's done with copper foil I believe, hand painted by experienced artists. I found it hard not to stare. You see them from time to time walking the streets. Some look awfully scary if you ask me.'

'Did he perchance sell you a goblet? With the lamp like?'

'He tried to.'

'Sorry,' Garfield looked confused. 'Tried to?'

'Well he wanted too much for it. He said he was taking it to the museum.'

'You mean the British Museum, right?'

'Yes.'

Garfield stood before the British Museum in the Bloomsbury area of London. The museum had opened its doors in 1753 as a public institution dedicated to the history of mankind. Garfield was in awe, only having read of its collections while in Egypt. Because of the war many galleries were closed due to staff shortages, however Garfield found a janitor prepared to be of assistance.

'If I were to ask for an item, like a Roman artefact, to be authenticated and say, evaluated, who should I ask for here at the museum?'

'Well that would be Thomas Bacon senior sir,' the janitor said, pleased with himself. 'There's the two of them what work here, Bacon senior and his son Thomas Bacon Junior. But he is fighting in France sir.'

Garfield was directed down a flight of stairs in the north wing where he found Thomas Bacon Senior deep in conversation with another staff member. Garfield stated his business. *Yes there had been an Australian soldier in the museum, three or four days ago. Yes he had with him a silver goblet of particularly fine craftsmanship. Yes, he tried to sell it. No, the museum has no funds. There is a war on you know.*

'So I directed him to Sotheby's who have regular auctions. My plan was to word up friends of the museum and hopefully someone will donate the piece to the museum. That's the best I could do.'

It took Garfield half an hour to walk from the museum to the River Thames where he found Sotheby's Auction House in Wellington Street, off The Strand. His blistered feet and the winter chill were only tolerated by the thought of seeing *that* goblet once more.

Once past the foyer Garfield found himself in the main showroom amongst what could only be described as organised chaos. Dozens of cabinets around the perimeter were filled with antiquities where the staff appeared to be in the cataloguing stage for an upcoming auction. However many others were engaged in packing crates of artwork and fine art. Garfield observed the high ratio of women to men. With so many of the auction house's male staff on the battlefields, Sotheby's was forced to employ more women.

'Can I help you?' the voice was pleasantly soft yet efficient and belonged to a society woman Garfield surmised. The young lady, not yet twenty, wore an A-line skirt with a white blouse incorporating sloped shoulders with a wide collar. As is the current fashion her hemline rose to mid-calf, saving fabric for the war effort. This was pleasing to the male eye, but traditionalists complained of immodesty. Immodest or not, the young lady's hair was less provocative, held back in a chignon. Garfield was captivated. 'Pardon?'

'I said, can I help you?'

Garfield was forced to jump aside allowing two staff members carry an alabaster urn to a showcase. 'My, you are so busy,' Garfield said. 'I'm surprised.'

'Surprised? Why?'

'With a war on that is.'

'War or not, business must continue,' the young lady was assertive and surprisingly businesslike. 'And good business generates profit, which generates taxes and we all know how Great Britain needs the money.' My, Garfield thought, we have a suffragette candidate here. 'Now,' the young lady continued. 'We have a major auction coming up and the fact that Sotheby's will be shortly moving from The Strand here to new premises at New Bond Street, Mayfair. So sergeant, how can I help you?'

'Oh, sorry. Ah ... yes.' Garfield removed his haversack and presented the oil lamp. If the young lady was affronted by the erotica she disguised it well and rose to the challenge. 'It's Roman I should imagine. You wish to sell it do you?'

'Yes,' Garfield lied. His own challenge was to find the goblet of which he was optimistic Archie had brought here to Sotheby's.

'You'll need to talk to Mrs Tunbridge, she is our Roman expert and should be able to give you an estimate.'

'Thank you.'

'It may take some time Sergeant ...'

'Sergeant Bennet.'

'Sergeant Bennet. As I said we are in the process of moving premises and we have another auction scheduled for Friday so things are a little hectic. I will be as quick as I can.'

'Sorry, but I didn't catch your name.'

The young lass turned and, allowing the faintest hint of a smile, said, 'No you did not.'

Garfield kept hold of his lamp, and watched the young lady weave her way through the disorder that was Sotheby's this day. Unobserved he moved amongst the showcases where hundreds of pieces were being catalogued and displayed. Cabinet after cabinet of Greek, Etruscan, though mostly Roman antiquities were being catalogued for Friday's auction. *So much history,* Garfield thought and muttered to himself, *and I have so little money.* Never would such items appear in the salerooms in Australia.

'Impressive, what?' an older woman, maybe fifty with a large chin and a wide mouth wearing excessive lip makeup that made her mouth appear wider than it already was, noted Garfield's interest.

Garfield turned. 'Impressive. I'll say.'

'Most of it is a deceased estate, Sir Wilbur Cadbury.'

'Really?'

'Yes. He was an avid collector but passed away three years ago. Now his family have decided to sell.' The woman studied Garfield briefly. 'You have the 'A' badge on your shoulder I notice. Anzac I believe?'

'Yes.'

'I lost my youngest son at Cape Helles. Dreadful business.'

'I'm sorry to hear that Mrs ...?'

'Cooper. The whole futile war is dreadful business.'

'I agree totally.'

'Are you now serving in France?'

'Yes.' Garfield tipped his head to his Red Cross armband. 'Field Ambulance with the twelfth battalion.'

Mrs Cooper nodded to the lamp still in Garfield's hand. 'Did you find that in France?'

'Ah ... no. It was found in Turkey actually, on Gallipoli.'

'Fascinating. All this killing and destruction and you find an old lamp. Roman is it not?'

'Yes, third or fourth century I'm led to believe.' Garfield had a thought. 'Maybe you can help me.'

'Oh?'

'I'm looking for a wine goblet, Roman silver about yay high,' Garfield drew his hands apart six inches. 'I believe it was brought in here very recently to be auctioned on behalf of another soldier.'

'Hmm. There is only one cabinet of independent lots. It wouldn't be an Australian soldier who's been badly injured in the face?'

'That's him.'

'And he wears a mask ... a reconstructed face.'

'Yes.'

'Well that would be in the cabinet I told you about, the independent lots that are not part of Sir Cadbury's. There.' And the woman pointed to a far cabinet at the back of the showroom. 'Now if you will excuse me, I had better get back to work before the boss comes back.'

***

The weather was deteriorating and the sun a faint orb behind black rain clouds rendering the gas ceiling lamps insufficient to light the entire showroom. Garfield shrank into the semi darkness, his gaze locked on the silver goblet, for there it was, lot 998, in the corner cabinet; an area neglected by the busy assistants cataloguing Sir Wilbur Cadbury's vast collection. Garfield checked his watch. He had been in the premises seven minutes. The attractive young assistant had been gone three minutes. Garfield felt a rush similar to a shrapnel bomb exploding overhead. He looked out from behind the cabinet ...

Young assistant? Nowhere to be seen.

Mrs Cooper? Busy with two others unwrapping a large marble bust.

It's now or never sport.

Garfield reached into the cabinet on the pretence he was inspecting the vessel. He raised it to inspect the base while surreptitiously scanning the room one final time. Garfield dropped behind the cabinet shoving the goblet into his haversack. The lamp followed. He swung the bag over his shoulders and walked as casually as he could towards the entrance.

'Oh Sergeant!'

Garfield froze. He turned. There she stood; the young beauty.

'Mrs Tunbridge is indisposed at the moment ...'

'Mrs Tunbridge?'

'Our Roman expert.'

'Oh yes.'

'She requested you leave the piece here for her appraisal.'

'It's fine ... thank you.'

'What's fine?'

'I've decided to keep it.'

'Really?'

'Really. Thank you all the same.' Garfield hooked his thumbs under the backpack straps and headed briskly for the main entrance.

'Sergeant,' that pleasant yet efficient voice chased him to the street. Garfield turned, his heart pounding. 'It's Molly,' she said sweetly.

'Molly!'

'My name's Molly.'

Garfield forced an anxious smile. 'Molly.'

Christ! He thought. *Now! Not now of all times.* He touched his slouch hat with a rakish tap of the finger.

And hurried off through the Strand.

***

London. May 1917. Liverpool Street Station.

As arranged Garfield met his mate Harry Barns, another field ambulance sergeant, outside the Liverpool Street Station. Terminus for the Great Eastern Railway. Harry turned heads. He was one of those quintessential shamelessly handsome Aussie diggers; tall, dark and handsome with a ripper square jaw and a country boy naivety about him.

'You took yer time.' Harry was hungry. He hadn't eaten since porridge at the billet at 9am. It was now ten after twelve, noon.

'Sorry cobber. Bit busy.'

'Oh yeh, an' I ain't?' Harry was also freezing cold. 'Jesus, it's brass monkeys. Let's get inside.' The two skipped up the grand steps of the main entrance to the station. 'What yer been up to any'ow, tryin' to flog that old rubbish you been cartin' about with yer?'

'Something like that. Tea Rooms then?'

'Yeh mate, but I just stuck me head in there ten minutes ago, and the joint's full.' He gave Garfield another reprimanding stare. 'Someone's late aren't they?'

'Come on digger,' Garfield slapped his mate on the back. 'They'll squeeze us in there somewhere.'

***

Liverpool Street Station Tea Rooms was packed. Then again, Garfield thought, every tearoom he passed was always packed. Since the Suffragette Movement there was a demand for moderately priced eating-houses and somewhere for young women to meet. Harry scanned the room. More than a hundred people busily ate, sipped tea and chatted, sitting in comfortable bow-back wicker chairs. The room was warm and inviting with a rare winter sun pouring through stained glass windows. Pretty glass shades hooded electric light bulbs hanging from the high ceiling. Every table had a fluted glass vase with purple pansies and yellow crocus flowers. The crescent-shaped buffet and cashier desk with painted panels and brass rail was adorned with exotic indoor plants. But it was the aromas of grilling bacon, frying potatoes and sugary treats like treacle tart and even chocolate that had Harry's belly rumbling.

Harry shook his head. 'Bugger, it's full up mate.'

Garfield surveyed the tables, when he saw exactly what he hoped to find. Two nurses sitting alone at a table for four. Garfield tugged at Harry's sleeve and together they weaved between the busy tables.

'Good afternoon ladies,' Garfield started in his most pleasant voice, sounding as gentlemanly as he possibly could. Bes and Janet looked up from their lunch, both poised with their Spode teacups mid-air. Bes looked affronted whilst Janet's wide smile gave Garfield the confidence to continue.

'Please excuse us for interrupting your lunch but ... well my friend Harry here and I were hoping we could share your table.'

Bes saw opportunists, whether that was true or not. She frowned and looked to Janet who by now gushed shamelessly at Harry. Bes kicked Janet under the table. 'Oh!' Janet twisted to look her friend in the eye before deciding to answer for both of them. 'Well ... why not.'

'Thank you so much,' Garfield continued. 'I'm Garfield Gardener and this is Harry Barns. We're both famished and as you can see the room is packed to the gunwales, as my uncle would say.'

'I'm Janet Stubbs and this is Bes Mulberry. Was your uncle a sea captain then?' Janet asked naively as the two mates sat.

'No,' Garfield looked confused, not seeing the connection. 'He was a postmaster ... oh, *packed to the gunwales*, now I understand.'

Janet, more so than Bes, suddenly felt awkward dressed in their nurses' day wear. The grey-brown ankle length skirts and matching jacket with a white collar and wide brimmed hats were hardly pleasing to the male eye. Harry noted the AANS brass badges. 'You girls were in Egypt huh?'

'Yes. And you?'

'Yep, but I missed Gallipoli. Garfield 'ere didn't.'

Janet. 'What an awful mess that was.'

'Were yous there?'

'No but we saw the damage. Bes and I were nursing at Heliopolis.'

'Fair enough.'

The waitress stopped at their table and Harry ordered eggs and chips for both himself and Garfield and extra pots of tea. Harry looked to the nurses' empty plates. 'And cream cakes for the ladies, extra cream,' he told the waitress. 'My treat.'

It took some smooth talking, mainly on Harry's behalf, but Bes finally warmed to the men by the end of their meal.

Garfield explained how he and Harry had ten days in *Blighty*, as the Tommys call any furlough back home offered by the army. 'And you?' asked Garfield. 'Are you here on leave?'

'No. We've been posted to the Queen Alexandra's Military Hospital in Millbank.'

'Oh, I see.'

'So when are you due back in France?' Bes asked Garfield.

'Flanders actually. Two days' time. Rumour has it we are to be sent to Ypres.'

Ypres was well known amongst them. Death had hung over the medieval walled city of Ypres since the beginning of the war. Occupied briefly by the Germans it was recaptured by the allies. In the following winter, at a terrible cost of life and property, the Germans reoccupied the strategic area.

And now Australia was ordered by the high command to fetch it back.

Ypres was not a pleasant place to be.

'Tell you what,' Garfield put a pound note on the table. 'Let's go to the electric theatre. I've never been.'

'Great idea,' Harry agreed turning to Janet. 'What d'ya reckon?' Janet was keen. Very keen.

'I don't know,' Bes plucked her calculated three shillings and ten pence from her purse and was about to put it on the table when Garfield took her hand, enclosing her fingers around the coins. 'Like Harry said, our treat.'

'Oh ... I can't ...'

'You can repay me by accompanying me to the moving pictures,' Garfield said, adding, 'Like I said, I've never been.'

***

After tramming to the Oxford Cinematograph Theatre, the four were able to lose themselves in a world of laughter, watching Charlie Chaplin starring in a film called *The Pawn Shop*. The following film, *Poor Little Rich Girl*, starring *Mary Pickford,* was more subdued however, with the story of a young girl neglected by her parents who almost dies of delirium, only to defeat her fears in the end.

'I think I could drink a glass of beer after that,' Harry said, lighting a Woodbine. What about you Janet?' It hadn't gone unnoticed by Bes and Garfield that Harry managed an arm around Janet's shoulders through the second film.

'I'd love a beer actually,' Janet said. 'Bes?'

'We really should be getting back.'

'Come on Bes ... Miss Mulberry. Just the one.' Harry noticed a flower girl peddling hyacinths. He bought two small threepenny bunches. 'Here.'

'Oh,' Janet smiled. 'Really? '

'Really.' Harry shot Garfield a wink.

Bes, not wishing to let Janet down, said, 'You're a smooth one you are sergeant.' She accepted the flowers and thought. *Janet will need a chaperone by the look of her.* 'Just the one beer then.'

'That's the ticket,' Harry said, pleased with himself. He took Janet by the hand. 'Come on then, I saw the Wagon and Horses nearby.'

'He's a bit rough around the edges,' Garfield told Bes as they followed the others, a dozen steps ahead. 'But he has a heart of gold. He's really a top chap.'

'You mentioned earlier you collected a few old things in Egypt,' Bes was fascinated.

'Yes.'

'What sort of things, I mean I was offered bits and pieces in the street in Cairo but someone told me most of it was fake.'

'Well yes. You've got to buy from the right people. I bought small items mostly, things easy to transport. Little figures looking like the pharaohs, statues of the gods.' Garfield went onto explain how he had made 'a few bob' on the side buying and selling.

'You're quite the business man aren't you?'

The nurses managed two small shandies each while the men drank two pints of bitter ale before bidding farewell. The beer had given Harry the Dutch courage to give Janet a peck on the cheek. Janet hardly held back. 'Say, let's do it all again tomorrow,' Harry grinned. Janet nodded her head like a pantomime puppet.

Truth known Bes enjoyed Garfield's company. He was an articulate and intelligent man who knew plenty about the time of the pharaohs. In fact he was knowledgeable on most ancient civilisations. Other than that, Bes wanted to remain friends, nothing else. For this reason a picnic was decided. The nurses would borrow a basket and rug and supply the food while the men brought beer and wine.

They met in Hyde Park at noon where a company of Irish Rifles was being drilled alongside the Northumberland Fusiliers; a noisy gathering sending the picnickers to a quiet pavilion where on weekends a band would play. Today it was deserted and although it was cold, the chilly breeze of the day before had vanished.

Cold pork pie, beer, cheese and pickle sandwiches along with a bottle of sweet French white wine Garfield managed to buy on the street. They all agreed that the pie was delicious and they were also unanimous on the jellied eel Janet had bought from a fish vendor that morning – it was an acquired taste.

After lunch Harry and Janet went for a stroll to the ponds to feed the bread crusts to the swans and ducks, but romance hung heavily in the air. Lying on his side on the rug Garfield reached out to touch Bes on the hand. 'Bes,' he said in a soft voice. Bes pulled away abruptly. 'Oh, I'm sorry … I …'

'Don't apologise. It's not you Garfield. It's nothing personal. It's just that … well … it's me. I lost my family in a tragedy at Christmas back in Hobart in '14.'

'How awful, your family?'

'Well my two sisters and mother. It was a bomb blast.'

'A bomb blast? In Hobart?'

'It was sabotage. The police caught the killer yet he was let out on bail on a technicality and escaped. He's never paid for what he did. My little brother survived but is maimed for life and my father died later in a mental institution.'

'Oh Christ! Excuse me blaspheming. That's terrible.'

'So I'm having difficulty adjusting you must understand.'

'Of course.' Garfield reached out to stroke Bes's arm, a sympathetic gesture, but thought better of it.

'I had a relationship at the time. But … well … I enlisted didn't I? So did he for that matter. Now I have a problem with men. As I said nothing personal.'

'Forget it Bes. I just enjoy your company. Just friends huh?'

'Just friends.'

'I actually have a favour to ask you, Bes.'

'Favour?'

Garfield opened a satchel he had brought with him. 'I need you to look after this for me.'

'What is it?'

Garfield withdrew the Roman silver goblet and explained its history. 'It would be safe with you here in London. I'm off to Flanders and from what I hear … well I don't want to lose this.'

'I don't know Garfield. Is it valuable?'

'Very, I should imagine. Bes, you would be doing me a great favour. It should only be a few months then we can meet again and, well ... I can take you out for a slap-up dinner.' Bes allowed a brief smile. 'Just as friends,' he added.

'Just friends.'

CHAPTER TWENTY-FIVE
A VICTORIOUS CROSS

Messines 1917

June 7th 1917 Messines was the first time the Australians and the New Zealanders fought alongside each other since Gallipoli. Strategically important, the Wyschaete-Messines Ridge was the main objective of this battle, for the Germans were using this ridge as a ten-mile long salient into the British lines. Nearby the medieval walled city of Ypres was in the thick of it. Australia's part in all this – the Australian 4th Division under the command of British officer Lieutenant General Sir Alexander Godley – was to capture the enemy-occupied villages around Messines and advance to the flat ground beyond.

For two years this attack was meticulously planned, with sappers digging deep tunnels, nineteen in all, beneath the German lines. Incredibly the enemy was kept in the dark. Zero hour was set for 3.10am, on June 7th. Prior to this, British and Canadian miners had engaged in subterranean warfare but when the Anzacs arrived they used these tunnels to advantage and packed them with explosive ammonal.

At precisely 3.10am the detonator switches were triggered.

Ned was there.

The earth lifted. Mounds of earth the size of small hills raised towards the heavens. The noise was unbelievable, heard across the English Channel it was said, and the sky rained clumps of earth the size of cabins. It was a cataclysm for the enemy caught totally unawares. The Australian diggers watched bodies cartwheeling through the air. Thousands of Germans were obliterated. Thousands more were wounded.

But this was only the beginning. This detonation signalled the start of a massive allied attack, advancing on the Germans while the enemy were disorientated, in shock and above all, demoralised.

The battle of Passchendaele had started.

Immediately waves of Australian, New Zealand and British soldiers under Godley's command climbed from the relative safety of their front line trenches and attacked the German front line through choking smoke and settling dust. However German machine gunners in the areas undisturbed by the explosions opened fire on the advancing allies. Although this attack destroyed any chance of a German salient, the allied victory came at a price – 13,500 Anzacs casualties alone.

Despite the fact Ned was with the sappers he was not about to miss the big push. Taking a .303 Lee-Enfield and bayonet he donned a steel helmet and joined the fray. Although the British 25th Division and the Third and Fourth Australian Divisions had a relative clear run to the enemy trenches, Ned found himself on the extreme southern edge of the battle. Ned was with the Australian 33rd Battalion under command of Lieutenant Colonel Leslie Morshead. Here, undisturbed by the allied bombing, the 33rd ran into determined German defences from beyond the flank of the attacking line. And to say the going was tough was an understatement. No man's land was a bog, a swamp of death and destruction. Deep artillery shell holes dotted the landscape and everywhere were signs of ruination.

Sunrise was still two hours away, but at 4.30am the attack was halted briefly, to allow allied back-up battalions to move forward. This, unfortunately, gave the German machine gunners a chance to regroup. By the time the advance continued the Germans were able to offer even greater resistance.

Ned was furious. He watched mates mowed down by the relentless machine gunners. Ned found himself in a situation. He had crossed hundreds of yards of no man's land without firing a shot. When he left the front line ramparts he was with hundreds of men. Now he was alone. But the fear that should have paralysed him turned to fury. Somehow, Christ knows how, he was positioned in a shell hole, lying on his belly with four members of the British grenadiers. Two throwers were dead, one bomb carrier was badly wounded and their NCO suffered shell shock, blabbering like a lunatic.

The fear on the face of the wounded man gave Ned strength. He crawled up to the crater edge. He could see the pillbox clearly, fifty yards away – thirty feet wide and ten feet deep. The walls were three feet thick reinforced concrete. Near indestructible for the artillery unless it was a direct hit.

Christ!

How on earth Ned got this close without being seen he had not a clue. Two machine guns inside the pillbox were mowing down mates a hundred yards to his right. They had no cover. It was a massacre. It was crazy. Surreal.

Ned could see the stuttering muzzles of the Maschinengewehr .08. Light rain steamed off the over-taxed barrels. No one seemed aware of Ned's presence. He aimed his rifle and squeezed off a shot, firing directly into the pillbox's firing-slot. The first gun stopped. Ned ducked. Immediately the machine gun burst back into life. Ned had no hesitations. He rolled back into the pit unclipping four grenades from the wounded Grenadier's bandolier – Mills bombs – pineapple-shaped killers that exploded into fragments of lethal shrapnel. Ned knew how to use them. He'd practised in Egypt.

Remove the safety pin, hold down the strike lever, and throw the bloody thing true and straight. And four seconds later ... Death!

Ned lay back across the inside crater lip. Squeezed off another shot directly into the pillbox firing slit.

Bullseye!

The gunner pulled back. If nothing else Ned had *scared the shit out of the bastard Hun.*

Ned cranked the bolt of his rifle ramming another .303 down the breach. He leapt to his feet and ran for the pillbox.

There wasn't even time to pray. The gunner spun the muzzle in his direction. Ned dived into a muddy ditch. He caught a gobful of mud and spat. A spray of bullets danced about the ditch. Ned counted to three. Aimed wild. Fired. And pounced from the ditch zigzagging towards the western end of the pillbox and out of sight. The machine gunner resumed firing at the easy targets. Ned slammed his back against the pillbox. He pulled the pin on a grenade and, crabbing his way to the first firing slot, he released the strike lever, counted ...One ... two ... And heaved the grenade through the slot.

Ned heard panicked shouts. He heard a muted thud. The first gun fell silent. Ned dived to the ground pushing himself along on his back with his boots. He paused directly under the second firing slit. Repeated the grenade action while the steaming muzzles of the German machine gun spat five hundred rounds per minute into his desperate and dying mates.

Ned felt the vibration beneath the earth as the second grenade exploded inside the pillbox. Instantly the gun was silenced. But Ned heard anxious soldiers trying to resurrect their machine gun.

Survivors!

Ned crawled beneath the slot, pounced to his feet and ramming another bullet into the breach he rushed the door. Booting it open he fired into the chest of the first man he saw.

A big bastard wearing a thick great coat and a terrified gape.

Ned cranked the bolt. Chambered another round and fired as another shadow sprang towards him. The man was an officer, hit in the face he crashed to the bunker floor. His pistol scattered across the concrete. Ned dived, scooped up the handgun and, kneeling low, he fired indiscriminately at anything that moved.

'Nicht schiesen! Don't shoot!' one man screamed in English. Ned blinked, his eyes adjusting to the gloom. He raised the Luger pushing the muzzle into the prisoner's forehead, forcing the terrified German against the wall.

'Nein, nein. Don't shoot. Please.' With the Luger firmly planted in the German's forehead Ned kicked out at the officer lying dead on the floor. But blood poured from a neat hole in his head.

He's goin' nowhere. Bastard.

'Ich habe Kinder. Bitte,' the prisoner blabbed.

I have children. Please. He pleaded. Ned smelt urine. *He'd pissed his trousers.*

Instantly Ned's face was sprayed with a mist of brain and blood. His prisoner's head exploded. An Aussie outside had managed a lucky shot through the firing slot. The prisoner crumbled to the floor. Ned heard a whimper behind him. He spun about and a German soldier who looked no older than sixteen stood with his arms high in the air. His rifle and ammunition belt were at his feet.

'I surrender!' he cried in English. 'I surrender.' Ned marched across the bunker, arm outstretched and jammed the Luger into the boy's cheek slamming his head against the concrete. The soldier closed his eyes and screwed up his face in a terrified grimace waiting the bullet. 'Nein, nein!' he whined.

A hundred yards away a second pillbox was murdering Australian soldiers. Shooting at the wounded lying in no man's land. The guns were relentless. Merciless.

Ned's hand was shaking in anger.

Suddenly, over the mayhem, Ned was aware two British grenadiers were in the doorway. He turned back to his prisoner 'Open yer eyes,' he yelled at the soldier. The German squeezed his eyelids even tighter. 'Open your fuckin' eyes!' Ned screamed in his face. The lad opened his eyes. Now they were wide. Ned glared into his soul. Killing the enemy was one thing but looking a man in the eye and shooting him in cold blood was another. 'On yer knees.' Ned buried the muzzle into the soldier's cheek and the Hun didn't hesitate.

'You,' Ned ordered a young a grenadier looking as terrified as the German. 'He's yours. Do with him what yer want.'

The first grenadiers took charge of the prisoner. Ned turned on the second soldier and tugged at his grenade bandolier. 'Give me the grenades sport.' Ned's eyes were glazed. Mad. He was not to be reasoned with. The soldier unfastened the grenade belt. Ned hooked it over his head. He rammed a fresh clip into the Luger magazine, and ran for the second pillbox.

But Ned had a hundred yards of trenches before the pillbox.

He holstered the luger, gathered four grenades and pulled the pin on each one. Holding them in a cluster Ned ran along the enemy trench lip throwing bombs into other machine gun posts. It was so brazen it was unexpected. Ned left a trail of death in his wake. At the second pillbox Ned dropped to his belly, pulled the pin on three more grenades and crawled like a stalking iguana. Ned dropped two bombs in the first slot and without waiting crawled to the second gunport. Three grenades exploded within a second of each other. Ned retrieved the luger, threw his back to the wall and shuffled around to the door. The door crashed open and a wounded gunner leapt out gasping for air. Ned shot him in the mouth.

Ned turned. A German came at him with fixed bayonet. Ned ducked right, managing to fend the barrel aside. The attacker tripped and Ned shot him as he fell. Ned caught the abandoned rifle and charged into the pillbox. Screaming obscenities Ned bayonetted the survivors.

But Ned was not done. Not yet. With the tide of war in the allies' favour, Ned had great sport running through the evacuating enemy trenches dropping bombs down any hole leading to an underground bunker where he fancied the Germans might be hiding.

With the village taken and the enemy retreating Ned had won the day. By the time his mates caught up with him Ned was standing on a pillbox wiping the blood off his bayonet with a felt hat.

Ned Kelly saved lives that day. No one could ever even estimate how many diggers he saved. But he would leave the battlefield a wounded man taking a bullet in his arm from a German officer before Ned put the man in his grave. Ned's courage didn't go unnoticed by the British or his own officers. He walked three miles to a dressing station behind the Australian lines feeling damned pleased with himself. Later a citation was agreed by all who witnessed Ned's courage on June 7th that he be awarded the Victoria Cross.

No one denied his bravery.

***

October 4th, 1917 Broodseinde Village.

The allies had successfully demoralised the German Army. This set the stage for the Third Battle of Ypres. But the following days the rains came. First drizzle, followed by showers and by the third day squalls in off the Atlantic delivered torrential rains turning the battlefields into quagmires. And the weather was predicted to worsen.

The Royal Engineers were exhausted; building roads, rails and laying miles and miles of duckboards to deliver the machinery of war to the front line. The mud of Flanders crippled infantry movement. Men had to pull one leg from the mud before they could make the next step. Men fell into putrid shell holes filled with brackish water and corpses. It was one door from hell.

A British war correspondent summed up the advancing Australian soldiers as looking like men who had been buried alive and dug up again.

The advance had already been postponed one day because of the weather. Now Field Marshal Douglas Haig, senior officer of the British army, and overall commander for the Western Front Allied Forces, was determined not to abandon the continuing attacks.

But with the allied forces having the upper hand the Germans were desperate to reinforce their forward positions. Now they hit their enemy with all they had.

And Sergeant Garfield Gardner, recently promoted to staff sergeant, was in the thick of it … standing in the most dangerous place on earth.

Garfield Gardner thought the guns had ceased firing. He was deafened by silence. But in reality a rare madness had smothered him. An artillery shell landed only yards away. This explosion he heard. It was louder than anything he had heard before. The ground beneath him shook. A clump of earth the size of a horse cart plumed twenty feet into the air. It was almost in slow motion. Garfield cowered, his hands over his head for protection. But the earth mound crashed back right beside him. His trench wall caved in.

And Garfield was buried under three tons of earth.

Thankfully he had mates who saw it all. They saw three others torn apart from the same shell burst. They had managed to dive aside. They heard Garfield's muffled scream … and he disappeared.

It took the diggers forty minutes to dig their staff sergeant free. Apparently Garfield was trapped with his head in a tiny air pocket. Two of the diggers pulled Garfield from the dirt like he was a freshly buried cadaver. Some tried to make light of the situation. A throw away joke. But this was lost on Garfield. His eyes were vacant. He may as well have been a cadaver. For Garfield the war was over.

Shell shock was a term coined by the battle-weary soldiers themselves. Doctors in the field spoke of the condition being caused by nerve damage from physical injury. Others thought it the constant exposure to heavy artillery bombardment. Symptoms included tremors, confusion, fatigue, impaired hearing, weakened vision and nightmares. *The nightmares were the worst.*

Despite the efforts of academic minds, Army doctors were having difficulty understanding this phenomenon of warfare. Unfairly, some medical practitioners believed shell shock was no more than the artful act of a coward or malingerer, suggesting it should be addressed by military discipline. So in the heat of battle Garfield Gardner found little sympathy when he cowered beneath a table in his tent quarters, his face taut with fear, tears rolling off his cheeks and crying for his mother.

***

Garfield in London at Seale-Hayne Hospital.
Seale-Hayne College, named after its patron Charles Seale-Hayne, started life as a training institute for the Women's Land Army – instructing women in farming during the war. But the imposing two-storey, red brick and grey slate roofed building, recently built between 1912 and 1914, was handed over to a Doctor Arthur Hurst for his ground-breaking treatment of these shell shock victims.

When Garfield came into Doctor Hurst's care he was child-like and in a wheelchair. Gradually, under the doctor's care most patients regained some sanity. Creativity was encouraged. The peace of the countryside in Devon was also a tonic. Doctor Hurst, a medical pioneer who understood shell shock, encouraged the patients to take up clay pigeon shooting. He recreated the battlefields of Flanders on Dartmoor to help relive their experiences; to face their demons and, much to the chagrin of fellow doctors, Hurst's therapies, in many cases, worked.

But for Garfield Gardner his past was a vague memory. His health deteriorated until one winter's morning, December 4th 1918, his body was found floating face down in a fishpond on hospital grounds. It appeared he was left unattended the evening before and had wandered to his favourite place in the gardens, only to die thousands of miles from friends or family.

CHAPTER TWENTY-SIX
AT WHAT PRICE PEACE?

1919

Bes woke in a lather. Sweat dripped from her forehead like wringing a wet sponge. Her pillow was damp and she was hyperventilating. Although she heard the detonation that shook the world about her, the flash had been secondary, exploding overhead like lightning. Catapulted against the back fence next to the kennel she had blacked out that horrific Boxing Day event back in Hobart in 1914. Bes never saw sister Frankie's body, torn apart by that terrible bomb. Yet the nightmares returned night after night, four years and forty-six days later.

The throb of the piston rod in the engine room of the steamship Marco *Polo* brought Bes back to reality. The vibrating calmed her. The judder of the keel from bow to amidships as the ship crushed a wave comforted her. Bes had grown comfortable with the old merchant trader taking her and her colleagues back home after the war. They were in their fifth week, crossing the Indian Ocean, but now, the closer they approached the homeland the more Bes was having reservations about returning home to Sandy Bay. So it was of no surprise to her fellow nurses, all keen to return to their families, that Bes volunteered for nurse's duty at The North Head Quarantine Station in Sydney; a long way from Hobart.

As if world war was not enough.

Australia alone had lost sixty thousand souls, mostly young men, to war. Now Mother Nature had further plans. Pneumonic influenza. A killer virus given the name Spanish flu for the simple reason it seemed prolific and widely reported in Spain before it infected the rest of the world. The virus mutated rapidly and constantly, spread by sneezing and coughing predominantly. Spanish flu was a highly contagious respiratory illness caused by the influenza virus. Categorised A, B and C, A was the worst.

Soldiers weakened by war, their immune systems struggling from poor food and sanitary conditions, were easily infected. And men confined to below decks aboard returning troopships for weeks on end were …well, sitting ducks.

The Spanish flu spread rapidly throughout Europe and the globe from October 1918. Its spread was impossible to prevent. Then, a few months later in January 1919, the deadly killer was first detected in Australia

***

North Head Quarantine Station, Sydney. February 10th 1919.
The ferry transferred Bes and six other volunteer nurses to the landing jetty. A neat and modern wooden construction pushing fifty yards out into a shallow bay in North Harbour. The Sydney quarantine station was a relatively small community of weatherboard and stone buildings dating back to the 1830s. It was settled on the remote Sydney North Head in a peaceful clearing amongst eucalyptus gums, semi tropical palms and grass trees. Bes found the jacaranda trees in full bloom particularly fetching. Long narrow dormitory buildings with their generous Georgian glass windows offered plenty of light for the inmates and shower blocks were bays separated by corrugated iron partitions.

The station was a short walk to Collin's Flat Beach and Cannae Point, landmarks of Sydney's immense harbour. Over the finger of land to the east were magnificent views across the vast Pacific Ocean. Sydney's northern beach suburb of Manly was also easy walking distance north, where the station shared sweeping views across to Dobroyd Head.

Bes and her colleagues were ordered into a straight line in the shade of a dormitory veranda, thankful they were wearing light linen skirts and blousons. They had returned to wearing bonnets after wearing straw hats in Egypt where the bonnet proved impractical; yet here they were in the heat of a Sydney summer and the air was uncomfortably still. Many had sewn their own uniforms together on the return voyage, and for this reason their dress exhibited varied styles of collars, blousons, skirts, footwear and headwear.

Doctor Frederick Wilcox stood with the head Matron, Matron Agatha Bridges, to welcome the new arrivals. The still air brought with it small annoying flies causing some discomfort, but not for Matron Bridges who swiped at the persistent pests with an African feathered fly switch. *No doubt a souvenir from Egypt*, Bes smiled to herself.

The doctor started introductions. 'Good morning ladies.' A varied response of murmured greetings was returned. 'I know you are all well advised on this world wide pandemic so I won't keep you too long before Matron Bridges gives you your duties. I would like to say how grateful we are here at the quarantine station for you ladies volunteering. We appreciate you have just returned from Egypt and France and understand your sacrifice. On behalf of the hospital and the Australian government, we thank you.' Doctor Wilcox lashed out at a particularly persistent fly before explaining, 'Because we are so distant from the rest of the world we have had time to prepare for this pandemic. Maritime Quarantine was implemented here on the 17th October last year, after reports of the Spanish flu in New Zealand and South Africa. These countries are also remote. Nowhere is safe.'

He explained how the first case of an infected ship arriving in Australia was the screw steamer *Mataram* sailing from Singapore to Darwin.

'We don't know what caused this influenza, but a vaccine has been produced that arrests the more serious secondary infection that is likely to cause death. The Commonwealth Serum Laboratories are manufacturing millions of doses of this vaccine, which are to be given to returning troops as well as civilians. Any questions?'

'Have the vaccines been successful Doctor?'

'So far our Northern Territory doctors have evaluated the vaccine to be partially effective in preventing death in the already inoculated individuals.'

Partially, Bes thought, the notion was terrifying. 'Doctor Wilcox.'

'Yes.'

'When were the first cases brought here?' Bes asked.

'Two weeks ago. You may already know that New South Wales declared the flu outbreak on the 27th of last month.'

Bes and the others knew all right. Sydney was like a ghost town with schools closed and all public events and gatherings cancelled. The few on the street going about business wore mandatory masks. To Bes it seemed like stepping out of the frypan and into the fire.

'However,' Doctor Wilcox went on, these precautions appear to be slowing the virus. Your work here, ladies, is invaluable. Wear your masks at all times, wash your hands regularly and be vigilant for your own sakes as well as your peers.'

The wards were stifling hot. Bes noted some electric fans spinning sluggishly. These proved to be hardly adequate. Although there was electricity the wards were illuminated at night by pear-shaped gas fittings. And with all the windows and shutters open in an attempt to catch a breeze stubbornly absent, the flies were numerous and irritating. Bes recognised the all too familiar smell of sickness and death. And the living smelt unwashed although the previous nurses did their best to sponge the patients.

'Masks on,' the matron ordered. 'No exceptions and keep them on at all times. We have lost fourteen men this past three days,' the matron said, and not too subtly. Bes would soon realise the older woman had a hearing impediment and speaking loudly was her only means of communication.

Most of the patients were too ill to stir, although some men vied for attention on their approach. There were two rows of single iron beds foot to foot with a central aisle.

'Water,' someone rasped. One young nurse broke away from Matron's tour to draw a mug full of water from a stone filter and help the soldier drink through a straw. Matron watched studiously. The nurse completed her task and made to join the others once more. 'Wash your hands,' Matron scolded. 'Now.' She pointed to one of several washbasins throughout the ward. The nurses waited. 'With soap.' The matron cried out.

Bes took the opportunity to look about the ward. Someone had put Pears Soap advertising posters on the walls to liven the atmosphere. Cheap decoration, she thought, but effective. One poster showed a woman in her dressing room inspecting her face in a hand mirror. Bes read the words beneath the image, *for the hands and complexion I use Pears Soap with the greatest satisfaction for I find it the very best*, and she wondered how many patients looked at this poster and thought of their mum, their sister or their wife.

They passed an operating theatre, which Bes thought more like an autopsy room. A narrow theatre table, built with a contraption of wheels for raising or lowering, was in the centre of the room. Iron wall brackets supported an electric hot water cylinder for sterilising equipment and Bes noted a shelf of various chemicals in jars; ether, chloroform and cylinders of nitrous oxide. There wasn't a great deal else.

Matron Bridges lifted her mask to rub an irritable itch on her nose before entering the second ward. 'Now ladies,' the matron *tried* to speak softly. 'This is D ward and we have eight secondary cases here.' The nurses knew a secondary infection was a death sentence in most cases. Doctors returning from the war had lectured the nurses aboard the *Marco Polo*. There was a reasonable amount known about pneumonic influenza, its contagious transmission and its symptoms – the body aches, muscle and joint pain, headache, sore throat, unproductive coughing with occasional harsh breathing – but very little was known about its treatment.

'The most common sign of infection is a fever ranging from 100° to 104° Fahrenheit that persists for days,' Matron Bridges told them. 'After the disease is established the mucus membranes redden from sneezing. In some cases there is a haemorrhage of the mucus membrane causing nosebleeds. Some patients are affected by psychoses with the infection causing mental disturbances.'

The matron stood at the foot of a bed watching its occupant silently a moment. The patient was rolled in a sheet reminiscent of a burial shroud. Bes watched on in silence. The man would only be in his early twenties. He struggled to breath, his windpipe rattling in near death. It was heartbreaking, to serve his country, survive, then come home to this. Bes fought back a tear. But now was not the time.

'Our greatest danger with this influenza is if the infection progresses into the often fatal secondary bacterial infection of pneumonia,' Matron said quietly as possible, as she led the new recruits away from the dying man. 'That's the killer. This occurs when the patient does not rapidly recover after three to four days of fever. They slip into irregular pyrexia due to bronchitis.'

'Pyrexia?' someone whispered.

'Raised body temperature,' Bes whispered back.

'The pneumonia then appears. The lobes of the lung become speckled with pneumonic consolidations. We know the causes of death are toxaemia, blood poisoning from bacterial infection, and vasomotor depression. It is these secondary complications that make the infection so deadly.'

'It is truly scary,' one nurse mumbled through her mask.

'So remember,' the matron went on. 'The infection is passed on through coughing and sneezing, so keep your masks on at all times. Also wash your hands regularly as a tiny amount of saliva or body fluid passed onto your lips could be your death sentence. Do I make myself clear?'

'Yes matron.'

'Matron.'

'Yes.'

'How *do* we treat these men?'

'With love and care and Aspirin.'

'Aspirin?'

'Yes. Call it acetylsalicylic acid if you want to sound more professional. Aspirin is our best remedy to reduce fever and pain. The bottom line is we have no cure. We must do our best to stop the victims going into the secondary infection. That ladies, is the killer. Secondary patients are given epinephrine and oxygen masks to aid breathing. Cinnamon powder with milk will reduce body temperature as will salt of quinine. Then it's plenty of sleep, plenty of fluids and nourishment.'

'Is that the best we can do?'

'Yes. That is the best we can do. Now, come,' Matron sighed and, taking a deep breath, she walked down the corridor. 'I'll show you to your quarters and you can check your rosters.'

***

Next day.

Bes and two colleagues, Sister Angie and Sister Heather, were the first on duty in B ward. Here, the first stage victims were treated *with love and care and Aspirin*. It seemed futile. On her first shift three men went into secondary bacterial infection of pneumonia. They were immediately wheeled into D ward where beds had been vacated by the dead.

Late morning Bes passed the operating theatre, noting a masked man in a full-length white laboratory jacket. She introduced herself. 'Good morning.' The man started, startled by Bes's presence. 'Sorry,' Bes said. 'I didn't mean to alarm you.'

'You did, rather.'

'Sorry.'

'That's all right. It's just that these things make me nervous.'

It was then that Bes noticed the petri dish in his hand. 'Is that what I think it is?'

'Depends. If you're thinking death in a glass dish then you would be one hundred per cent correct.' The scientist placed the dish carefully on the bench. 'You're one of the new nurses I take it?'

'Yes. Bes Mulberry.' Suddenly Bes was astutely aware of how muffled her voice sounded through her mask.

'Albert Grahams.' The man was in his mid-thirties and also masked. 'Resident chemist. But I'm not getting anywhere I'm afraid.'

'It's terrifying,' Bes said. 'All this death and no one has a cure.'

'More than terrifying.' Albert Grahams studied Bes a moment. Bes, at five-foot-ten had maintained her slim figure throughout the war. But with her fair hair styled into a chignon and that ubiquitous mask covering her nose and mouth, it was difficult to assess her beauty.

'So what have we here?' Bes alluded to the dish.

'I've taken samples from many of the patients ...'

'Samples?'

'Saliva and blood. I use the Petri dishes to grow sterile cultures of bacteria and then investigate the bacterial culture as it grows. Vaccines have been created for this bacterial infection.

'You've lost me I'm afraid.'

'Serial passage is a virus attenuation technique developed by Lois Pasteur back in the 80s.'

'Louis Pasteur, of course, I've heard of him.'

'Yes, well. It is similar to selective breeding, and can be used to create an attenuated strain of virus to develop vaccines.'

'I'll have to take your word for it.'

'Yes, well, it *is* more complicated than that.'

'I had better get back to my patients.'

'Bes.'

'Yes.'

'Be careful, won't you.'

Bes watched the soup wagon being pushed between the beds and caught the aroma of chicken broth reminding her of how hungry she was. Mrs

Appleby the cook placed bowls of the hot liquid next to the beds, placing spoons in each before moving on, the threat of influenza always present.

'Best we help these poor devils eat,' Angie muttered through her mask. Bes took up the task at one end of the ward when ....

'Bes!' one man spoke with a rasping chest. 'Bes. Is that truly you?' Bes had been too busy to notice the sleeping man earlier. Certainly she noted the soldier had a reconstructed face, an all too familiar sight after her short spell in English military hospitals before she sailed home. But this man slept peacefully, his face mostly covered by a sheet. Bes stood at his bedside, incredulous that she was recognised. It could only be one man.

'Archie?'

'Yes, yes. Remember me?'

Bes certainly did remember the man who wanted to marry her. The man who declared his love for her only to turn bitter when he was rejected. The same patient in Cairo who exposed the Heliopolis Doctor Galloway as a married man, effectively destroying any romance between doctor and nurse. Even though Bes later discovered that Galloway's relationship with his wife back in Australia was an estranged one.

'Yes Archie. I remember you. How could I forget?'

'Look at you,' Archie reached out to take Bes's hand but Bes pulled away; the thought of his contagion being the perfect excuse for her rebuff. 'Still as beautiful as ever,' he said.

Suddenly Bes felt awkward. 'We must be careful Archie,' Bes reddened. 'You are ill.'

'Yes, this damned flu.' If Archie was annoyed, Bes couldn't tell under his mask. 'But I'm getting over it, I just know it.'

'So you had a face reconstruction,' Bes said. Her words seemed hollow, announcing the obvious.

'What do you think of it?' And Bes imagined him beaming behind his mannequin like face.

'You look very handsome Archie.' Then as an after-thought, 'Did you meet the famed surgeon, Doctor Harold Gillies?'

'I certainly did. I have nothing but praise for the man. He is helping thousands I'm told.'

'He has been nothing less that miraculous Archie. You are a lucky man.'

'Lucky,' Archie said sourly. 'Do you think having my face blown off lucky?'

Bes recoiled. This was the other side of Archie she had experienced in Cairo.

'You know what I mean Archie.'

'Sorry.' The single word slipped from his expressionless mask. 'May I have some water please nurse?'

Nurse. Not Bes ... nurse.

Bes fetched a tin mug from the water filter, propping Archie's head so he could drink from a straw. 'Here, take it slow. Do you need aspirin?'

'Yes please.' Archie reached out once again, taking advantage of Bes's close proximity. Suddenly Bes noticed a deformity she had not noticed about Archie in Egypt. He was missing part of his little finger on his left hand to the second knuckle. Bes felt faint. She stepped back to scrutinise the man like she had never done before.

'What happened to your finger?' Bes asked, forgetting protocol and lifting Archie's hand into her own. 'Did that happen on Gallipoli also?'

It would be a long shot to lie to a nurse who could see the stub was well heeled over a period of years. 'No. I caught it in some machinery well before the war.'

Bes felt ill. Her sister Frankie's killer, Leroy O'Connell had exactly the same deformity. His, the police had told her, had been caught in the crankshaft of a tractor. Surely this was not he. But he escaped justice. He was never caught and what better cover could there be, than enlisting in the war effort. Bes felt her heart quicken.

She must be mistaken.

If Archie was suspicious he didn't show it. Once again that damned mask was convenient. Besides, Bes told herself, she had never met her sister's brother-in-law and he had not met her.

Bes's continued her duties in a daze. The situation plagued her and the more she thought it possible the more confused she became. And no one could answer any questions about the man in bed 27, ward B.

'He came in off the *Parramatta,*' was all matron could tell Bes. 'We isolated thirty men from that ship,' Matron Bridges recounted. 'All I know is he was badly disfigured at Gallipoli Peninsula and spent time in England with his face reconstruction. I must say they did a wonderful job. Why the interest nurse?'

'Nothing,' Bes floundered. 'I ... I actually nursed him in Cairo and I was just ... wondering.'

'You nursed him in Cairo. Well, well. Isn't it a small world?'

'It certainty is Matron.'

Bes propped the borrowed pushbike against the wall outside the Manly Post Office in Corrie Road, well back from the beach. The ride had taken her nearly an hour and the exercise had done little to clear her head.

Old George Smith stood behind the cashier bars at the telegraph counter dutifully wearing his mask, sitting awkwardly over a full beard. With his public dealings he was taking no risks.

'A telegraph you say. To Hobart.'

Bes nodded. The fact she was wearing her nurse's uniform seemed to unnerve the man. He fidgeted with his mask making certain it was well secured. 'It's going to cost you twopence a word.'

'Fine.'

'Who to?'

'Detective Charles Lloyd at Police Headquarters, Hobart.' George Smith scratched the information onto a page in a well-used book especially for telegrams.

Enquiry – Fugitive Leroy O'Connell – request any disfigurements or personal markings – tattoos etcetera – Miss B. Mulberry – sister of Frankie Mulberry deceased.

'Nineteen words. That'll be ah … three shillings and twopence.' Bes fished about in her purse. 'Are you certain you don't want to delete a word or two?' The efficient postal worker asked.

'Here.' Bes pushed the correct change under the bars and Smith hastily swept the coins into an open drawer using his pencil.

'Very well then. One moment.'

Bes watched as the old man tapped out the message in Morse code. 'There,' he said proudly, his mask bobbing up and down as he spoke. 'Done. That message will be in Hobart already. Fascinating days we live in, huh?'

'Fascinating,' Bes answered. 'Can the return telegraph be delivered to me, Miss B Mulberry at the quarantine station?'

'I'm afraid not miss. Flu an' all that you see. But I'll telephone your matron when it arrives and you can collect it from her. Is that suitable?'

'It'll have to be.'

Detective Charles Lloyd's reply was telephoned from the Post Office to the Quarantine Station later that afternoon. Matron Agatha Bridges was not in good temper when she wrote the message onto a sheet of writing paper.

'What's the meaning of this Nurse Mulberry?' Bes imagined the corners of her mouth curling down beneath her respiratory mask. The woman waved the paper before Bes.

'May I see it please?' Bes asked.

'Answer my question first. Why are you telegraphing police in Hobart, police of all people, requesting information on one of our patients?'

Bes thought long and hard. She was a volunteer here, working at the quarantine station at her own risk. Damn the woman.

Matron. 'Well?'

'Frankly matron, it is not your business.'

'Well I never.' The matron's chest rose like a ruffled rooster.

'I have reason to believe the man to be an imposter.'

'Rubbish girl. Archie Bryant is a war hero no less.'

'Then I will not trouble you further matron.' Bes snatched the notepaper and walked away.

'You may be a volunteer nurse Mulberry,' matron screeched under the mask. 'But I'll not have your shenanigans in my hospital. Do you hear me?'

But Bes was already reading, and on the move.

Police Headquarters Hobart.

Reply to Miss B. Mulberry.

Fugitive Leroy O'Connell – observations made at time of first arrest when finger-printed – 27th December 1915. Half small finger missing – left hand – right forearm small birthmark shaped like a bean and same size – two inches from elbow – I must insist on asking Miss Mulberry – why this request?

Signed Detective C. Lloyd

The last question threw Bes and stupidly she found herself adding up the words multiplying them by twopence each. *It's not his money!* She chose to ignore the detective's query at the end of his telegram, *why the request?* There was only one thing to do and that was to inspect Archie's right forearm. Excitement grew into fear. What to do if it *was* her sister's murderer? If so she would have to act fast, as this man, by all appearances, was convalescing and would be discharged.

Bes didn't know why but she felt she was not alone. She felt Frankie's presence as if her sister was channelling through her, giving her strength. Striving for answers and justice. Bes had had an hour to calm herself before once again coming face to mask with this Archie Bryant. Bes wanted to call out the name Leroy O'Connell. To watch his head turn in recognition and then cut the man's throat ...

But could she do that? Cut a man's throat. Become the killer herself. Bes stopped in the corridor, her mind clouded. Stop. *Deep breathe in. Concentrate. You can do this. Get proof. Get the police.*

Yes. The police.

Bes's strength returned and she entered the ward.

Her heart skipped a beat.

'Where is he?' she snapped at Heather who was changing bed 27's linen.

'Who?' Heather said stupidly. She was a ditherer this day.

'The patient.' Bes couldn't bring herself to say the man's name, to say aloud, Archie Bryant.

'He's in the garden. He's improved greatly and matron ordered him out into the sun.'

Bes stepped into a position where she could see into the courtyard garden. Archie Bryant sat in a wicker wheelchair staring down at the bay where the late afternoon sun glittered across the water like some giant hand had scattered cut diamonds across the surface. Bes's palms felt sweaty; she wiped them down each side of her skirt and headed out.

***

Out of doors the air was still and sultry, a brief breeze rushed up from the beach rustling the brush trees, before dying off once more.

'Hello Archie,' Bes forged a smile. It was not easy but she managed to force the horrors of Boxing Day 1914 out of her thoughts.

'Bes!' Archie had the strength to wheel about and face her. 'This is a surprise.' Archie held up his little finger and wiggled what remained of it. 'I thought I had scared you off with me little pinkie.'

Bes huffed a nervous laugh. 'Huh! It would take more than that to scare me off Archie.' Bes had a sudden thought that her comment sounded flirtatious and quickly added. 'I'm back from Egypt remember … saw some dreadful sights there.'

'Yes, haven't we all.'

'So you're on the mend.'

'Yeh Bes, I'm feeling much better. Thanks for asking. Mind you I'd love a smoke but I'm not too certain me lungs could handle it. Not yet anyways.'

Bes looked into Archie's eyes behind the faux reading glasses holding his mask in place, the eyes looked moist and dark behind the copper foil cheeks and she noted tiny beads of perspiration trickle down his neck.

'Be a love and push me into the shade,' Archie said. 'I'm fair melting under this mask.'

Push yourself into the shade, Bes wanted to say. *You* are *capable*. But Bes restrained herself and dutifully wheeled the patient across the flagstones and into the late afternoon shade, under the washhouse awning. She stood a moment, hands remaining on the wheelchair handles, and together they shared a moment as the sun reached the horizon, like the yolk of a huge egg vanishing behind the Blue Mountains somewhere off to the west.

'Beautiful isn't it?' Archie said breaking the tranquillity. He reached back over his shoulder to place his hand on Bes's.

Bes slipped her hand away. 'So, you'll be off home then?'

'Yeh.'

'Melbourne isn't it?'

'You remember.'

'I remember you saying you don't have family there anymore. What will you do?'

'I'm a mechanic, I'll find work. Might even move to the country.' Bes felt that icy cold chill run down her spine, chasing a trickle of sweat as it pooled at her tailbone.

I'm a mechanic.

Was not Leroy O'Connell a mechanic? 'Have you ever been to Melbourne?' Archie asked.

'Only Williamstown and Port Melbourne when the *Benalla* docked there on our way to Egypt. Did you grow up there?'

'Yeh.'

'What school did you go to?'

'School? Ah ... Fitzroy. But I left when I was fifteen to take an apprentice as a mechanic.'

Bes planned her next question carefully. 'I'll bet you were a good football player.'

'Yeh. And who doesn't love footy?.' Archie was speaking from the heart. Football was a passion. 'Use to go every weekend to watch the Roys play. All season. Never miss a match.'

'Oh ... the Roys?'

'Yeh, Fitzroys.'

'They're the black and white jerseys aren't they?' Bes asked, having already gleaned from Heather, who hailed from Melbourne, that the Roys' colours were Maroon and Blue.

'Ah ... yeh. My uncle played half-back with 'em a few seasons.'

'Really? What was his name?'

Archie paused a moment. His tone changed. 'Fred ... Fred Bryant. Why d'yer ask?'

'Well he would have known Geoff Moriarty then?'

'Who?'

'Geoff Moriarty.'

'Oh yeh, sure.'

But Bes wasn't so sure Archie knew who Geoff Moriarty was. Heather had told her Moriarty was famous for becoming the first official football coach in Australian sporting history. Every Melbournite worth their salt knew that.

If Archie felt discomfort Bes couldn't tell. But his tone had a slight hard edge to it. 'You never talk about yourself Bes.' Archie cleared his throat. 'I think you told me once years ago that you was Tasmanian?'

'Yes. Hobart. Have you ever been to Tasmania?'

'Nar. I believe it's real pretty.'

'Yes. Very.'

'Cold though, eh?'

'Only in winter. We have four distinct seasons in Tasmania. But the weather varies. I had an auntie who always said of Tasmanian weather, *if you don't like it come back in ten minutes.*'

'Where in Hobart do you live then?'

'Sandy Bay.'

Silence followed. Bes twisted the wheelchair slightly and took a garden bench seat off to Archie's right where she could look him in the eye, but Archie remained fixed on the view towards the harbour.

'You must be hot in that pyjama top,' Bes said. 'It's wet with perspiration.'

'I am hot, actually.'

'You're still running a temperature. I'll fetch you a clean one.'

If Archie had any inclination this nurse was asking strange questions this one act of kindness negated any negative thoughts. 'That's real kind o' yer Bes.'

Bes returned minutes later with a clean pyjama top. 'Here, let me help you take this one off.' Archie held his arms high and Bes lifted the soiled nightshirt over the patient's head. Archie had a fine physique. Although war had taken its toll, any sign of malnutrition was replaced by the improved diet from his time in hospital. He even had toned muscles. Bes circled the wheelchair. 'Arms up again.' As Bes made to slip the new top over his torso, she saw the proof she needed.

Right forearm small birthmark shaped like a bean and same size – two inches from elbow.

Proof that this man before her was Leroy O'Connell. Her sister Frankie's killer. The murderer of her mother and little sister Molly. Bes fought a wave of nausea. A dizziness overcame her. She fought the light-headedness, floundering slightly on her feet.

'Are you all right? Bes?'

Bes tried to speak but her voice was choked. She must at all costs keep it together. Now was not the time to let loose with accusations, let her temper fly. It was not the time. Not yet. Deep breath in.

Bes pulled the nightshirt over Archie's head. 'I'm fine ... I ... I just had a dizzy spell.'

'Are you sure you're all right?'

'Yes ... I'll be fine.' What Bes had to say next tore at her heart. It pained her to speak of Boxing Day 1914 but she had to continue at all costs. 'There is something you don't know about me, Archie.'

'Oh.' Archie suddenly felt close to Bes. Was he about to be entrusted with a family secret? A personal nuance maybe. Was this attractive nurse confiding in him because she actually had feelings for him? 'Well please Bes, don't keep me in suspense.'

'My sister was killed in a horrific bomb attack. Boxing Day 1914, in her own home in Queen Street Sandy Bay.'

These words spat from her like machine gun bullets. Bes stared directly at the mannequin-like face of her sister's killer. The eyes blinked but that mask hid all emotions. Bes wanted to tear the damned thing from his mutilated face and claw at him. Instead she remained calm and collected.

'The police have never caught the man,' she said. 'He escaped and has never been seen since.' Bes looked away, not wanting to look accusingly at the patient.

'Th-that's terrible ... how awful,' Leroy O'Connell was choked with guilt. Or was it the fear of exposure. He cleared his throat. He could not believe what he had just heard. All this time, all these years he had been acquainted with Bes he had never enquired, or heard her surname spoken. Mulberry.

'My mother and little sister Molly were also killed in the attack,' Bes continued, facing the beach once more to allay suspicion. 'My little brother Ben was badly wounded and my father eventually died of a broken heart, having had a mental breakdown and a stroke from all the stress.'

Leroy was speechless. His thoughts now went to escaping, leaving this god-awful quarantine hospital and vanishing. Head to North Queensland maybe. He could still work as a mechanic, handicapped or not. 'I need to rest,' was all he managed. Leroy O'Connell turned his wheelchair about and started wheeling back to the ward.

Bes was not reading any emotion. No emotion at all from this callous murderer. She had just told the man she lost most of her family in a bomb attack and *the heartless bastard wheels away.*

Now Bes knew what she must do. 'Let me help you,' Bes caught up and took the reins.

'It's all right.'

'No I insist.' Bes wheeled him back to bed 27 where Leroy O'Connell climbed without difficulty back onto his bed. 'I'd like to see the matron about being discharged.'

'Certainly,' Bes said with surreal calm. 'You still look hot Archie. Would you like some water?' Leroy O'Connell nodded his head, careful to avoid eye contact. 'There are no fresh mugs,' Bes lied looking over at the stone water filter. 'I'll fetch some and tell matron you wish to see her.'

Bes hurried along the corridor. She knew exactly what to do and felt a coldness she could only imagine a psychopath like Leroy O'Connell would experience. Fetching a tin mug from the scullery she made for the operating theatre. If Albert Grahams the resident Chemist was on duty, he was nowhere to be seen. Bes found what she was after, saliva samples incubating in the Petri dishes. Heart pounding she lifted the lid on a 'healthy' specimen and with the aid of a swab, carefully removed enough to wipe around the inside of the mug. Bes hurried to the kitchen, filled the mug with water and was at bedside 27 within minutes. Leroy O'Connell drank without hesitation. 'Matron?' he asked, after draining the mug and wiping his mouth on his sleeve.

'She's retired for the night but will see you first thing in the morning. Now you rest Archie.'

Back in her quarters Bes took the Gideon's Bible from the drawer in the bedside cabinet – a moral offering from the hospital - and held it to her chest. She had considered herself a good Christian until the events of Boxing Day 1914. Now she too was a killer. She squeezed the good book tight and prayed that justice would be swift and that god would forgive her.

CHAPTER TWENTY-SEVEN
JUST DESSERTS

The wait was terrifying.

Archie (Leroy) stared at the trench wall. He was only inches away. The weather had been hot and dry the past days and the dirt crumbled before him. He watched the fine cascade of dirt, loosened by the vibration of artillery shells, trickle like sand down the trench wall. Crumbling dirt turned to tiny pebbles and dried clay. Suddenly a tiny face appeared; a spiky black-eyed face with hair-thin pincers each side of the mouth. The fat maggot wriggled into the light dragging more crumbling turf and soil with it. The hole widened and other maggots poured from the opening. Larger pieces of earth turned to chunks when without warning an arm flopped free. A human arm, dangling from the widened hole held by a thread of skin to the torso beyond. Archie jumped back, choking a scream, when the entire trench wall caved in and what remained of the fragmented, shredded cadaver dropped to his feet in a gush of rotting gasses. Severed legs, torn arms and bomb torn body parts folded in on itself at Archie's feet and then he recognised the body of Frankie Mulberry ...

And Archie's scream woke the patients in the ward about him.

Minutes later he was dead.

***

Hobart 1919

Bes stood in the doorway of the Queen Street family home. *Bah!* She thought, mulling the words around in her head. *Family home ...*

Hardly. Family to Bes now, was only her brother Ben and herself. Sixteen-year-old Ben stood at his sister's side. How he had grown the past four years while Bes had been on service. He was still passionate about his cricket, being a right-hand bowler worked reasonably, but with his left arm amputated he was no batter. It had been difficult for Bes to recognise Ben at first; not only had he grown into a fine young man, but he had visible scars of the explosion. His left cheek resembled leathery dried seaweed and he wore a pirate's patch over his left eye where the shrapnel from the bomb had gouged his eye socket. This had only proven to build his character at school, to make him resilient. And Bes had heard from teachers at Hobart State High School in North Hobart, where he schooled the past few years, that he was pretty apt at throwing a one-armed punch at any boy who bullied him in the schoolyard.

Ben read Bes's hesitation. 'Come in sis,' This had been the first time his big sister had returned to Queen Street since that fateful day. Outwardly it looked an innocent weatherboard home; freshly painted white, neat garden of rose bushes and pansies bordered with a picket fence. Bes had heard how the neighbours all chipped in back in '15, many of them tradesmen, and rebuilt the house where the explosion had done so much physical damage that day. But the mental damage was another matter altogether. Ben gave Bes a gentle shove and followed her down the passage, dragging Bes's kit bag behind him with his one arm. 'In yer go then, Auntie's so excited to see yer.'

Auntie, being Jessie. She wasn't really an aunt. Jessie was the wife of Uncle Johnny – Ben's Godfather. Johnny had gone off to fight on the Western Front in 1916. He never made it back. *Hit by artillery,* the letter said. They never found the body. *Lost beneath the Flanders's mud.* Auntie Jessie had moved in to the family home and taken up guardianship of Ben when his father Frank died.

Bes swallowed hard and took the first steps into the family home; the first steps since their lives and the house were so violently torn apart.

The sweet smell of baking cakes welcomed Bes down the hallway towards the kitchen where she could hear the banging of pots and pans. Bes reminisced, her mother always made a racket trying to extract a pie tin or a baking tray from the inadequate sized drawer. In the kitchen Jessie was bent over the drawer and, as Bes guessed, she was struggling with a difficult baking tray caught at the bottom. The late afternoon sun had moved towards the mountain off to the west, making the kitchen gloomy. Aunt Jessie had not switched on the electric overhead bulb as yet. Maybe she was used to the dim light. Bes said nothing and turned on the light. Jessie, a frugal woman never to use this new-fangled electricity unless it was necessary, stood sharply, straightening her aching back before turning. 'Bes!' she cried out.

'Aunt Jessie.'

Bes had a tear in her eye. It multiplied. They hugged. Bes had grown up with this woman and her husband, Uncle Johnny, who had always been dear friends of the family. Now Jessie, too, was all that was left. They hugged. Jessie held Bes at arm's length and looked her up and down. Bes was a woman now, twenty-three. 'Look at you Bes, so ...' Jessie wanted to say grown up but that seemed so inappropriate now. The two held hands a moment, each with thoughts of their own losses. It was time to move on.

Ben hoisted the kit bag over his shoulder, having become quite useful with his one arm. 'I'll leave this in your room Bes.'

Bes gave her brother a warm smile before looking around the kitchen. It had been completely rebuilt, except for the fittings that were not damaged, like the stubborn baking tray drawer, and the stove of course. That cast iron stove-oven would survive anything the Western Front threw at it.

'Golly,' Bes said of the reconstruction. 'They did a wonderful job.'

'Yes Bes,' Jessie said soberly, wiping floury hands on her apron, suddenly realising she had flour everywhere, including on Bes. 'Mr Brooks at number 47 acted as foreman and they rebuilt all this over six weekends.'

'Then I must thank them,' Bes said. They had certainly done a wonderful job but in reality she was struggling to decide whether she could live here at all. Bes looked to the cake tins brimming with batter on the kitchen bench; now more alert to the treacle deliciousness that was Aunt Jessie's baking. 'Maybe we could invite them over for a tea party,' Bes said.

'Good idea,' Jessie loved company. 'Tea for the ladies but you best buy some beer for the men.'

Truth be known, Bes knew the neighbours had primarily rebuilt the home for her father Frank, but he would never move home, having died of a broken heart some time ago before she returned home. Bes opened the back door and looked across the yard to the empty kennel. 'Maybe we should get another dog,' she said. Jessie nodded and an awkward silence followed.

Ben broke their reverie. 'What's this sis'?' Bes turned to see Ben holding up the ancient Roman goblet left in her care two years earlier by that sergeant

Garfield Gardener she met in London. She had never found out what happened to him, and god only knows she tried to find out. The only information she could glean from the army was that he was not listed as killed in action.

'Looks old,' Ben held it to the light.

'Ben!' Jessie was horrified. 'You shouldn't go through anyone's private property, even if it is your sister's.'

'That's all right Auntie.' Bes explained what it was and how it came into her possession.

'Goodness. Silver you say. Then I must clean it.' Bes knew Auntie would prepare a solution of spirits of ammonia and turpentine to polish it, like all the good housekeepers did, to polish silverware.

CHAPTER TWENTY-EIGHT
MELBOURNE BECKONS

It would be two months before the letter was delivered. Bes was starting to believe it would never arrive, suspecting Doctor Harold Gillies in England had simply forgotten her plight. Bes looked at the envelope addressed to her personally:

Sender; *Doctor J. Bird. The Royal Melbourne Hospital.*

She felt the tears well once more. Bes had been very emotional since returning home. But here at last was some hope for Ben. Before leaving England Bes had managed an audience with the famed surgeon Doctor Harold Gillies at the Cambridge Military Hospital, England, and he explained that he was already in the process of sending a portfolio of his many successes – with detailed instruction on how to proceed with these life-changing facial reconstructions – to colleagues in Australia and New Zealand; New Zealand being his home country. Bes's enquiry was unusual as it was a request for her civilian brother and not a war victim. However Gillies sympathised with this hard working nurse and recommended his protégé in Melbourne, Doctor Jeremy Bird, do what he could for the lad. Doctor Bird conducted his research with the aid of local police and, having pity on the young bomb victim, decided to accommodate Ben Mulberry. Bes read part of the letter aloud:

And it is with great pleasure that myself and the hospital board of surgeons have come to the decision we would like to reconstruct Ben's face, and with our compliments. Would you kindly contact the hospital at your earliest convenience to book an appointment for yourself and Ben to meet here in Melbourne for a preliminary examination.

Bes had no desire to head back to sea so soon, but the date was set. Her Auntie Jessie saw to it, personally pulling a few strings and drawing on favours owed to her deceased husband Johnny, who had worked at the Hobart Docks as foreman to the apple merchants prior to the war. Ben and Bes sailed from Hobart on the 13th November for Melbourne as steerage passengers on board the Union Steamship Company's steamer SS *Loongana*. They arrived on the 15th after crossing a calm Bass Strait.

Bes would finally experience Melbourne, arriving at Port Melbourne then on to Flinders Street Station late on a warm spring afternoon. Sister and brother walked to a tram stop, captivated by the hustle and bustle of the big city; especially Ben who had never travelled further than Austin's Ferry, north of Hobart. At Bourke Street the sun washed over the stone and brick buildings like a goldsmith had recently plated them with gilt. The streets were busy – although some pedestrians still wore masks against the now diminishing pandemic, the pneumonic flu. People were gay, the city looked prosperous and Bes felt positive about her future and that of her brother, for the first time in a long time.

Bes and Ben shared a laugh boarding a tram, sitting on a wooden bench seat and facing out the port side onto the street, a street rushing by at fifteen miles per hour. From here they would be transported up Swanston Street to the corner of Lonsdale Street to meet Doctor Bird at the Royal Melbourne Hospital.

Although the Spanish flu pandemic was relatively lenient on Melbourne, the memory was fresh in everyone's mind and even now in November Bes had read in the newspapers that auxiliary hospitals – especially set up for quarantine – were still taking in pneumonic flu patients.

It was while travelling on a rattling tram along Swanston Street that Bes's life took a positive turn. Maybe it was Ben's distorted cheek and the eye patch that captured the tram conductor's attention, for he too had been in the wars. Literally. At first Bes took little notice of the conductor, working his way along the seats; taking coins in exchange for tickets. At the corner of Franklin Street and Swanston, the stocky red headed conductor skipped off the moving tram as it pulled to a stop.

'Tickets madam?' he asked of Bes, who was already plucking a florin from her purse. The conductor discreetly studied Ben's injuries; his first thoughts being, Ben was too young to have been in France, surely. Bes saw the conductor staring at her disfigured brother and immediately took offence. 'Here!' she said defensively, thrusting the coin foreword; too annoyed to look the man in the eye, dare she scold him.

'Nurse Mulberry!' the conductor's mouth dropped open. 'Bes?'

Bes was as surprised as the conductor. 'Ned!'

'I don't believe it.' Clearly Ned was pleased to see her. 'What … what are you doing here? I seem to remember you telling me you were a Hobart lass, didn't you?'

'My brother Ben …' Bes's words trailed off. Suddenly an explanation seemed superfluous looking at Ben's injuries. Ned was the perfect gentleman. 'Nice to finally meet you Ben. Your sister told me all about you.'

'She did?'

'Yes. We met in Cairo. I was wounded and your wonderful sister patched me up.'

'Goodness,' Bes felt a thrill she had difficulty expounding to herself. She felt a connection, something she had not felt in a long time. Ned remembered his post.

All clear.

Ned stepped aboard, gave the cord two sharp tugs and the driver jerked the tram foreword. There followed a brief pause when Ned started,

'Are you …'

'How's your arm?' they said in unison. Both laughed nervously.

'You first,' Bes said.

'Are you living here, in Melbourne?'

'No, just here for Ben.' Bes was now acutely aware that the hospital approached. 'We have to get off at the Royal Melbourne Hospital actually.' There was an anxious edge to Bes's voice and Ned read it correctly. She was nervous, as was he.

'Maybe we could meet for afternoon tea,' Ned suggested. The hospital stop approached. Bes looked at Ben who simply winked at his older sister. 'To catch up on old times like,' Ned added. But the chemistry between them knew better.

Bes, 'That would be lovely.'

The passengers within earshot on the busy tram smiled approvingly. Romance reaches to everyone at some stage in his or her life.

And it was after all, spring.

The Lonsdale corner approached. Ned pulled the cord and the tram slowed. 'Crystal Café,' he said. 'Bourke Street. We passed it a moment ago.'

The tram stopped. 'I'll find it,' Bes said, stepping from the running board to the street. Ned tugged the cord. 'Three o'clock tomorrow then,' he called out, steadying himself on a seat rail as the tram pulled away again.

'Three o'clock then.'

Bes stood a moment and watched Ned go about his business collecting fares as the tram turned the corner, before realising she still held the fare in her hand.

Ben interrupted her thoughts. 'I think he's keen on you sis.'

'I didn't pay him the fare,' Bes said, trying to change the subject.

'So, you just saved two bob.'

'That's not the ...'

'You're keen on him too, aren't you?'

'Nonsense. We're just old friends, that's all.'

'Hmm. We'll see.'

***

Royal Melbourne Hospital. November 1919

Doctor Jeremy Bird turned the pages of Doctor Gillies portfolio; an album of black and white photos of soldiers with horrific head wounds. It had finally reached him from colleagues in London working with the Red Cross. 'These are nothing less than remarkable,' Bird told Bes and Ben. 'Simply remarkable.'

Most were photos of facial damage from shrapnel where entire cheeks had been torn away. Many, like Ben, had lost an eye. Noses were either missing or simply twisted skin. Now, as they healed, they were having faces reconstructed in prosthetics by talented sculptors.

'It is in its infancy Ben, you must understand,' the doctor said. Ben understood, but for so long he could not look at his own reflection in a mirror, he would take any risks for the procedure. 'Being only sixteen, your body still grows, Ben. It is my plan to reconstruct your cheek with the copper foil method and you will be fitted with a custom-made glass eye, however you will have to wear glasses, cosmetically that is, to hold the glass eye and cheek in place. But, as I said, your body still grows. You will have to return every two years until you are twenty-two. Do you have any questions?'

'Just one sir, when can we start?'

***

Next day. Crystal Café Melbourne. 3pm.

Bes had maintained the slim figure of her pre-war years and turned heads, both male and female, in her high-waisted tunic style dress worn with harem pants. Not exactly the latest in fashion but at a David Jones sale price of ten shillings and nine pence it was all she could afford. Ned had arrived at the tearooms early and stood clumsily as Bes approached the table. He was still standing, fumbling with the rim of his hat when Bes suggested they both sit.

'Of course.'

They sat.

'You look ... very nice,' Ned said lamely. He wanted to say *beautiful* but thought the word a little too forward on this, their first date.

Date! Was this truly a date?

'Thank you,' Bes answered. 'You look quite the striking figure yourself.' Ned too, had done himself proud, wearing a grey waistcoat over a white collarless shirt with a woollen flat cap. However he had borrowed the trousers from a mate and they were a little on the large side.

'Where's Ben?' Ned asked, starting the conversation.

'Ben!' Bes laughed. She actually laughed. 'Why, was he invited too?'

'No!' Ned said a little too smartly. 'I mean ... no ... I just wondered, that's all.'

'Oh. Ben is at the hospital. The doctor admitted him and he will be there most of the week.'

'Oh.'

Ned of course, knew Bes and Ben's history. The parcel bomb. The devastation. She had told him all this in Cairo all those years passed. But Bes went on to explain how Ben was being fitted with prosthetics.

They shared their stories to date, drank two pots of tea and Ned polished off five scones, strawberry jam and cream to Bes's one.

But Devonshire tea at the Crystal Café in Bourke Street was never to be a one afternoon affair. Both Bes and Ned knew this after their first rendezvous. They had both experienced so much during the war years. They had so much in common, so much to offer each other and when Cupid's arrow struck it struck hard.

Ned too, had lost his father, not in France but to the pneumonic flu. Jim Kelly had been one of the first to die in Melbourne some nine months earlier. So it was of some relief to Ned's mother, Flo, that her son had found a companion in his life, for she had seen too many returned soldiers go down the path of drunkenness.

'You're a protestant then?' Flo asked Bes, *fishing* on their first meeting.

Bes was blatantly honest. 'I was born Protestant but lost sight of god some time ago.'

'Oh.'

Bes went on to explain to Mrs Kelly what had happened those four long years ago.

'How awful,' was all the old woman could say and Bes now understood how this woman – not the sharpest pin in the cushion – could aimlessly name her son Edward, when her married name was Kelly.

While Ben was being fitted with a reconstructed cheek and a glass eye, to return some normality back into his life, Bes and Ned met daily.

Ned proposed marriage to Bes the eve before Bes and Ben were to sail back to Hobart. Bes accepted on the spot.

CHAPTER TWENTY-NINE
TILL DEATH DO US PART

Flo Kelly's sister Kate – who also lost a husband, a schoolmaster fifteen years her senior, to an aged care home – moved into the Kelly home. This freed up Ned to relocate to Hobart, the plan being to open a market garden. It was something Ned knew about. It was something he was good at. *Greenfingers* his friends called him. Together on a trip south Ned and Bes found land at Woodbridge for sale and all about were apple orchards.

'There's a big market for apples Bes,' Ned told his fiancée. But the fifty-acre farm, with cottage, was valued at five thousand pounds, far more than the nine hundred pounds they could manage between them. Weeks turned to months. Ned found work managing a nursery in Sandy Bay and Bes earned extra money as a local midwife when requested.

Bes and Ned were married on February 14th 1920 at St Peter's Church in Grosvenor Street Sandy Bay. Ned moved into the Queen Street family home until they could afford the deposit on an orchard. This would take years by which time Bes's brother Ben brought his own bride into the family home. Sandra Mulberry, nee Smith, would give Ben three sons and a daughter.

But the most amazing experience for Ned had been the first day he walked into the Queen Street living room and stared at the mantelpiece.

'Bes,' he said in a reverent whisper. 'Where did that come from?'

Bes watched Ned reach for the ancient Roman goblet. But something stopped him. It was almost spiritual; then again it was as if Ned was afraid to touch it.

'Why, that old thing. I do believe it's Roman.'

'Yes, yes. But where did you get it.'

'Well it was given to me.'

'Given to you! Well sort of. I was asked to look after it.'

'By whom?'

'A sergeant I met in London.'

'Sergeant who?'

'Ah … Garry … no Gavin … ah, no … Garfield. That's it Garfield.'

'Garfield bloody Gardener.'

'Yes. That's him. Did you know him?'

'Know him? I certainly did.'

Bes explained how the goblet came into her possession and Ned explained how he found it in a crater, avoiding explaining how he helped create the crater.

It was beyond coincidence. A rare and yet fortuitous moment. Ned finally picked up the goblet with the reverence it now deserved; like handling the cup of Christ. The Holy Grail.

Ned told of how he left the goblet and an ancient lamp found with it with another soldier called Archie.

'Archie?' Bes felt a sickening in the pit of her stomach. Surely this could not be the very same Archie Bryant, AKA Leroy O'Connell! 'What did he look like?'

'Who? Archie?'

'Yes.'

'Ah … well … he was about five foot eight, had broad shoulders, a strong devil by all accounts. He was a nice enough bloke but had a short fuse.'

Bes felt a shiver up the spine. 'Did he by chance have half a finger missing; left hand little finger.'

'By Jove Bes. You're on the money. How did you know him?'

'He was one of my patients at Heliopolis,' Bes said flatly. And to that extent she was telling the truth.

***

April 11ᵗʰ 1920. Queen Street, Hobart. 4pm.

Ned had turned the backyard at Queen Street into one large glasshouse. There was little space remaining around the garden's perimeter and the glasshouse housed an army of budding pot plants at various stages of propagation; all in neat single file aboard a fleet of trestles. Ned was gaining experience for the future orchard and possibly a nursery in the planning. He found the plants better company than most humans and spent hours beneath the glass panelled roof, alone with his thoughts for the future, while putting the past behind him. A tap on the glass withdrew Ned from his reverie; his mind wandering afar with watering can in hand.

'Mr Kelly I presume.'

Ned recognised cops when he saw them and instinctively tensed. 'Who wants to know?'

'Well, Mr Kelly, I'm Detective Lloyd and this is my subordinate Senior Constable Freddy Stawell.' Ned thought the older cop looked tired and imagined his job stressful. *The name Lloyd also rang a bell. Had Bes spoken of a Detective Lloyd sometime in the past? He thought so.* The young cop was strong-jawed and handsome in a mainstream way.

Ned felt uncomfortable. It was not every day police made a visit and it usually wasn't a visit for tea and scones. 'What can I do for you?'

'We are looking for your wife, Bes.'

'Oh?'

'We knocked at your front door and there was no answer, then your next-door neighbour, who confirmed that you both lived here, suggested we come down your side lane.

'My wife is sleeping, we're having a baby.'

'Congratulations.'

'Thank you. She's six months gone.'

'Wonderful. My children are all grown up.' Ned didn't suffer fools lightly. He wanted to say *cut to the chase* but Lloyd, no fool, read his mind. 'We have some important news for your wife Ned. To do with the Boxing Day incident in 1914. Would you be so kind as to wake her?'

'No need.' Ned's eyes looked beyond the two policemen to Bes who stood at the top of the kitchen steps, her back arched, stomach stretched forward and with her hands resting on her rounded belly.

'You better come in Detective,' Bes said as the two coppers turned to face her.

Inside Lloyd was amazed to see the restoration. The kitchen looked larger than when he was here last. 'The neighbours all chipped in and rebuilt it,' Bes said, remembering Lloyd's connection with the case and his prior visits to the bombsite.

'I'm having tea, can I offer you a cup?'

'Tea sounds wonderful, thank you.'

Bes dragged the kettle of simmering water off the stove plate but Ned quickly relieved her of the chore, filling a family sized teapot past the spout.

Moments later they sat about in the front living room, the *good room* as Ned preferred to call it. Lloyd looked at the urn on the mantelpiece with interest but said nothing.

'You are a Victoria Cross recipient, are you not?' Lloyd asked Ned who nodded reservedly. 'Yes, I read it in the paper. You are a brave man. I was too old to enlist but ...'

Ned fidgeted, clearly uncomfortable and impatient.

'Look,' Lloyd sat forward on the edge of his chair. 'I won't keep you too long. Ah, Bes, did you know an Ed Shelley, he used to work for the O'Connells at their farm at Coal Valley.'

'No, the name's not familiar.'

'He would have been nineteen then, by all means a good-looking lad. He's twenty-three now.'

'What's this to do with the bombing detective?' Ned asked impatiently, thinking of his pregnant wife's well-being.

'Well he was known to your father, Bes. And it's a shame your father is no longer with us to testify ... to shed light on the matter so to speak. You see he threatened your father in the weeks leading up to the bomb attack.'

'Oh god! How ... I mean why?'

'Ed Shelley's mother, Edith Shelley, by all reports, is a piece of work. By that I mean not a particularly nice person. Now she ran a bawdy house in South Hobart up near the Cascade Brewery ...'

Ned interrupted. 'You mean a brothel?'

'Exactly. And she had a market for younger women and many under age.'

'God no!' Beth gasped. 'What does this have to do with father?'

'Fear not Bes, your father's reputation is intact. He was no less than a good citizen. One evening in March 1914 your father, Frank Mulberry, was the driver on tram number sixteen on the Cascades tramline when he saw Mrs Shelley chasing a man down the street from her bordello and on to your father's tram, slashing him several times with a cutthroat razor before Frank managed to subdue her until police were called.'

'My Father ...'

'Yes. He saved this man's life. You did not know of this?'

'I remember talk of a kerfuffle on the tram. An assault father stopped. But I never knew it was that serious.'

'You told me yourself Bes,' Ned said, 'what a modest, quiet man your father was.'

Bes nodded slowly. 'But what has this to do with what happened?'

'Well the man who was attacked was married and Edith Shelley was trying to extort money from him ...'

'Blackmail?'

'Yes blackmail. And when he confronted her she lost control, attacked him and your father was the prime witness – there were no other witnesses on the tram the evening this occurred – the prime witness, your father, saw Edith Shelley fetch a five-year sentence for attempted murder.'

'And the son Ed Shelley?'

'Revenge. He was a vengeful mongrel with a temper to match.'

'Are you saying it was this Ed Shelley who made the bomb?'

'Exactly.'

Bes felt instantly ill. She hurried from the room and down the passageway to the outdoor lavatory where she dropped to her knees and threw up. Leroy O'Connell AKA Archie Bryant had died by her hand. She poisoned the man with the pneumonic flu virus.

Bes's pregnancy excused her actions before the police, and five minutes later Ned managed to return Bes once more before the lawmen.

'You alright?' Lloyd asked.

'Fine.' Bes remained standing and stretched, her hands on her hips and pouting. 'I need you to tell me everything.'

'Certainly.'

'Are you saying that this ... this evil person Ed Shelley decided to kill my entire family as a vendetta against my father?'

'No Bes. He only intended to kill your father. The parcel was addressed to Frank Mulberry, not Frankie Mulberry. But Ed Shelley was illiterate, he copied the writing and his hand was no more than a scrawl, and together with the pink ribbon he used everyone assumed it was a present for Frankie.'

'It was meant for your father,' Constable Stawell said. 'No one else.'

'How do you know this?'

'He has confessed.'

'So why was it left with the Randall's across the street?'

'Because he had the wrong address. He knew it was the corner house but he got the wrong one. And in doing so he trod in the rust-stained mud in the Randall's driveway. The same mud that told us the wearer had been on the Randall's property. It turned out that the three men who mucked out the sties, Brady, Leroy and Ed, had the same boot size and often wore one or the other pair, where the boots were always left on the front porch.'

'So how did you catch this man?'

'Forensics took another look at the evidence and lifted one thumbprint belonging to Ed Shelley from a bomb component.'

'But at the time you found Leroy's prints on some components?'

'Yes, we know Leroy O'Connell was party to the crime and now we know why.'

Bes felt a measure of satisfaction. 'So Leroy was involved?'

'Yes.'

'Why ... how?'

'You had better sit Mrs Kelly.'

'I'm fine.'

'Trust me,' Lloyd said. 'I'd be happier if you sat.'

Bes sat heavily. Ned pulled his chair alongside and took Bes's hand.

'Your sister Frankie was having Leroy's child.'

'N ... no!'

'I'm afraid it's true.'

'It's impossible. Frankie would never ... never cheat on Brady. She loved him ... no I cannot believe that.'

'Mrs Kelly ... ah, Bes. Your sister did not cheat on anyone. She was forced by Leroy.'

'Forced!' Bes's voice was breaking. 'Forced? You mean she was raped.'

Lloyd need not repeat the repugnant word. He simply nodded. 'October 10th 1914, a Saturday. That was Brady's twenty-second birthday ...'

'That's correct. I remember it well,' Bes was surprised at her own memory of events. 'I remember it because Frankie came home angry. She said both Brady and Leroy got quite drunk. Frankie was mad as hell.'

'Ed Shelley told us during his confession that at Brady's birthday picnic alongside the creek near Ed's shepherd's hut, Brady went to fetch more beer from the homestead and while he was away Leroy coaxed Frankie into the hut on some pretext and forced himself upon her.'

Bes sat silently a long moment. 'Are you alright?' Ned asked.

Bes didn't answer. 'Why didn't she tell me? We were best friends. My sister and I had no secrets.'

'Ed Shelley also said Leroy threatened Frankie if she spoke up.'

'Bastard,' Ned spat.

'And she would have been ashamed,' Lloyd added in Frankie's defence. 'She knew Brady would not believe her. We know that Brady and Leroy were thick as thieves. Frankie kept the whole thing a huge secret because she thought she would lose Brady.'

'Then she discovered she was pregnant.'

'Yes, she was having Leroy's baby.'

'But how ... I mean how would she know it was Leroy's?'

'Woman's intuition, the timing. She just knew.'

This was something Bes totally understood. Women's sixth sense.

'And the longer she kept quiet about it the less likely Brady would be to believe the truth.'

'So she told Brady she was having *his* baby and they secretly married,' Bes said quietly. 'And then they planned to tell Mum and Dad in the New Year.'

Detective Lloyd nodded. The complexities of crime never ceased to intrigue him.

'But where does this Ed Shelley bloke come into all this?' Ned asked.

'Well as I said, Ed Shelley saw Leroy lure Frankie to the hut. He saw everything and this is when he hatched his plan to make Leroy help him make a bomb.'

'Blackmail?'

'In a nutshell, yes. Ed Shelley was seething about what happened to his mother and desperately wanted revenge against your father. I am really sorry to be the bearer of bad news but you must know the truth.'

'Yes ... yes. Thank you.'

'Ed Shelley confessed you say,' Ned said.

'Yes, yesterday. You see we had an unsolved crime from back in early December 1914, a woman was found dead in bushland not that far from the

O'Connell's farm. She was finally identified as a woman from the north of the state whose car had broken down in the country. This led her to seek a mechanic in the area and who was the closest?'

'Leroy.'

'Yes. And his sidekick Ed Shelley.'

'Unfortunately this woman was a little too independent for her own good. A lonely widow who succumbed to Leroy's charm. It was a late afternoon in summer, when Leroy suggested they have a romantic get together, somewhere private away from the workshop and away from his wife. The woman, by all accounts, was a bit of an adventurer. But somehow things got ugly, she must have changed her mind, Leroy lost his temper and choked the woman with a handkerchief. He panicked and left the woman's body amongst a copse of trees where she was not found until months later.'

'How awful.'

'And what happened to her car?'

'Leroy broke it down for parts and sank the remains in a creek near the farm.'

'What a piece of work.'

'But we lifted finger prints from a beer bottle discarded at the crime scene,' senior constable Stawell said. 'And when we checked our files the same print, Leroy O'Connell's, turned up as a match.'

Did you ever discover her identity?'

'Bertha Green.'

Lloyd shot his subordinate a displeased glance. Protocol usually called for privacy unless the deceased was a relative. But then he thought it *was* some time ago.

'We advertised in the paper,' Lloyd continued. 'Missing persons, and her estranged husband in Launceston came forward and identified her belongings, what little there was. You see she moved to Hobart and took up lodgings with a Mr and Mrs Bentwood in West Hobart. But over a short period she had, shall we say, more than one male visitor. This did not sit well with Mr Bentwood, a devout Baptist, and he asked her to leave. That was just before Christmas 1914. Now Mr Bentwood thought Mrs Green had vacated his lodgings but she was in fact by this time deceased. Mr Green let himself into her room and there wasn't much left behind, certainly nothing of value he assured me. Consequently the landlord forgot about her. Initially we thought the woman was of means, but the pearl necklace was fake and the cameo, an heirloom, was not of particularly good quality.'

'However we have evidence leading to Leroy O'Connell. By this time he had left his wife and child and the pig farm, and escaped with thirty-eight pounds they had in a savings account.'

'Nice man,' Ned said with undisguised sarcasm.

Lloyd looked at the young senior constable. 'Constable Stawell.'

'Sir.'

'Step outside please. You too Mr Kelly. I'd like a word in private with your wife.'

'Oh?' Ned looked at Bes and she attempted to return a reassuring smile but seriousness prevailed.

'It'll be fine Mr Kelly. Please.'

The young policeman stood by the door waiting for Ned to join him. 'We'll meet you in the glasshouse shortly,' Lloyd added. Ned shook his head slightly, gave the older cop a fixed stare, closed the door and walked off down the passageway.

'Now I must address, Mrs Kelly, a certain telegram I received last year in February,' Detective Lloyd sounded menacingly formal all of a sudden. Bes stiffened. 'A telegram sent to me from Manly in Sydney in regards to identifying a certain Leroy O'Connell. A telegram from you no less, Bes.'

Using her Christian name had a note of leniency about it.

'Yes.'

'And I replied to the effect the man had a section of his left small finger missing and a bean shaped birthmark in the crook of his right forearm. Is that correct?'

There was no denying it. 'Yes Detective Lloyd.'

'But I never received a follow-up.'

'Oh, I ... I ... ah ...'

'Well I do believe it was a soldier who was badly wounded in Turkey, at Quinn's Post my sources tell me.'

Bes swallowed hard. She did not like this line of inquiry. Not one bit.

'He was enlisted as Archie Bryant and by all accounts was a sapper.' Bes tried to look blank. 'Got to be a brave soul to be a sapper, eh Bes? But you'd know that, being a nurse during the war.'

'Why are you telling me this Detective Lloyd?'

'Please call me Charles, we've known each other some time now.'

'Charles.'

'Well I'm a family man Bes. I have a lovely wife and three children, all grown up now. But I'm also a policeman. And Joan, my wife, says I always think like a policeman. So when you sent me that enquiry and when I did not receive a reply to my enquiry I started asking questions. I contacted the Manly police and they sent an officer to the Quarantine Station to meet up with you, have a little chat if you like, but guess what? You had resigned and left abruptly the day before and there was no forwarding address. I assumed you were maybe sailing back here to Hobart. Then, on further enquiry, my contact in Manly, the officer, discovered that this Archie Bryant died the same day. He died of pneumonia complications from a secondary virus of that terrible pneumonic flu.'

'So what's that got to do with me?' Bes found the courage to be defiant.

'Well, the matron told my officer that this Archie Bryant was on the mend, that he was due to be released. But then he becomes very ill once again and dies. The matron also told the officer that she feared Archie Bryant was contaminated by missing virus samples taken from the chemist laboratory at the Quarantine Station.'

'Impossible!'

'Is it Bes? Your name came up in the enquiry. But of course this could never be proven. Could it?'

'Don't know what you're talking about.'

'My only concern is, what if this imposter, Archie Bryant, who we now know was Leroy O'Connell, what if he was innocent? What if he had nothing to do with your family's death?'

'But he did. You said so yourself.'

'Yes, I did. The bottom line is the man was guilty and he died an awful death at the hand of god. So if the contamination was an accident, then he still got his comeuppance.'

Detective Charles Lloyd stood and helped Bes to her feet. She arched her back and stretched, her hands back on her belly. 'It must be a boy by the size of me,' Bes said, keen to change the subject.

'Yes indeed,' Lloyd said. 'And a fine boy indeed I should imagine, with such a brave mother and father. You take care Bes Kelly, and enjoy a wonderful life.'

EPILOGUE

After four years picking up work where possible, Ned and Bes managed to save twelve hundred and sixteen pounds; a small fortune but not enough for the banks to lend them the remainder. They were still nearly four thousand shy of enough to purchase a moderate orchard with a comfortable family home; as number two was on the way. Barrie Kelly was nearly three – middle name Edward – and Bes was certain she was having a girl second time around. If so, they both agreed she should be named Frankie.

Some evenings, usually a Saturday or a Sunday after Barrie was put to bed, Bes and Ned would relax after their evening meal in the living room. Ned would read the weekend papers and if Bes wasn't reading she would knit and catch up on the sewing and darning. Often they discussed finances.

Ned looked to the mantelpiece. Alongside the ancient Roman goblet – that most visitors thought an unsightly item to have on display – were Ned's medals, including his Victoria Cross.

'I think I'll sell me medals Bes,' Ned said out of nowhere.

'You'll what?' Bes was incredulous.

'Sell me medals. We might get enough to convince the bank to loan us the rest.'

'You'll do no such thing Ned. The Victoria Cross! That must be passed on to Barrie when he's old enough to hear your stories.'

Stories!

It was not something soldiers spoke of. War was something to forget. How could Ned tell his son he strangled men with his bare hands or shot men in the face?

Nar. Barrie could have his medals, but there would be no stories. Ned stared at the goblet. It never failed to fascinate him, how it found its way halfway around the world and into his home. It was fate or fortune. It was meant to be.

'I wonder what the goblet's worth?' Ned said as much to himself as to his wife.

'That Sergeant Garfield who gave it to me for safe keeping told me it was valuable,' Bes said.

'And where is this Garfield now Bes? I think we could safely do with it what we wish. Besides, as I've told you it's more mine than his anyway.'

They had discussed this often.

'Then let's find out!'

***

It was six months before the letter from Sotheby's in London arrived. Bes had prepared a photograph of the goblet and a letter of provenance, including drawings of all markings. Their reply was positive. Yes we believe the goblet would fetch a good price, maybe as much as one thousand pounds.

It was an opportunity too good to resist. Bes and Ned both agreed they had enjoyed the goblet's company over the years but they needed to establish their future.

Maybe this was its purpose.

On the 2nd of October 1924 little Frankie Kelly was born, six pounds three ounces. The following day a letter arrived from their bank in Hobart to notify them one thousand four hundred and thirty pounds had been wired into their account from Sotheby's in London. The last paragraph in the letter went something like this;

... and if you would like to make an appointment at the bank at your earliest convenience we would be only too happy to discuss approving your loan.

Bes and Ned, Barrie and Frankie, and Garfield the red setter moved to an orchard, not far from the one they first looked at, two months later.

***

1930s

During the 1930s a German became more and more dominant on the world stage. Adolf Hitler became chancellor of the Nazi Party in 1933. 'Adolf Hitler, Adolf Hitler,' Ned said over and over to Bes. 'I've heard the name before ... in France.' Then it all came back to Ned. He remembered the beady eyes of hatred, the corporal who was left to guard him in the bungalow prior to the Battle of Fromelles.

'Yes. That was him. I clobbered the beggar with a Luger and stole his uniform.'

Of course, Ned had told Bes the story a few times over the years.

But Hitler?

She found it hard to believe.

ABOUT THE AUTHOR

After decades in the hospitality industry, and the best part of forty years since opening the Drunken Admiral Seafood Restaurant, Craig hung up the apron to leave family at the helm and indulge in his other passion, writing fiction.

Craig was born in Hobart in 1952, and travelled extensively giving him the experiences and escapades he so enjoys putting into print. This includes working as a chef for a restaurant owned by Sydney underbelly figures in the early 70s, and cooking in Darwin when cyclone Tracy destroyed the city in 1974. Life has been busy and interesting to say the least.

In the 90s, Craig independently shot two feature films, a murder mystery set in Southern Tasmania which aired on television, and a splatter comedy still available online. He wrote, produced and directed both.

Having led a 'normal' life of work and duty, Craig Godfrey decided to follow his real passion of writing fiction, and with Tasmania's fascinating past, he has plenty to write about.

Using Tasmania's history as a blank canvas, Craig loves nothing more than to weave adventure, mystery, and mayhem involving colourful characters from all walks of life. He has published 20 previous titles.

NOTE FROM THE AUTHOR

Word-of-mouth is crucial for any author to succeed. If you enjoyed *On the Devil's Knee*, please leave a review online—anywhere you are able. Even if it's just a sentence or two. It would make all the difference and would be very much appreciated.

Thanks!
Craig

Thank you so much for reading one of our **Historical Fiction** novels.
If you enjoyed the experience, please check out our recommendation
title for your next great read!

The Reckoning by Jeffrey Pierce

"Eloquent and hard muscled, deeply researched and deftly imagined,
The Reckoning is an entrancing, fantastical journey to an end you will
never see coming. The good news is it is just the start."
–Michael Connelly *(The Lincoln Lawyer, The Harry Bosch series)*

View other Black Rose Writing titles at
www.blackrosewriting.com/books and use promo code
PRINT to receive a **20% discount** when purchasing.

THE INN OF TEARS

ALICE TÉLOT (1861-1918), who wrote under the alias of "Jacques Fréhel," was the author of eight books, five of which were novels and three of which were collections of stories. Though details of her life are scarce, she was said to have been born in Saint-Malo in Brittany, and was from a family of mariners. She was the lover of the anarchist novelist and philosopher Han Ryner and a regular contributor to the feminist journal *La Fronde* and, despite her book *Les Ailes brisées* having been awarded the Prix Jules Favre by the Academie Française, her work fell into great neglect and she is almost forgotten today.

BRIAN STABLEFORD's scholarly work includes *New Atlantis: A Narrative History of Scientific Romance* (Wildside Press, 2016), *The Plurality of Imaginary Worlds: The Evolution of French roman scientifique* (Black Coat Press, 2017) and *Tales of Enchantment and Disenchantment: A History of Faerie* (Black Coat Press, 2019). He has translated more than three hundred volumes from the French, mostly in the genres of *roman scientifique, contes de fées* and Romantic and Symbolist fiction. His recent fiction includes the visionary science fiction novel *The Revelations of Time and Space* (2020) and its sequel *After the Revelation* (2021); the last in his long series of "Tales of the Genetic Revolution," *The Elusive Shadows* (2020); and the comedy fantasy *Meat on the Bone* (2021), all published by Snuggly Books.

SNUGGLY BOOKS